Ezili Coeur Noir smiled at the noise, enjoying the terrible, familiar song of death reversed. All of the corpses had done this when she had revived them; each had sung a beautiful note of pain. It was so pure, so absolute, she wished to one day make an orchestra of these corpses, killing and reviving them to create the music she heard echoing in her black heart.

Already she was walking down the road, instinctively searching for another dead body, feeling herself drawn to it as she repopulated the Earth with her army of the undead. But soon she would not need to search. Once the Red Weed batch was completed by her lackeys, Ezili Coeur Noir would have an endless supply of the dead to reanimate, a perfect orchestra to scream her beautiful songs of death. And prized among those singers would be the three humans she had found in the underground bunker of the redoubt, the three who had challenged her with the brightness of their living souls.

Other titles in this series:

James Axler
Outlanders®

SCARLET DREAM

A GOLD EAGLE BOOK FROM
WORLDWIDE®

TORONTO • NEW YORK • LONDON
AMSTERDAM • PARIS • SYDNEY • HAMBURG
STOCKHOLM • ATHENS • TOKYO • MILAN
MADRID • WARSAW • BUDAPEST • AUCKLAND

Recycling programs
for this product may
not exist in your area.

First edition May 2011

ISBN-13: 978-0-373-63870-3

SCARLET DREAM

Printed in U.S.A.

Call no man happy till he is dead.
—*Aeschylus, 525–456 B.C.*

The Road to Outlands—
From Secret Government Files to the Future

Almost two hundred years after the global holocaust, Kane, a former Magistrate of Cobaltville, often thought the world had been lucky to survive at all after a nuclear device detonated in the Russian embassy in Washington, D.C. The aftermath— forever known as skydark—reshaped continents and turned civilization into ashes.

Nearly depopulated, America became the Deathlands— poisoned by radiation, home to chaos and mutated life forms. Feudal rule reappeared in the form of baronies, while remote outposts clung to a brutish existence.

What eventually helped shape this wasteland were the redoubts, the secret preholocaust military installations with stores of weapons, and the home of gateways, the locational matter-transfer facilities. Some of the redoubts hid clues that had once fed wild theories of government cover-ups and alien visitations.

Rearmed from redoubt stockpiles, the barons consolidated their power and reclaimed technology for the villes. Their power, supported by some invisible authority, extended beyond their fortified walls to what was now called the Outlands. It was here that the rootstock of humanity survived, living with hellzones and chemical storms, hounded by Magistrates.

In the villes, rigid laws were enforced—to atone for the sins of the past and prepare the way for a better future. That was the barons' public credo and their right-to-rule.

Kane, along with friend and fellow Magistrate Grant, had upheld that claim until a fateful Outlands expedition. A displaced piece of technology…a question to a keeper of the archives…a vague clue about alien masters—and their world shifted radically. Suddenly, Brigid Baptiste, the archivist, faced summary execution, and Grant a quick termination. For

Kane there was forgiveness if he pledged his unquestioning allegiance to Baron Cobalt and his unknown masters and abandoned his friends.

But that allegiance would make him support a mysterious and alien power and deny loyalty and friends. Then what else was there?

Kane had been brought up solely to serve the ville. Brigid's only link with her family was her mother's red-gold hair, green eyes and supple form. Grant's clues to his lineage were his ebony skin and powerful physique. But Domi, she of the white hair, was an Outlander pressed into sexual servitude in Cobaltville. She at least knew her roots and was a reminder to the exiles that the outcasts belonged in the human family.

Parents, friends, community—the very rootedness of humanity was denied. With no continuity, there was no forward momentum to the future. And that was the crux—when Kane began to wonder if there was a future.

For Kane, it wouldn't do. So the only way was out—way, way out.

After their escape, they found shelter at the forgotten Cerberus redoubt headed by Lakesh, a scientist, Cobaltville's head archivist, and secret opponent of the barons.

With their past turned into a lie, their future threatened, only one thing was left to give meaning to the outcasts. The hunger for freedom, the will to resist the hostile influences. And perhaps, by opposing, end them.

"Call no man happy till he is dead."

—Aeschylus, 525-456 BC

Chapter 1

She had surrounded herself with dead things, for she found their company more agreeable now than that of the living.

Her name was Ezili Coeur Noir and she was the queen of all things dead, the flower of carnage. She stood over six feet tall and her limbs were bird-thin sticks, like the tools of some perverse surgeon. Her skin clung so tightly to those limbs that it seemed as if it would crush the stick-thin bones that were visible beneath. That skin was the rippled leather of a lizard, discolored and rotten with oozing wounds, as if in sympathy with the dead things she had elected to surround herself by. She stood upon two spindly, emaciated legs at an odd angle, as if no longer able to hold herself straight, which left her looking like some hideous mannequin discarded by its satanic puppeteer.

Along her torso, beneath her taut skin, her pronounced ribs showed like the keys of a piano, before finally disappearing beneath two misshapen breasts that hung like deflated balloons. Her elbows and knees were jagged points, like shards of broken glass, and her fingers curled arthritically in on themselves, their thick, jagged nails a sickly yellow.

Ezili Coeur Noir's yellow eyes showed the intolerance of a lizard, twin black slits like the eyes of an alligator, watching inscrutably above a hideous smile that, like the eyes, was more reptile than human. The yellow of those eyes almost seemed to glow within the darkness of her skin, weathered and aged to a leathery mahogany brown.

Her clothes, like her body, had rotted, their dust-caked remnants clinging to her dark flesh in tattered rags. Death and entropy were all her body understood now, and thus nothing that came into contact with Ezili Coeur Noir could remain intact.

She stood knee-deep in the swampland of Louisiana, where the plant life was so thick that it almost blotted out the rays of the rising sun. The plants nearest to Ezili Coeur Noir were dying as she stood and breathed in their proximity, wilting their life away in supplication to the queen of all things dead, who now stood gloriously among them.

Ezili Coeur Noir had been there all night, watching as her people, her legion of the dead, went about their work. Her people had come from the ground, locked now in various states of decay as she had revived them. They shambled, lurching to their tasks as they dug at the marshy ground, clawing at it with withered hands that ended in broken yellow nails.

Ezili Coeur Noir closed her eyes as her legion of dead dug at the spongy soil, listening to their groans of complaint, their grunts of interest. Most of them had no real capacity for speech anymore; their tongues had shriveled away in death, no longer able to create the shapes needed to turn sound into form. Still, they made noise, the way humans will make noise, as if—even in death—they feared this dead place where the insects made their home. There were other things here, of course—amphibians, birds, some hardy types of fish that swam in the deeper pits of water among the marshes—all of whom seemed to fill the air with creaking and cawing, the hideous shrieks of a child's nightmare.

Two centuries before, there had been other things living here, too—humankind. Out here in the depths of the bayou, Army men had cordoned off an area of this sweaty habitat to develop a research station located in the back of beyond, far from the nearest town, with just a single dirt road leading to it. The road endured in patchy remnants, a mud track lined with little sunken posts that stuck out of the earth like sharks' teeth. The patches of road were uneven, and what remained survived from sheer tenacity and nothing more, for it had barely been used in two centuries and it led, categorically, to a patch of nothing amid a swamp full of the same. Or so it appeared.

In fact, the swamp had grown to cover the single-story entrance to the redoubt that had once stood at the end of the road. Nature had buried it, either through choice or when the nukecaust of 2001 had rewritten all the maps. Either way, the entrance to the redoubt was hidden beneath layers of marsh and concrete. But far below that, far below the entrance itself, lay the thing that Ezili Coeur Noir was searching for, the toy she wished to play with. She felt it calling to her.

Instinct had brought her here—instinct, arcane knowledge and an all-pervading sense for death in all its beautiful forms. For, to Ezili Coeur Noir, death was a thing of beauty, the perfect punctuation to conclude the statement called life.

All around the queen of death, the corpses worked at the soil, pulling and wrenching, tossing aside sodden chunks of earth that hit the ground with wet slaps. As the ground was sifted, black-shelled, multilimbed inhabitants crawled from the soil, disturbed by the outrage. The undead men ignored the beetles and the worms and the termites as they scrabbled from the upturned sod, letting them land and feast on their decaying flesh with hungry mouths. There were other things here, too, finding their way in the early morning gloom, flying insects that buzzed incessantly as they sought out the rotten flesh of the moving living-dead things, yearning to gnaw at it and to lay their eggs in rotten muscles, in ragged ears and between the gaps of the undead men's smiles. The undead ignored them, or perhaps chewed on those insects that landed between their lips, an old instinct from the days when they had needed to eat, just muscle memory now playing its cruel tricks. The undead care not for the needs of the flesh, are undisturbed by such things as turn the stomachs of the living.

There came a noise then, a single, sharp thump that sounded of metal. Ezili Coeur Noir opened her eyes to slits, wide black vertical stripes crossing the yellow as she looked out at her people. They looked at her expectantly, twenty corpses that had once been men and women, and two of them just children, recently dead things now who barely stood tall enough to nose at the oyster entrance to her lifeless womb. She saw the expectation in their blank expressions where others would just see the rotting faces of the butcher's blade. They had found it, she knew—the door to the redoubt.

Ezili Coeur Noir stepped forward, her spindly legs flicking out uncomfortably, like the long limbs of a house spider, trotting forward with a disquieting gait. Despite her skeletal form and the hideous way her decomposing legs ground against the sockets of her hips, the queen of death still strode with an indefinably regal air, her head held high. She dominated all that she saw; there could be no question that here was the ruler of all that her reptilian eyes surveyed. Even through their dead orbs, her corpselike minions saw this and several of them genuflected in appreciation as she tottered past them, the upper half of her body swaying as though a leaf on the mildest breeze.

The door was buried amid the sludge of the swamp, hunks of powdery concrete clinging to its surface. Reinforced steel, the door lay in front of the queen of death, nine feet by twelve, not flat but at a slight angle that made it a locked portal in the ground. A few brave rays of sunlight sneaked through the thick plant cover to glimmer on its metal surface, and pools of water began leaking over it even as Ezili Coeur Noir looked. Here was the entrance to the redoubt, the entrance that had been hidden for over two centuries.

Without taking her eyes from the gleaming surface of the steel door, Ezili Coeur Noir issued an instruction in a voice with all the vibrancy of ashes crushed in the palm of the hand. "Open it."

The corpses hurried to obey, pushing past one another in their haste to serve their terrible mistress. Groaning and mumbling, Ezili Coeur Noir's undead workers pulled at the door, struggling to make it move on its hinges. The door resisted. Not only had it been designed to withstand the impact of a nuclear blast, but also its hinges had been undisturbed for two hundred years; to move such a thing now was like trying to lift a mountain.

Ezili Coeur Noir observed with but the mildest of interest, barely watching as her favored subjects worked at the door, throwing themselves at it, ripping at the seals with the broken nails of their decaying hands, tugging away the concrete debris that had amassed there. The corpses felt no pain and could never tire, for they were at the peak of tiredness, the tiredness that comes only with the grave. And so they simply followed the instructions of their mistress without question, working at the door with all their effort until at last something moved. There had been a magnetic seal in place here, operated by an electronic lock, but even a magnet can be conquered, given enough force, facing an opponent with relentless and tireless ambition, limitless reserves of strength.

It took half an hour, but finally the corpses stepped aside as the door glided back on its tracks, grinding slowly to the side to reveal the shadow-filled interior of a long-forgotten military base. Two of the corpses had lost limbs in their struggles with the door, and one his head, but the others had used the broken bodies as props and levers until the door finally gave. Now the broken corpses simply waited with the others, blessedly unaware of how their incompletion might make them inferior. Ezili Coeur Noir strode forward, the sunlight playing in the jutting spikes of yellowing bone that poked upright atop her head in a crest.

This close to the door, she could smell the stale air, which had been trapped within the redoubt since it had been sealed all those years before. Her stub of nose wrinkled for a moment in her decaying face, and her lips pulled back from sharp teeth as she was dealt the full force of that putrid air. Ezili Coeur Noir chuckled then, reveling in the stench of the absence of life. Here was a part of the Earth that had been hidden so long that it had been effectively taken from the living. Now it stood as a shrine to death, proof positive of life's inability to truly conquer her planet.

As the stale air dissipated, the queen of death stepped into the shadow-drenched interior of the redoubt, her long toenails clacking against the hard concrete floor. Obediently, her little army followed, their loyalty to their mistress beyond reproach. They were recently dead things, and yet they still moved, for she had granted them life, after a fashion.

Despite being unoccupied for over two hundred years, the redoubt reacted to the movement within. The motion-sensitive strip lights flickered on along the floor and high in the ceiling, illuminating the vast, slope-walled corridor that Ezili Coeur Noir and her people now found themselves in. The light mattered little to the queen of death; she needed nothing but her inherent sense of all that kills and rots and dies to guide her way. Corpses to the left of her, corpses to the right, Ezili Coeur Noir strode down the redoubt corridor, lights flickering on with her every step, the footsteps of her posse echoing into the darkness ahead as the distant lights winked on. In such close proximity to the corpses, Ezili Coeur Noir could smell their rotting flesh as it clung to their bodies, insects burrowing among its rotten folds. The corpses reeked of death and the smell pleased her, its perfume a scent she would bathe in given time.

Wide enough to fit two automobiles, the tunnel sloped downward at as light incline for a long time, with no visible breaks, no doorways or recesses. From far at its dark end there came a low rumbling, as ancient generators groaned back into life and machinery began to whir. Here and there black wiring led down from the overhead lights or up from the floor, ending in a junction box set at the midpoint of the otherwise blank walls, each one cased in black plastic with a little door that worked on a simple spring-loaded hinge. Every thirty paces there was a small red box covered by a glass panel, the fire alarm system that had been installed centuries earlier.

Here, Ezili Coeur Noir knew, buried deep in the sublevels of the forgotten redoubt, was a thing that could do her bidding on a colossal scale. She could sense it, in the way that she could somehow sense all things that brought decay, a flaming beacon in her mind, calling to her with siren song.

The blank-walled tunnel sloped for almost three hundred paces, and by the time the group had reached its end, the motion-sensitive lights behind them had begun switching off, leaving the area by the entry door in darkness once more. The walls were a bland gray, smoothed concrete and plaster left unpainted. Here and there, notations had been scratched on the walls, tiny markings in pencil, the initials of a soldier or a workman scrawled lightly into the plaster in a spot close to the curved ceiling beside one of the recessed strip lights.

At the end of the tunnel the group stopped at a set of steel double doors that were set horizontally like the jaws of an immense trapped animal. The grinding, whirring noise came from behind these closed doors, and Ezili Coeur Noir halted in front of them. In silence, her undead entourage waited obediently behind her.

Then, the horizontal double doors split, one shunting upward while the other retreated into the base of the floor, and a steel-walled box was revealed. Small halogen lights flickered on in the ceiling as the doors disappeared from view. It was an elevator, reinforced and large enough to hold a supply truck. The tunnel leading here had one purpose only, which was to take people to this elevator, and so the redoubt was designed to automatically call the elevator once the entry doors were opened.

With all the grace that the dead can muster, Ezili Coeur Noir stepped through the doors, and her undead companions shambled behind her, walking into the large box-like construction of the elevator cage. Behind them, the elevator doors rumbled closed on tracks that hadn't been used in two hundred years, and then the elevator began to descend into the core of the buried redoubt.

Standing in the shaking elevator, the sound of long-unused pulleys whining in her ears, Ezili Coeur Noir glanced around her, taking in the dead figures who had come to form her entourage. Ezili Coeur Noir had granted the dead life, but truly she wanted the reverse—to give the living the glorious gift of death.

Ezili Coeur Noir was the queen of all things rotten, all things dead, and in that lay her power. For all things must rot, and all things must die. And so they would, and so they shall.

Chapter 2

In another military redoubt, high in the Bitterroot Mountains of Montana, a warning light was blinking urgently on the computer monitor screen of Brewster Philboyd. In his midforties, Philboyd was an astrophysicist by discipline. His blond hair was swept back from a receding hairline. A lanky six feet tall, he looked faintly uncomfortable as he sat in the swivel chair, hunched in front of his monitor in the central operations room of the redoubt with its twin aisles of computer terminals, its walls dedicated to the monitoring equipment that defined the hidden base's function.

Behind Philboyd, a vast Mercator map dominated the wall above the doors into the operations room, showing every continent of the world, each one connected by dozens of different colored lines like the old flight plan maps that had existed before the nuclear holocaust had all but destroyed civilization. The map was just one part of a monitoring system that was dedicated to the upkeep of the mat-trans project, a transportation system developed in the late twentieth century by the U.S. military. The mat-trans units scattered around the globe could be used to move goods and personnel from location to location in the blink of an eye.

Like the map and the monitoring equipment in the control room, Brewster Philboyd was a relic from the twentieth century. He, along with a number of other military personnel, had been cryogenically frozen and placed in hiding on the Manitius Moon Base just prior to the outbreak of nuclear hostilities between the USA and the old USSR. Like many of other people who manned the redoubt now known as Cerberus, Brewster had been awoken two hundred years later into a new and dangerous world, where a once proud civilization had been replaced by the veiled manipulation of humanity by a poisonous alien race called the Annunaki. In recent years, Cerberus had set itself against this alien threat in a series of dangerous skirmishes, though the odds of actually defeating such a technologically superior enemy seemed astronomical.

Philboyd leaned forward slightly in his seat, adjusting the black-rimmed glasses he wore above his acne-scarred cheeks as he studied the warning pop-up that had appeared on his monitor. Philboyd's fingers played briefly across his keyboard as he brought up the details of the alert, scrolling through the data swiftly as he scanned the information it imparted. It appeared that there was life— or movement at least—in a long-abandoned redoubt out in Louisiana. According to the scrolling information on his screen, the old military base was designated as Redoubt Mike, adhering to the ancient military protocol of naming redoubts after a phonetic letter of the alphabet.

Turning in his chair, Brewster attracted the attention of his superior, a man called Mohandas Lakesh Singh, who was busy at a terminal that sat at the back of the room, overlooking the operations center.

"Lakesh?" Brewster began. "Do you know anything about a redoubt out near White Lake, Louisiana?"

Lakesh's blue eyes glazed over for a moment as he contemplated the question. He was a well-built man of medium height who appeared to be in his midfifties, with refined features and an aquiline nose. Known to his friends as Lakesh, Dr. Singh was in fact over 250 years old, and he had been with the Cerberus redoubt before the nuclear conflict that had ended the twenty-first century one cold January day. A cyberneticist and accomplished physicist, Lakesh had been involved with the mat-trans project from its earliest days, and it was with some sense of irony that he found himself in the same monitoring room several centuries later.

"Redoubt Mike," Lakesh mused, his eyes coming back into focus. "I have visited it several times." When Brewster looked at him curiously, Lakesh inclined his head with self-deprecation, and added noncommittally, "In my youth. Why do you ask about it, Brewster?"

Philboyd gestured to his flickering terminal screen. "According to this, Mike has a visitor. Maybe an intruder."

"That's quite impossible," Lakesh protested, rising from his seat. "That redoubt was sealed in the 1990s. Sealed and buried."

"Buried?" Brewster intoned.

"Redoubt Mike was a staging area for one of the earliest mat-trans units," Lakesh explained, "a prototype via which some of our initial exploration was done. Mike's mat-trans acted primarily as a sending unit, rather than a receiver, but this was in the early days of the project when the colossal amount of power required to operate a chamber was still being investigated. Mike's mat-trans operated using a cold-fusion generator—a nuclear system that was ultimately considered too problematic for the strains placed upon it."

"Problematic, how?" Philboyd queried.

"Mike's was a working prototype in operation while the whole process was still at its teething stage," Lakesh explained. "Ultimately, the idea of powering the units by cold fusion was judged too dangerous to continue to use, and so other avenues were pursued. Of course, several early systems were being tested at this stage. It was a prestige military project, and as is often the way in such cases, money was in place to ensure it would work."

Philboyd nodded in understanding. "But you said it was buried?" he asked.

"Redoubt Mike was abandoned once the cold-fusion system was deemed unsuitable," Lakesh explained. "The base itself was primarily belowground, with only the entry at ground level. They concreted over those doors and left it to the mercies of the swamps. Which means no one should be inside."

Brewster glanced back at his monitor screen where the warning pop-up continue to blink. "Well-lll," he began, stretching the single syllable, "either we have a glitch in our monitoring system or a caller has come a-knock-knocking for Mike."

Casting aside the paperwork he had been looking at on his own desk, Lakesh strode across the room and joined Brewster at his monitor, running through the alert data that had appeared there. As he read the details, the old cyberneticist's expression darkened.

LOCATED HIGH IN THE Bitterroot Mountains in Montana, the Cerberus redoubt was an ancient military facility that had remained largely forgotten or ignored since the nuke-caust. The isolation was only reinforced by the curious mythology associated with the mountains, their dark, foreboding forests and seemingly bottomless ravines. The wilderness area surrounding the redoubt was virtually un-populated; the nearest settlement was found in the flat-lands some miles away and consisted of a small band of Native Americans, Sioux and Cheyenne, led by a shaman named Sky Dog.

Hidden beneath camouflage netting, tucked away within the rocky clefts of the mountains, concealed uplinks chattered continuously with two orbiting satellites that provided much of the empirical data for the Cerberus team within the redoubt. Gaining access to those satellites had taken many hours of intense trial-and-error work by the top scientists on hand at the base, but their efforts now gave Lakesh's team a near limitless stream of feed data from around the planet, as well as providing global communications links.

Hidden away as it was, the redoubt required few active measures to discourage visitors. It was exceedingly rare for strangers to approach the main entry, a rollback door located on a plateau high on the mountain. Instead, most people accessed the redoubt via the mat-trans chamber housed within the redoubt itself.

Employing a quantum window, the mat-trans exploited the hyperdimensional quantum stream, transmitting digital information along hyperdimensional pathways. Though eminently adaptable, the system was limited by the number and location of the mat-trans units, much as a train is restricted by its tracks and the location of its stations.

More recently, the Cerberus personnel had refined an interphaser unit, which functioned along similar principles but relied on naturally occuring parallax points, intersecting lines of intense energy. Requiring no external power source, these parallax points existed across the Earth—and beyond—and could be exploited by use of a portable device called an interphaser, which could be carried by just one person using an attaché-style case. Although not limitless, the interphaser had the distinct advantage of portability and a wider array of receiver locations.

Having read the data on Brewster's screen, Lakesh

stumbled back into the empty chair behind him, almost falling as he sat. Several of the other personnel on shift in the command center turned at the noise, expressing concern for their operational leader.

"Is everything okay?" Brewster asked, although he feared that he already knew the answer.

"This is very bad," Lakesh said, his voice little more than a whisper. "Once the decision had been taken to decommission Mike, the redoubt was used as a storage facility for other projects of dubious worth. Which is to say, it became a dumping ground, since the impending secure closure of the site meant that whatever was left there could not be accessed ever again."

"What sorts of things?" Brewster asked.

Lakesh shook his head, feeling weary as the enormity of the breach in redoubt security struck him. "The sort of things the military always involves itself in—weapons, the means of destruction.

"Sooner or later, all our sins come back to haunt us, Mr. Philboyd," Lakesh pronounced, standing once more. "I think we had better assemble a team and investigate this intrusion at our earliest opportunity."

ON ANOTHER LEVEL of the hidden mountain base, Kane stood in front of a punching bag hanging on a rigid spring from the ceiling of the communal gymnasium. Kane gritted his teeth as he attacked the hanging bag with a series of swift, bare-knuckled blows: first right, then left, then right again.

Kane was a powerfully built man, with no-nonsense blue-gray eyes and dark hair cropped short to his collar. Dressed in a black T-shirt and loose slacks, Kane was an outstanding example of physical fitness. His wide shoulders and muscular arms powered his punches with incredible force, smashing the punching bag back on its spring so hard that it rattled in its metal housing. It had been observed that Kane was built like a wolf, sleek and muscular with exceptional power concentrated in his upper torso. He seemed to have the temperament of a wolf, too, for he was both pack leader and a natural loner, depending on the situation.

An ex-Magistrate, enforcer of the laws of the walled villes that dominated the U.S. landscape of the twenty-third century, Kane was a trained fighter, with a razor-keen mind and exceptional combat prowess. What distinguished Kane among his contemporaries, however, was something he referred to as his point man sense, an uncanny awareness of his surroundings that verged on the supernatural. In actuality, there was nothing unearthly about Kane's ability—it was simply the disciplined application of the same five senses possessed by any other human being.

As Kane worked at the punching bag, each mighty uppercut, jab and cross forcing the leather teardrop to shake in its mountings, he became aware of another person entering the otherwise empty gymnasium. Kane's blue-gray eyes flicked across the room as he looked over his shoulder, his fists still working at the high punching bag. The newcomer was a woman, her body sheathed in a skin-tight white jumpsuit that accentuated her trim curves and athlete's body. A cascade of curling red locks flowed past her shoulders to the midpoint of her back.

Brigid Baptiste and Kane shared a long history. Where Kane was a man of action, Brigid's background was as an archivist. Which wasn't to say that Brigid could not hold her own in a fight—far from it, as she could handle herself with fists or guns, and she had proved to be a hell-cat when riled. However, Brigid Baptiste had one trait that had proved immeasurably useful in the adventures she had shared with Kane: a mental talent known as an eidetic, or photographic, memory, which allowed her to visually remember in precise detail everything she had ever seen.

For almost half a minute Kane continued to beat at the punching bag, working rhythmically in a tarantella of swift punches as beads of sweat glistened on his skin. As he drilled his final right cross against the leather bag, Brigid Baptiste stopped in front of him, eyebrows raised in an inquisitive expression that betrayed her mocking humor.

"Feeling a little frustrated today?" she asked as Kane stepped back on the balls of his feet, leaving the punching bag swinging to and fro from its mounting between them.

Kane looked at her and smiled. "Aw, it had it coming," he said, indicating the swaying bag as it slowly returned to a static position, waiting for its next opponent.

Brigid looked at the punching bag and laughed, creases of delight appearing momentarily around her emerald eyes as she did so. "What, did it outsmart you at chess?" she asked. "Again?"

Brushing a hand through his sweat-damp hair, Kane reached for the hand towel that he had left on a nearby bench. "What can I do for you, Baptiste?" he asked, ignoring her friendly taunt.

"Lakesh is asking us to meet in the ops room," Brigid explained as she watched Kane wiping the sweat from his powerful arms. "I don't know the details yet, but it seems there's trouble out there in paradise and he wants us ready to ship out in the next hour."

Kane tapped at the side of his head, indicating the subdermal Commtact unit that was hidden there beneath the skin. "Guess I didn't hear the call," he explained.

Commtacts were top-of-the-line communication devices that had been discovered among the military artifacts in Redoubt Yankee some years before. The Commtacts featured sensor circuitry incorporating an analog-to-digital voice encoder that was subcutaneously embedded in a subject's mastoid bone. Once the pintels made contact, transmissions were picked up by the wearer's auditory canals, and dermal sensors transmitted the electronic signals directly through the skull casing, vibrating the ear canal. In theory, a deaf person would still be able to hear, after a fashion, using the Commtact. The Commtacts had other properties, too, including acting as intelligent, real-time translators on the condition that a sufficient sample of a language had been programmed into them to decipher a dialect.

"You didn't miss anything," Brigid assured Kane. "I told him I'd come find you."

Kane fixed Brigid with his most mischievous look as he slung the towel over one shoulder. "You just can't keep away, can you?"

In reply, Brigid leaped from a standing start, high into the air, and kicked the punching bag that hung between them, making it rebound so hard that it almost clipped Kane in his smugly smiling face.

"You wish," she told him as she landed in a graceful crouch.

Despite their outward antagonism, Kane and Brigid had the utmost respect for one another and they shared a very special bond. That bond was known as *anam-charas,* or soul friends, and it referred to a connection that transcended history itself. No matter what form the two found themselves in, no matter the nature of their reincarnations throughout eternity, the pair would remain unequivocally linked, tied together by some invisible umbilical cord that meant they would always be there for each other. Some had interpreted this link to mean that they were lovers, but the *anam-chara* bond was something more than that—the friendship and love of siblings or respectful contemporaries, with Brigid the yin to Kane's yang.

While Kane and Brigid had been partners for a long time, there was a third integral member of their group, as well. Grant was also an ex-magistrate and had been Kane's original partner in his Magistrate days. Grant was as much Kane's brother as any blood relative. Together, the three of them formed an exceptional exploration group who seemed able to handle themselves in any given situation. Which was fortunate, as the situations they encountered while working for Cerberus had ranged from the improbable to the outright impossible.

FIFTEEN MINUTES LATER, Kane strolled into the operations room dressed in a clean shadow suit, his hair still damp from the shower he had taken on leaving the gym.

As Kane walked through the doors beneath the Mercator map with its multicolored lines of light, Lakesh stepped forward to greet him. "I am glad you could make it so quickly, Kane," he said briefly.

As with Brigid Baptiste, Kane had known Lakesh for a long time and he recognized when the formidable scientist sounded worried. Behind Lakesh, Brigid and Grant waited along with several other personnel who were prepping the mat-trans for use. The mat-trans chamber was located in an antechamber at the far corner of the large room, well away from the entry doors. The unit itself was situated within a small, eight-foot-high cubicle surrounded by armaglass walls tinted a brown hue. The door to the

unit operated using a numeric key code, and the use of the
unit was monitored by a computer terminal located just to
the side of its entry door. Right now, Lakesh's deputy, the
copper-haired Donald Bry, sat at the mat-trans terminal,
a look of deep concern on his features. Normally, Kane
would not take Bry's expression as a reliable indicator
of the situation. The man was a compulsive worrier and
Kane struggled to recall an instance when his brow wasn't
furrowed beneath his untamed mop of copper curls. However, the atmosphere in the room was such that Kane knew
immediately that he had entered a serious situation.

"Well, I aim to please," Kane replied as Cerberus
weaponsmith Henny Johnson rushed over to arm the
ex-Mag for the field. "What's going on?"

Briefly, Lakesh outlined the situation regarding the
intrusion alert at Redoubt Mike and how the Louisiana
redoubt potentially contained any number of decommissioned weapons along with its outdated mat-trans unit.

"This may be a simple glitch in our system, or in
Mike's," Lakesh concluded, "but there's an adage that I
think applies here—it is better to be safe than sorry."

"I quite agree," Kane said as he strapped a familiar
wrist holster to his right arm and checked that the Sin
Eater pistol that Henny handed him was fully loaded.

Henny glared at Kane as he checked the pistol, as if
offended that he would, for even a moment, believe she
might send him out into the field with equipment that
wasn't fully prepared. She was a small woman, five foot
five with blond hair cut into a severe bob that ended just
below her ears.

"What's wrong?" she asked as Kane placed the compact pistol snugly in its wrist holster and shrugged the
sleeve of his black denim jacket over it to conceal it.
"Don't trust me anymore, cowpoke?"

Kane glanced up at the armorer. "I trust you, Johnson," he said, "but I'd also expect you to double-check my work if your life was about to depend on it."

"Thanks… I think," Henny said as she passed Kane a handful of spare ammo cartridges and flash-bang globes for use in the field.

"Well, then." Grant's voice rumbled from where he sat, perched on the edge of one of the computer desks. "Let's get this show on the road." Grant was a huge man, well over six feet in height and broad like an oak door. A little older than Kane, he was a solid wall of muscle, with skin like polished ebony and a gunslinger's mustache curling down from his top lip. Grant wore his hair cropped so close to his skull that he seemed almost bald, and he had placed a dark woollen cap over his head now, pulled low so that it met with his thick eyebrows, enhancing his permanent scowl.

Like Kane, Grant had dressed in one of the remarkable shadow suits beneath his long, Kevlar-weave black coat. Though they appeared to be made of the thinnest of material, the tight-fitting one-piece shadow suits acted as artificially controlled environments that regulated a wearer's body temperature and offered protection from a variety of environmental contaminants. Additionally, their weave was superstrong, creating an armored shell that could deflect knife attacks and even small-arms fire within reason. While not impregnable, the shadow suits gave a Cerberus agent a distinct advantage when out in the field.

Standing across from Grant, Brigid Baptiste had donned her own shadow suit, its sleek black lines clinging to her trim body beneath a suede jacket with a tasselled back. Where Grant's choice of weaponry was hidden amid the folds of his heavy coat, Brigid wore her own blaster—a TP-9 automatic—prominently in a low-slung hip holster, its grip pointing upward and ready for quick access.

Kane peered around the room for a moment, his eyes searching before he turned back to his partners where they waited at the desks. "Was I meant to bring the interphaser?" he asked.

"No interphaser this time, buddy," Grant advised in his deep voice.

Lakesh gestured to the doorway in the far corner of the room. "Ah, yes, you weren't here when I explained this, old friend," he told Kane. "We've used our remote access to power the receiver unit at Redoubt Mike," he stated briefly.

Kane felt a familiar sinking feeling in his stomach. "Oh, no," he groaned.

Brigid smiled brightly as she looked over her shoulder, encouraging Kane to follow her toward the armaglass cubicle that dominated a corner of the operations room. "Oh, yes. We're going via mat-trans for this one," she told him. "Old school."

"Oh, great," Kane muttered sarcastically as he followed his two companions through the doorway into the ancient mat-trans unit. "If there's one thing I miss, it's doing things the really shitty way."

"We'll briefly activate the outdated system by remote," Lakesh told Kane as he peered through the open doorway. "It's risky, but every second counts, so the closer we can get you to the site of infraction, the better."

"Right blindly into the thick of it, huh?" Kane said, shaking his head. "Yeah, that plan can't go wrong."

"For our security, the mat-trans will power down immediately after you've materialized at Redoubt Mike,"

Lakesh said to assure him. "Which means you'll need to comm us when you're ready to return."

Kane nodded irritably. "Got it."

Kane closed the door, locking the three companions in the ancient mat-trans chamber and enabling the jump sequence. Donald Bry's fingers worked the computer keyboard and the trio were reduced to their component atoms, digitized and sent across the quantum ether to the receiver unit in far-off Louisiana.

At least it's quick, Kane reasoned as his substance ceased to exist.

Chapter 3

Traveling via mat-trans was a little like waking in the middle of the night to the awful realization that you had contracted food poisoning. A moment earlier, one's life was a restful dream, then suddenly it had turned into a bewildering nightmare, colored only by one's need to vomit.

Almost doubled over, Kane took deep breaths as he stood in the mat-trans chamber that he and his companions had materialized in an instant before. His heart was pounding, his stomach was doing some crazy kind of acrobatics and he could taste bile at the back of his throat. For a moment he stood hunched over, staring at the white-tiled floor as he tried to bring himself back to a state of calm.

The tiled floor at Kane's feet was familiar, exactly the same as the one that the companions had left in Montana just an instant earlier, dusty white tiles glinting beneath harsh overhead lighting. White mist floated in the air like fog, slowly dissipating as extractor fans began their designated task of clearing the glass-walled chamber.

While mat-trans travel was possible for humans, it had not initially been designed with people in mind. Rather, it was intended for the movement of matériel, and its application to transporting the human form could be traumatic. Despite the churning of his stomach, Kane was fairly used to this ghastly system of travel, and had made his peace with it years before. Grant, by contrast, had never liked traveling via mat-trans, and he endured it with a determined mixture of bitterness and hostility, even after all these years with Cerberus.

"Everyone arrive in one piece?" Kane asked, straightening to check on his two companions.

They stood behind him, one over each shoulder in the manner of a fighter pilot's wingmen. Brigid Baptiste had her hand to her mouth and was biting down on her knuckle, her skin visibly paler than even its usual near-alabaster hue.

Realizing that Kane was looking at her for an answer, Brigid nodded, still biting down on her knuckle.

Across from the red-haired former archivist, Grant had his teeth gritted and his eyes screwed up tight, and his breathing was coming in ragged bursts.

"Grant?" Kane urged, reaching for his other companion.

"Present," Grant muttered, his eyes still closed.

Kane felt his own stomach lurch then, and he gagged for a moment, holding down its contents with considerable effort. "You okay?" he asked once he had got himself back under control.

Grant opened his eyes, the dark orbs looking bloodshot, focused on some far distant point. "That was…that was really something," he said through gasping breaths.

"Lakesh said this was a prototype unit," Brigid reminded them both. She had removed her hand from her mouth now, but she still seemed unsteady on her feet as she staggered forward, the chunky heels of her cowboy boots clacking loudly against the white tiles. "I guess they didn't iron out all the kinks on this one."

"Guess not," Kane agreed as he recovered himself.

The pale transportation gas had almost disappeared now, the extractor fans whirring loudly above the companions' heads, and Kane turned to face the door. The door was offset from center in a bank of tinted armaglass, its panes colored a golden yellow. When traveling via mat-trans, the differently colored armaglass was one rudimentary way to recognize that a person had actually been shunted to a new location. In the direct manner of the military mind, each location had differently colored glass, a coded sequence that identified each mat-trans and its location. Presumably, when the system was still in its earliest days and the number of units was small, one might say, "I'm going to gold," which meant the individual was traveling to Redoubt Mike in Louisiana. As a general rule, what a military force seemed to lack in subtlety it more than made up for in effectiveness. The speed and ease of identification could often be crucial in such situations, where goods and personnel were effectively being shoved through the unknown.

Still a little woozy, Kane stilled his mind and went into the near trancelike state that put him on high alert, powering his Sin Eater pistol into his hand with a flinch of his wrist tendons as he stepped over to the sealed door. The Sin Eater was the official side arm of the Magistrate Division, and both Kane and Grant had kept them when they had fled from the barony of Cobaltville that they had been tasked to protect years before. The Sin Eater was an automatic handblaster, less than fourteen inches in length at full extension, firing 9 mm rounds. The whole unit folded in on itself to be stored in a bulky holster just above the user's wrist, in Kane's case one tucked beneath the unbuttoned sleeve of his darkly colored denim jacket. The holsters reacted to a specific flinch movement of the wrist tendons, powering the pistol automatically into the user's hand where, if the index finger was crooked at the time, the pistol would begin firing automatically. The trigger had no guard; the necessity had never been foreseen that any kind of safety feature for the weapon would ever be required, for a Magistrate's judgment was considered infallible.

Kane and Grant were schooled in the use of numerous different weapon types, from combat blades to Dragon missile launchers, but both of them still felt especially comfortable with the Sin Eater in hand. It was an old and trusted companion, a natural weight to their movements, like wearing a wristwatch.

Kane worked the electronic lock, ordering the others to stay alert as the door slid open. Grant still looked decidedly uncomfortable, but Kane knew that they didn't have the luxury to wait around if there were intruders on site. "You ready?" Kane asked his old Magistrate partner.

Slowly, Grant nodded, ordering his own Sin Eater blaster into his hand with a well-practiced flinch of his wrist tendons. "Yeah, let's go crash this party."

Beside Grant, Brigid Baptiste unfastened her own pistol from its position at her hip, the bulky block of the TP-9 looking large in her delicate, feminine hands. Unlike the two ex-Magistrates, Brigid had not grown up being schooled in the application of weaponry. However, she had learned swiftly as an adult, her eidetic memory allowing her to perfect the techniques of combat far quicker than an average person. Her TP-9 was a compact semiautomatic, a large hand pistol with the grip set just off center beneath the barrel and a covered targeting scope across the top, all finished in molded matte black. With its grip so close to the center, it looked a little like a square block, the bottom edge of that square completed by the holder's forearm. Weapon now in hand, Brigid nodded her own silent agreement.

Kane stepped into a large, ill-lit room that lay beyond the mat-trans chamber, his companions close behind. As

Kane entered the main area of the room, a handful of fluorescent tubes flickered on from hidden recesses in the high ceiling. The lights were widely spaced, lighting the room while still leaving it in a gloomy sort of half light.

Leading the way in a semicrouch, Kane took two swift paces to the right and dropped to the floor, scanning the room with his eyes, his gun held out in front of him in a steadying, two-handed grip. Behind Kane, Brigid had peeled off to the left, her head ducked down as she swept the room with her own weapon, searching for any targets. At the back of the group, Grant paused just inside the open doorway to the mat-trans chamber, his own Sin Eater held at shoulder height, ready to back up Kane or Brigid and blast any hostile intruders they might flush out.

The room appeared empty, and after a moment Kane eased himself up from his crouch, never loosening his two-handed grip on the Sin Eater. The room was roughly square in shape, and Kane estimated it to be perhaps forty feet from wall to wall. Beneath the insubstantial illumination, Kane saw a long aisle of monitoring equipment facing the mat-trans cubicle. The aisle was split into two, a gap wide enough for a person to walk through at its center. Still alert, Kane stepped through the gap and peered at the dead equipment there. The aisle was made up of various computers and sensor arrays, including several rather old-fashioned banks of needles and dials alongside the digital monitors. Although the equipment had been shut down long ago, the low lighting would have been ideal for its users, Kane realized, as the majority of these monitors and sensor displays would have been backlit. In fact, other than a visible layer of dust, it looked as if they had been turned off just minutes before. It was kind of eerie, Kane thought, like walking through a graveyard at night.

The rest of the room contained one single desk set back from the others. Six old dial telephones sat to one side, their wires trailing down into a circular port at the edge of the desk, along with what appeared to be twin computer terminals. Kane peered closely at them for a moment, and he realized that one was in fact some kind of television monitor, most likely used for security purposes back when the base was live. Now, both screens were blank, powered down two centuries earlier.

To the rear of the large room were six tall banks of monitoring and recording equipment. Each of them towered above Kane to perhaps eight feet, their size and shape reminiscent of the cold-drinks machines common in hotel lobbies and schoolyards in the final years of the twentieth century. Kane glanced over them briefly, acknowledging the rows of long-unused lights and the ancient, rotten magnetic spools of tape that had presumably been used to store recordings of the mat-trans unit in operation. The banks of recording equipment ended off to the far right, where Kane spotted an open doorway that led from the room into darkness beyond.

Over to the far left corner of the vast, windowless room, Brigid found the majestic unit that powered the mat-trans. The unit ran floor to ceiling, with rounded sides stretching wider than her arm span; it reminded Brigid a little of an old-fashioned pillbox sentry post. Thick pipes emerged from the sides and top of the unit, and a dust-caked monitoring display glowed at roughly head height. Presumably, this display was a failsafe backup as the main monitoring would be conducted via the powerful computers in this underground control room. A sealed steel door stood in the center of the cylinder, with rounded corners and a raised lip that reminded Brigid of the doors one would see inside a submarine.

Tentatively, the titian-haired woman placed her hand against the metal sides of the unit, but even though it had just been activated, no vibration could be detected. Within that towering steel cylinder, the cold-fusion process for creating nuclear energy was in operation, Brigid knew, a product of the Manhattan Project research of the 1940s.

After a moment Brigid stepped back, eyeing the manner in which the piping connected to the mat-trans chamber. Since the nukecaust, anything involving nuclear energy set off alarm bells as being dangerous or risky, and yet here was an artifact that predated that paranoia, from when nuclear power was still being explored as a viable source of energy. In many ways, this generator was as much a relic from another society as anything the Cerberus team had encountered in ancient civilizations like the Mayan and the Sumerian.

With his gun held high, Kane used the weapon to gesture toward the open doorway. "We're all clear here," he said. "Let's move out."

Following Kane from her position at the far wall, Brigid slowed for just a moment to examine the neat, unmarred desks that ran across the axis of the room. It was both curious and intriguing, seeing all this monitoring equipment for the mat-trans, reminding her that there was a point not so very long ago where the whole concept had been nothing more than a theory to be explored by brave physicists.

"Come on, Brigid," Grant urged as he sidled up beside her. "No point keeping the man waiting."

Brigid nodded and trotted off to where Kane waited at the open doorway leading into shadow. Grant followed, seemingly more himself now, the wave of nausea from the hard trip having mercifully passed.

Kane crept out into the corridor beyond the open doorway,

noticing that a heavy rollback door there had jammed halfway out of its wall recess. Presumably, the door should lock while the prototype mat-trans unit was fired, but Kane could see that the door was now caught where the cracked walls had moved just enough to lock it in place. Time, he realized, eventually wore down everything, not just animals and plants. Kane continued, entering the corridor with Brigid a few paces behind him and Grant warily bringing up the rear.

As they entered the corridor, lights began to flicker on in recessed alcoves above, motion sensors detecting their movement. The corridor was typically bland, its walls finished in a two-tone design, primarily an off-white that had turned gray over time, while the bottom third was shaded with a thick red stripe. The stripe was some kind of section identifier, Kane theorized, perhaps relating to the mat-trans-testing facility. The corridor was empty, stretching off toward the doors of an elevator, their metal gleaming as the motion-sensitive lights at the end of the corridor flickered on in bursts of brilliance.

The corridor smelled faintly of burning, where ancient, long-settled dust was being heated by overhead lights that had presumably not been switched on in over two centuries. Kane glanced up, wondering if something might actually catch alight up there, but he could see nothing smoldering and so dismissed the thought. He walked slowly forward, the Sin Eater raised in his steady grip, checking for signs of movement or for any other indication of life. The corridor was silent, the only noise coming in the brief tinkling sounds of the fluorescent tube lights winking on as Kane approached them.

There were several doors leading off from the corridor, each one pulled closed. Kane tried a few of them, as did Brigid along the opposite wall of the corridor, and they found the majority of them unlocked and leading into what appeared to be storage rooms. The rooms stank of vinegar and were stacked full of boxes, their ancient cardboard tattered and torn. A few of the stacked boxes had toppled, spilling their contents of paper files and tape recordings over the floor. Ignoring them, Kane moved on, Brigid and Grant following.

Certain that no one was hiding in the straight corridor or the storerooms that branched from it, Kane stopped in front of the elevator doors and eyed the call button thoughtfully. The silver button glowed invitingly with a circle of faint orange around its rim. Kane knew that if anyone was in the redoubt—something that was by no means certain—using the elevator was a sure way to alert them to his team's presence.

Brigid and Grant caught up to Kane as he waited, and Grant voiced what his ex-Mag partner was thinking.

"Stairs?"

Kane nodded. "I think so," he said, leading the team toward a recess at the side of the corridor wall that ended with a heavy fire door.

"Looked like we were the first to use the mat-trans in a long time," Brigid said quietly, "but Brewster said they couldn't be sure where the intrusion had come from."

"Could be topside, then," Grant muttered.

Sin Eater ready, Kane pushed his free hand against the fire door, hoping he wasn't about to trip some unseen alarm.

With Brigid right behind him, Kane pushed open the door and waited for a moment until he was reasonably certain no one was standing in the stairwell in front of him. Dim lights placed at every third popped on. It was enough to make them clear, but hardly dazzling. In the day-to-day running of this redoubt, the staircase would have been for emergency use only, so there had been no need to keep it permanently or brightly lit. The moving of the door must have tripped the switch for the floor lights, but no noise accompanied this. Could be a silent alarm, of course, Kane realized distrustfully before tamping down the paranoia he felt.

At the rear of the group, Grant had adopted a ready crouch, scanning the corridor they had just traipsed down, just in case any sudden surprises materialized. Grant had never been comfortable leaving an operational mat-trans at his back; it meant that potentially anyone could sneak right up behind you, even from a previously empty room.

"Stairs are clear," Kane stated shortly before he stepped through the doorway and disappeared into the empty stairwell. They appeared to be at the bottom level of the redoubt, the hard concrete steps echoing Kane's every movement. Swiftly, Kane climbed the stairs, taking them two at a time, his Sin Eater pistol nosing ahead of him.

Brigid followed, entering the stairwell immediately in Kane's wake, but holding back at the lowest step so as to keep Kane covered while he hurried up to the first landing, the midpoint between floors where the staircase abruptly turned on itself. Brigid watched as Kane whipped the Sin Eater around and surveyed the next set of stairs before making his way up to the next floor. After three seconds Brigid followed Kane up the stairs, the hollow heels of her cowboy boots clip-clopping loudly in the stillness of the vertical shaft.

Grant waited patiently at the bottom of the stairs, standing so that his back wedged the door open and he could peer out to the corridor that led to the mat-trans. The echoes of his companions' footsteps came back to him, and once he judged that they had both reached the next floor he slipped back from the door, letting it slowly close before he hurried up the stairs.

One flight above, Kane stood in front of another fire door, peering through a vertical rectangle of reinforced glass, approximately twelve inches by two. There was nothing but darkness beyond, and he realized with irritation that, without something out there, the motion-sensitive lights of the ancient redoubt would remain off. He held his empty hand up in a halting gesture so that Brigid could see. "Stay here, keep me covered," he said in a low voice.

Then Kane pulled the heavy door toward him and dashed out into the corridor beyond, the solid black muzzle of his Sin Eater poised and leading the way. Brigid stepped forward, wedging the door open with her foot as she watched Kane jog down the corridor, the overhead lights sparking into life. Like the one below, this corridor was painted a dull off-white. A horizontal bar of green ran in a continuous line along the bottom third of each wall.

With the overhead lights sputtering to life ahead of him, Kane swiftly and meticulously checked each door leading off from the gray-green corridor, trying the handles, peering inside those that were unlocked, and then moving on. Brigid held her TP-9 semiautomatic out and ready, tracking Kane's movements, her steadying left hand gripped just beneath the wrist of her outstretched right.

Kane felt instinctively that this whole level was empty, and he made short work of checking as much of the area as he could. It appeared to be primarily a storage level, with several offices and a quartet of bunk rooms at the far end close to the restrooms. Other than dust and a half-full box of now-perished canned food, the level was inoffensive in its emptiness. Had anyone been here, Kane concluded, the lights would have been on already—the only

real risk was when he came to the bunk rooms, whose
lights worked on a manual switch. As such, they may just
contain someone lurking in the darkness.

Warily, Kane entered the first of the bunk rooms, ducking low as he stepped inside, conscious of the lit doorway
at his back that would illuminate him as an ideal target
for anyone hiding in the shadows. Crouching in the darkness, Kane stilled his breathing, listening for any sounds
of movement, any indication of another presence within
the room. There was nothing, he felt sure, and he edged
his left hand along the wall behind him until he found the
light switch, flicking it on.

Illuminated, the room was empty. It contained three
Army cots, one each to his left and right and a third over
against the wall farthest from the door. There was a footlocker at the end of each bed; two of them were closed,
their lids scarred and chipped. The third lay open, and
Kane peered briefly at its contents—several garishly colored comic books, a dark pair of socks with a toe missing
and a well-thumbed paperback with a man's booted feet
on its bright red cover. The open lid to the footlocker had
attracted a layer of dust, through which a two-inch yellow
circle peeked like the sun. Kane leaned down, wiping his
finger through the dust until he could see the circle in full;
it was a sticker bearing the legend "I heart Atlanta". Kane
wondered idly if the owner would still "heart" Atlanta
half as much if they saw what the nuclear devastation had
wrought there shortly after this redoubt had been sealed.

Kane turned, leaving the room as he had found it and
made his way farther along the corridor to check the other
rooms. There were three other bunk rooms, and each contained two or three Army cots along with occasional belongings that had been left behind when the redoubt had
been closed, nothing but forgotten antiques now.

Head down, Kane took long, swift strides back to the stairwell where Brigid and Grant waited. Brigid had her gun trained on the corridor as Kane approached. Behind her, Grant appeared tense as he surveyed the stairwell, up and down.

"Level's clear," Kane explained, keeping his voice low. "Guessing no one's interfered with this junk in two centuries. Whatever Cerberus was reading, it may just be a wild mutie chase."

"Might be," Grant agreed, sounding less than convinced. "Want me to take the next one?"

"I've got it," Kane assured him, taking the lead once more as he trotted up the concrete stairs.

As he turned the right-angle in the stairwell heading up, Kane saw a sliver of light eking through the rectangular glass of the fire door that faced him. Kane slowed as he climbed the stairs, checking the higher levels with a swift glance before focusing on the illuminated rectangle of light. "Could be company," he stated, his voice little more than a whisper.

At the tail of the group, Grant peered back over his shoulder, making sure no one was following them from below, while Brigid pushed herself close to the outside wall as she slowly followed Kane.

At the penultimate stair, Kane ducked, keeping his head lower than the bottom of the glass panel, pressing his knee against the step in front of him. Kane stared, trying to make out what was going on on the other side of the tiny window as its light played against the wall. He could see the familiar off-white paint of another corridor and the edge of one of the overhead strip lights showed, glowing firmly in its ceiling mounting. Kane waited, doing a slow count to ten in his head—now was not the time to rush in where angels feared to tread. As he waited, a shadow crossed the rectangle of glass, and Kane instinctively crouched lower, the barrel of the Sin Eater held at eye level, pointing upward to where the door would open.

Nothing happened.

Warily, his breathing coming slow and steady despite the tension he felt, Kane inched forward, his eyes still on the clear glass panel. Behind him, Brigid hugged the wall, the TP-9 semiautomatic poised on the closed door.

Still in a crouch, Kane sidled up to the door until his head was just below the edge of its small windowpane. For a moment he watched the square of light that was projected on the wall to his side, waiting to see if anything else crossed the gap, all the while listening intently for the sounds of movement. There was nothing; it was quiet as the grave.

Almost a minute passed with Kane just waiting there, searching for any further indications of movement. Then he peered back, his eyes glancing past Brigid and fixing on Grant's. Grant recognized the question in the ex-Mag's face, and he nodded, indicating he was ready.

Kane turned back to the fire door, standing to his full height and reaching for its cool metal handle. As he did so, the face of a man appeared at the window. Or, at least, the remains of a face—for the man appeared to be decomposing even as the empty sockets of his eyes fixed on Kane.

Chapter 4

With a sudden crash, the reinforced glass pane shattered inward as the eyeless thing's decomposing hand smashed through it, reaching for Kane through the window in the fire door. Kane leaped backward, staggering down two steps in his haste and yet still just barely avoiding the lancelike fingertips as they clawed the air, grasping for his face.

"The hell is that?" Grant swore from his position on the lower level.

Kane raised his Sin Eater, targeting the door. "Whatever it is, it's about to be a whole lot of dead," he snarled.

The heavy fire door swung open as far as the safety hinge would let it, and the creature staggered into the stairwell. His tread was unsteady, more a series of lurches than a regular stride. As he approached, Kane barked an order at it, employing the authoritative voice he had used back in his Magistrate days.

"Restricted area, perpetrator—down on your knees."

The eyeless corpse gave no indication of adhering to Kane's instruction but merely took another shaky step forward, negotiating the first stair with a rumbling groan from deep in his throat.

It was clearly a man—tall, thin and wearing a dark suit of some sort. It was hard to tell more than that, however. The suit was moth-eaten and parts of it looked burned. As for the man's flesh, that also looked moth-eaten, rotted meat clinging to jagged bones in some perverse mockery of life.

The walking corpse took a step closer to the Cerberus team. Smelling him for the first time, Brigid Baptiste began to gag. He stank of rotting, infected meat, and as she watched she saw something dark appear between the wasting muscles of his neck; a hairy caterpillar, its black body thick as a man's thumb and longer than Brigid's hand. Poised against the wall, the former archivist reared away, watching as the ghastly thing took another staggering step past her, reaching out toward Kane.

"On your knees," Kane repeated, gesturing with the muzzle of the Sin Eater pistol in his hand. "You take one more step and I will shoot." He didn't have any authority here, that was true, but Kane was pretty damn sure that the dead thing that stumbled in front of him didn't, either.

Behind the creature, the fire door had eased itself closed on its slow hinges, effectively shutting off the noise of movement here from the rest of the redoubt. The rotting thing took another lurching step toward the ex-Mag.

Kane gritted his teeth. "You're about to end up a whole lot deader if you don't back off," he snarled.

Then, with a surge of incredible speed in the dim lighting of the tight stairwell, the corpse-thing lunged for Kane. More literally he fell at Kane, arms outstretched, using weight and gravity to propel himself at the ex-Mag.

Kane depressed the trigger stud of his Sin Eater and a stream of 9 mm slugs rammed into that cadaverous body even as he fell forward. The sounds of gunfire echoed throughout the stairwell as Kane was slammed backward by the falling corpse, and he felt his feet slip off the step, throwing his balance. Then Kane found himself crashing against the metal-barlike banister that ran around the inside turn of the stairwell, striking it with his lower back in a spasm of sharp pain.

Kane's feet kicked out as he finally lost his balance, and suddenly he was toppling backward, the corpse still flailing at him as they both began to drop over the side of the stairs.

Moving on instinct alone, Brigid reached out and grabbed for the undead thing that was pushing Kane, seizing the creature's legs as she watched Kane descend over the banister. Held in Brigid's grip, the corpse-thing found himself dragged off his victim, and he turned to face her even as his head slammed into the metal banister with a resounding clang. In that instant, Brigid produced her TP-9 and drilled a cacophony of bullets into the thing's decomposing face, reducing it to pulp. Chunks of rotted flesh sprayed the walls around her as bullets mashed into the remains of the thing's hideous features.

At the same time, one floor below, Kane dropped headfirst toward the next flight of stairs. Twisting frantically in midair, he stretched his arms out in front of him in an effort to break his fall. He landed badly—it was hard to do otherwise, landing as he did on the uneven incline of the stairs—taking the impact in his strong arms and rolling over onto his back with a grunt of pain.

"You okay?" Grant asked, peeking down the stairwell at his partner as Brigid continued struggling with the corpse on the floor above.

"Help Brigid," Kane replied without hesitation.

Grant didn't question the order—he knew that Kane only used Brigid Baptiste's first name when he was really concerned for her. He figured that being knocked over a balcony by an animated corpse will do that to you.

Brigid, however, had matters well in hand. The corpse-like figure staggered in place as she peppered his decomposing body with bullets, until he finally slouched against the banister and sunk to the floor in a heap, emaciated limbs flailing in all directions.

"I think it's dead," Grant said as he hurried up the stairs to join Brigid.

Brigid looked at him, one ginger eyebrow cocked in amusement. "I think it was dead before it met me," she said.

Grant leaned down, getting a closer look at the messy, foul-smelling remains of the creature. Clearly human but visibly decomposing, he reeked of death. Using the barrel of his gun, Grant prodded the corpse a few times, but the dead thing didn't react.

As Grant pushed at the unmoving corpse in the dim lighting of the stairwell, Kane trudged back up the stairs, a spatter of blood marring his forehead. "Did we get it?" he asked.

Grant nodded while Brigid checked Kane's wound. It was just a graze; the thin line of blood made it look worse than it really was. Once she wiped that away, Brigid could see the scratch, and it had already dried.

"If Stinky here has buddies," Kane noted, "that shattered window is going to draw their attention. But if we move quick, maybe we can get the jump on them."

With that, the Cerberus trio headed for the fire door, leaving the remains of the dead man sprawled across the stairs. They didn't notice him flinch, struggling to pull himself up from the floor after the heavy fire door had inched closed, his ruined face dripping away in gobs of muscle and dried-up skin.

AN ALIEN RACE called the Annunaki had first visited the Earth aeons ago and had been surreptitiously involved in human affairs ever since the emergence of humankind.

To man, these beings from the stars, wielding technology far in advance of anything he could comprehend, had seemed divine, and so man had served and worshipped them without question.

But the Annunaki, alarmed at the proliferation of humans, initiated a wave of destruction to purge the Earth of humankind and start afresh. Recorded by various historical documents, that purging is perhaps best known as the Great Flood of Judeo-Christian tradition, and although it decimated the local population it failed to totally destroy it.

The Annunaki had spent the subsequent millennia observing from the shadows as man had grown bold, had proliferated at an alarming rate and learned how to tame his environment for his own ends. While the Annunaki had weaponry that had seemed magical in its capability, they had been fascinated to see how man developed his own terrible weaponry, things that could hurt and maim and kill.

Ultimately, the Annunaki had played their hand once more to begin the second great purging, utilizing fire this time where water had failed before. The brief nuclear war of 2001 had utterly changed the landscape of the planet Earth, creating vast tracts of irradiated land known as the Deathlands, and all but destroying the population. This was the world's legacy that the Cerberus rebels inhabited.

But while the nuclear bombs had marked the end of civilization, they had not been the only means of destruction developed by man. In fact, in the centuries since the Annunaki had first tried to extinguish him, man had excelled in developing the means with which to kill his fellow man, and many and varied ways had been created that might be used to that terrible end.

Deep in the subterranean complex of Redoubt Mike, Ezili Coeur Noir had just uncovered one such terrible weapon. The queen of all things dead, Ezili Coeur Noir had an inherent ability, something like a homing instinct, that drew her to the things that would destroy life. She had sensed this thing down here, deep beneath the Louisiana bayou, and she found herself drawn to it. In her mind, it was like some almighty magnet drawing her down into the earth, down where the dead men lay.

MOVING STEALTHILY, Kane led the way into the corridor with Grant and Brigid just behind him. The undead thing that they had encountered had shaken them all up, and Kane felt unsettled as he trekked down the corridor.

The overhead lights flickered here, and though the motion sensors responded to the presence of the Cerberus rebels, several of the fluorescent tubes had blown. In places the lights flickered in staccato bursts, leaving the corridor in a sort of half-light of lightning flashes. Like the ones they had encountered on the lower levels of the redoubt, the corridor itself was painted off-white, with a boldly colored stripe lining the bottom third of the walls. This stripe was finished in a bright sky blue, and with the flickering illumination it gave Kane the eerie illusion of being below water.

There were no other corpse-things, but the corridor was littered with broken crates and boxes, with ancient paperwork strewed across the carpet tiles of the floor.

"Looks like they used this level as a dumping ground," Grant muttered.

"Guess they wanted to get rid of this stuff," Brigid pointed out, kicking at one of the stacks of paperwork with her toe. The topmost papers of the stack slid to the floor, and Brigid saw a bold red stamp marked Top Secret across several fluttering pages. "It's just so much landfill now."

Kane moved on, passing two open doorways to his left, both of them opening out into storerooms stacked with old furniture, chairs with broken backrests and wheels missing from their runners, computer desks stained with centuries' old coffee.

This corridor proved much shorter than the ones he had explored on the preceding levels, and it ended in a solid wall on which hung a lone fire extinguisher painted a bright bloodred. Beneath the flickering light, the extinguisher seemed to flash like some fleshy cut in the wall, vying for Kane's attention.

Off to the right, Kane saw a wide corridor set at a right angle to the one they were in. The corridor stood in darkness, and Kane peered into it trying to make out details. He could discern faint noises coming from its far end, distant shuffling sounds. With a swift hand gesture, Kane led the way silently down the corridor, his companions following at a wary distance, their guns ready.

The white-blue corridor ended in a sharp turn that opened directly into a large room the size of an aircraft hangar. The exit came so abruptly in the intermittent tube lighting that Kane very nearly stepped straight out into the open before he realized what he was doing. The sole of his boot scraped against the floor as he came up short and pulled back to the edge of the wall. He had managed just the briefest of glances ahead, but in that half second he had seen plenty, his regimented brain automatically taking in details from years of discipline.

It was a vast room, perhaps eighty feet square with scratched metal decking that glinted beneath harsh spotlights hanging on high catwalks. There were figures moving around the vast room—fleshy, shambling figures like the corpse-thing that his team had tangled with in the stairwell.

Grant and Brigid caught up with Kane and he gave them a look, indicating that someone was on the other side of the wall. Brigid lowered herself behind Kane until she knelt in a crouch by the near wall. Grant, meanwhile, silently eased himself across the wide corridor until his back was flush against the far wall, just out of sight of the opening but with the gap firmly in the sights of his poised Sin Eater.

Kane inched forward, bringing himself in low to peer once more around the edge of the whitewashed wall. He saw now that the room beyond was lit in patches, but it was enough that he could make out even the far corners, where stacks of crates towered haphazardly against gray-licked walls. Three aging Army vehicles were parked off to the left of the room. Two were jeeps, their tires long since perished or removed, one with its engine on blocks in front of its open hood, and the third was a heavy artillery truck, its olive paintwork caked with mud that had dried there two centuries ago, its tires flat.

At the rear of the room, Kane spotted the twin metal doors of a goods elevator. They opened like jaws, and the elevator looked wide enough to hold a truck. This was doubtless how the vehicles had been brought here, Kane realized, and presumably they had been left when the redoubt had been closed down.

The central strip of the room was empty. Painted lines marked out a "road" and designated safe walkways. Corpselike figures wandered around this vast arena, some of them carrying bulky crates in what seemed to be an effortless manner despite their wasted musculature. Kane counted more than a dozen zombies, for want of a better term, before his attention was drawn to the far side of the room. There, off to the right, a large glass-walled area took up almost one-third of the floor space, and Kane could see movement within. A towering figure strode among the other corpses, rotting like them and yet somehow demanding Kane's attention. As he watched, Kane realized it was a woman, her flesh almost entirely rotted away, what remained a dark shade of brown like licorice beneath scraps of clothing.

There was an incessant buzzing coming from the hangar, low but present all the same, from the insects that flew close to the dead things, drawn to their rotting stench. It was incessant, like the sound made by someone running a finger around the rim of a wineglass. But for the woman it was different. Nothing flew around her.

Kane stepped back from the opening, swiftly attracting the attention of his companions. "There's something going on out there," he told them in a sharp whisper, "but I need to get closer if we're going to find out what it is."

Grant nodded sternly once and, after a moment's hesitation, Brigid did the same. Briefly, Kane outlined the layout of the room and explained where everyone was to go before he led the way on swift, silent tread, into the vast, hangarlike chamber.

All the while, Kane couldn't shake the feeling that there was something very familiar about the corpselike woman he had spied in the glass-walled office. Emaciated and almost fleshless, she had a certain presence he recognized, a certain bearing he felt that he somehow knew.

Quickly, his head ducked low between his shoulders, Kane sprinted to the nearest wall of the glass-lined area, crouching where a bank of filing cabinets had been placed against the wall on the far side.

Across the hangar, Brigid and Grant made their way through the shadows at the edge of the room, posting themselves among a pile a dismantled crates atop which a crowbar had been discarded. From here, they could see the doorway to the glass-walled area, as well as most of the vast, hangarlike room without exposing themselves.

Now poised beside the glass wall, Kane edged himself up from his crouch and peeked through the glass. This close up he could see that it was smeared with dust and grime, but he could still see through it clearly enough to observe what was going on within. The room itself seemed to be some kind of office with a laboratory attached, and files of paper had been left haphazardly over several surfaces while the lab was now in an obvious state of disrepair. The spindly corpse woman who had drawn Kane's attention continued flicking through the pages of the file she held in her clawlike hands as other undead figures wandered throughout the room.

Kane watched incredulously as a fly, its bloated black body like a blob of ink, left the gaping eye socket of its host, a dead child no taller than Kane's navel. It flew around in that strange, hard-angled-turn manner that flies will until they find somewhere to go. Then, the inkblot fly seemed to spot the woman, darting in the air to buzz toward her. But as it neared her, attracted by her reeking decrepitude, the fly's wings ceased moving and it simply dropped, plummeting to the ground where it landed with a sharp whisper, now just a dried-up husk. Kane saw another fly do the same thing a moment later, this one a fat bluebottle with body like shimmering glass. This, too, dropped in the presence of the corpse woman, falling to the floor as though in supplication.

Machinery whirred behind her within the glass-walled room, ancient lab technology that was being operated—perversely, it seemed to Kane—by another of the shambling undead figures, this one a short, stocky woman whose skin had wrinkled into a black smear that clung like tar to her dead flesh. She was operating some kind of mixing device, Kane realized, and he moved a little to his right so that he could see what the device was doing. He watched as test tubes spun, their luminous contents bubbling and frothing with each rotation of a spinner arm. There were four test tubes at each end of the arm, eight in total, each clamped there by holding pincers, a stopper cap preventing their contents from spilling free as the arm rotated.

"What the hell are they mixing up in there?" Kane mouthed, his voice something less than a whisper.

Kane watched as the eight glass tubes were whirled around once again within the centrifuge unit, like a tiny funfair ride. The spinner arm itself was located behind reinforced armaglass, like a little glass display cabinet at the side of the room. Presumably, the cabinet was designed to both dampen the noise of the machinery and to protect the user from dangerous chemicals, for the door could be sealed to prevent any leakage. However, Kane spotted a crack in the glass and the lock appeared to have been wrenched off, a brown smear across the front panel—the woman's flesh, he acknowledged with a growing sense of nausea.

A digital timer at the top of the mixing unit glowed, proudly counting down from a little over twelve hours, its green numbers marching slowly toward an inevitable zero. Whatever it was that was being mixed there, it would be ready at sundown, Kane calculated.

His interest piqued, Kane shifted his position, turning his attention back to the taller, corpselike figure who seemed to dominate the room. The corpse woman was working through a file of papers, and Kane swallowed hard as he saw the pages begin to crumble in her hands, tiny flecks of paper sailing away on the air, now nothing more than dust. Wrapped in its brown cardboard sleeve, the file was marked U.S. Army and several notations appeared on its foremost page.

Kane edged closer to the glass, trying to make out the designation on the front cover where the corpse woman held it with vomit-yellow talons. *RWI077-093-d.*

Kane committed the number to memory as he watched the woman flick through the file, a rictus grin fixed on her hideous features. With each turn of the page, flakes of paper drifted from the file like ashes from a fire; it was literally rotting at her touch.

Kane turned at a nearby noise, ducking out of sight. Across the hangar, the animated corpse of a male was pacing toward the glass-walled room, rolling gait uncomfortable as he balanced a heavy metal cylinder in his outstretched arms. The man was wide-shouldered and must have been over six feet tall when he was alive. He still seemed formidable even with so much of his body rotted away beneath the ragged remains of his dark clothes. Despite himself, Kane smiled when he noticed that the corpse wore a leather patch over his left eye, even though the evidence of the right eye was just an empty socket now. Whatever it had worn in life, the man now wore in death, Kane realized.

Eye Patch stomped through the open doorway and into the glass-walled area, and he stopped in front of the woman, showing the cylinder for her approval like some mockery of an old-fashioned door-to-door salesman.

Kane hunkered down, watching the transaction from behind the concealing cabinets. The woman leader stared at the cylinder for a long moment, reading the coded markings there with lizardlike eyes yellow as egg yolks. There were several brightly colored haz-chem labels on its side, Kane saw, including one showing a cross through the black silhouette of a slope-sided beaker on a burned orange background—poison.

The woman ran her hand along the metal canister, her ragged nails playing across its surface like nails on a chalkboard. Kane gasped as he saw the paint begin to peel and flake away as if it had been prematurely aged by the elements.

Then the ex-Mag heard the corpse woman speak for the first time, in a voice like dried leaves. "Yes," she told the figure with the eye patch. "Find more. Do this for your mistress. Do this for Ezili Coeur Noir."

The partially decomposed male figure placed the canister on the floor, leaving it at Ezili Coeur Noir's feet. Then he turned and made his way from the glass room before halting in the doorway. Kane got the impression that the broad-shouldered corpse was sniffing the air, as if he had sensed something. Kane crouched, pressing his back against the glass as the broad figure stood there, searching the room with his eyeless socket.

From his position, Kane could see only the figure's boots—holed and wasting away. He felt his stomach turn as the dead thing made some hideous sound from the back of his throat, the noise of a man choking on his own blood.

Across the room, crouching among the stacked crates, Grant and Brigid watched furtively as Kane huddled closer to the wall, trying to keep out of the eye line of the dead thing standing in the doorway. They heard him make that terrible sound deep in his throat, and they watched with concern as three figures seemed to answer, moving toward him from their work at a stack of matériel near the glass office. Ungainly but purposeful, the figures made their way over to the area where Kane was crouching, one of them using an ebony walking cane to help balance the stride of his wasted legs.

Grant tapped on his Commtact. "Kane, you've been spotted," he whispered. "Abort."

Even as Kane heard Grant's words amplified through his mastoid bone over the subdermal Commtact, the eye-patched figure at the doorway turned to face him, showing the fearsome remains of its broken teeth as it snarled at him. Kane's eyes widened as three more rotting forms joined Eye Patch, standing in a semicircle at his back. As Kane began to push himself up from the wall, the figure with the eye patch raised his sickening, rotted hand and his bony index finger extended to point at the ex-Mag, like the accusing finger of judgment.

"Guess you've got me dead to rights," Kane muttered as he stood in front of the four accusing, wasted figures.

Chapter 5

Kane took in the figures who faced him in an instant.

The one with the eye patch pointed at Kane with a skeletal index finger as if in accusation of the living.

Behind Eye Patch, three other forms loomed, rocking on their heels as they watched him with dead eyes. The one farthest to the left was tall and scarecrow thin, wearing tattered clothing. He was so unsteady that he used a crooked walking stick.

Beside Walking Stick, Kane saw an emaciated figure with the straggly remains of long dreadlocks. The wide hips of her pelvis confirmed that she had been a woman, and a powerfully built one at that. When the woman bunched her fists, a gob of discolored and rotting flesh hung down between her ragged fingers like a teardrop. Mentally, Kane tagged the woman Dreadlocks before turning his attention to the last of the undead creatures.

This one was shorter than the others, a little over five feet tall, and had adopted a fighting stance, pitching his legs wide to lower his center of gravity. He had wispy hair, and his skull peeked through the rotted flesh of his long-dead face. Kane tagged this one Shorty, and figured him to be the least trouble if it came to a fight.

Pointing at Kane, Eye Patch curled an index finger, folding it inward, like the beckoning finger of fate. A twisting knot in his stomach, Kane recognized the movement; the corpse wasn't pointing but was pulling the trigger of a gun, an old flinch reaction from whatever brutal life he had lived.

As the realization dawned, Kane took a quick step to his left, away from the glass wall. The tall corpse with the walking stick took a step to his right, holding the stick out to block the ex-Mag's way. Behind the clutch of corpses, the twisted form of Ezili Coeur Noir had appeared, moving like a specter from the glass-fronted office into the main hangar. Her mouth opened, black tongue writhing amid rotting gums, as she spoke.

"Life."

Kane heard the word, and felt the nagging at the back of his mind that somehow he knew this woman. The eye-patch-wearing corpse took another step toward Kane, so close now that Kane had to step back to avoid him. The corpse's dead companions stepped forward, too, boxing Kane in. Behind them, more of the undead figures had begun amassing, acknowledging the perverted condemnation of the queen of death.

Taking another lurching step forward, the figure with the eye patch reached for Kane once more, and Kane found himself backed up against the wall.

"Back off, Eye Patch," Kane snarled.

The corpse ignored him, reaching up with his rotting left hand and grabbing a fistful of Kane's jacket. The instant the corpse grabbed him, Kane rammed his Sin Eater into the corpse's belly and squeezed the trigger. Gobs of desiccated flesh spurted from the figure's back as 9 mm bullets blasted through rotted flesh. The corpse staggered backward several steps, wrenching a square from Kane's jacket, two brass buttons flying off into the glass wall to Kane's right.

Freed of the corpse-thing's grip, Kane kicked out with his left leg, striking the tall man in the midsection. Eye

Patch bent over himself with the impact of Kane's kick, and the ex-Magistrate pushed off, flipping over the toppling body and bringing his gun up to deal with the next of the clutch of zombies.

A short way across the hangar, Grant spoke to Brigid where they hid, watching the frantic showdown from the cover of the stacked crates. It had been less than ten seconds since Grant's Commtact warning, and it was clear Kane was in trouble.

"Come on," Grant snapped.

Brigid trotted out from cover in Grant's wake, blasting bursts of bullets from her TP-9 at the looming pack of undead creatures that traipsed across the room toward their partner.

A fleshless woman standing close to the crates staggered over as Grant drilled her with bullets from his Sin Eater, flipping the weapon around to smash her in the face with its grip. Brigid leaped over the woman's corpse as it flopped to the floor.

And then, the one thing Brigid had most feared happened. As she leaped the fallen figure of the corpse, a skeletal hand whipped out and grabbed her ankle, pulling her to the ground.

Brigid spun, unleashing another burst of bullets right into the undead thing's withered face at near point-blank range. The corpse woman shook in place as Brigid's bullets drilled into her, ripping away the gory stump of her nose and rattling against the empty sockets of her eyes. Yet still the undead thing clung on, ignoring the effects the bullets were having on her face, and Brigid reached a sudden, awful realization—bullets weren't stopping these things.

A little way across the hangar, Kane had just come to the same conclusion. Still in motion, he had blasted a volley of 9 mm steeljackets at the scarecrowlike figure holding the walking stick, only to see him stumble a pace back before regaining his footing, glowering at Kane with those lifeless eye sockets. Kane spun, dropping low as his leg swept the scarecrow, knocking him from his feet. The corpse's walking stick whipped out as he fell with a ghastly hiss from peeled-back lips as black as night.

Kane continued the leg sweep, catching the woman with dreadlocks just behind her ankle. She stumbled a pace forward, but despite her apparent unsteadiness, she refused to fall. She turned on Kane then, reaching down at him with long arms as he scooted across the metal plating of the floor. Kane grunted as the woman's hands snagged the torn front of his jacket, and she demonstrated incredible strength as she pulled him from the decking in one swift jerk.

The hideous figure of Ezili Coeur Noir let loose a deep, throaty laugh as Kane was yanked from the floor, nodding her approval as he was thrust up in the air by her dead servant. With clawlike, fleshless hands, Dreadlocks lifted Kane high over her head as her mistress laughed, and Kane tried desperately to bring his pistol up to shoot her.

Just then a stream of bullets slammed into the woman holding Kane and she stumbled back, her dreadlocks whipping around her face. Kane felt her grip loosen, and suddenly he was hurtling through the air before crashing an instant later into—and through—the glass wall of the office. Kane rolled across the office as glass shards shattered all around him. Then, bringing his gun up, he blasted a stream of fire across the remaining windows behind him, sending a burst of shattering glass at the five corpselike figures who were just turning to follow him. He watched in grim satisfaction as three of the figures dropped back to protect Ezili Coeur Noir, with only the shorter individual leaping over the barrier of the filing cabinets amid the smashing glass.

Kane engaged his Commtact, instructing his companions in a hurried explanation. "They ain't living and they ain't dying. Anyone have any ideas?"

The zombie he'd named Shorty was in the office now, hurrying past a doorway through which Kane could see the closed doors of an elevator, and Kane saw that he had grabbed two long shards of broken glass, wielding them like knives as he hurried at Kane. Still on the floor, Kane pushed himself back on his shoulders before springing up into a crouch and unleashing another stream of bullets at his onrushing attacker. The short zombie was knocked backward by the impact of the bullets, and he held one hand up as if to protect his ruined face.

STRUGGLING in the mantrap-like grip of the dead woman holding her ankle, Brigid Baptiste was a little too preoccupied to answer Kane's question. The undead thing wrestled with Brigid's foot as they lay sprawled on the floor, even as Brigid's TP-9 blasted another burst of gunfire in her face. Kane was right; bullets were having almost no effect, and they needed some other way to deal with these deathless things.

With a determined shriek, Brigid kicked the zombie girl's arm with her free leg, snapping the brittle bones with a determined boot. From somewhere deep in her rotting chest, the undead thing growled. Brigid ignored her, kicking out again.

GRANT WAS PEPPERING the area with bullets, turning this way and that as additional corpses descended on him from all around the hangarlike room. One, a child with a wilted stump for an arm, ran straight into Grant's line of fire, his decomposing body shaking in place as he staggered closer to the ex-Mag.

They aren't stopping, Grant realized, but maybe we can drive them away somehow.

THE GLASS SHARD in the zombie's raised hand shattered under the impact of Kane's bullets, spraying glass over the undead man's ruinous face. Instantly, Shorty lunged out with his other hand, and Kane saw the lethal shard of glass leave the creature's other hand and cut toward him through the air. In flinch reaction, Kane's right hand whipped up, bullets lashing the ceiling from the muzzle of the Sin Eater as he tracked the hurtling glass knife.

His shots missed, but Kane managed to bat the lethally sharp blade out of the air with the barrel of his pistol, turning his head as the blade shattered into a dozen smaller, onrushing blades. Then Shorty was upon him, and Kane saw the other corpses clambering over the filing cabinets as they followed the most direct route to assist their companion.

THE CORPSE CHILD grabbed the end of Grant's Sin Eater, shuddering in place, ignoring the stream of bullets that drilled through his tiny hand. His other arm, withered to something like a twig-thin branch, jabbed at Grant, stabbing him in his side so hard he felt it through the protective weave of his shadow suit.

With a single mental command, Grant sent his pistol back to its housing in his sleeve, and the corpse child stumbled as he lost his grip. Grant was ready, however, and he drove the hard end of his bent knee straight into the undead child's face, knocking him to the floor.

An instant later Grant was turning, shoving another

walking corpse aside as he sprinted toward the far side of the room, away from the glass-walled office.

"Kane, Brigid—hang tight," Grant ordered over the Commtact. "I just had an idea."

"Make it quick," Kane responded as he threw the attacking zombie over a desk, knocking a bulbless lamp and an empty filing tray flying.

Behind Kane, three more undead figures were making their way toward him in their unwieldy but determined manner, the one with the black walking stick thrusting it in front of him like some kind of sword.

BRIGID LEAPED from the floor, the undead woman's hand still clutching at her ankle. It didn't matter as Brigid's second kick had wrenched the rotten limb free of its socket, and now she dragged the hand and arm along with her as she ran back to the crates where she and Grant had hidden. Behind Brigid, the fleshless woman flapped her remaining arm as she struggled to pull herself up from the floor, moving with all the grace of a drowning man.

Brigid shoved her TP-9 back into her low-slung hip holster, reached for the crowbar resting atop the crates.

As the corpse woman staggered toward her, maggots visibly writhing in the stump now hanging in place of her arm, Brigid lashed backward with the crowbar, smashing it against the corpse's face with all her strength. The undead creature rocked on her heels, and Brigid kicked out hard into the corpse's pelvis, forcing her backward. Then Brigid swung the crowbar once more, this time from low to the floor, bringing the metal tool up in a vicious arc that rammed the claw end straight into the woman's ruined face.

The corpse-thing whined in some approximation of pain or surprise—Brigid didn't know which—and stumbled backward, pulling at the metal bar now lodged in her face.

Bunching her fists, Brigid took a pace toward the stumbling undead woman, preparing to knock her down once more, only to hear a growling noise from far off across the hangar bay. But this time the growling wasn't coming from a recently dead thing's long-dry throat. Instead it was coming from an engine as Grant started up the artillery truck that had waited in the redoubt for over two hundred years.

Sitting in the cab, Grant pumped the accelerator and the truck rumbled to life around him. The vehicle was rusted and worn, and all four tires were flat as road kill, but at least it operated along the same basic principles as the Sandcats he had driven back in his days with the Cobaltville Magistrate Division.

The corpse figure of a man was slammed against the hood and disappeared from view beneath the body of the truck as the vehicle picked up speed.

As he urged the artillery truck across the metal decking toward the distant glass walls of the office-lab, Grant glanced out to his right and his eyes met with Brigid's. The corpse-thing with the crowbar in her face sinking to her knees in front of her.

"Want me to get the door for you?" Brigid asked, her words amplified over the medium of their linked Commtacts.

"Say again?" Grant asked.

But Brigid was already sprinting across the room, rushing behind the truck as it picked up speed. Grant glanced to his left and saw Brigid running onward deftly avoiding the shambling undead figures as she hurried toward the closed doors of the goods elevator.

"I figure we have only one exit," Brigid explained over

the Commtact, but before she could continue Grant cut her off.

"I gotcha," Grant assured her. "Be there in a tick. Kane," he added, alerting his other colleague. "You might want to duck down."

"Roger that." Kane's voice snapped back instantly, not bothering to question his best friend's left-field advice.

Grant was at the wall to the office then and he slammed on the brakes as the truck smashed through the floor-to-ceiling panes of glass. He saw Kane leap back just in time as the glass shattered all around him, twinkling shards surging across the office like some beautiful, man-made tidal wave.

The truck slapped into the corpse wielding the walking stick like a weapon, knocking him flying in an instant, and its front tire bumped over another before it came to a halt, chairs, desks and office debris toppling in front of its hood.

Commanding his Sin Eater back into his palm, Grant snapped off a quick burst of covering fire from the truck's window as Kane vaulted over a dust-caked desk and scrambled toward the waiting vehicle. A moment later Kane had clambered up into the high rig, the figure with the dreadlocks lunging after him.

"What kept you?" Kane asked breathlessly, delivering a swift back-kick into the grasping corpse woman's chin.

"Traffic," Grant replied, working the gearshift into reverse and pumping the gas.

A moment later the Army truck was hurtling backward across the hangar bay, rotten rubber tires screeching on the metal decking as Grant wrestled with the wheel. They hit something behind them, and Kane leaned out of the window, peering to see what it was. A stack of crates toppled over, and two undead corpses were knocked from their feet. Ezili Coeur Noir watched, well away from the path of the rushing vehicle.

Over by the elevator, Kane spotted Brigid jabbing at the control panel with her free hand as she sprayed staggered bursts of bullets at a half-dozen undead men who threatened to overwhelm her. With a cheerful chime that seemed utterly out of place in the nightmarish surroundings, the elevator arrived, its jawlike metal doors sighing open while Brigid's sweeping bullets knocked another zombie off his feet.

Grant's foot pumped the brake, and he gripped the steering wheel as the truck threatened to go into a skid on its bald flat tires. As the vehicle screamed across the metal it knocked three corpse figures from its path, but there was no time for celebration. Brigid Baptiste leaped aside as ten tons of truck hurtled past her and crashed hard into the edge of the open elevator, metal-on-metal kicking up a lightninglike burst of sparks. As the truck drew to a stop, its left side flush with the wall of the goods elevator, Brigid rushed into the elevator cage and jabbed at the control panel with the heel of her hand. In front of her, the doors began to close on their pneumatic motors as several undead figures struggled from the floor toward the fleeing Cerberus team.

Behind Brigid, Kane had jumped down from the cab and was adding bursts of gunfire from his own weapon to hers as she fended off the approaching figures until the shining metal doors finally closed. As they did so, Brigid let out a long breath. "What on earth…?" she asked.

"RWI077-093-d," Kane replied, flexing the tension from his shoulders as the elevator shuddered and began to rise.

"What does that mean?" Brigid asked him, baffled.

"It was the code on the file that crazy-looking woman

was studying," Kane told her. "She called herself Ezili Coeur Noir."

"Ezili of the Black Heart," Brigid said in translation. "Voodoo *loa,* the spirit of death."

"No." Kane shook his head. "That's no voodoo spirit."

Brigid looked up at Kane querulously as she discharged the near-empty clip from her TP-9 and loaded a fresh one. "No?"

"Don't ask me how," Kane told her, "but that there— that's Lilitu, Annunaki dark goddess and royal pain in the ass."

Brigid's eyes widened as she stared at Kane, utterly dumbfounded.

Chapter 6

In her guise as dark goddess of the Annunaki pantheon, Lilitu had been manipulating humankind almost from the day that she had first emerged from the water and begun to walk on two legs.

Her story had been told in a hundred different ways across the different religions of mankind, where she had been Lilith, Lilu and even the Queen of Sheba who seduced wise King Solomon. The ancient Sumerian records cast Lilitu as a terrible harlot-goddess who reveled in the extremes of carnality. As Lilith, Lilitu was reputed to sexually take men by force as they slept, and in Talmudic lore she was believed to be the first wife of Adam.

While mythology was often mired in interpretation, it was clear that Lilitu was a shrewd and ruthless manipulator with a sadistic streak. Thousands of years ago, when the Annunaki had first walked the Earth, Lilitu's family holdings had become a sprawling empire near the Red Sea. Wishing to acquire the territory, Overlord Enlil had wed Lilitu in a pact that had resulted in betrayal and usurpation. Thus, Lilitu had embarked on a millennia-long war with the Annunaki Supreme Council, a sprawling game of chess with humanity as pawns. And so Lilitu was rightly renowned for her utter ruthlessness, the possessor of a callous streak that recognized no limitations.

Several years ago, Lilitu had emerged from her chrysalis state where she had hidden for ninety years in the guise of Baroness Beausoleil, ruler of her own self-named ville in the Outlands. She had caused trouble for the Cerberus rebels—both as Baroness Beausoleil and in her true form—since almost the day of their inception.

However, although she had assumed many forms in her near-immortal lifespan, the last time the Cerberus rebels had dealt with Lilitu she had been in her true body, a graceful humanoid goddess with a snakelike aspect to her crimson-scaled skin and black-vertical-slit yellow eyes, a magnificent crest atop her skull.

Less than a year ago, the Cerberus team had dealt what had appeared to be a final, decisive blow against the Annunaki's mothership, *Tiamat*. During the scuffle, Lilitu had been shot—and apparently killed—by her brood sister Rhea, and her corpse had still been aboard *Tiamat* when the magnificent organic spacecraft had been destroyed in an almighty fireball. Kane, Brigid and Grant had seen that with their own eyes, and yet they knew that the Annunaki had a nasty habit of surviving even the most dire and absolute of circumstances.

Kane climbed back into the cab of the artillery truck as the elevator doors opened in front of them, and he shot Brigid an inquisitive look. "You going to say anything, Baptiste?" he asked. "Or are you just going to let your jaw hang like that until the wind changes?"

Brigid Baptiste brushed a lock of her red-gold hair behind her ear as she finally spoke, now seated between Kane and Grant. "Lilitu," she said, as if quite unable to comprehend what Kane had said. "That…*thing*…was Lilitu?"

Kane nodded. "I think so," he said. "She's been through a few changes."

"A few changes?" Grant repeated, amused. "She looked awfully *dead,* my friend."

Placing his hands on the steering wheel, Grant pushed down gently on the accelerator and the truck idled out of the elevator as the doors opened to their full extent, a long, ill-lit shaft yawning in front of before them. As the truck rumbled along a few feet, motion-sensitive lights popped on overhead, lighting a little more along the wide tunnel. In the flickering lighting, the three Cerberus teammates saw they were in a gray-walled corridor that angled upward toward the surface. The corridor was wide enough to accommodate the truck twice over, and as they watched the lights pop on ahead of them, the team became aware of dark figures lurking in the shadows. These figures, like the ones they had left below, stood at strange angles like once-proud trees struck by lightning, their bodies rotten, creamy bone visible amid the perished skin of their emaciated faces. The undead.

"How much gas do we have?" Kane snapped as he wound down the passenger side window and recalled his Sin Eater back into his right palm with a slap.

Grant looked at the fuel gauge that was set beneath the speedometer on the dashboard display as the cab shuddered in time with the idling engine. The needle stood at empty. "Not much," Grant said.

Kane cursed as he began blasting a stream of 9 mm slugs at the nearest shadowy form. The zombie thing to their right fell in a hail of bullets, but Kane watched with revulsion as it began to struggle back to its feet. Up ahead bright sunlight was just visible through a huge rollback door that stood open at the end of the tunnel.

"Think we have enough to get outside?" Kane asked, peering at Grant and seeing the twisted wires beneath the ignition where his colleague had hot-wired the ancient truth.

"We're running on fumes," Grant admitted, "but what

the hell." With that he slammed his foot down hard on the accelerator and the truck lurched forward, bumping over the struggling corpse and knocking another rotting figure from his feet like a bowling pin.

The truck rocked so much that it felt as if it might shake itself apart as they picked up speed. Leaning from the passenger window, Kane snapped off swift burst of gunfire as another rotting figure loomed into view.

The truck now snugly within the tunnel, trundling along at a steady clip as Grant wrestled to keep it on course. The vehicle's bald tires struggled for traction, pulling the heavy machine toward the walls as Grant held the accelerator down. The cab stank of diesel, and Grant eyed the fuel gauge on the dashboard once again—the needle seemed to be stuck at empty, and Grant tapped the plastic several times to see if it was a genuine reading or whether it had simply become jammed over time. The needle didn't move.

"Kane," Brigid urged, pointing up ahead.

Kane saw what was worrying Brigid—a zombie stood close to the rollback door, his skin peeled away from his face, skull held at an odd angle atop his broad shoulders. The undead thing grasped a thick tree branch—wider than a man's leg—and as Kane watched he hefted the branch forward like a jousting pole, swinging its sharp point at the windshield of the cab.

Grant stomped on the accelerator, knocking another corpse flying in the air until the undead thing slapped against the low ceiling. Grant peered in the mud-caked side mirror, watching as the corpse fell from the ceiling and dropped into the back of the truck. He could not tell if it was still moving, and he turned his attention back to the doors ahead.

Up ahead, the broad figure lunged with its jousting

pole branch, driving the sharp end into the grille of the truck with a rending of metal. Beyond the windshield, the engine began to pour a cloud of steam, obscuring Grant's view as he struggled with the wheel. Behind them, the undead corpse in the back grabbed onto the flatbed of the truck with clawlike hands, the ancient paint there flaking away with each scratch of his ragged nails.

As they hurtled over the lip of the redoubt doors, Kane swung open his passenger side door, using it like a battering ram to knock the broad-shouldered zombie off his feet. Bald tires spun on the dirt track beyond the redoubt, and suddenly the truck was out in the open. Outside the external door they found themselves bumping along a dirt road that carved a path through the dense swamp. Although dense, the plant life in the immediate vicinity of the doorway looked brown and ragged, as if it had been touched by poison.

As soon as they left the shadows of the underground redoubt, the heat of the Louisiana swamp struck them like a wall, the thick, heavy atmosphere of late morning like some physical blanket weighing down upon them. The breeze through the open passenger side window didn't feel refreshing at all; it felt oppressive, hitting Kane in the face like hot liquid. Sweat beaded on his brow immediately, and his companions shifted in their seats, sweat running down their backs. Kane pushed the collar of his jacket back off his neck, wiping away the perspiration that was already forming there with an irritated hand. Threads hung from the shredded front of the jacket where the undead creature with the eye patch had grasped him.

As they continued along the overgrown dirt track away from the redoubt entrance, they became aware of other shambling figures moving through the undergrowth, and

Kane peered in his side mirror to see more corpselike forms massing at the rollback doorway of the redoubt.

Warm air sullied the cabin, and the smell of the bayou came to them through the open window. Sitting between Grant and Kane, Brigid held her hand against the dusty vent in the center of the dash, feeling the stream of warm air there like breath against her skin.

Suddenly the remains of Grant's side window shattered entirely as a charcoal-black skeletal hand reached through, grabbing for the wheel. It was the undead thing who had landed on the bed of the truck as they sped out of the redoubt, Grant realized. As the wheel was pulled out of the ex-Mag's grip, the truck lurched to the left, screeching off the dirt road and crashing through a clump of saplings, thin branches snapping as they struck the grille and windshield.

"There's one on the roof!" Grant shouted as the truck bumped through dense leaf cover that hung like a green curtain ahead of them, obscuring their way.

Grasping the steering wheel with both hands, Grant fought with the wheel, struggling to right the old artillery truck's path as the bald tires spun for traction in the marshy ground underfoot. Grant eased up on the accelerator as he felt the truck threaten to roll, pulling the vehicle back toward the dirt road, even as the undead figure batted at his face with his clawed hand.

On the other side of the cab, Kane thrust open the passenger door and clambered out, the road rushing by just a few feet below the soles of his boots. "Come on, you ugly son of a bitch," he snarled as he pulled himself up onto the roof.

The undead figure on the cab hissed as he saw Kane, dark-colored spittle spraying from his black mouth. Dressed in tattered rags, the figure had stick-thin limbs and dark rubbery skin so taut that it looked as if it had been stretched over a drum. He lay on the cab roof, legs splayed out behind him for balance, reaching into the driver's window with one bony, emaciated arm.

With his left hand reaching back to cling solidly to the edge of the truck, Kane clambered toward the undead thing in a crouch, powering the Sin Eater back into his free hand as he did so. "Ride's over," he snarled. "Don't forget to tip your driver."

The undead creature grabbed for the muzzle of the Sin Eater as Kane's finger tightened on the guardless trigger, and his rotten hand was blown away in a burst of bullets. The walking corpse seemed surprised for a moment, the dead pit eyes gazing in astonishment at his ruined hand. Kane brought the pistol around and blasted off another stream of bullets as the truck bumped over the uneven road, and his shots went wild.

Then the undead thing flipped his legs out in a such a way that they almost seemed to be dislocated, and Kane found himself tumbling off the roof and over the front of the truck. Everything seemed to whirl around him, and Kane reached out blindly until his left hand found purchase. As swiftly as it had begun, Kane's fall stopped, and he found himself lying prone on the front of the truck above the engine housing, his hand grasping one of the wide side mirrors that stuck out like an elephant's ears from the truck's hood.

Through the dirt-streaked windshield, Kane saw Brigid's eyes widen. Then Grant was shouting something to him, indicating that he needed to get out of Grant's field of vision, even as the truck bumped once more off the strip of bayou road, careening onward at an angle, vegetation brushing against its side.

Low-hanging branches snapped against Kane's back,

jabbing into the protective weave of his shadow suit as the truck hurtled onward down the road. Then the undead figure that had been atop the cab crawled feet-first over the windshield. In a moment, the moving corpse was sitting with his back propped against the dusty windshield glass, and he kicked out at Kane even as the ex-Magistrate struggled to pull himself back onto the hood. The undead thing's foot slammed into Kane's face, the torn remains of his shoe falling apart as it struck him. Kane fell backward, his grip slipping fractionally on the wing mirror.

Another good kick, Kane thought, and I'll be—

But there was no time to finish his thought. The moving corpse kicked out again, and Kane found himself rolling off the hood, the roar of the engine close to his ear as he toppled over the front of the truck.

Inside the cab Brigid had produced her own blaster from its holster as the corpse kicked Kane from the hood. She thrust it against the windshield glass and began firing, fractured bullet holes appearing across the glass like heavy raindrops as she sprayed the back of the undead figure with everything she could. The mobile corpse shuddered with each shot, chunks of desiccated flesh disappearing in clouds of dusty dry skin. He turned, a disquieting movement of his emaciated body, somehow not quite the way a person should move, and then opened the black jaws of his rotten mouth, hissing out a curse at Brigid as she continued to drill him with bullets. Then the moving corpse butted his head against the ruined glass of the windshield, slamming against it like a ram as the truck hurried on through the bayou.

"Where the hell did Kane go?" Grant shouted over the sound of Brigid's semiautomatic, only now seeing his friend was no longer on the hood.

The frantic answer came in an unlikely form. The

undead figure that was butting itself against the wind-shield seemed to suddenly slip away, slumping to the right of the hood before falling from the vehicle entirely. Kane pulled himself up over the side, using the wheel rim and bumper to kick himself up from where he had been clinging just seconds earlier. Hanging on the hood, he watched the corpse-thing fall from the truck and roll across the road in a tumble of ruined limbs before he was caught up in the double wheels at the rear of the truck and was crushed beneath their tread.

Brigid pushed open the passenger door as the truck sped on through the bayou, and Kane clambered back inside, his jacket and face smeared with dirt.

"What happened to you?" Brigid asked.

"Ducked out for a sec. Thought I saw someone I knew," Kane said with a lopsided grin.

Grant tapped at the needle of the fuel gauge once again and glanced in the side mirror, hoping that they had enough fuel to outrun anything else that intended to follow them until they could at least regroup and come up with a plan. The engine growled unhappily as Grant moved the old-fashioned gearshift, holding the clutch at the biting point as they struggled around a tight bend that ran on an incline.

"So?" Grant finally asked, his eyes on what passed for a road amid the greenery. "You think that thing was Lilitu?"

"When we last saw her," Kane offered, "she *was* dead, remember? Blasted by an ASP gun, then caught up in *Tiamat*'s fireball."

"And yet she still walks," Brigid muttered, her voice quiet with concern, fingers still playing against the warm stream of air from the broken air-conditioning vent.

"You sure that's Lilitu?" Grant persisted, as the buried

entrance to Redoubt Mike disappeared around a bend in the road behind them.

Kane nodded sullenly. "I never forget a pretty face," he said.

Grant sneered. "I didn't get a real close look, but it did seem like a face you'd never forget."

In myth, Lilitu was renowned as a sexual predator. In reality, Kane had suffered at the hands of more than one deranged would-be goddess during their adventures, and while Grant wasn't sure of the details, it had been a pattern so frequent it had become almost comical for a while. Even so, Grant knew better than to rib his partner about it.

Kane turned to Brigid, seeing the look of vexation that marred her features. Brigid's eidetic memory was such that she should have recognized the dark goddess straight away had she got as close as Kane had, even with the desiccation of her old, lizard skin.

"I wonder what happened to her?" Brigid said, thinking out loud. "The Annunaki are almost immortal, but she looked barely alive."

"Their mothership, *Tiamat,* has regenerated the snake-faces before now," Kane pointed out.

"Regenerated, yes," Brigid agreed, "but that is... well..."

"One bastard ugly regeneration," Grant suggested.

"Straight to the bottom of the regeneration class," Brigid agreed. "Besides, the Annunaki pantheon may have proved irritatingly hard to kill, but *Tiamat* is no longer in orbit. She's dead. Isn't she?"

"She may be," Kane mused, "but bits of her are still cropping up. We found that chair, remember?"

Brigid nodded, remembering only too well. A little over a month ago, she and Kane had come into contact with an individual called Papa Hurbon, a voodoo priest who practiced the dark arts of the Bizango. Hurbon had a handful of seemingly undead zombies at his beck and call, but Kane and Brigid had reasoned these away as created through drug use, the Bizango practitioner's standard way of sapping the will of the living to create what appeared to be a walking corpse. During that escapade, Hurbon had revealed himself to be in possession of something he called a vision chair, but which Brigid had identified as a working astronavigator's chair from the deck of *Tiamat*. The chair had been alive, bonding with any sitter to generate a series of highly detailed star maps within the mind's eye. In discovering this fact, Brigid had very nearly been killed by the chair as it attempted to consume her and control her will. The chair itself had subsequently disappeared when its owner had returned for it, and Papa Hurbon had found himself maimed at that owner's hands, left alive but with both of his legs removed for her sadistic pleasure. Hurbon had, Kane recalled, referred to that sadistic owner as Ezili Coeur Noir.

"How far away was that?" Brigid asked suddenly, gazing out the windows of the truck as if seeing their surroundings for the first time. The shrubbery here seemed lush and green, moisture glistening on its leaves like beads of sweat. They had left the strange dead zone that surrounded the redoubt, with no clear explanation yet of what it meant.

Considering Brigid's question, Kane did a swift calculation in his head, then stopped as the realization dawned. They were very close to Papa Hurbon's voodoo temple and the last known location of the vision chair. "Shit," Kane swore through gritted teeth. "A dozen miles, maybe less."

"And this is old Louisiana," Brigid pointed out. "We're

not actually that far away from Beausoleil, which is where Lilitu was reborn in hybrid form."

Grant growled with irritation as he turned the wheel of the old artillery truck. "You guys ever get the feeling you could see something coming but you never bothered to look?"

Brigid was about to respond, but with a sudden lurch the engine spluttered and the heavy vehicle shuddered to an abrupt halt. Cursing, Grant pumped his foot on the gas pedal several times, but there was no response. He reached beneath the steering column, untwisting and re-knitting the wires he had used to engage the truck but, other than a spark from the wires and a cough from the engine, nothing happened.

"Whatever's going on," Grant explained, "we'll be meeting it on foot."

Kane turned to the passenger door and, Sin Eater still in hand, pushed it open and hopped out of the cab. Grant did likewise from his own side, while Brigid shuffled across the bench seat and dropped down beside Kane. The dark-haired ex-Mag was already back in point man mode, huddling in on himself as he studied the surrounding foliage, listening to the orchestra of birds and insects all around them. Off to his right, some distance from where the truck had shuddered to a halt, Kane heard heavy, dragging footsteps, and he turned that way, urging his colleagues to remain behind him. Kane trotted forward, moving with the silent surety of a sleek jungle cat, pushing aside branches as he made his way toward the noise.

Ahead, through the low-hanging fronds of the plant cover, Kane saw another of the hideous walking corpses. This one was about five feet tall with a stocky build, and he seemed to be walking in a circle. At first, Kane thought his head was ducked low to study his steps, but as he turned Kane saw that the thing had no head, just a ragged stump of desiccated flesh within which the ex-Mag saw several bloated insects rummaging.

Still disguised by the branches of the nearby tree, Kane held a hand up in silence, shooing his companions back before turning himself and scurrying quietly away from the circling corpse.

"What is it?" Brigid asked as Kane emerged from the undergrowth.

"Something that should have been buried a long time ago," he advised. "Whatever's going on here is definitely against the laws of nature."

"It wouldn't be the first time those have proved malleable in the hands of the Annunaki," Brigid reminded him.

"No." Kane shook his head. "This is something else. Lilitu was always a twisted bitch, but this is more like some morbid compulsion, raising the dead. If left unchecked, the dead around here could well outnumber the living."

"That seems unlikely," Grant muttered.

"There was a time," Brigid reminded them both, "that this whole country was called the Deathlands, so many corpses had been created by the megachill. If Lilitu or Ezili Coeur Noir or whatever she's calling herself is trying to raise an army of the dead, there are plenty of people just waiting to enlist."

"But dead things deteriorate over time," Grant pointed out, glancing up at the sounds of movement nearby. "She might have an unlimited supply of names, but no one can revive dust. Can they?"

Suddenly the thick undergrowth parted just behind Kane and the headless corpse lumbered through, arms swinging as if to keep his balance. Kane leaped away, turning to face this eerie vision.

"There was a code," Kane said as the headless zombie plodded toward the three rebels. "The number RWI—"

"RWI077-093-d," Brigid repeated, recalling the string of numbers Kane had quoted to her earlier.

As Kane stepped away from the shuffling, headless thing, the leaves parted a little way across on the other side of the dirt track, and another walking corpse stepped into the sunlight, followed by two more.

"Shit." Grant spit as he turned to face the newcomers. "These things are all over."

The lead corpse was tall, almost inhumanly so, while one of his companions was no bigger than an eight-year-old child. The third was roughly Brigid's height, and he walked with the aid of a branch, propping it beneath one arm in the manner of a crutch.

"They must be smelling us out somehow," Kane realized, taking in the newcomers before turning back to the weird headless figure shambling toward him from the other direction.

"Opposites attract," Brigid pointed out. "True for magnets, maybe true, too, for the dead to the living."

With professional exactitude, Grant and Kane formed a perimeter while Brigid pondered the code reference Kane had reminded her of moments earlier. Inspiration struck an instant later and she engaged her Commtact, calling up Cerberus. "Brewster? This is Brigid out in the field," she began. "I need you to check something for me."

Then, in front of Brigid's startled eyes, the headless corpse lunged forward. Kane kicked out, his foot striking him hard in the upper chest and forcing him back several steps. The corpse-thing regained his balance and lunged again at Kane with bent, clawlike hands.

At the same time Brewster Philboyd's steady voice came over Brigid's Commtact receiver, its calmness at odds with the situation unfolding in front of Brigid's eyes. "What can I help you with, Brigid?"

"See if Lakesh knows anything about the following," Brigid stated into the hidden Commtact. "RWI077-093-d. It's a military code, prenukecaust."

On the other side of the road, Brigid saw, Grant was tracking the towering corpse-thing with the muzzle of his Sin Eater, watching warily he took another step toward them while Kane fended off his headless colleague. Meticulously, Grant began to fire, single rounds puncturing the rotted skull of the towering brute, tossing chunks of wizened brain matter high in the air. The thing kept on plodding toward him.

"Everything okay, Brigid?" Brewster asked over the Commtact. "You sound a little distracted."

"Just get back to me with the information, Brewster," Brigid replied before disengaging the Commtact and lending her own firepower to Grant's attack on their lumbering opponents.

A moment later the creaking, eerie insect song of the bayou was joined by the loud symphony of gunfire, splitting the air for miles around.

Chapter 7

"RWI077-093-d."

Brewster Philboyd read out the sequence of numbers from his notepad as he stood beside Lakesh, who was seated at a desk in the ops center of the Cerberus redoubt.

Sucking thoughtfully at his teeth, Lakesh shook his head. "The number means very little to me, I'm afraid," he said in his mellifluous voice, "other than the string at the end. It's certainly nothing to do with the mat-trans development project."

Adjusting his black-framed spectacles, Philboyd looked up from his notepad with disappointment, realizing that the chances of finding an easy answer had evaporated with Lakesh's statement. "And the string at the end?" he asked.

"The 93 refers to the year—1993," Lakesh explained patiently. "And the *d* is an acknowledgment that whatever the project was it had been decommissioned. It was no longer active at the time this file was created."

"I see," Philboyd acknowledged.

"The old database would likely be able to give you a summary of the project," Lakesh suggested.

Philboyd blushed, ashamed he had not concluded this himself. "Of course," he muttered, making his way back to his own console. Cerberus dealt with so many esoteric and downright weird things that now and then the presence of an artifact about which they might genuinely have information seemed almost more baffling than those they had to piece together from sketchy data.

Lakesh watched as the tall man returned to his place in the double line of desks in the high-ceilinged ops room, sat and began accessing the powerful Cerberus databanks. Still under Lakesh's scrutiny, Philboyd tabbed through a series of screens to access the legacy system on which the current Cerberus databank was built, tapping quickly at the keys as a password prompt appeared. As Philboyd continued to work, Lakesh's clear blue eyes flicked to the clock in the top right corner of his own computer display, and he saw it had been almost two hours since they had been alerted to the initial incursion at Redoubt Mike. Two hours was a long time in military terms; two hours could both start and end a war.

Lakesh shook himself, dismissing such morose thoughts. He was tired, despite only being on shift for four hours. It seemed that, more and more, he was wearying in the most ordinary of situations. Things he had once taken for granted seemed to be taking that little bit longer, that little bit more concentration and effort.

Working the keys of his computer, Brewster Philboyd entered the relevant password codes and brought up the file on RWI077-093-d. The data was vague, and the details of the project it referred to were highly restricted. But just the basic summary invited a sense of dread as Philboyd's eyes skimmed the page.

RWI077-093-d.
Project: Red Weed Initiative (decommissioned 1993). File ref. 077.
Subject: Airborne biochemical weapon.
Strand/Type: Bacillus-compound.
Project aim: Eradication of organic life (plant and animal) in enemy territory.

Effectiveness: Total (99.8%, lab conditions). Humans, canines, cattle, avian, insects, plants (including moss; fungus; gut flora).
Time required: Less than three hours from deployment for initial effectiveness.
Projected use: Restricted areas only. Red Weed is a highly virulent airborne weapon, able to regenerate rapidly, with a lifespan of (+/-) 12 hours.
Usage: Laboratory conditions only. Field test unattainable.
Computer model: Yes. Conclusion: Highly effective.
Restriction: Not for use on domestic soil under any circumstances.
Exception(s): Def Con One by Presidential release.

Brewster Philboyd stopped reading, his heart pounding and his throat suddenly dry. RWI077-093-d, or the Red Weed Initiative, involved a weapon designed to eradicate all forms of life in the space of just a few hours. While it could exist out of the test tube for a maximum of twelve hours, that did not matter; according to these notes, the weapon was so effective it didn't need any more time to utterly eradicate anything it encountered. This thing had been tested in the lab—Philboyd paused at the line that suggested it would be effective on humans, wondering how they had tested this—but never used in an external area. No wonder it had been decommissioned, since a biological weapon this vicious could, unchecked, destroy the world in a matter of days.

He peered again at the screen, taking in the details a second time. The words "Bacillus compound" nagged at him and he turned to Cerberus physician Reba DeFore where she worked at a terminal close to the main doors of the room.

"Reba?" Philboyd asked.

The physician peered at him, her brown eyes twinkling in the harsh lighting of the ops center. She was a stocky woman with long, ash-blond hair that trailed halfway down her back. Today, DeFore had tied her hair back in an elaborate French braid, with twin corkscrews of hair trailing down beside her ears.

"Do you happen to know what a bacillus compound might refer to?" Philboyd asked.

DeFore nodded. "Bacillus is the basic bacterial component of anthrax," she said. "Potentially lethal to humans and animals."

Thanking the physician, Philboyd turned back to his monitor and read the details over once again, his eyes gradually losing focus as he realized the enormity of the data there. File RWI077-093-d was a modified version of anthrax, ramped up to destroy everything it came into contact with. Coming as he did from the era that had been all but destroyed by nuclear war, the word *everything* held a terrible resonance for the twentieth-century astrophysicist.

Pulling himself out of his lament, Philboyd stabbed at the call button on his desk and placed a headset over his ear, preparing to alert Brigid Baptiste to his horrifying discovery. As he did so, he became conscious that Lakesh was standing behind him, and he flipped over to speaker phone so the Cerberus leader could hear Brigid's responses.

"Your file number is for something called the Red Weed Initiative, a lethal airborne cocktail that can literally kill anything in its path, plant or animal," Philboyd explained.

"Sounds just dandy," Brigid replied. She seemed a little out of breath and her words were labored.

"Once unleashed, this thing works like anthrax," Philboyd continued, "only about a hundred times more thorough."

"Is that an accurate estimate," Brigid queried, "or just a figure of speech?"

Despite himself, Philboyd smiled. "Believe me, if you're in the way of this thing once it's unleashed, it won't matter. Red Weed's efficiency was over ninety-nine percent under lab conditions."

"What about in—uh—the field?" Brigid asked after a pause. It was clear her attention was being called elsewhere.

Philboyd and Lakesh looked at one another, wondering at their colleague's struggle, and Philboyd asked what was going on.

"Just a little local trouble," Brigid explained tersely. "Keep going."

"Red Weed requires a catalyst compound to become active. It was never tested in the field," Philboyd elaborated. "Looks like the project was decommissioned before that ever came about."

"So it's untested," Brigid confirmed.

Lakesh leaned close to the communications array at Philboyd's desk. "I wouldn't rely on that as any kind of saving grace, Brigid, dear," he said, his eyes scanning the file still illuminated on Philboyd's monitor screen. "Work on the presumption that if you do get in the path of this thing when it's unleashed, you'll die."

"Avoid dying," Brigid acknowledged. "Good plan. Gotta go."

Abruptly the communication ended, leaving Philboyd and Lakesh staring at the speakers like faithful hounds waiting for the return of their master.

"Why do you think it was decommissioned?" Philboyd

asked after a half minute, his voice seeming too loud as it broke the silence between the two scientists.

"Conscience," Lakesh said with a teasing smile, turning from Philboyd's desk and striding across the room to the exit doors beneath the Mercator map.

Philboyd called after him as Lakesh reached for the doors. "Do you really believe that, Lakesh?"

"Given what you yourself know of the military mind," Lakesh said, "what do you think?"

With those enigmatic words, Lakesh exited through the doors and disappeared into the corridor beyond the ops center.

Feeling alone, despite the numerous personnel busy at their own desks with their own projects, Brewster Philboyd shook his head. There were occasions, without doubt, where Lakesh could prove insufferable.

OUTSIDE THE BUSTLING ops room, Lakesh found himself in a huge corridor that served as the central artery for the Cerberus redoubt. He glanced toward the heavy, rollback exit doors at the end of the corridor. It felt cold out here, after the heat of the busy ops room, and Lakesh reached his hands around himself and rubbed at his upper arms for a moment, feeling the chill through the white jumpsuit he wore while on duty.

The corridor had been bored into the rock of the mountain itself. Lakesh had visited many redoubts during what he thought of as his first life, over two hundred years before, and while they were each unique in certain respects they seemed uniform in their brutality, the ruthless efficiency with which they had been constructed from whatever materials existed in a given location. Despite its familiarity, Cerberus could seem a harsh environment, an unforgiving place to spend one's time, all hard surfaces and heavy doors.

Entering the personnel elevator, Lakesh was soon on the floor that contained his own apartment, the one he shared with wild child Domi. Though many years younger than him—even in the relative terms that ignored Lakesh's cryogenically compounded age—Domi was Lakesh's lover and the most cherished friend he had in this strange new world.

As Brewster Philboyd had been running through the horrors of this Red Weed Initiative and everything that it might entail, but Lakesh had been struck by how much he needed a break from the ops room. He had not even spoken to Donald Bry, his second-in-command, to inform his lieutenant to take over the supervision of the ops center, he noted with surprise. Lakesh sighed, shaking his head—he would comm Bry from his apartment rooms in a moment, explain the situation. He needed familiar surroundings but not those of the bustling, harshly lit ops room.

There's something going on with me, Lakesh told himself. Something terribly familiar and terribly wrong. I'm getting old again.

Though ancient, Lakesh had had a degree of his youth restored by the Enlil, the Annunaki lord, while in his guise of Sam the Imperator. Over recent months, Lakesh had begun to suspect that that blessing had in fact been a curse. He feared that he was beginning to age once more, and at a far more rapid pace than was normal. Now, it seemed, he was becoming more and more tired, dogged by a bone-weariness that threatened to overwhelm him with no warning, coming upon him with the speed of a storm.

"I should talk to Reba," Lakesh muttered, saying it

out loud as if that might make him acknowledge what he knew already deep down. Reba DeFore was the Cerberus physician and she would be more than happy to give him a once-over, Lakesh knew, and yet he had walked out the ops center, past her desk, ignoring her. Now, he remained here, lurking outside his own apartment, frightened somehow of facing this dark shadow that threatened to overwhelm him.

His chest felt tight as Lakesh pushed at the door and entered his private quarters, smelling something burning even as he stepped through the door.

His feet hurried across the carpeted floor, head turning left and right as he searched for the source of the smell. There, in the walk-in kitchen area, something was burning beneath the overhead broiler. Lakesh took two long strides that brought him to the small oven, switching off the broiler as smoke billowed from the bread that had been left there to toast. The bread was charcoal-black.

"Domi?" Lakesh asked, raising his voice but careful to keep the edge out of it. Removing the burned bread from the grill, Lakesh turned and paced through the little, self-contained apartment unit.

Domi was sitting on the floor of the bedroom, naked and staring into space. She was a curious sight. An albino by birth, her skin was alabaster-white and her hair the color of bone, cut short in a pixie style that framed her sharp, angular features. At barely five feet tall, Domi's small frame was like that of a child, her bird-thin limbs and tiny, pert breasts more like those of an adolescent girl going through the first flush of puberty. Strangest of all, however, were Domi's staring eyes—colored bloodred, they made her look like something eerily satanic, a demon from some terrible hell.

Domi was a true child of the Outlands, her manner

and fierce temper the legacy of an upbringing where survival was a daily challenge, and where one lived by one's instincts alone. Domi had been with Cerberus since its early days, though her adoration of Lakesh had developed much later. While a trusted member of the team, Domi remained something of a loose cannon, her actions unpredictable, her morality far more malleable than that of Kane, Grant or the others.

Right now, Domi was sat cross-legged, staring at the floor, her eyes unfocused. Lakesh took a step closer, wondering what the remarkable girl had seen or sensed. Domi relied on her instincts in a way few could truly comprehend, and Lakesh had known those infallible instincts to save his life on more than one occasion. Tentatively he spoke her name again, this time pitching his voice a little above a whisper so as not to disturb her.

"Domi? Dearest one? What are you doing?"

"Hmm," Domi responded, her murmur noncommittal.

"Dearest," Lakesh tried again. "Is there trouble?"

For a moment Lakesh suspected Domi wouldn't answer, but then she turned her head and, as if seeing him for the first time, smiled, her white teeth dulled to cream by the proximity of her chalk-white skin. "I cannot get it to work," she said.

Confused, Lakesh watched as Domi jumped up from her sitting position, brushed off her rump with a slap and paced over to kiss him.

"Dearest one," Lakesh said, holding her at arm's length and looking at her strange, statuelike features with utter bewilderment, "I have no idea what it is that you are talking about."

"The rug," Domi said, using the big toe of her bare right foot to point to the carpet that lay across the floor of the bedroom to the side of the bed. "Brigid's rug. I cannot get it to work."

The rug was one of the strangest and most esoteric items that the Cerberus team had encountered in their recent adventures. Although it was found in a disused Soviet military installation in Russia, the rug itself was Persian and ran to almost eight feet in length. Threaded with vibrant colors, its design showed a series of expanding golden circles and squares that originated from its center. The gold design rested on a cerulean background, colored like a cloudless sky, and the intricate design was decorated with similar repetitions all over its surface, each finished in green or red amid the blue-and-gold body. The design was called a mandala, a device used to facilitate meditation. In memorizing every complicated detail, it was said that a person might transcend the physical plane and achieve a certain spiritual dimension, reaching deep within to attain a higher level of human consciousness. The remarkable design had proved to be the gateway to a hidden area of the human mindscape dubbed Krylograd, but only Brigid Baptiste's phenomenal eidetic memory had been sufficient to memorize the exceptional design with the necessary speed to allow access to this dimension. What happened in Krylograd had been the catalyst for a whole series of problems for the Cerberus team, including an assassination attempt on Lakesh. The Cerberus rebels had decided the best thing to do with the rug was to store it in the redoubt, where it could do no further harm.

Quite what had possessed Domi to attempt meditation using the carpet, Lakesh could not begin to imagine. She was without question, a fascinating combination of contradictions.

"Oh, my dear," Lakesh soothed, resting his hand gently

on the milky flesh of her collarbone. "Some of us, I fear, are not destined to reach higher planes of consciousness..."

Domi's brow furrowed and she bared her teeth savagely. Was Lakesh patronizing her?

"Myself included," Lakesh added as he saw the simmering anger begin to show on his lover's features. "Don't think I haven't tried, in my idle moments here with this remarkable rug."

Domi smiled then, staring into the eyes of the taller man. "Stupid trick rug," she said with a chuckle.

As Domi laughed, Lakesh seemed to sway, and he stumbled two steps backward until the back of his leg met with the bed. With a thump, he fell to a sitting position on the edge of the mattress, still swaying in place.

Domi's smile broadened. "Is that your idea of subtlety?" she chided.

But Lakesh seemed to look past her, his hand reaching up to press against his forehead.

"Lakesh?" Domi asked, an edge of concern coloring her voice. "Are you okay, lover mine?"

After a moment a tentative smile crossed Lakesh's features and his eyes met with Domi's once more. "Just tired," he assured her. "It's nothing."

Domi continued studying Lakesh warily. "You sure?" she asked.

"I should contact Donald," Lakesh announced, dismissing Domi's question. "Tell him to take charge of the ops center in my absence."

Domi stepped forward, crouching in front of Lakesh and staring at him with those fiercely penetrating eyes of her. "Are you okay?" she asked again, her words coming more firmly this time.

"Just not feeling as young as I used to," Lakesh told

her. Technically, it was the truth, but even he recognized the lie in the casual way he had phrased it. What was it that he was so scared of? Did he think his friends would reject him if they knew he was becoming an old man once again? Or was it something more fundamental than that? Did he fear that this was not age catching up with him so much as Death stalking him? Was that what Mohandas Lakesh Singh truly feared?

Chapter 8

More of the living dead had emerged from the surrounding undergrowth as Brewster Philboyd related what he had learned of the Red Weed Initiative to Brigid Baptiste. The three Cerberus rebels now found themselves very much outnumbered, with fifteen of the undead humans lumbering toward them in their slow, relentless way as they stood beside the stalled truck.

Kane blasted another stream of hot lead from his Sin Eater, snarling as the undead creature in his sights staggered under the force of the blows before shrugging them off and renewing his slow, relentless advance.

"Our shots aren't having enough effect," Kane said.

"Yeah, I noticed," Brigid agreed as she blew a chunk of brain matter from the skull of the woman standing just three feet in front of her, avoiding the undead woman's grasping hands.

"Any ideas?" Kane snapped as he struck out with his left fist, knocking the deathless creature that reached for Brigid across her sagging jaw. The monstrous, rotting thing staggered backward before toppling over, her legs shuddering as it hit the dirt.

"I had a dream like this once," Grant admitted, unleashing a cacophony of bullets at the lumbering corpses from his own Sin Eater. "Covered in sweat and surrounded by faceless, unstoppable things."

"Yeah?" Kane urged, taking a step back and finding

himself almost walking into Brigid where she stood beside Grant. "What did you do?"

"I woke up," Grant replied acidly.

"Well, I don't think that's going to work, partner," Kane told him as he ducked beneath a swinging branch that one of the fleshless creatures in front of him was using like a club. "Any other bright ideas?"

The jagged end of the branch cut the air just over Kane's head, the breeze created by its passage ruffling his dark hair. As the branch continued its arc overhead, Kane jabbed out with his left fist, driving his punch upward and into the zombie's slack jaw. The punch connected with a loud clack of mashing teeth, and Kane watched as three of the creature's teeth burst from his mouth, rotten brown squares hurtling through the air.

The zombie lurched backward, issuing a low hiss from his emaciated throat between the new gaps in his smile. Then he was swinging for Kane again, the hefty branch cleaving the air with incredible power. Kane took the blow full to his upper right arm, and he felt the reverberation through his shoulder blade like the tolling of a bell. Stumbling sideways, Kane centered himself and spun, lashing out with his foot to deliver a mighty roundhouse kick to the moving corpse's chest, front and center.

With a howl of whatever it was that passed for pain in these terrible creatures, the walking corpse fell backward, letting go of the heavy branch he had been using as a club. Kane drove himself forward, peppering the zombie with a burst of fire from his Sin Eater pistol before turning to face his next attacker.

A few paces from Kane, Grant stepped forward as two more of the lumbering creatures emerged from the thick undergrowth. With a blur of movement, Grant thrust his right hand—the one still holding the Sin Eater—into the closer creature's gut and pulled the trigger of the blaster. The undead thing shuddered, leaping from the ground as Grant's solid punch drove him into the air, his guts spraying out as the stream of bullets split him apart. Hunks of rotting human flesh spattered against trees and ferns as the zombie sailed through the air, but there was no time for Grant to congratulate himself. The second undead thing was already upon him, a clawlike hand scraping down the weave where his shadow suit protected his chest. Grant beat it away with a sharp jab of his elbow, before bringing the Sin Eater to bear once more.

Nearby, Brigid staggered her bursts of fire as the lumbering army lurched toward her teammates, threatening to cut off their final avenue of escape.

"We need to find some cover, somewhere we can hole up," she shouted over the sounds of gunfire. For a second she thought she saw a tall figure move through the distant foliage—Ezili Coeur Noir on the prowl. Then, one of the zombies was upon her, too, either a child or a dwarf, it was hard to be sure, such was the shocking state of the creature's atrophy.

The creature stood four and a half feet in height, with long arms and stubby legs like a gorilla. His face was charcoal-black, scrunched up, the skin stretched taut over his skull like the old leather of a baseball catcher's mitt. His clothes were nothing more than grimy, soil-stained rags. As the eyeless sockets met Brigid's gaze, the undead monstrosity opened a dark mouth and unleashed a hideous ululation, like some terrible, discordant crow's song. Then he was leaping at Brigid, fleshless fingers entwining in her long hair as his head rushing toward her face.

In an instant the zombie head-butted Brigid full in the forehead, and she saw bright spots flash before her vision as she staggered backward.

The terrible corpse-thing was still clinging to her as she danced in place, and Brigid shoved him away with both hands, using the hard edge of the TP-9 handgun like a lever. With a savage scream, Brigid pushed the zombie off of her, and he rolled away into the dirt, a clump of Brigid's bright red hair still in his hands like some perverse trophy.

As Brigid swayed in place, trying to recover from the harsh blow to her head, the dwarflike corpse righted himself and began to lumber toward her on his abbreviated legs.

Driven by combat instinct alone, Brigid swept out with the pointed toe of her right boot, kicking the charging zombie in his black-skinned, scrunched-up face. Her foot connected with fearsome accuracy, and the undead creature seemed to fall over himself as he took the hard impact. Brigid watched in disgust as his head was wrenched from his neck, hanging there from a torn ligament as the monstrous thing tumbled to the ground. Lying on his back, the zombie kicked his legs against the ground, arms slapping at the floor as he struggled to right himself. His head rolled to one side, the neck not just broken but actually torn apart.

"And stay down," Brigid commanded, turning her attention to the next wave of the undead creatures massing toward the Cerberus warriors in increasing numbers.

With a hideous, choked growl, another of the zombies reached out from Kane's side, grabbing for him with brittle, dirt-brown nails as he blasted bullets at several of other attackers. Kane cried out as those ragged nails rent against the flesh of his cheek, and he found himself struck with a wave of sudden nausea, staggering sideways on the dirt path as if drunk.

Brigid spun, drilling bullets into the undead creature's

face as he reached for Kane once again with those sickening, flesh-free hands. The bullets ripped at his ruined face, the skin there blackened with age, and he held up skeletal hands as if to swipe the bullets away. As he did so, Brigid drove a powerful knee into the undead thing's groin, using the force of her blow to knock him backward even while he registered no pain. The corpse fell back, unleashing another gurgling grunt as if choking on his own saliva.

"Come on," Brigid snapped at Kane as he reached for her proffered hand and pulled himself from the ground, "this is no time to take a nap."

As he stood, Kane engaged his Commtact, calling on Cerberus headquarters once more. "Brewster? This is Kane. Can you zero in on my location?"

Brewster Philboyd's voice came over the Commtact a moment later. "I have you on screen, Kane."

Every member of Cerberus was equipped with a subcutaneously implanted transponder. Each transponder broadcast a telemetric signal that provided the Cerberus nerve center with a constant stream of information about an individual's health and well-being, including heart rate, blood pressure and brain-wave activity. At a keystroke, these blips could be expanded to give full diagnostics for each member of a field team. With satellite triangulation, the transponders could also be used to track down an individual to within almost a hairsbreadth of their actual physical location.

At the Cerberus redoubt, an operator like Brewster Philboyd had access to two main satellite systems, which allowed for near-real-time communication, as well as monitoring facilities. Accompanied by a map overlay, infrared and other standard camera analysis, the satellite surveillance could provide much-needed spot reports on an otherwise unknown area for field teams like Kane's.

"We're in a bit of a jam here, Brewster," Kane explained as another zombie shambled toward him, swinging a thick hunk of piping. "Do we have anything nearby, a building of some sort where we might take refuge?" Kane reached out, grabbing the swinging club, shoving its wielder backward with a grunt.

"There's a lot of leaf cover," Philboyd replied. "Bear with me while I switch views."

"Take your time," Kane muttered sarcastically into the subdermal Commtact as he swooped out a low kick at his attacker's ankle. "No rush."

Beneath Kane's blow, the undead creature's leg snapped with an audible crack, but there was no time for celebration. Even as one fell back, another undead monstrosity was looming to take his place.

A few paces behind Kane, Grant and Brigid were dealing with a whole host of assailants that continued to swagger from the bushes. Grant's Sin Eater clicked on empty and he automatically sent it back to its hidden wrist holster without a moment's thought.

Brigid blasted another burst from the TP-9 as Grant stepped forward and reached for the two nearest undead humans, grabbing them by their rotten skulls. With astonishing speed and brutal efficiency, Grant slammed their two skulls together, striking them so hard that one of the creature's jawbones fell to the ground with a tearing of tissue-thin skin. The jawless creature fell to his knees in the soil. Grant drove himself forward, kicking the remaining zombie in the gut as if punting a football. The zombie drooped like a ragdoll over his boot before being slammed back into the trunk of a tree. Grant was still moving, and he followed through his punt with a savage kick to the jawless figure's head, driving the thing's skull down into the ground.

"Kane, you got anything?" Grant shouted, not bothering to look behind him as he stamped on the undead creature's head.

Across the clearing, Kane was punching another of the undead things in the skull, unleashing a burst of bullets into its face as he pulled back his fist for a second strike. "Any second now," Kane assured his partner. In front of him, the zombie staggered under Kane's blow, reeling for a second like a gyroscope running out of energy.

Then Brewster Philboyd's familiar voice echoed through Kane's skull once more, a palpable sense of pride in his tone. "Kane, I've found somewhere. It's about a half mile to the north, close to the main roadway there."

"What are we looking at, Brewster?" Kane asked.

"Some kind of a... Well, it looks like a big old mansion," Philboyd replied. "Run-down, but it's still standing."

"We're not planning on holding a dinner party there," Kane snarled. "Just give me the directions."

"Either follow the road you're on until you hit the main highway, or you could cut through the undergrowth—"

Kane cut him off. "Going through the undergrowth is out of the question," he explained as he saw yet another rotting corpse step from the overhanging branches of a tree. "Thanks for the assist—keep us on visual if you can."

"Copy that," Brewster acknowledged.

"One more thing," Kane said as he eyed the walking corpse. "Heard you tell Baptiste something about there being a catalyst for this Red Weed stuff. They have a lab operating here mixing up a little potion. It looked like just a handful of test tubes. Reckon that's our catalyst?"

Philboyd was silent a moment as he pondered Kane's

observation. "I'll see if I can pinpoint the last known location of the Red Weed supplies," he told Kane. "We can talk it through once we know for sure."

Then the Commtact reverted to silence.

Kane lashed out with his fist once again, knocking another undead human figure aside in a spray of dislodged teeth. "Keep on the road," he instructed his companions, raising his voice to be heard over the gunfire. "We've got about a half-mile trek to shelter."

"Is it safe?" Grant asked as he tossed aside another walking corpse with a powerful yank of her rotted clothes. He snarled, wrinkling his nose in disgust as the clothing shredded at his touch, leaving threads all over his hands and fingertips.

"We'll see," Kane snapped as he blasted a stream of bullets into the side of the stalled artillery truck where another of the undead forms was lunging toward the trio.

Then a figure came over the low, dropdown side of the truck and seemed to not so much leap as fall at Brigid, even as she stepped back to avoid him. The corpselike thing struck her shoulder, knocking her backward as he fell to the ground. Without a moment's hesitation, Brigid blasted a stream of bullets into the monstrosity's head at point-blank range. After a couple of seconds beneath the lethal impacts, the corpse-thing's brittle skull began to pop, splitting apart along deep seams that showed through the tortured skin that barely held it together.

"When all of this is over," Brigid noted, pulling herself from the undead thing's embrace, "I am so going to need a bath."

Kane smashed his fist into the face of another of the shambling creatures as he hurried to join Brigid at the side of the truck. "Ah, you're repulsed too easy, Baptiste," he told his beautiful redheaded companion. "Nothing like a good workout to get the blood pumping."

Brigid fixed Kane with an irritated glare. "I'd prefer to get the blood pumping against things that actually have pumping blood," she complained before turning and trotting a few paces down the dirt road past the truck. More of the undead figures waited there, moving along the mud track in their unsteady, shambling way.

"Kane," Brigid called back, "we have more company."

Kane turned as he finished drilling another clutch of bullets at a struggling undead thing that scuttled ahead of him on broken legs had become turned inward at the knee. "Nothing like being popular," he muttered before turning his gun on the nearest of the undead forms blocking their path.

Still on the far side of the truck, Grant faced three more shambling forms, one of them the almost decapitated dwarfish figure that Brigid had dealt with just moments earlier. Grant looked at the freshly reloaded pistol in his hand, shook his head and reached up for the handle of the truck door, yanking it open with a hard pull. Set high off the ground, the door swung open and smashed into the head of the closest of the undead figures, caving in his half-rotten nose and knocking him backward.

Grant placed his foot on the wheel rim of the truck and swiftly climbed up, pulling himself past the door and up onto the roof of the cab. Behind him, the less agile figures of the undead grasped at the empty air where he had been just seconds before.

On the other side of the truck, Kane and Brigid stood together, staring down the half-dozen shambling forms lurching along the road toward them, flies and other insects buzzing about their rotting flesh in the heat of the bayou. Even as they pondered their next move, another undead form lumbered out of the undergrowth, growling some inhuman curse from deep in his ruined throat.

Then, from overhead, Grant's sturdy form came hurtling through the air as he leaped from the roof of the truck's cab and dived into the nearest pair of undead. The ex-Mag had returned his Sin Eater to its hiding place beneath his sleeve, resorting to brute strength to overpower these ghastly undead things and clear a path for his colleagues.

Kane appreciated the logic. There was no doubt that bullets were having the most minimal effect against these awful things, and it seemed that again and again he and his partners had had to resort to physical contact to genuinely turn the tide of battle against each shambling wreck that had once been a human. With the briefest thought, Kane returned his own pistol to its hidden wrist holster and charged at the nearest clutch of walking dead, barrelling into them like an angry bull.

Though eminently capable, Brigid Baptiste found herself at something of a disadvantage in using the same tactic as her partners. Kane was a powerfully built man, and Grant's strength might, in a simpler era, have formed the stuff of legend. Brigid could hold her own in any combat situation, but against an enemy who simply wouldn't fall, she knew she was best advised to back her plays with more force than her fists. In an instant she scampered back to the stalled truck, pulled herself up over its low side where the khaki paint was chipped and ruined and clambered on the open, flat back. There was a long metal bar on either side that held the dropdown panels in place like a bolt. Swiftly Brigid kicked one of the bolts back so that the side panel dropped down in front of her. As the panel dropped, Brigid felt the truck shake and she saw two figures pulling themselves up from behind her,

climbing onto the flat body of the truck with their emaciated, rotting arms.

Brigid turned swiftly, striking the first across the face
with a well-placed kick. The zombie lurched backward
but clung on to the side of the unmoving truck, making
the vehicle shake and sway.

Brigid pulled her foot back and booted the thing again,
this time jabbing down with her solid heel and driving
it into the corpse-thing's cavelike eye socket. The creature struggled and fell, dropping back to the dirt path, her
awful face fixed in anger.

Before Brigid could move, the second undead thing
had pulled himself over the lip of the side panel, and
he grasped her other foot in a terrible death grip. Brigid
found herself pulled down, and she struck the metal body
of the truck with a heavy blow, feeling the force of her
landing hammer through her elbows and knees.

Brigid spun then, rolling herself on the bed of the truck
as the undead thing pulled himself up her body, tearing
at her pant leg. Brigid jabbed the muzzle of her TP-9 into
the corpse-thing's open mouth and held the trigger down,
watching the undead creature shake in place as the volley
of bullets drilled through his skull, bursting out the back
of his head in a rush of bloodless flesh and dry, powdery
brain matter.

Yet still, incredibly, the zombie kept coming, even with
half his skull blasted to dust. And then, from Brigid's
right, the other undead creature, the one she had only just
kicked from the side of the truck, pulled herself up over
the side panel and began to stagger toward Brigid again.

Chapter 9

Lying on her back on the bed of the artillery truck, trapped by the weight of the undead form scrambling up her legs, Brigid Baptiste heard a cawing sound. Looking directly up into the sky above her, she saw the dark blur of a crow swooping overhead, its black feathers like the Grim Reaper's shroud in the light of the balmy day. It had been a day, she thought—hell, it had been a life—of omens and portents.

The undead thing was still clawing up her leg, despite the fact that Brigid had just dispatched a whole clip of ammunition from her TP-9 semiautomatic right into the ghastly monstrosity's skull. To her right, the second zombie, the one she had kicked from the edge of the truck, clambered over the side panel once again The creature's movements were jerky, like some terrible stop-frame film, time-lapse photography projected in front of her into the air.

Brigid swung the semiautomatic around, pressing at the trigger as she targeted the thing clawing over the side of the truck. Brigid bit back a curse as she realized the gun was empty.

Then the creature whose head she had almost destroyed with her first salvo grabbed at her chest, one rotting hand mashing against her breast as he pulled his way up her struggling, supine body. Brigid lashed out, driving the heel of her left hand into the thing's forehead, slamming hard against the deteriorating flesh that clung there.

The undead creature lurched back and Brigid pumped her knee up, powering it into the undead human's body. The creature flipped off of Brigid, rolling onto the metal bed of the artillery truck with a hideous shriek.

Brigid pushed all her weight back onto her shoulders, arching her back as the second undead thing lumbered toward her across the body of the truck. The first was still moving to her left, trying to right himself where Brigid had flipped him off her body.

With a tensing of her muscles, Brigid drove herself back, then sprang forward to land in front of the second shambling figure in a crouch. Still moving, Brigid drove her left fist into the zombie's hip, hitting her with such force that the undead figure was forced to turn, staggering backward as she lost her balance.

Brigid spun in place, sweeping one long, slender leg around her until she connected with the undead thing's legs where she struggled to remain upright. The awful creature was knocked from her feet like a skittle in a bowling alley, falling sideways into the side panel of the truck where she lay as if snapped in two. The undead thing groaned, a low, bubbling sound like a man trying to scream under water.

Brigid leaped up, ramming her TP-9 back into its hip holster as she finally grabbed for the boltlike bar that she had spied a few moments earlier. She was standing just a foot away from the other zombie as she yanked the metal rod free from its housing in the side panel. The rod was just an inch in diameter, but it stretched a third of the truck's length and was made of solid steel. Brigid pulled but the end of the rod was stuck, and she saw a deliberate stopper there to prevent it from being accidentally pulled from the siding. As the undead thing behind her began struggling upward and her colleague lifted himself from the opposing side of the truck, Brigid kicked out with all her might, breaking the rusted old bracket that held the metal bar's stopper in place.

Freed, Brigid swung the metal rod out in front of her like a staff. It stood almost four feet in length, coming up to the bottom of Brigid's ribcage as she stood in place on the bed of the vehicle. The undead man with the shot-to-pieces skull was struggling to pull himself up from the floor of the truck, fat flies buzzing around his rotting flesh. Brigid swung the length of metal at the undead man's head, batting him across a cheekbone whose milky whiteness was visible through the patchy skin of his face, knocking the lumbering figure sideways. Then the beautiful Cerberus warrior raised the steel bar over her head and used it like a club against the struggling figure, slamming the undead thing again and again, like someone swatting a fly. The long length of shining metal whistled as it cut through the air, clunking viciously against the animated corpse.

The second undead figure lurched toward Brigid, arms outstretched in an attempt to claw Brigid's face. Brigid reared back in disgust, recalling the hideous dwarf thing that had torn at her hair. Then she was swinging the pole once again, this time in a horizontal arc to smash its length against the lumbering thing's torso. There was a clang of metal on bone, and the zombie fell onto her back, viscous liquid seeping from her open mouth.

For just a second Brigid stood there over the fallen corpse, catching her breath, and once again a movement in the distance caught her eye. She watched as the dark, skeletal figure of Ezili Coeur Noir strode along the dirt path on long, emaciated legs, trotting like a bird in the snow. And all around her, clawing from the ground, figures seemed to be emerging—human figures, each one accompanied by a horrible, bone-chilling scream.

"Shit," Brigid murmured under her breath before turning and placing her foot against the far side panel of the truck's rear, even as the zombies on the truck bed shook, trying to right themselves.

A moment later Brigid had leaped over the open side of the truck, the metal pole clutched in both hands, and she hurried to join her two companions as they fought back the undead hordes that waited in the road.

On the dirt-track road, Grant and Kane stood back-to-back, fending off the last of the undead figures. More had appeared while Brigid had been engaged in furious battle atop the truck, and she could see a heap of ruined corpses scattered around the edges of the road, their crumpled bodies stuck at terrible, unnatural angles. Even as Brigid hurried to help, a towering undead figure swung a mighty arm at Grant's head; it was like a slab of rotting meat hurtling through the air. The ebony-skinned ex-Mag sidestepped, narrowly avoiding that savage blow, and then stepped forward, his arms outstretched.

With a mighty shove, Grant slammed the monstrous figure in the chest and, using both arms, ran forward, his feet powering against the dirt of the road, pushing the undead form back toward the edge of the tree-lined roadway. Before the figure could counteract Grant's move, he found himself shoved into the side of the road where the low-hanging branches of a tree reached out like the talons of an eagle. With one last brutal shunt, Grant forced the zombie into the sharp end of a low-hanging branch, skewering the undead thing. The towering corpse struggled, the branch poking from his broad chest, unable to get himself free. It spit something the color of dried blood from his dry mouth, desperately reaching for Grant as the ex-Mag stepped back.

Grant turned away, dismissing the corpse-thing that struggled at the branch. Shaking his head, he muttered just one word as he walked away, "Fail."

Brigid, meanwhile, was helping Kane with the last of the shambling figures, using her pole like a staff to herd the undead creature away until Kane was in the ideal position to break his legs with two low ram's-head punches. They left the animated corpse struggling in the mud, dragging his crippled legs behind him.

"Figure it won't be long until more of these damned things arrive." Kane spit. "Let's get moving."

Brigid turned back to the truck one last time, recalling the dark figure she had seen moving in the swamp. "Wait," she instructed, slowing her pace.

"What is it, Baptiste?" Kane asked, looking fiercely in her direction, his face red with anger and exertion.

Brigid had stopped in the middle of the bayou path, searching behind her with her clear, emerald eyes. "I saw her," she said. "Lilitu—or Ezili Coeur Noir or whatever we're calling her. I saw her."

"She must have come out of the redoubt to follow us," Kane conceded.

"Her and her army," Grant rumbled, checking the immediate undergrowth for further signs of ambush.

"We should keep moving," Kane reminded Brigid, a note of urgency creeping into his usually professional tone.

"These…dead things are coming from somewhere, Kane," Brigid said, her eyes still roaming the path that led back to the redoubt. "I think she's creating them."

"Creating…?" Kane and Grant responded in unison.

"I don't know." Brigid shook her head. "I only saw for a

second, just a second. But she seemed to be pulling them out of the ground. Dead people sprouting like weeds all around her—awful, awful weeds."

Kane reached for Brigid, pulling her around to look at him, physically shaking her out of her reverie. "Come on, Baptiste," he insisted, "this is no time to get maudlin."

"Kane," Grant urged, indicating movement nearby. "We need to get if we're getting."

Brigid looked at Kane, her *anam-chara,* her soul friend, and he saw that her eyes were welling with tears. "What kind of monster would do this?" she asked.

"The kind we make a habit of slaying," Kane assured his beautiful companion, brushing a stray lock of her red-gold hair from her face. "Now, come on. Let's get to cover and see if we can't put all the pieces into the right order, figure us a way to end this horror show."

Brigid nodded, wiping self-consciously at her eyes with the heel of her hand.

A moment later the Cerberus trio were moving once more, jogging along the dirt road toward the spot indicated in Brewster Philboyd's communication.

THE CORPSELIKE FIGURE of Ezili Coeur Noir stalked through the sweat-heavy air of the bayou. Her yellow lizard's eyes were narrowed, their dark slits focused on the warm, living things that scampered away ahead of her and her people. There were three of them, running from destiny.

She smiled at the thought of these fools, running away from death as if death could ever be outraced.

Beneath her feet, the ground was breaking as another figure clambered from his resting place under the earth. Broken fingernails clawed at the sod, dragging against the muddy ground as another undead human struggled to free himself from the soil.

Ezili Coeur Noir looked down, peering at the animated dead thing as he wrenched himself from the moist loam and hefted himself up into a sitting position, damp soil still clinging to his rotted body. This one had no face, just a bare skull without a shred of skin other than at the scalp, where long strands of white hair clung like sap to a tree. When he reached up out of the ground with his other hand, it was clear that he was missing some fingers; just a thumb and the little finger remained, while the others were removed at the second knuckle. The undead thing wore the clothes he had worn in life, a long black coat that had ripped and torn so as to give the appearance now of a bat's wings. He hunkered down, shaking himself like a dog as the soil clung to his body and clothes. Dry soil fell from his clothing along with the shining black bodies of several beetles, scurrying away from the light, their underground lives disturbed.

Ezili Coeur Noir waved one of her spindly hands across the undead thing's brow, brushing against it just for a moment, the soil crumbling at her touch. As she pulled her hand away, more of his form seemed to appear, tendrils of flesh budding on his skull as if pulled from the very air itself. The undead thing opened his mouth to scream, but he had no voice box yet, no tongue; he could not cry out at the agony of this unholy rebirth as he felt his body being pulled back from the ether, re-created from the atoms that remained in the soil and the atmosphere.

Ezili Coeur Noir stepped away then, continuing to follow the warm, living things that scurried away down the long dirt road leading from the redoubt's doors.

Behind her, the revived-and-once-dead thing stumbled forward, unused to moving his legs after so long at rest, his scarred boots too big to comfortably accommodate still-fleshless feet. The flesh was re-forming there, too, reknitting between skeletal toes, and suddenly he found he could lift his feet once more. For a moment he lurched in place in a spastic, uncoordinated dance, his mouth still open in a soundless scream.

Around the moving corpse, other undead things walked, keeping pace with their mistress. The one-eyed corpse walked in something approximating a stride, his eye patch a mirror of the dead socket it was strapped beside. The others followed: Dreadlocks and Walking Stick and the little one whose face was a spectral mask of bone, two glass shards clutched in the fleshless fingers of his dry hands.

Suddenly the newly reanimated corpse made a shrill noise. His throat had finally regrown and at last he could give voice to the agony of his rebirth. His screech sounded like nails on a blackboard.

Ezili Coeur Noir smiled at the noise, enjoying the terrible, familiar song of death reversed. All of the corpses had done this when she had revived them; each had sung a beautiful note of pain. It was so pure, so absolute, she wished to one day make an orchestra of these corpses, killing and reviving them to create the music she heard echoing in her black heart.

Already she was walking on down the road, instinctively searching for another dead body, feeling herself drawn to it as she repopulated the Earth with her army of the undead. But soon she would not need to search. Once the Red Weed batch was completed by her lackeys, Ezili Coeur Noir would have an endless supply of the dead to reanimate, a perfect orchestra to scream her beautiful songs of death. And prized among those singers would be the three humans she had found in the underground bunker of the redoubt, the three who had challenged her with the brightness of their living souls.

KANE, GRANT AND BRIGID HURRIED along the dirt road, keeping to the middle of the path and away from the dense foliage, wary of whatever it might now be hiding. As they jogged toward the distant road, Brewster Philboyd's voice came over the Commtact once again, giving Kane the information he dreaded.

"Production of Red Weed was very limited," Philboyd confirmed. "It was still at test stage when the initiative was abandoned, probably a funding issue. Donald here has done a back-door hack to find us the location of the supplies that exist and—well—you won't like it."

"It's in Redoubt Mike, isn't it?" Kane huffed as he jogged along the dirt track beside his two companions.

"It is," Philboyd confirmed. "It was stored in one of the lower levels of the underground bunker for safety. Essentially the place became a secure dumping facility once the redoubt itself was abandoned. But if the catalyst is released into the atmosphere there, it will travel through the air vents and could potentially set off the Red Weed, turning the virus live."

"And once live," Brigid observed, "no one else will be. Not for very long, anyhow."

"That's about the sum of it," Philboyd agreed dourly.

"What about a counteragent?" Brigid asked as she jogged beside Kane and Grant. "Is there something of that nature that we could employ to halt the chemical reaction, stop the virus?"

"Got nothing showing up in the file," Philboyd said slowly as he scanned the information he had pulled up on screen at the Cerberus base. "I'll see whether anyone here has any ideas. Because once that thing's loose, there won't be much time to do anything."

Kane bit back a curse as another shambling corpse came staggering out of the bushes beside the track. "Thanks for the heads up, Brew," he said. "Keep on it."

Then Kane he cut the com link and turned his attention to the rotten human figure approaching his team from the distance. Before Kane could react, another rotting figure came crashing out of the undergrowth. Brigid dispatched him with a flick of the metal pole she had ripped from the truck, flipping the figure on his back and mashing his skull with a second, savage blow. Another undead man had appeared as they jogged past, and Kane had simply urged they pick up the pace, outrunning the shambling figure and leaving him behind them—it beat getting slowed down by another pointless scuffle during which the zombie's comrades could well appear.

The Cerberus field team reached the end of the dirt road and found themselves on the verge of an old highway. The blacktop was scarred and cracked, with weeds growing from holes in its surface, but it still looked pretty durable. The field team were breathing a little harder, sweat glistening on their skin from the heat of the bayou as much as their exertions, but they were otherwise intact.

Kane checked the position of the sun as he engaged his Commtact once more, calling on Cerberus to give further directions to their make-do shelter. The road around them appeared to be empty, a line of blacktop out in the middle of nowhere, far from the towering spires of the nearest ville.

"Hang a left," Brewster Philboyd's calm voice directed over the radio contact in Kane's skull. "The road curves gently away from the coast. You'll find the house about one-fifty, one-seventy-five yards along. It's set back a little from the road but it should be visible."

As Kane spoke, Grant recalled his Sin Eater to his hand with a whirring of motors from its holster and, without warning, drilled three rapid bursts of fire into the foliage by the dirt track they had just exited. Something lurched out of the bushes about fifteen feet down the road, a woman dressed in rags and struggling along with her lopsided gait—another of the undead. Grant's shots slammed into her right shoulder and her torso, and the undead woman spun in place like some nightmarish ballerina, absorbing the impact of the shots as if they were nothing more than snowballs.

"Dammit," Grant stormed as the undead woman fixed him with her eerie, dark gaze, raising one withered hand and pointing at his group with a fleshless finger.

Grant's shots couldn't do much, he knew, but keeping these things at a distance was preferable to tackling them up close.

Then the undead woman began to shout, or at least what passed for shouting from her dry, rotten throat. It sounded like the brushing of reeds in the wind, but amplified a hundredfold into something terrible. As she called out, more of the undead forms stepped from the bushes and hurried along the dirt road to join her in their sickening, unbalanced way.

"They're learning," Brigid stated ominously. "Calling to their friends."

Grant carefully sighted down the length of the Sin Eater once more and pumped a shot into the throat of the screaming woman, silencing her despite the distance between them. As a Magistrate, Grant had been highly trained in the effective use of many weapons;

he considered there was nothing remarkable about his marksmanship under duress.

To Grant's side, Brigid added a hail of bullets from her TP-9, cutting the woman down as she reached for her ruined throat. Already other undead figures were lurching ominously along the dirt track, heading relentlessly onward toward the Cerberus teammates.

"Come on," Kane urged, "let's keep moving."

With that, Kane led the way at a fast jog along the ruined blacktop, Grant and Brigid hurrying at his heels. Grant kept checking over his shoulder as the group rushed down the curving road, and finally he spotted more of the shambling, undead figures emerging from the entrance to the dirt track. Others came lurching out of the vegetation along the side of the road, until Grant counted nine of them making their slow, relentless way toward the retreating Cerberus warriors.

Then Kane spotted the mansion house, exactly where Philboyd had advised. It was set back twenty feet from the road's edge, a gravel drive made up of pale stones the color of sand leading to its wide front door. The door was painted a rich maroon, its luster like bruised flesh. The house itself was three stories, with high windows arrayed across its front, reflecting the rays of the late-morning sun. A small flight of steps led to the magnificent front door, which was framed by twin columns holding aloft a portico.

Kane stopped at the edge of the driveway for a moment, examining the building and its dark slate roof. Despite Brewster's description, it didn't look run-down at all. In fact, it seemed to be in wonderful condition.

As the Cerberus trio made their way along the path, Kane and Brigid walking abreast with Grant walking backward to keep his eyes on anything that might be following them, the majestic door to the house swung open and the wide figure of a portly woman stood there, her face hidden within the shadows of the hallway beyond.

"Welcome, weary strangers," the woman called, and her voice was as rich and as dark as coffee sweetened with muscovado sugar. "Welcome to the House Lilandera."

Kane and Brigid exchanged a confused look as they continued to stride up the pathway toward the open door, Grant trailing behind them as he watched the entryway to the drive.

"No need to be worried," the woman assured them from the shadows. "Every stranger is welcome here, be he waif or stray." And then she let out a laugh, a deep, throaty chuckle that sounded faintly perverse.

Kane offered the woman in the doorway a smile and a wave. Through his clenched teeth, he muttered to Brigid, "Keep your eyes open."

Out of options, all three Cerberus warriors made their way up the steps and into the House Lilandera.

Chapter 10

At the Cerberus facility in Montana, Brewster Philboyd was busy explaining the situation to his colleague, Donald Bry, as they sat together in the operations center. Bry, a short man with a mess of copper-colored curls atop his head and a permanent expression of concern, nodded in sour agreement.

"If this Red Weed virus is unleashed, the death toll would be catastrophic," Bry said. "We'd be looking at a megacull the likes of which hasn't been seen on this planet since the nuclear hostilities in 2001. Maybe worse."

"So what can we do?" Brewster asked. "Once this catalyst is formulated, the Weed effectively goes live. It doesn't even need to come into direct physical contact. So long as enough of the catalyst is in the air of the facility housing, the Red Weed will set it off."

"And the Weed is so virulent," Bry noted as he scanned the file on Philboyd's terminal screen, "that it would spread like wildfire. Could we close down the entire redoubt, do some kind of remote lockdown on the place, sealing the virus inside?"

"Difficult verging on impossible," Philboyd concluded, shaking his head. "The door's already been broken open, so we'd be looking at serious reconstruction work to make it airtight. This catalyst cycle completes in eleven hours."

"But there must be…" Bry began, scratching at his

head as he pondered. "Dammit, we need Lakesh. He's been to the facility."

"Where is he?" Brewster asked, peering around the hectic operations room.

"He's taken a couple of hours to himself," Bry explained. "Domi said he was exhausted, though I can't think why."

With a "humph" of acknowledgment, Philboyd turned back to his screen. "We need a counteragent, just as Brigid proposed," he said.

"I'll put a team on it," Bry agreed. "You look into the possibility of sealing the redoubt." Then he made his way across the room to where Reba DeFore, the Cerberus physician, was working at her terminal close by the entry door. "Reba, how is your knowledge of toxicology?"

"So-so," DeFore said, holding her hand out, palm down, and tilting it in the air.

"We need to find a way to turn back this Red Weed," Bry said, "and it seems that the catalyst is the weak link. If we can find a way to break that, we could prevent any outbreak of this virulent bioengineered anthrax. Your thoughts?"

"Get the chemists together," DeFore said, brushing a loose strand of her ash-blond hair from her face. "We'll see what we can do."

KANE AND BRIGID RUSHED through the door and past the woman holding it open in front of them, with Grant following a moment later.

"Welcome, welcome," the woman said in her treacle-rich voice.

Kane looked at her, seeing her in the light for the first time. She was a little over five feet tall with coffee-dark skin. Although she was short, the woman was wide, mak-

ing Kane think of her almost like some second door made
of flesh that would open and close to allow callers entry
to her domain. Her thick hair seemed uneven, brushed in
such a way as to clump around the center line of her head.
She was dressed in a floor-length dress of a red like blood,
low cut over the bosom to show off an ample décolletage.
A string of glistening pearls was wrapped double around
her neck, the second loop hanging low to her navel. Her
fingers seemed to flash with lightning where rings of
silver, platinum and gold encircled each of her stubby
digits. She even wore rings on her thumbs, two on the
right thumb and one on the left, a flat gemstone laid in the
latter's center twinkling with the purple of amethyst. Her
chocolate-rich eyes met with Kane's, sitting in pools of
white turned yellow, and a broad smile lit her face, bringing with it the cracks and wrinkles of age. At a guess,
Kane would say she was in her fifties, maybe older.

"And what brings you to the House Lilandera, handsome stranger?" the woman asked as she openly admired
Kane.

Still standing close to the open doorway with his Sin
Eater clutched in his hand, Kane peered back outside,
warily observing the shambling undead as they stalked
along the gravel drive toward the vast house. They seemed
to have slowed, walking less purposefully now as if they
had lost track of their quarry. Grant and Brigid had taken
up positions to either side of the open doorway, Grant's
own weapon trained on the shambling creatures as they
lurched nearby, Brigid with the steel pole poised and
ready in her grip.

"You might want to close this door," Kane urged the
dark-skinned woman. "We don't seem to be keeping the
best of company today."

The woman followed Kane's line of sight, squinting

slightly as she peered out the door; she was short-sighted, Kane realized.

"Them?" the short woman said, and there was a note of laughter in her rich voice. "They won't come in here, my darling. This place is only for the living. The beautiful, beautiful living."

Grant and Brigid exchanged looks before turning their attention back to the shadowy figures outside the door.

"I'm not sure they make the distinction," Kane said, firmly pushing the door closed with a press of his hand.

Once Kane shut the outside door, it seemed as if the interior itself took on new light. A low-hung chandelier warmed the place with its creamy glow. The Cerberus rebels found themselves standing in an old-fashioned hallway, mock Victorian with wood paneling in a rich chestnut, polished so that it gleamed beneath the rich glow of that ornate chandelier. A wide staircase led upward into the second story of the building.

The hall was decorated with paintings, each one mounted in a golden frame that had been enlivened with velvets of the richest reds and purples. The way the material hung gave the impression of drapes, as if the paintings were windows half hidden from view. Kane took a step closer, the better to appraise the nearest painting between its rich, velvety curtains. It showed a well-proportioned man, naked and glistening with sweat, sodomizing a braying goat with his phallus. The man had dark hair, cut short like Kane's own, and for a moment Kane felt a strange mixture of repulsion and embarrassment, as if the painting showed himself committing the sin, as if some terrible inner desire had been laid bare for all to see. The broad brushstrokes of the face looked eerily like his own.

Kane turned away, focusing his attention on the round woman who had welcomed them to her house. She had moved from the door, leaning now against the banister to the wide staircase. The stairs were thickly carpeted in the deep, rich red of autumnal leaves, and Kane saw human figures had been carved into the banister, their rounded shapes polished so they shone. Like the painting, these, too, were engaged in graphic sexual acts, and Kane struggled to turn away, fascinated and repelled all at once. Though static, the carved figures seemed animated, as if they might move at any moment.

"What kind of house is this?" Kane asked, his voice low and wary.

"A celebration of life," the dark-skinned woman said, smiling her broad smile. She intertwined her fat fingers in front of her, and their rings glittered as they caught the overhead light. "A place where everyone can find a friend, my darling. Just you see."

"We're not looking for friends," Kane assured her, "just a place to catch our breath while we figure out what's going on."

The round woman gestured with her stubby arm, indicating a lounge that resided through an open door along the wide, warmly lit passageway. "You stay as long as you like," she told Kane, taking in his companions with an incline of her head. "As long as you like."

Standing close to the front door, Grant was peering through a side window there, watching the driveway outside.

"Grant?" Kane said.

Grant turned from the window. "They're still out there, but they don't seem to be approaching the house yet. I guess they didn't see us come in."

"Won't take them long to figure it out," Brigid stated dourly. "It's not like there's a myriad of places we could have gone."

Before Kane could reply, the woman who seemed to own the house spoke up. "They won't come in here," she explained, shaking her head confidently. "They're drawn to the living, but they're afraid of them, too. Afraid of meeting the same fate they suffered once before. I imagine it must be a tremendous burden, knowing what it feels like to be dead."

Kane's eyes narrowed as he assessed the woman in front of him, realizing there was much more to her than met the eye. "Have you seen a lot of this? Dead folks getting up and walking around?" he persisted.

"Since as long as I can remember, though that isn't very long," the woman replied cryptically. "People call me Ellie, by the way, so you nice folks might as well, too."

"Well, Ellie, I'm Kane," Kane told her, before indicating his companions. "Grant, Brigid Baptiste…"

Brigid offered her hand to the shorter woman, who grasped it firmly, the bracelets on her wrist clattering as they shook hands. Brigid's slender hand looked small in Ellie's paw.

"Well, well, aren't you just pretty as a cloud," Ellie said, eyeing Brigid with approval. "A pale child as beautiful as you would be a treat to our honored gentleman callers."

Brigid dismissed the comment, not quite sure of how to take it. "What do you know about the things outside?" she asked. "They are dead people, aren't they?"

"Don't need me to tell you that," Ellie assured her, "not a sweet and clever young lady like you."

Brigid found herself taken aback by the compliment. While it was no doubt a social grace, she felt as if it meant something more, that this Ellie woman had looked into

her soul with those chocolate-rich eyes, seen the aspects
that came together to make her. It was weird. "Th-thank
you," the beautiful Cerberus warrior stuttered, feeling
disconcerted.

Still peering through the side window, Grant saw the
corpselike figures meandering along the shingle track.
Just a few minutes before, they had been savagely determined, relentless in their pursuit of the Cerberus field
team under the tutelage of their rotting mistress. Now
they seemed idle, confused, as if they had forgotten their
purpose for coming here. Whatever effect this house had,
it seemed to be the equivalent of stealth tech, hiding it
from the view of the walking dead. There was something
very peculiar going on here; that was for certain.

With a sweep of her skirts, Ellie led the way into the
lounge. Like the hallway before it, the lounge was richly
decorated, its walls painted a lustrous red, the lighting
low and intimate.

"You all make yourselves at home," Ellie instructed,
indicating the cushioned seating of the cozy room. She
turned then, exiting the room to give them some privacy.

There were several couches, each of them plumped
up with cushions. Kane walked across the room, feeling
the soles of his boots sinking into the thick carpet. The
room smelled of vanilla, and he noticed incense burning
from three sticks in an ornate holder on the low coffee
table, their smoke trails puffing languidly into the air. A
well-stocked drinks cabinet with a glass front lined one
wall, and beside it a bookcase towered almost to the ceiling. The shelves of the bookcase were lined with thick
volumes bound in leather, and Brigid Baptiste couldn't
resist taking a step toward it, eyeing their titles for a
brief instant.

"What is this place?" Kane muttered, keeping his voice low.

Grant slapped Kane on the back and laughed. "I think we just hit the honey pot, partner. This here is what they call a house of ill repute, where a boy becomes a man."

Brigid looked at them both and rolled her eyes once more. "Let's just get on with it," she said, "and get out of here." With that, the red-haired former archivist took up a position on one of the luxurious couches, resting the steel pole beside her, propped at an angle against the seat.

"Something's not right here," Kane stated, his voice quiet.

"We've come to the conclusion that one of our arch foes has come back from the dead and is proceeding to *raise* the dead," Brigid concluded sarcastically as Grant took up a seat beside her. "Yes, I think you're correct, Kane—something isn't right here."

"No," Kane said, turning to examine the low-lit room they were now in. "This place. There's something—"

Kane stopped himself as Ellie returned, bustling through the doorway carrying with her a silver tray on which rested a bowl of dried fruits. She placed the bowl on a low table in the center of the room, within reaching distance of Brigid's seat, before shuffling over to the drinks cabinet. "Help yourself," Ellie cooed encouragingly. "Now, what would you nice folks be drinking today?"

"We're not—" Kane began and stopped himself.

"I'm sure there's something here you'll like," Ellie insisted as she stood in front of her drinks cabinet.

Kane did see something he liked there, reflected in the glass of the drinks cabinet. He turned to see more clearly and watched as, striding down the stairs in the hallway, a shapely woman appeared, dressed in whispers of white lace, her long blond hair trailing past her shoulders and down, over the swell of her breasts. The thin whisper of her white garment ended at her hip, leaving those long, shapely legs bare as she strode slowly to the foot of the staircase, her smooth skin shining in the warm glow of the chandelier. Meeting his eye, the blonde woman played her tongue slowly over her lips, her blue eyes narrowing and the hint of a smile tugging at the edges of her painted mouth. Her eyes were the color of a cornflower's petals, the color of the assassin.

"I see you're interested." Ellie's voice broke Kane's thoughts, but when he turned he realized she was addressing Brigid Baptiste. Chewing one of the dates, the red-haired former archivist was watching the older woman as she pulled a thick leather-bound book from the bookcase. "Here," she said, handing the book over to Brigid, "take a look at this if you wish."

Brigid took the book, her fingertips brushing against the softly rippled surface of the leather binding. Automatically she opened the cover, turned over the flyleaf and looked at the title page. There, printed in thick black ink, Brigid read *BUTTERFLY* by S.X. Roamer.

Brigid read the words, wondering at the title and the curiously named author. She was about to put the book aside when her eye was drawn to the frontispiece on the opposite page. It was a line illustration, full of delicate ink strokes, with pointillism to give it definition and depth. The black-and-white illustration showed a woman, her flowing locks trailing like a lion's mane down her naked back. The woman in the drawing was unclothed, but there were straps tied to her wrists and ankles where she knelt on the rumpled sheets on an unmade bed. Though her arching back faced the reader, the woman in the illustration was looking coquettishly over her shoulder out from the page, and her eyes seemed to meet with Brigid's as she stared at the picture.

"What kind of story is this?" Brigid asked, her voice quiet, timid. She already knew, she was sure. And she knew the woman, too, didn't she? She knew the woman in the illustration. That slender athletic form, those long locks of flowing hair and the emerald eyes that stared out at the reader.

Emerald eyes?

Hadn't the illustration been black-and-white just a moment before? Brigid asked herself.

Across the room, Kane found himself standing and walking toward the blonde woman in the wisps of white lace, his booted feet sinking into the luxurious carpet beneath them. The blonde stood at the bottom of the staircase, her pale hair shimmering beneath the glow of the chandelier. She was beautiful, like an angel.

Grant raised himself from his position on the couch, motioning toward Kane as the ex-Mag made his way toward the shapely blonde standing just beyond the doorway. "Uh, Kane?" Grant called. "You think maybe you want to get back here and…?"

The plump woman at Brigid's side tsked, shaking her head. "You've all had a long day," she told Grant, stepping closer to him as he rose. "Your friend just needs to take a load off."

Grant fixed her with a look, his lips curling in a sneer. "We don't have time for this," he told Ellie as she swirled the liquid around in the wide brandy glass she held in her bejewelled hand. "We came here to find—"

"Sanctuary," Ellie finished for him before taking a mouthful of the honey-colored brandy from the glass she held. "And you've found it, if only you'll open your eyes."

Grant could taste something in *his* mouth then, felt the

burn of alcohol on *his* breath. He watched as the woman took another drink from her glass, feeling the liquid wash around *his* mouth and down his own throat. "No," he said. "This isn't…this isn't right.…"

Ellie took a step closer, her smile never faltering. Then she was standing directly in front of Grant, her hand pressed against his elbow, her head tilted to look up at his far above her. "A brave man like you shouldn't be afraid," she told him, her voice like warm treacle in his ears.

Grant watched as she took another deep swig from the glass of brandy, felt it strike his own tongue, swirl around his head the way brandy will. "What are you…?" Grant began, feeling himself sway in place.

Ellie placed her finger to Grant's lips, fixing him with a motherly look. "Hush now, brave man," she told him. "Nothing will hurt you here. Nothing will hurt you in the House Lilandera."

Then she stepped away, and Grant stood in place in front of the couch, his head swimming. He needed to sit, he knew, could feel his legs trembling, his body swaying.

Kane, meanwhile, took another pace toward the hallway, his own eyes fixed on the gorgeous blonde at the foot of the stairs. She smiled at him, her lips colored a pale pink as if they had been dipped in ice. Then the blonde beauty ran her hand up the side of her body, gently cupping her breast for a long, sensuous moment.

"Go on, child," Ellie whispered to Kane, and her voice seemed to be just inches from his ear. "Kirsten there likes you. Go make a friend. There's no need to be scared. We are celebrants of life. Nothing can hurt you here."

Kane didn't turn, his attention was fixed on the leggy blonde at the bottom of the stairs—blue-eyed Kirsten. As Kane watched, taking another step forward as if drawn by a magnet, Kirsten turned and began to scale the stairs once more, her long legs kicking out in front of her like some magnificent racehorse, whispers of lace shimmering in the light like cobwebs glistening with morning dew. Kane watched her walk away, watched the way her body moved.

When Kirsten reached the top of the stairs another woman appeared, as achingly beautiful as the first, dressed in a cream-colored bodice and stockings, her blond hair shimmering like the rays of the sun. Where Kirsten's eyes were cornflower-blue, this one had green eyes, the color of the ocean, and a mouth so perfect that Kane yearned to kiss it. As if sensing Kane's wish, the green-eyed woman turned to Kirsten, reaching her arm to the back of her neck and pulling her close until their faces almost touched. Kane watched from the foot of the staircase, his heart drumming as the two women closed their eyes, long lashes blinking down like the dark wings of a crow, and began to kiss, probing at one another, open mouths joined in passion.

"Pretty mouth and green my eyes," Ellie muttered, the words echoing in Kane's head as he began to scale the stairs.

On the couch, Brigid was still looking at the illustration that formed the frontispiece of the book she held— *Butterfly*. In the illustration, the woman's lustrous hair seemed to ripple slightly in the breeze, and Brigid peered more intently, utterly transfixed.

She had red hair now, the young woman in the picture, hair the color of the sunset in late summer, and those locks cascaded down her back like a waterfall, a waterfall made of sunsets. Brigid wondered what the straps were for on the woman's arms, wondered if she had placed them there voluntarily or if they had been placed upon her.

As she thought it, Brigid became aware of the pain at

her wrist, something digging in there where her sleeve ended. Her eyes turned to look at her left wrist and she saw the dark leather strap that had been tied there, felt it pinch her skin and noted the way her flesh had reddened around it. Beneath her wrist she saw the rumpled bed-sheet, and her eyes lost focus for a moment as she looked at its creases and folds, the way it seemed to be like some static ocean laid out in front of her.

It was just the illustration, Brigid realized. The illustration in the book, not her. And yet for a moment it had seemed as if—no, it was impossible.

Brigid stroked her hand across the facing page, turned it over so as to cover the illustration of the woman on the bed, as if shutting her out of her mind. There was text there, the start of the story, and Brigid wanted to look away but already, without even meaning to, her photographic memory had taken a snapshot of it, was carving the words into her brain.

Chapter 11

Mary should not have accepted that invitation, she knew, Brigid read, *even as she felt herself being drawn from the warmth of her bed to the leaded window of her bedchamber. The need within her was like a splinter in her heart, an ache born of desire. Her eyes opened, blue as sapphires, and she felt the cool night air dance across her face, painting her features in like a sirocco on the desert sands.*

In the faraway distance, Mary—or was it Brigid?—heard the tolling bell of the village clock tower, its chimes slowly droning out the 3:00 a.m. call.

Her nightdress clinging to her like a second skin, Mary pushed back the bedcovers, felt the chill of the January night air even as she began to clamber out of her warm bed, its sheets rumpled beneath her girlish frame.

Brigid, too, felt the chill, the downy hair on her arms standing upright as she turned the page of the book called *Butterfly.*

There was a gap in the curtains, and a full moon peeked through, bathing Mary's room in a shaft of beautiful silverlike liquid. Beneath that eerie line of light, the room appeared to be the bedchamber of a child, Mary thought, the mirror with flowers painted on its surface, the glass-eyed dolls that sat on the seat in the corner, their noses turned up in feigned disinterest.

Outside, it was a January moon, alack; the Wolf Moon

as the old washerwoman had called it when they had spoken just a few days before, that morning when she had found Mary trying to hide the evidence of the ruined bedsheet. Despite the chill air, Mary felt her face warm at the thought, her cheeks reddening as she recalled the way the sheet had been torn, the blood of her maidenhead spilled upon its snow-white weave, spilled from the very core of her being. Her mind still reeled at the thought of the fire that had been lit deep within her on that night, the desire that felt like a lightning strike at her very core. Now he was calling to her once again, this handsome enticement who made her so curiously light-headed, this wolf who was also a man. She heard him howl, in her head, beyond the window—it was hard to tell where the noise truly came from now, within or without.

Silently, Brigid pushed herself from the bed, the covers arrayed before her like the waves of the ocean, finally halted by Canute. Despite herself, she almost cried out as her bare foot touched the old floorboards, for the floor was icy to her touch, like the fingers of Jack Frost playing across her sole. Outside, she knew, the wolf was waiting, and he, too, would want to play similar games.

Brigid Baptiste walked slowly across the room, the gossamer-thin nightdress clinging to her fragile body, her nipples hardening as the night air caressed the paleness of her exposed throat. He was outside, she knew, the wolf, the man, the one who had taken her on the heart-rending journey from girl to woman just a few nights before, when the January moon had first opened the fullness of its wicked silvery eye. It was as if she had been a chrysalis, a thing forming in the darkness, growing and shaping itself into something new and wonderful. And now, having felt his touch against her skin, felt his body

*pressed against hers, Brigid was no longer a chrysalis
but a beautiful butterfly.*

*Brigid stopped before the leaded window, feeling
a tremor course through her body as she reached for
the heavy curtain there, where the moon's eye peered
within. The Wolf Moon could see her, her once girlish
body that had seemed to change three days before, that
had taken on new curves and swellings as that wolf-man
had pushed her to the bed and straddled her, the light of
the moon making his fur glisten. Her breath was coming
faster now, her heart beating more rapidly, and again she
heard the call from outside, that long, deep howling as
the beast cried out to her to join him, to abscond to the
forest where they could be animals together.*

*She pulled back the curtain and the brightness of
the Wolf Moon seemed to turn her hair to liquid fire, a
raging volcano erupting over her head and shoulders, the
lava cascading down the swell of her breasts, lit bright
through the gossamer weave of her nightgown. Brigid felt
the burning there, the fire burning within her outthrust
nipples.*

*Outside, just emerging from the tree line, a lone figure
padded out into the open. Brigid narrowed her emerald
eyes for a moment, holding one dainty, porcelain-colored
hand up to shade her from the glare of the full moon.
Already pale, her hand became alabaster in the quick-
silver light of the Wolf Moon. Down there in the garden,
close to where the mighty oaks cast their dark shadows
like spectres, there stood a man. Alone, his clothes were
dark as his hair, which tumbled past his collar in thick
curls. Oh, but how she longed to run her hands through
that mane of hair, to rub her fingers across his broad
chest once more until they were tangled in the down that
seemed to cover him where it was absent from her own*

smooth curves. This man, this beast, this animal already possessed something of her, a glistening shard of her virgin heart, which he had taken when he had taken her three nights before.

Brigid put her hand against the handle of the door to the balcony, feeling the icy coolness of the metal that served to link the outside to the house, like a shaft driven through some willing maiden. She pushed down on the ice-cold handle, pressed her body softly against the door as the longing within her swelled like crashing waves. Her heart pounded, racing within her breast, and her breath caught in her throat so sharply that she could hardly bear to take another. An icy shiver went right through her body then, from the tips of her toes and the crown of her head, two surging winds rushing to meet, crashing together at her center, her womanhood.

Brigid relaxed herself, struggled to right her breathing, to slow her fluttering heart. She wanted him now, wanted him so badly that even the thought of having him, of holding him, made her want to fall to the floor and sob. The moon at her back, she peered once more into the room where she had spent her childhood, where she had been but a caterpillar waiting to cocoon itself before it emerged into a bright and brilliant woman. The dolls by the fireplace seemed to watch her with their glass-bead eyes, accusing her of betraying them, of betraying her childhood.

Then she turned once more, defiantly placing her childhood behind her, and opened the door. Brigid took a single step out onto the balcony, paying no attention to the cool night air as it rushed across her newfound woman's body. The nightdress fluttered around her, its white silk clinging there like a second skin.

The girl took another step forward, then another and

*another, all the while the rays of the Wolf Moon play-
ing like fingers through her beautiful auburn hair. Then
Brigid had reached the balcony's edge, as if it were
some strange purgatory between girlhood and the final
embracing of her womanhood, and she leaned down
until her elbows met with the stone balustrade outside
her window. She had played with her dolls out here as a
child, on summer afternoons when the days were warm,
the sounds of her little-girl laughter jabbering through
the branches of the oak trees that overlooked her bedchamber's window. Now she desired just one game, an
amusement that required two players for its ultimate
fulfilment. Leaning down, her hair whipping around the
oval of her face in the night breeze, Brigid spoke one
word to the beast that waited far below in the palace
grounds. "Come." It was a whisper, nothing more than
that, a sound made as much with the heart as with the
lips.*

*The man at the edge of the trees turned his head at
the sound, and Brigid saw the way his eyes twinkled
beneath the moon's silvery light. He was so handsome,
his shoulders wide and strong, his chest like one of the
carved marble statues she had seen in the museum when
her nanny had taken her there just a few years before.*

*"Come," Brigid said once more. "Come to me, pre-
cious splinter in mine heart."*

GRANT FELT AS IF his feet had been rooted to the spot as
he stood in front of the couch in the lounge of the House
Lilandera, the rich taste of brandy still lingering in his
mouth. He was aware of what was going on around him—
that Kane had just departed the room, that Brigid was sitting to his left, thumbing the pages of the leather-bound
tome, that the large woman called Ellie was standing at

the doorway—and yet he seemed unable to react. It was like being trapped between sleep and wakefulness, his mind alert but with his body unwilling to respond.

In a swish of skirts, Ellie paced across the room, and Grant watched out of the corner of his eye as she checked on Brigid in an almost maternal way. Brigid didn't seem to react, even when Ellie brushed the woman's red hair from her face, admiring her flawless skin with a smile. "Such a pretty one," Ellie said. "So, so pretty."

Grant could not perceive why Brigid hadn't responded, had not reacted in any way to the woman's physical intrusion into her personal space. Brigid Baptiste seemed oblivious to it, as if her attention was captivated by the open book resting on her lap.

Something's not right here. That's what Kane had said, Grant recalled. Whatever "here" was, it was more than just some old whorehouse on the outskirts of the bayou. After all, who would come to the bayou for the services a place like this would provide? This area was a dead zone, and in more ways than one.

Grant urged himself to move, to take a step forward, to break whatever spell he had been placed under that was forcing him to stand in place. He felt his muscles tense, felt the fingers of his right hand begin to curl, to form a fist.

"Oh, my goodness, but you're a tough one, aren't you?" Ellie uttered, her rich voice flowing into Grant's brain like hot fudge over ice cream. Then her hands reached over and stroked the back of Grant's hand. Somehow the touch made his fingers unfurl. The fist he had been trying to form ceased to bunch and he couldn't seem to muster the will to re-create it.

Ellie stepped back, and Grant watched, unable to move, as her dark chocolate eyes played over his body, admiring him like a work of art. In her hand, she swished the brandy in its glass, the rich honey color swirling around and around. Slowly, with something that amounted to a sense of ceremony, she brought the wide-brimmed glass up to her nose, sniffed at its contents in a long drag, filling her wide nostrils with the scent of the vintage. Grant could smell it, too, he found, as he watched the woman inhale in front of him. Then, with equal precision and ceremony, she took a taste of the liquor, swallowing it before breathing out though her open mouth with a sigh, letting the rich aftertaste run across her tongue a second time. Somehow, Grant could taste the liquid in his own mouth, feel its alcohol burn down his own throat, the aftertaste on his own tongue.

"Now," Ellie said, "we need to help you get rid of all that tension, don't we? Poor brave soldier who's lost his way."

Grant's face scrunched up as he tried to reply, tried but found he could not get the words out. Leave me alone, you witch, he wanted to tell her. But the words just wouldn't form in his throat, would not burst free of his lips.

Still smiling, Ellie ran one of her pudgy hands softly down the side of Grant's face, just barely stroking him, the sparkling rings like sunbursts in his eyes. "Come with me," she instructed, and she turned to exit the room.

Despite all rational explanation, Grant found himself following.

PRETTY MOUTH and green my eyes.

Kane heard the words swirling through his mind as he reached the top of the staircase, where the two blonde women waited. They had stopped kissing and now just seemed to be waiting for him, their eyes playing over his body, feasting on his good looks.

He had been with beautiful women before, of course. Indeed, Kane's life seemed to involve a steady flow of gorgeous women, the vast majority of whom turned out to be deadly, duplicitous or downright demonic. The fault was partly his, of course. There was something of the wolf about him, it was said; he was a natural loner, never fully letting his guard down to really make a connection with another human being, to find a lover he could trust. In fact, it seemed strange sometimes that Kane had stayed with Cerberus, that he had come to trust Brigid Baptiste, his *anam-chara,* his soul friend, with a bond that seemed to be something more than love.

Ahead of him, the two shapely women were leading the way down a hallway that, like the rest of House Lilandera, was painted in rich colors, warm reds and purples, dark, sensual hues that spoke of primal desire, of sweat-drenched dreams and of blood-letting. Kane stopped for a moment, his boot soles sinking into the thick red carpet, seeing the wood doors leading off the corridor. Something seemed strange about all this. Hadn't there been something else he was supposed to do?

The blonde with the cornflower-blue eyes reached back, her pale hand grasping for Kane's as she looked at him over the curve of one milky, slender shoulder, and a promising smile played on her perfect pink lips.

"You don't need to choose," the blonde called Kirsten said.

"And you won't ever want to leave," the other one, the one with green eyes, added.

But there was a choice, Kane realized, and it wasn't the one they spoke of. He couldn't put his finger on it, but he knew there was something about this that was still a choice, and maybe a bad one. He was neglecting something, forgetting something, ignoring something that was so terribly obvious it was almost as if he was staring right at it and still not seeing it.

Kirsten pulled at Kane's hand, her fingers wrapped around his. A few steps in front of her, the other woman, the one whose name Kane had never even asked, pushed open a door of rich walnut, turned and backed into it, bending low and curling her finger to entice Kane and Kirsten to follow.

"Come on, lover," Green Eyes intoned encouragingly, her voice breathy.

Kirsten tugged at Kane's fingers again, taking another step toward the room with a stride of her long, bare legs. Kane followed, his hand tingling at the beautiful woman's touch.

The one with green eyes ducked past the door, disappearing into the room beyond. A moment later, still pulling at the very tips of his fingers, blue-eyed Kirsten led Kane into the room.

A magnificent bed stood in the middle of the room, a deep mattress sitting so low that it remained close to the floor. Candles were lit all around the room, and incense burned in one corner, a thin trail of smoke drifting from it in a languid swirl toward the ceiling. A wide sash window overlooked the bed to the left side, and the light that came past the red-velvet drapes seemed to be the light of sunset as it ebbed into night. The blonde with green eyes was already relaxing on the bed, lounging back, her long legs stretching out in front of her. She caught Kane's eye and gave a long, slow blink, her dark lashes coming down to cover her eyes like the night sky that was hurrying over the window behind her.

Desire had never been a motivating factor in Kane's makeup. Others had often wondered, occasionally to his face, why he and Brigid Baptiste had not officially become a couple. They had failed to understand the psychological makeup of the man, how his Magistrate training had taught him a discipline that was so ingrained that he would always put the mission first.

But now, faced with these two beautiful creatures in this house of carnal desire, Kane felt himself drawn into their web, felt himself unspooling, coming loose at the seams, losing a part of the very thing that made him.

Kirsten had joined her friend on the mattress and, with both women's eyes still fixed on Kane's, she worked the clasp of her friend's stocking, slowly unravelling it and curling the wispy material down her partner's shapely leg.

Kane was unravelling, too, he realized, somehow losing something of his essence in the face of everything he was being offered here. He could hear his pulse in his ears, feel himself being dragged toward the promise that lay in front of him.

With the mess of thoughts swimming drunkenly in his head, Kane found himself drawn to the bed, the two beautiful temptresses encouraging him to join them in their games of lust.

ELLIE WALKED DOWN the red-walled corridor beyond the foot of the stairs, and Grant followed like some obedient hound. The round woman eyed each painting that hung on the wall as she passed it, pushing back the velvet curtains here and there to examine several more closely before moving on. There must have been a hundred paintings in frames big and small, each frame gilded with a rich gold as yellow as butter.

When Ellie halted in front of yet another of the pictures, Grant struggled to break whatever trance he knew he was in. Kane had explained to him about the trancelike

creatures he and Baptiste had met at Papa Hurbon's, and
Brigid had told him of the drugs used by the Bizango
practitioners that could enslave a man's mind, making him
like a zombie of voodoo lore—not a reanimated corpse,
but a walking dead man all the same. Grant had met with
Papa Hurbon, too, at a later date, once his followers had
finally departed, and he wondered now if they had had to
break the spell that they were under, battle through the
miasma induced by the drug cocktail that they had been
dosed with. Was this woman a Bizango, a practitioner of
the darkest form of voodoo arts? Whatever it was, Grant
needed to break this fix that Ellie had on him—now,
while her back was turned, before she could ensnare him
further with another potent, impossible sip of the brandy.

Grant could not comprehend how it truly worked, this
trick with the brandy glass. He had heard of deceptions
that involved hypnosis, where a stage magician would
somehow make his subject walk through fire or bark like
a dog or strip naked in front of an audience of strangers,
but this was no stage trick. The woman had needed to say
no words to ensnare him, seemed to plant no trigger in his
regimented mind to exercise her control of him.

Desperately, Grant bunched his fists, the movement
feeling as if he had overstretched, as if a muscle had been
pulled, a ligament torn. If he could do that much, he reasoned, he could break the spell; it was all just a matter of
willpower.

Then Ellie turned to him, her broad face and uneven
bonnet of hair filling his vision. "This one, I think," she
said, smiling wickedly as she tapped her index finger
against the glass that covered the nearest painting, its
velvet drapes pulled open to reveal its contents.

Automatically, Grant's eyes followed where the woman
tapped, observing the picture that was framed there. It

was a small picture, six inches by eight, finished in dark hues, browns and blacks. Pale, tiny figures waited in the picture, naked bodies copulating in a dark forest as, in the distance behind them, a hilltop city burned, billowing black smoke into the indigo sky beneath the waning moon.

Ellie took a step back, leaving Grant standing alone in front of the strange painting. "Close your eyes," she instructed. "The transition is easier that way."

Thus told, Grant found his eyelids shutting in a long, slow blink as if overcome by sleep. Then he heard Ellie laugh, a hearty sound close to his ear. But as the laughter continued it seemed to get farther and farther away.

Grant felt the cool night air playing on his bare skin then, and when he reopened his eyes, he found he was no longer in the scarlet corridor. Instead, he was in a dark forest, the indigo night sky looming high overhead. From close by, the familiar moans and cries of sexual desire played like an orchestra tuning up, and as he stepped out of the trees Grant saw the pale figures of the painting clenching one another in their desperate trysts, caught up in the urgency of desire as their city burned in the distance. The ex-Magistrate turned, looking all around him and seeing more and more figures engaged in this moonlit orgy, sweat glistering off their skin.

"Oh, crap," Grant muttered. He was inside the painting.

Chapter 12

"So I'm stuck inside a picture," Grant snarled. "How the hell does that work?"

He turned around, watched the dark smoke as it billowed into the sky from the distant city, flames reflecting against the clouds. The smoke was moving, so whatever this painting had been when he had first looked at it it was now animated, a viable world with which he could interact. The moans of desire from the copulating couples between the trees confirmed that, too. High above, wisps of clouds rippled in front of the waning moon, drifting slowly across the night sky.

Grant turned 360 degrees, looking for an exit, the edge of the picture, the window of its frame. There was nothing; he appeared to be standing in a moonlit forest that stretched on as far as he could see. There were several pale figures just a dozen or so paces away, locked in embraces, their naked bodies moving rhythmically as fornicating partners pressed against each other.

Grant checked himself, saw that he was still dressed in his shadow suit and the long coat made of Kevlar weave. A moment later he was warily approaching the nearest of the couples. The couple was deeply involved with each other, kissing and tenderly stroking each other as Grant strode across the soil and halted in front of them.

Up close, the couple looked remarkably alike, and Grant saw that it was a young dark-haired man with a girl who appeared almost to be his twin. Their eyes were the pale blue of ice, and there could be no mistaking that they were related when one saw them together side by side— related or perhaps simply drawn by the same hand. The man looked somewhat girlish, with a soft face and long, dark hair trailing past his neck in a cascade of curls, a full mouth with the kind of bruised lips that suggested a pout no matter what he did. The young woman had identical coloring, but the soft lines and full lips of her face seemed more appropriate in a woman, and her hair trailed farther down her naked back and over her shoulders to her breasts. Grant wondered if they were related or if this was merely a deficiency of the painter who had created the picture he was now standing in.

"I need some help," Grant stated as the couple turned to him. "How did I get here?"

The couple looked at him blankly, as if unable to comprehend the question. Grant wondered if they were more like automatons, unable to do anything other than move within the confines of their roles in the painted bacchanalian tryst. He decided to try a more direct question, one they would certainly know the answer to. "Okay, then how did *you* get here?"

The man's thin eyebrows rose, and the trace of a smile crossed his full lips. "We walked," he said, as if it were obvious.

"From where?" Grant asked.

"The city," the woman replied, inclining her head as she admired Grant with her ghostly, ice-blue eyes.

"When?" Grant asked, but already he had the sinking feeling that he was not getting anywhere with these people.

"When the inferno began—" the man said.

"And the people started burning," the woman concluded for him.

"When was that?" Grant asked, his sense of irritation growing.

"Oh, before the moon rose," the man told him.

Grant turned away, shaking his head in despair. He wasn't just trapped in a painting; he was trapped in a riddle. The occupants spoke in circles, most likely because they had no knowledge of the world beyond the contextual frame of the painting. The city was alight and they were out here, naked in the forest, as part of some mass orgy under the light of the waning moon. Everything they said was merely restating the details of the painting. There was no depth to their comprehension, nothing beneath the surface of the brushstrokes that had made them.

As he considered this, a woman stepped out from behind a tree. She was naked, shorter than Grant by more than a foot, and her skin glistened in the moonlight a golden color, like the skin of a peach. She smiled as she met Grant's eye, then turned away as if with shyness.

It was hard to tell in the soft moonlight, but Grant wondered that he recognized her. Her trim, athletic form, her dark hair and golden skin—the woman looked like his lover Shizuka.

In annoyance, Grant turned away, scouring the surrounding forest and wondering how to escape. Should he go to the city? Or walk in one direction until perhaps he met with the edge of the picture? Could such a thing be done?

The woman strode closer, her body moving like liquid in the moonlight, and placed her hands around Grant's waist from behind, pulling herself close to him and rubbing against him like a cat. "Don't leave," she said, as if reading his thoughts. "We have so much we can do right here, while the city burns forever."

Grant turned his head, looking at the ill-lit but familiar face of Shizuka over his shoulder. Even as a painting she was beautiful, and despite his suspicions, he felt the desire welling within him.

KANE LAY BACK ON THE BED as the two women stripped him, pulling away his torn jacket and peeling off the shadow suit that clung to his muscular body like a second skin. The smell of incense clouded his senses, and its scent was now joined by the proximity of the women, the clean smell of their flawless, beautiful skin. He reached for one of them, Kirsten of the blue eyes, pulled her to him like a man plucking a ripe fruit from a tree. As the other blonde laid kisses upon his body, Kane brought Kirsten's face close to his own, planted kisses on her neck, gorging on her smell.

Then he moved, reaching up to kiss her lips, and Kirsten seemed to tremble in his arms, kissing Kane back with more and more desperation, her kisses fierce and urgent.

The other girl joined them both, running her hands up the ex-Mag's body, and Kane watched as she placed soft, wet kisses along Kirsten's spine, making the gorgeous blonde arch her back with delight.

Kane felt the need inside him, his lust increasing so that it crowded out every other thought. He pulled for the girl with the green eyes, dragging her from Kirsten by her hair, yanking her to him with no gentleness, just urgency.

"I want you," he breathed.

"I'm yours," she replied, but her words were stifled as Kane kissed her mouth, coiled his fingers in her silky hair.

INSIDE THE PAINTING, the woman looked like Shizuka.

And yet she didn't, Grant realized as he moved to kiss her. The simple strokes of the paintbrush had rendered an impression that could be Shizuka, nothing more, and as Grant saw her up close he noted the way the illusion had been created, the swift strokes of the brush to make the illusion of a face, a body. We see what we want to see in paintings, he thought, bring what we have inside of us as viewers.

Grant shrugged out of her grip and, with a practiced flinch of the tendons in his wrist, brought the Sin Eater into his palm.

"Keep away," he instructed, jabbing the muzzle of the pistol at the painted woman. "Whatever you are, keep the hell away from me."

The Shizuka look-alike laughed, a musical trilling in the nighttime forest. "Oh, you surely don't mean that, lover," she chided. Then she took a pace closer to Grant once more, the moonlight playing off of her bare flesh.

"What's my name?" Grant asked, the gun still poised in front of him.

Instead of answering immediately, the woman stepped against the gun, letting its cold metal rest against her breastbone, her nipples jutting out. Then she dipped just slightly, rubbing the end of the gun with her naked chest. "Whatever you want me to call you, lover," she told Grant, a catlike grin on her beautiful mouth.

Without a moment's hesitation, Grant pulled the trigger of the Sin Eater, drilling a burst of 9 mm bullets into the Shizuka pretender who was reaching out for his embrace. There was an explosion, and a cloud of dust blocked Grant's vision for a moment as the bullets struck home against the chest of his would-be lover. Then he stood back and watched, incredulous, as the temptress deteriorated the layers of paint that made her real falling away as if they had never been there. First the beautifully sculpted lines of her skin, the golden tan losing its depth and becoming a simpler shade of pink, thin yellow brushstrokes providing its highlights. Then the flesh itself disappeared and a white outline stood in its place, an outline in the shape of a beautiful woman, just two dark smears showing the hair atop her head, the triangle at the meeting of her legs. In place of her beautiful face there was just a cross now, lightly scrawled onto the canvas, showing roughly where eyes and nose would sit. And then the edges of the woman shape blurred and the whiteness that had once been Shizuka's form became just a scribble in space. And then the forest behind her began to show through, appearing like an image seen through wet tissue.

Grant let out a breath he hadn't realized he had been holding as all evidence that the woman had ever existed finally disappeared. "Okay," he muttered, "it's like that, is it? New world, new rules."

New world, new rules, no way out.

"No," Grant stormed. There was always a way out. He just needed to trust in his friends. And then he realized what it was that he really needed to do.

"TAKE ME," the woman with the green ocean in her eyes whispered when Kane broke away from their kiss, and it seemed as if her words were running through his skull.

And then another voice was running through Kane's skull, a man's voice, deep and familiar. "Kane? Kane, do you copy?"

Kane's eyes seemed to blur, and the room and the women within it lost focus for a moment as the voice drilled through his head.

"Repeat. Kane, do you copy?"

It was Grant, speaking to him. Not in his head, but through the Commtact link that ran along his jawbone and into his skull casing, a link that bypassed the normal aural channels.

"This is Kane," Kane said, screwing his eyes tight to better concentrate on the communication that seemed so desperately out of place in the love nest. "What's happening, Grant?"

INSIDE THE PAINTING, Grant smiled as he heard Kane's voice reverberating through the Commtact in his skull. At least that still worked right. The broad-shouldered ex-Mag held his free hand to his ear as he strode through the unlit forest away from the sounds of the orgy, his booted feet sinking into the soft earth beneath them.

"We're under some kind of hypnosis," Grant explained. "I'm not sure how, but I think Ellie's managed to trick us into seeing things that aren't there. This ringing any bells with you?"

"A few," Kane responded over their shared Commtact link.

Within the lush bedroom of the House Lilandera, Kane opened his eyes just a fraction, seeing the bright red walls and the flickering candles once more, the two beautiful women whose naked bodies were stretched taut in their desire for him.

"I'm stuck in some kind of freaky painting and I can't get out on my own," Grant explained over the Commtact. "You and Brigid have to break this spell right now or we're all screwed."

Kane closed his eyes, shutting out the vision of the room and the desirable women. "When this is over, remind me to tell you about your timing," Kane returned in response.

"Count on it," Grant said before letting the Commtact link go dead.

The smell of burning incense still in his nostrils, Kane ignored the cooing of the women on the bed, ignored the feel of their warm flesh against his skin. He had felt himself being broken apart earlier, unraveling as the women called to him, losing his integrity in some indefinable yet terrifying way. Grant's call over the Commtact had brought him back to reality; he just needed to hold on to his sanity long enough to stay there.

With that, Kane engaged the Commtact link once again, shutting out everything that was going on around him.

"Baptiste?" Kane began. "It's Kane. Can you hear me?"

IN THE MOONLIT GARDEN, the man stepped fully out of the shadows cast by the towering oaks and Brigid gasped, her heart racing as she saw him properly for the first time since the night of their first joining just three evenings before. He was broad of shoulder and long of leg, and he walked in a way that made her know, truly know, that here was a man who commanded all he surveyed. As he was the master of his territory, so, too, was he the master of her, heart and soul.

Her heart drummed against her breast, so hard it felt as if it would break through the flimsy garment that she wore. Brigid watched as the wolf who was a man came for her, answering her siren song. At the bottom of the trellis, he placed one powerful foot on its lowest bar and, like a deckhand, began to ascend it like a ladder, hurrying so swiftly and with such surety that Brigid wondered if his weight might pull the whole thing loose from her father's wall, bringing Daddy's precious roses with it. In silence, the man climbed, the dark, liquid shadow of his body hurrying toward her like an arrow aimed squarely at her beating heart. This was how he had come to her before, she realized, when he had taken her maidenhood as she'd struggled beneath him, scared and confused, her pale body arched in both pleasure and pain.

"Oh Lord, forgive me," she whispered, her hands coming together for a moment in front of her heaving breasts. She desired him so surely now that it pulled at her from within, threatened to disable her, to pull her apart at the seams.

Persephone descended into the underworld for love, Brigid recalled, a silly story from her childhood. But this man—this beast—ascended and thus brought the underworld to her, sowing the taint of that underworld deep inside her, planting the infernal flames deep inside her womanhood.

When he appeared on the balcony, Brigid recoiled, her whole body trembling with fear and anticipation. With the moon behind him, he seemed to be crafted of the inky shadows themselves, only the slightest glint playing where she knew his eyes must be. Brigid stepped back farther, until she met with the cool edge of the door that led into her bedchamber. Familiar with every step of this dance, the man stepped forward, his eyes fixed on her, watching the pulse that throbbed at her pale throat. She felt so small in front of him, her body tiny when placed so close to his.

He took another step closer, foot crossing foot, peering around the small balcony as if scenting his territory, and Brigid found herself backed into her bedroom. The glass-eyed dolls watched her like artifacts from another's life. When the man stepped through the balcony doors and over the threshold Brigid let out the tiniest whimper, suddenly fearful of having this creature here, of what he might do. Yet, she wanted to feel him within her, to feel his body pressed against hers.

"Oh, wicked, wicked heart," her mind cried out, and there was a voice in her head asking to be heard.

She took another step back, passing the mirror with the flowers painted across its surface. Where the moonlight seeped into the room from the open doors of the balcony, Brigid saw her reflection in the mirror's surface, saw her pale lips and long hair, honey-blond curls flowing down her shoulders, her blue eyes catching the light.

The man reached for her, his hand grasping her wrist and—

Brigid threw the book aside, found herself sitting in the lounge of the strange mansion house out in the middle of the Louisiana bayou. She was alone in the room now, candles flickering and the vanilla smell of incense assaulting her nostrils as she looked all around her in confusion.

"What the hell just happened?" Brigid asked, her voice just a whisper.

"Baptiste?" Kane's voice drummed through her skull over the Commtact link. "I repeat, it's Kane. Do you read me?"

"Kane?" Brigid replied, her voice breathy as if she had been running fast. "I'm…"

"We all are," Kane reported. "I'm upstairs. At least, I think I am."

"I'll find you," Brigid told him.

Then Kane cut their link, busy with his own dilemma once more.

Warily, Brigid looked down to the carpet at her feet, saw the leather-bound book lying there, its pages open but pressed facedown into the thick pile of the scarlet weave.

"That book," Brigid affirmed, mouthing the words to reassure herself that she was real. Her voice seemed strained, a sound that she had almost forgotten. She had been inside the book, reading it and yet living it. A girl—Mary—no more than sixteen years old, with blond hair and sapphire eyes, had somehow become her, or perhaps Brigid had become Mary; it was hard to tell, since the whole thing was blurred like a waking dream. She had been romanced—was that the word for it?—by some sort of nether creature, a man who was also a wolf.

Trying to recall it felt strange, like a dream half remembered, piecing together something that had no substance, that had never been real. As she thought of the man-wolf she felt a tremble of desire deep within her, immediately followed by stinging embarrassment flushing at her pallid cheeks.

Fixed by her gaze, the book seemed to loom on the floor, tempting her to pick it up, to reengage with the world within.

Brigid looked away, peering around her, her hand reaching for the hip holster that still held her TP-9 semiautomatic. She had been left alone in this room, held in place somehow by the uncanny book. It was only on seeing her reflection—or, more accurately, seeing the reflection of another woman, of Mary, the book's heroine—that she had realized all was not as it should be. Had Kane's voice been speaking to her inside the book? Perhaps. And so she had broken the spell, the same way that one can flinch oneself awake from a nightmare. But, just like waking from a nightmare, Brigid struggled to suppress the feeling that the horror had not gone away.

Standing, Brigid reached for the metal bar that remained at her side, propped against the couch she had sat upon. Semiautomatic in one hand, metal staff in the other, Brigid warily made her way toward the open doorway and out into the hallway that ran beside the magnificent staircase of the house. She had to find Kane and Grant before they, too, got sucked deeper into some kind of nightmare over which they had no control.

BUSINESS REPLY MAIL
FIRST-CLASS MAIL   PERMIT NO. 717   BUFFALO, NY

POSTAGE WILL BE PAID BY ADDRESSEE

THE READER SERVICE
PO BOX 1867
BUFFALO NY 14240-9952

NO POSTAGE
NECESSARY
IF MAILED
IN THE
UNITED STATES

Send For
2 FREE BOOKS
Today!

I accept your offer!

Please send me two free
novels and a mystery gift (gift
worth about $5). I understand
that these books are completely
free—even the shipping and
handling will be paid—and
I am under no obligation
to purchase anything, ever, as
explained on the back of this card.

366 ADL FDJR   166 ADL FDJR

Please Print

FIRST NAME

LAST NAME

ADDRESS

APT.#   CITY

STATE/PROV.   ZIP/POSTAL CODE

Visit us online at
www.ReaderService.com

© 2010 WORLDWIDE LIBRARY ® and ™ are trademarks owned and used by the trademark owner and/or its licensee. Printed in the U.S.A.

GE-GF-11 ◄ Detach card and mail today. No stamp needed. ▲

Chapter 13

What you see is what you get, or so the saying goes.

Kane had been born a Magistrate and he would die a Magistrate, if not in name then doubtless in nature. He had been born Kane, named after his father, who, had also been a Magistrate, a defender of the laws of Cobaltville.

The Magistrates were not recruited; rather they were born, selected before they had even been conceived, chosen to follow in their father's footsteps for when the old men got too old to pound the streets of Cobaltville or enter the Tartarus Pits where the human detritus lived in squalor. Thus, being a Magistrate was quite literally in Kane's genetic makeup, a part of his DNA. He was not so much born as crafted, bred like livestock to do the job of a Magistrate.

Kane had been trained from birth, schooled in the ways of the Magistrates so that he could defend Cobaltville from the insidious forces that might topple its carefully balanced regime. Where other children had grown up in an environment where they learned through play, Kane had grown up in one of stern discipline, and his mind had been schooled to embrace and employ that discipline.

There had been exercises from the very earliest days of Kane's life, drills to make his body firm and strong. And there had been other exercises, too, mental tools that made his mind strong, that kept him fiercely focused on his goals, whatever they may be. Part of that had been to teach him to accept the word of Baron Cobalt as immutable fact, a teaching he had had to break in later life, but there had been more to it than that—he had been taught to retain facts, to compartmentalize and to apply logic no matter how dangerous or tense the situation.

In time, Kane had broken that indoctrination, and he and his partner Grant had found themselves exiled from Cobaltville, defending freedom once they learned that what they believed in was nothing but a sham, a scheme designed to trick humanity and to make them obey.

Yet still Kane remained a Magistrate, deep down in the core of his being, his mind a disciplined, structured landscape that respected boundaries and could place things in sections and subsections, file experience within boxes.

And so now he found himself lying atop the mattress in one of the beautiful bedrooms of the whorehouse called Lilandera, with two stunning women pleading for him to take them, to satisfy them that he might satisfy himself, and he reluctantly closed his eyes and ignored all extraneous detail, trusting the disciplined aspect of his mind to take control where his surface thoughts had become distracted.

To stop looking was easy; that only required the closing of one's eyes. Kane had done that when Grant had alerted him to something not being right here, had ignited that fear that had preyed at his mind with almost every step he had taken into the House Lilandera. His heart was still racing, adrenaline coursing through his veins with the desire he felt for the two incredibly beautiful women who had thrown themselves at him, who still promised delights beyond imagination. In his mind's eye, Kane clung to that surge of adrenaline, for he knew he would need it before this moment was passed.

He slowed his breathing then, consciously taking deeper breaths, slower and more controlled, enforcing a calmness on his body that it yearned to break from. The smell of the incense was still strong in his nostrils, creating mood, enticing the ex-Magistrate to succumb to the needs of the flesh. Smell is that strangest of senses, capable of affecting one's thoughts, one's appetite, even one's mood. With the application of abrupt logic, Kane switched to breathing through his mouth to tune out the incense smell; doing so didn't matter, he wouldn't be here long.

Eyes still shut, Kane next blocked out the murmurings of desire from his ears, wilfully ignoring the crude whisperings of blue-eyed Kirsten and her friend with the prettiest mouth and the greenest eyes. Instead he tuned in to something deeper within him, the rhythm of his body, the pace of his own breathing, of his beating heart. It was an old Magistrate trick, a way to still one's thoughts as the surrounding world became chaotic; it was the very same trick he used when he went into high alert and employed what he called his point man sense. Thus, the murmurings of desire faded from Kane's ears, and instead he heard the organic music within him, the beating of his heart, the pumping of his blood.

With the blocking of the sounds, Kane forced himself to block out the touch of the women's bodies against his, making them just a minor irritation that he could simply ignore for his resolve was strong. An individual can block out a lot merely by allowing the mind to rest; the way one is not conscious of the feel of a seat once one is comfortable in it. So Kane employed the same sensibilities as the sitter, letting all his concerns float away, and thus stilling his mind.

He was at peace now, the world around him no longer important.

And yes, it's true—what you see is what you get. The thing is, you have to know what it is that you're looking at.

Four seconds later, when Kane opened his eyes, he saw the room for the first time. It wasn't a candlelit bedchamber, with ornate decorations and a window looking out at the reddening ball of the setting sun. No, in fact the description that came to Kane's mind was "a rat hole."

The mattress he lay on was soiled and torn, and it sat low to the floor not through some convention of the bed but because there was no bed. The walls of the room showed expanses of green mould and dark patches of damp assaulted the deteriorated plasterboard across two of them. The polished walnut door was no longer polished nor walnut—Kane saw it now as a broken thing with panels missing, an eczema of peeling paint marring its surface. Additionally, there were black streaks across the door frame where it had been damaged by smoke; presumably the door itself had been replaced after that.

In the corner where the incense sticks had once appeared to be burning, Kane saw now just a hole in the bare floorboards. As he watched, a mouse scurried from the hole, scrambling across the room on its tiny pink feet until it disappeared in a hole in the skirting board, peering back out at him with its twitching nose.

All of this, Kane took in in a matter of just a few seconds, his eyes wandering over the room as he stilled his tremulous heart.

However, the biggest revelation hit Kane like a punch to the gut. The two women, with their radiant skin and long blond hair, had been replaced. They were no longer the divinely beautiful creatures that Kane had been almost unable to keep his eyes—or hands—off. In their place, clambering on the soiled mattress, Kane saw two hairless, emaciated things, their flesh incomplete, their faces malformed. They reminded him of fetuses, with their large eyes in dark pink sockets and the whole thing not fully formed, as if they had somehow grown to adulthood without altering from their early fetal state. The darkness around their eyes, the way their skin seemed tight in places yet sagged in others, reminded Kane of newborn birds, just waking in the nest for the first time.

With a kick of his feet, Kane shoved himself back on the bed, pulling away from the fetuslike women as they watched him, smiling with their lipless mouths. The one to the left had blue eyes the color of cornflowers while the one on the right had eyes as green as the ocean. Stripped naked, sharing a bed with these things, Kane felt sick.

As his stomach turned, Kane felt his self-control slip, and for just a single flashbulb instant he saw the women as beautiful once more, the cozy warmth of the red room vying for attention in his muddled senses. He took another breath through clenched teeth, tried to stay in the moment, to see things as they truly were. A man with less discipline would find such a thing impossible, the illusion was so pervasive, but Kane knew it was an illusion now, and so he knew he must hang on to whatever tentative grip he had on the reality or he would lose himself to this perverse dream that sucked at him like quicksand.

The unformed things that had once seemed beautiful made their way toward Kane, the one with blue eyes reaching for him with a fleshy hand of pink so dark it looked as if the skin had been scalded. She reached for Kane, walking her short pudgy fingers up his leg toward his groin, a coquettish twinkle in her eye. Kane batted her hand away, rolling himself from the bed and out of the creature's reach.

"Keep away from me," he warned, backing to the mould-dappled wall.

"Come back to bed," the one with green eyes pleaded. Her voice was soft, husky, laced with desire. If Kane didn't look at her, hadn't seen her for what she really was, he could still believe she was that beautiful woman who had enticed him here. Instead he had no idea what she—what either of them—were. They weren't human, not really. They were more like something that had been aborted before it could achieve true life. Succubi perhaps, those mythological prostitutes who drained the life from their lovers, left them as nothing but empty shells. Even as the thought occurred to him, Kane was struck by the similarity of the classical succubus to Lilitu, the Annunaki goddess who had been reborn as Ezili Coeur Noir. Were these things somehow a part of her, related to her in some way? It was like seeing pieces of a puzzle with only the scantest idea of what they formed.

Swiftly, Kane moved across the room, reaching for the pile of his clothing. Curiously, he still wore his Sin Eater in its wrist holster—all thoughts of it had evaporated while he had been under the spell of the house and these malformed creatures had obviously considered it no threat to them while he was under the spell. The things that had once appeared as women watched him, cooing to him and pleading he stay in bed with them, satisfy them, abuse them. For a lightning-flash moment he saw them again as he had seen them before, beautiful and alluring, and the room was painted red and lined with candles once more.

Kane screwed up his eyes, forcing the illusion out of his head as he concentrated on pulling on his pants. The women continued to taunt him, asking him to return to the bed, to come, to be with them.

"Keep away from me," Kane told them again, opening his gray-blue eyes to slits so as to watch them. "I can see you now."

The emaciated, sticklike things writhed on the bed, pressing their mouths to one another as if kissing, the noises they made as they touched no longer alluring, sounding now like grinding bones to Kane's ears. He could see them if he looked hard enough, if he kept his mind disciplined and held the illusory power of the house at bay.

"Baptiste?" Kane called, engaging the Commtact as he pulled the sleeves of the shadow suit over his arms. "How are things with you? Still on top of it?"

DOWNSTAIRS, Brigid was just making her way to the foot of the staircase beneath the orange glow of the chandelier.

"I'm right here, Kane," she responded automatically over the Commtact. "Be with you in a minute."

"Any sign of Grant?" Kane asked, his voice piping straight into her ear as if he stood right next to her.

"Nothing yet," Brigid replied as she took the first stair. As she did so, she heard a noise coming from the corridor and she halted, the metal pole in her hand resting against the next riser like a walking cane. She dipped her head, peering back down the corridor that led into the depths of the house. It was hard to see, the corridor was lost to shadow after just a dozen paces. But as she looked, she heard the noise again, a thumping as if of a heavy tread.

"Wait, I'm going to check something out," Brigid whispered into the hidden Commtact pickup.

"Negative, Baptiste." Kane's voice rasped over the Commtact. "We need to stick together."

Brigid took a step back, peeking over her shoulder to make sure no one was sneaking up on her. "Pipe down, Kane," she instructed in a harsh whisper. "I'll be one minute and I'll be sure to take care, I promise."

Kane grunted an acknowledgment but Brigid chose to ignore it, tuning out the Commtact receiver.

Cautiously, the titian-haired warrior made her way into the corridor that ran along the staircase. Pictures lined the walls here, and Brigid's eyes flicked to them for just a moment. She was wary now, conscious that this house had many subtle traps that could snag the mind with the most casual of efforts. The pictures, she saw, were masked by velvet curtains, like tiny theatrical stages, as if each one contained a whole story just waiting to spring to life.

Brigid heard the noise again, more clearly this time—footsteps coming from the shadowy end of the corridor. She waited in place against the side of the stairs beside a door handle, silently peering into the darkness as the footsteps became slowly louder. Then she spied the figure in the shadows, recognized it as the wide form of housemistress Ellie.

"That you, brave soldier?" Ellie called as she strode toward Brigid.

Brigid saw that the woman was squinting, and she recalled how she had struggled to make out the moving figures beyond the house when her team had arrived. She was short-sighted, and that might just be the only thing that Brigid had on her side at that moment. It seemed that this woman could somehow hypnotize with a look. It wouldn't do to be caught by her, not without some kind of plan in place. Brigid was armed, but that was no use—for one thing, she did not have a blood-thirsty temperament, and killing this woman in cold blood did not appeal to her, despite the mind-trickery on display in this house.

For another, Brigid realized that killing someone with the power to instantly make one see whatever they wanted would be about as easy as catching dreams in a paper cup. Even Perseus had needed a trick to kill the gorgon, Brigid reminded herself.

With a swift decision, the beautiful Cerberus warrior reached for the door at her back and pulled it open. The door opened outward, and in a moment she had ducked her svelte form inside, pulling the door quietly shut behind her.

With the door closed, Brigid found herself in darkness. She stilled her breathing, listening to the heavy footsteps as Ellie's shadow flickered past the edges of the door where the light seeped in, and then moved along the corridor, muttering to herself about imagining things and about handsome gentleman callers.

Brigid turned then, trusting her eyes to adjust to the darkness. What she had at first taken to be a cupboard was actually a small, boxlike landing that opened out into a staircase leading into the basement of the old house. Balancing her metal pole against her side, Brigid ran a hand along the wall until she located the light switch and flicked it on. Nothing happened—either the bulb was dead or there was no power coming into the house. However, as her eyes continued to adjust to the darkness, Brigid realized she wasn't absolutely blind in this environment. There seemed to be something glowing at the foot of the stairs, glowing with a slow pulse, first soft, then bright, then soft once more.

Cautiously, Brigid took a single step down the wooden staircase, ducking her head at the low ceiling, hearing the stair creak as she applied her weight. The glow below her was faint, but it was surely there.

"Kane," Brigid whispered over the Commtact, "I've

found something. Down in the basement. Something glowing like it's—I'm not sure—alive, maybe. I'm checking it out."

"Baptiste…" Kane began, a note of irritation in his tone.

"You haven't cornered the market on impetuous decisions just yet, Kane," Brigid reminded him in a brisk whisper. "I think this may be important."

With that, Brigid stole her way down the stairs, taking care to keep her movements light and still wincing every time the old wooden boards creaked. As she watched, the glowing continued to throb, like some slow pulse, dull then bright, dull then bright, making the dark basement pop into brightness and long black shadows every ten seconds or so. As she reached the foot of the stairs, Brigid saw the glowing more clearly, and she began to define the shapes as they became brighter before fading away. It was not just one item that glowed, but over a dozen, all pulsing in unison as if they were somehow linked despite being strewed across the copious area of the basement.

The glowing pieces were arranged in a roughly semicircular, radial pattern with a large glowing hunk dominating its center, so that when they glowed it seemed reminiscent of a sunburst. Close up, Brigid saw that the small pieces were jagged, and it seemed as though they had been broken off from the main body of the item that rested in the center of the otherwise ordinary basement room.

That central item was familiar to Brigid Baptiste, and she had to stifle a gasp of surprise as she recognized it. It was a chair, its back to her. But not just any chair. This was the so-called voodoo chair that she had seen and become ensnared by when she and Kane had met with Papa Hurbon, local practitioner of the dark voodoo arts.

In actuality, it was an astronavigator's chair from the starship *Tiamat,* a part of the literal mothership of the Annunaki, and it possessed the ability to project images of star maps into a user's mind.

When Brigid had last seen the chair, it had been missing its lower section and had been propped up on bricks. The lower section was still missing, but now panels from the side and back had gone missing, also, and there was just a strut where the headrest should be. Peering around the room, Brigid saw the missing parts all around her, they were the other items that seemed to pulse in time with the chair's glowing palpitations. It had been taken apart with some degree of finesse she saw, despite the rough edges of the breaks, and its parts arranged in a manner that seemed almost as if they had been planted, sown into the floor of the grand old house's basement, like the points and convergences of a pentagram. With its known ability to project images into a sitter's brain, Brigid realized that the scope of the chair's abilities may very well include overlaying illusions into a person's mind, making them see whatever it was programmed to make them see.

Suddenly the nature of the book she had been reading and, presumably, whatever weird experiences Kane and Grant had been through in the House Lilandera, began to make a strange, alarming kind of sense. The book she had held had been a prop—all the things in the house were props—and the chair projected its illusions into the minds of anyone who interacted with those props.

"I think I've found the source of our trouble," Brigid whispered, trusting the Commtact to enhance her voice for Kane's ears wherever he now was in the house.

After a moment Kane's voice came to Brigid. "Care to elaborate, Baptiste?"

"It's that chair," she subvocalized. "Papa Hurbon's chair. It's here."

Brigid took another pace forward, aware of the creeping tension in her muscles. The chair may be casting the illusion but there was one part of the puzzle that remained unanswered—when Brigid had encountered the chair before, it had needed to physically bond with her before it began to project its information for her brain to interpret. Like much Annunaki machinery, it was organic technology, and it required a person's touch to make it operate.

Cautiously, Brigid paced around the edge of the chair, the TP-9 semiautomatic held out steadily in front of her in a one-handed grip, the metal pole she had snagged from the artillery truck prepped in the other.

Just as Brigid had guessed, there was a figure sitting in the chair. It was an elderly woman, with white hair and skin so pale that, in the glowing pulsation of the chair and its parts, it looked as if it may never have been touched by the sun's rays. As far as Brigid could tell, the woman was sleeping.

Chapter 14

No matter the size of a prisoner's cell, the prisoner will eventually examine every inch of it. And so it was with Grant. At first, he had dismissed the place he found himself in, aware that it was a painting somehow brought to life through means he could not begin to comprehend. But, having alerted Kane to his predicament via their linked Commtacts, he decided to search the place, to find out a little more about this odd trap he had been placed within.

The first thing that struck Grant was how real it all felt. Yes, there was a sense of unreality about it, the way the people had appeared to be loosely of the same appearance, the way that the Shizuka analog had broken down when he had shot her. But on a surface level it seemed to be real. Grant could feel the wind on his face, and he watched as it rustled the leaves in the trees and the branches above him swayed with the breeze. The place smelled like a forest, too, a cold, damp smell as if there was moisture in the air. Yet when he examined the trees up close, he saw the brush marks there, like a backdrop from a stage play.

Grant walked deeper into the forest, leaving the fumbling couples behind him, dismissing their pleas and groans of ecstasy. Behind him, the city continued to burn, lightening the sky. The flames acted as a fixed point, like north on the compass, and Grant kept them at his back at all times to ensure he walked in the same direction. In theory, he was walking toward the external frame of the painting and hence an exit, since the burning city had formed the distant background of the picture as he looked at it on the wall of the House Lilandera. As theories went, it was the best he could come up with given the unreality of his situation.

The forest was like a dark streak, only defining itself into individual trees when he got close to them, as if the details didn't really exist until they were within arm's reach.

On the ground, twigs and a few fallen leaves lay on the loam. Grant halted, crouching to examine one of the fallen leaves. It was as big as his spread hand and a yellowish green in color. He picked up the leaf, its three prongs stretched out like the fingers of a cartoon character's hand. Close up, the leaf didn't have veins as leaves should; instead, it seemed untextured, like a flat sheet of colored paper in the shape of a leaf. The green of its surface was not complete, and Grant saw now that white peeked through where the paint had not been applied evenly. It was curious—in his mind, he comprehended this as a leaf from a tree, but his eyes could see the defects, the limitations in the artist's work.

Grant cast aside the leaf, pushing himself up from the ground on powerful legs. The sounds of coupling had become distant now, and the forest was instead a place of forest sounds, owls hooting, foxes barking and other nocturnal things prowling for food and shelter. Grant walked on, striding through a copse of trees and onward, in the opposite direction to the burning pyre of the city.

IN THE CONFINES of the House Lilandera, Kane was concentrating on keeping a level head as the only way that he could think of to hold the house's strange illusions at bay. He shrugged into his jacket, sighing and shaking his head when he saw the frayed rip across the front where the undead thing with the eye patch had torn it during their earlier scuffle. That seemed like days past, and yet it had been perhaps ninety minutes. Which reminded Kane—the Red Weed was even now being mixed in the laboratory of Redoubt Mike, the glowing clock counting down atop the centrifuge spinner in the glass-walled room. Kane and his companions had less than eight hours to halt it.

From the well-worn mattress, the two fetuslike figures reached for Kane, a haunting sense of desperation in their childlike expressions.

"Don't leave us," said Kirsten, still recognizable because of her vibrant blue eyes.

"We would love you here forever," the one with green eyes added.

"Yeah," Kane grumbled, "that's what I'm afraid of."

The woman creatures, unable to comprehend that Kane had truly broken their illusion, cooed to him once more, making a performance of touching each other's naked bodies, pudgy fingers playing through dark flesh with the texture of dough. Repulsed, Kane turned away and made his way to the door.

"I'd like to say it's been nice knowing you, ladies," Kane said without turning back, "but let's just say it's been an experience."

With that, he pulled open the remnants of the rotten door and stepped out into the corridor. Like the bedroom, this previously impressive hallway now looked like hell, the last proud hurrah of a struggling dumpsite.

The window at the end of the corridor was missing, shards of glass clinging to the wooden frame like spiders hanging to the remains of a broken web. The walls were speckled with mold, and here and there toadstools were growing in pools of moisture, the floor and walls beside them sprayed with their black spores. The floorboards were bare, with wide streaks of dirt worn into them.

Kane made his way toward the staircase, passing the doorways that led to the other bedrooms of the bordello. Several featured doors, though two of them were half rotted away, while the third had paint scarred across its surface and a small hole in its lower panel where someone—or something—had put a foot through it. Peering into one of the rooms, Kane saw a man lying on the bed with another of the dark-skinned fetuslike things riding astride him, teasing his body as wind blew through the shattered remains of the window. The man was naked and delirious, wailing in either pleasure or abject horror, Kane didn't care to think about which.

For a moment Kane's concentration slipped, and he saw the bedroom as he was supposed to, in the vivid colors of the shared illusion. The man seemed to lie amid a circle of flickering candles as moonlight spilled through the window, a gorgeous woman with dark hair and dark looks teasing his body to extremes of pleasure. It was easy to get sucked into the illusion.

Kane halted, closing his eyes and recentering himself. Without consciously thinking it, his wrist muscles flinched and he called the Sin Eater back to his hand. He opened his eyes then, and the illusion of the beautiful room had evaporated like steam. Without hesitating, Kane drilled a single shot through the back of the head of the woman-thing, and she toppled from the man's body, a bloody circle appearing on her forehead. What the man on the bed saw, Kane couldn't imagine.

"Get up, get dressed and get out," Kane instructed. "This place isn't safe."

The man looked startled. "What are you? Some kind of magistrate?"

"Yeah." Kane nodded. "Now get your stuff and get out. I'm closing this rat hole down."

Perhaps the man recognized the Magistrate tone in Kane's order. Perhaps he just saw something that wasn't really there. Whatever it was, he pushed himself from the bed and started gathering his clothes, looking timidly at the slumped body of the woman who had been bringing him pleasure just a moment before.

Kane moved on, ignoring the fact that the half-formed woman was twitching. Hard to kill, maybe? Didn't matter now, he had bigger fish to fry.

Then he saw a woman standing at the top of the staircase, blocking his exit as she glared at him, her skirts still glamorous despite the squalor of her true surroundings. It was Ellie.

"And just what do you think you're doing?" she asked, her voice still rich.

"Getting out of here," Kane told her.

Ellie shook her head indulgently. "Oh, no, that ain't how things happen 'round here, sugar," she said. "This here is a celebration of life. You don't want to be leaving that, now, do you?"

Kane raised his right hand, showing Ellie the Sin Eater blaster he held. "I broke your spell," he explained. "Without that, this joint looks a little too members-only for my liking. So me and my friends are going to have to be on our way, I'm afraid."

Ellie tsked, shaking her head heavily. "No one ever gets out alive," she told Kane. "That's the charm."

Before the ex-Mag could respond, Ellie became a blur

of motion, rushing forward the four steps between her and the muzzle of his blaster. She yanked it to one side as Kane clung on to its grip. Kane's finger squeezed at the trigger, and a 9 mm burst whizzed past Ellie's head and drilled into the wall, kicking up dried-out plaster where they struck.

"No one ever gets out alive," Ellie repeated, pulling Kane close to her by the end of his own pistol. Her other pudgy fist struck out, ramming into Kane's gut with such force that he felt the breath burst from his lips.

If he had had any lingering doubts, it was at that moment that Kane felt sure that there was a little more to the motherly Ellie than he had initially presumed.

Something of the old magistrate code came back to Kane as Ellie drove her pudgy fist into his gut for a second vicious punch. Never forget—everyone's a suspect.

GRANT WALKED FOR A WHILE, passing more and more of the painted trees, his soles sinking into the moist earth with each step. But finally he came to a little wooden shack in the woods, beside which waited a cart on a simple dirt track. Lights burned in the windows of the shack, and Grant could hear faint noises coming from within. Although he didn't recall seeing it in the painting, the shack seemed as if it had been in the forest forever, not incongruous with what else he had seen around him. As he neared, Grant became conscious of cheering and laughter coupled with strains of up-tempo music. It sounded like a party.

Grant pushed aside a low-hanging branch that barred his way, and he walked up the dirt track to the shack itself. It was a single-story building, and he estimated that the interior would be no bigger than two family-size rooms, a modest accommodation for a woodsman and his wife.

Grant peered through the nearest window, from which bright light glowed and dimmed as if with the flickering flames of candlelight. Through the window, much to Grant's surprise, he saw nothing other than the changing hues creating the illusion of the flickering of candle flame.

Like strokes of paint on a canvas, Grant realized, the illusion of something not really there.

On a whim, Grant tried the door. Finding it unlocked, he pushed it open and, without a moment's hesitation, walked into the shack.

Inside it wasn't a shack at all. As the door swung closed behind him, Grant found himself standing in what appeared to be an ancient Greek temple, with a troupe of dancers taking center stage as its lone patron reclined in a cushioned seat, nude serving girls tending to his every need. The patron had the dark skin of an octoroon, and a frame so corpulent that it made him look like one of the cushions he reclined upon. Most notably, however, he had no legs, both limbs finishing at stumps above the knee. Grant knew who the man was, for they had met just two months ago.

Glancing behind him, Grant saw that the exterior door of the shack had disappeared. Instead there seemed to be a beautiful wood door, lacquered and decorated with a painting of swirling flames bursting from an idealized sun. Flaming sconces lit each corner of the room, casting their light and heat through the stone-walled building.

Warily, Grant stepped away from the door and walked through the main hall of the temple, through the cavorting dancers as their lithe bodies swayed and dipped to the strains of the simple music that a quintet played in one corner of the temple's open hall.

The man at the seat clapped his hands together, delighted

to see a newcomer in their midst. "Fresh entertainment," he bellowed. "And what do you do?"

The man stopped as he saw Grant's face for the first time, and his broad, gap-toothed grin turned to a look of fear as he saw the scowl on the ex-Magistrate's face.

"Papa Hurbon," Grant said to the man reclining on the couch. "You remember me?"

The dark-skinned man with no legs swayed a little in place as if drunk, and his mouth dropped open as he tried to form a coherent sentence. "Yuh…?" he began.

Impatiently, Grant waited.

"You can't be here," Hurbon finally managed to say, his hand sweeping through the air as if to brush Grant from his sight. "How can you be here? This is mine."

Grant grunted. "Perhaps it's time you learned to share, huh?"

But Hurbon had turned his attention away, clapping his hands to get attention as he called over his shoulder. "He shouldn't be here," he shouted. "Kill him!"

Automatically, Grant took a step back, planting his feet in preparation for battle as six guards, tall men whose skin was so dark it seemed almost to absorb all light, stepped from the shadows and pulled short swords from the leather scabbards they wore at their belts. Off to the side of the room, the quintet continued to play their music, but the dance troupe stepped back, sheltering close to the walls.

"Whoa, let's not be hasty," Grant began. "See, I want to help you get out of this place."

Papa Hurbon laughed, a deep sound like distant thunder. "And why would I ever want to leave?" he challenged.

Before Grant could respond, the six muscular guards began to close in on him, their short swords glinting in the flickering firelight of the room.

As THE LIGHT CAST by the astronavigator's chair grew brighter in the basement of the House Lilandera, Brigid Baptiste stared at the sleeping woman resting within its embrace. The woman was locked in the chair by tendrils that had spread across her body like a creeping vine. The woman was definitely still breathing, and she was old, Brigid realized, really old. Blue veins showed in the pale skin of her face and hands, and her clothing looked like something from another era, layers of taffeta and lace finished in creamy whites like something a bride might have worn two hundred years ago.

The woman's face was drawn with age, but she still retained a certain aristocratic air in her aquiline nose and the sharp angles of her cheekbones. Up close, Brigid saw that she wore a little blush on her cheeks, a whisper of silver eye shadow. At a guess, Brigid estimated that she was at least eighty years old.

Another pulse went through the chair and its disconnected parts strewed across the room, and with it the basement lit up once again. Its mildewed walls and the dust bunnies that scarred the concrete floor of the basement became visible in the pulsing light. Feeling paranoia creeping into her thoughts in that eerie, ever-changing light, Brigid peered around the room, confirming that just the two of them were there.

The chair's parts had been placed at deliberate intervals around the room, the headrest here, the side panel there, each one forming a part of the clear pattern that was impossible to ignore once it had been seen. The pattern was a pentagram, a five-pointed star made up of lines so as to form a pentagon in its center. It was a potent symbol in both magic and the subset of magic known as voodoo. The chair with its dozing occupant had been placed in the center of the pentagon.

Brigid eyed the staircase before she put down the bar in her hand, making sure that the door remained closed. Then, with the TP-9 semiautomatic still held loosely in her other hand, she approached the dozing woman as the lights pulsed bright once more.

"Wake up," Brigid said, keeping her voice low and reassuring. "Wake up now. I believe you're in danger here and I want to help."

The elderly woman did not wake up. Indeed, she showed no signs of reacting at all to Brigid's whispered plea.

The lights in the cellar dimmed again, and Brigid took another step closer in the darkness, until she was standing right next to the chair. Then she placed her left hand gently upon the woman's shoulder, shook her ever so slightly.

"Wake up," Brigid whispered, her voice a little louder this time. "Please wake up."

The woman didn't even flinch; she seemed dead to the world. It was almost as if she was in a coma.

Though she was no expert, Brigid knew a little about magic, enough at least to know that the pentagram symbol being created by the placement of the chair's parts held significance. She stared at the pattern as the lights flickered on and off, wondering if their very specific placement was casting the illusory spell that operated within the house.

As THE SWORD-WIELDING guards stalked toward him, Grant noticed something peculiar about them. Their clothes seemed to be made of curling material, and their hair was the same, tight curls like cresting waves. As Grant noticed this, he saw, too, that their graceful movements seemed to follow those curving lines and he realized at last what it was—he was still in a painting, albeit a new one from where he had begun, and the curls were an affectation of the artist who had drawn it.

"Kill him!" Papa Hurbon repeated as he snatched a mouthful of black grapes from one of his serving wenches.

The first two guards leaped at Grant then, swinging their swords at him, the twelve-inch blades slashing the air. Grant stepped hastily back, and the swords cut the empty air where he had stood a fraction of a second earlier. Then he was leaping forward again, driving his right fist into the jaw of the first guardsman with the force of a pounding jackhammer. The guard went down at the blow, toppling backward to strike the marble floor. Grant ducked his partner's sword as it rushed for his face. Then Grant moved in a short, three-step run, ramming his shoulder hard into the gut of his would-be executioner, knocking the sentry off his feet.

As the sentry landed against a white marble column, the next two guardsmen had moved to take his place, jabbing with their own short swords as Grant weaved agilely between them. The swords flashed in the air, cutting through the same curling arcs as the hair on the guardsmen's heads. Grant dropped, slapping his left palm on the floor and using it as a pivot to swing his legs around and knock both of his new attackers off their feet. The pair of them tripped and slammed against the floor like skittles, but there was no time to finish them. Already the final two guards were bearing down on Grant as he leaped back to his feet.

Grant was a big man, but still tremendously agile. He kept himself in the peak of physical fitness, and his strength was formidable. Being struck full force by Grant was little different from being swatted by a hurtling locomotive.

With grim determination, Grant slapped the next guardsman's sword out of his way, knocking the blade from the man's hand with a savage back-handed blow. Before the astonished guard could react, Grant drove a ram's-head punch into his nose, driving the hard cartilage there into the man's brain with such force that his eyes went bloodred as he collapsed to the floor.

Grant turned, dropping low as the sixth guardsman jabbed his sword at him. Behind the guardsman, three of the fallen guards were recovering, picking themselves up and readying to join the battle once more.

"This is crazy, Hurbon," Grant shouted as the sentry in front of him swung his sword again. "I just came here to talk."

Lounging back on his cushioned seat, Hurbon barked a laugh, reaching out for another grape from the serving girl who knelt by him. "Oh, but this is so much fun," Hurbon insisted, "don't you find, *mon ami?*"

Hurbon grabbed the wrist of his serving wench and pulled her onto the cushion beside him. Grant cursed, turning his full attention back to the scuffle as a flashing blade cleaved the air just by his ear. He could see how the voodoo priest might think this was all just fun and games, but Grant himself was not comfortable with the sinister implications of the scenario they both found themselves in. In Grant's experience, it was rare that illusions were ever used for genuinely positive means.

The nearest guard lunged again with his sword and Grant felt the blow graze the armor plate of his heavy coat. As the guardsman pulled back the sword, Grant ducked down and powered a shoulder into him, knocking him with such an almighty blow that there came the loud sound of ribs cracking. The guard scooted backward as Grant drove on, his own feet slamming against the floor as he charged at his foe. The guard struggled to take a breath as Grant shoved him into the nearest wall with a crash. The wall was decorated with a mosaic that showed the curling, stylized waves of the ocean, and a dozen tiny fleck tiles fell from the picture as Grant smashed his foe against it with bone-jarring force. The guard tried to recover, pulling his sword up to defend himself, but Grant's hand grabbed his wrist, breaking it in a second and turning the sword away. Then Grant drove his knee into the sentry's solar plexus, and the guard doubled over as if wrapped around an iron bar. Pulling the short sword out of the sentry's grip, Grant stepped away and, no longer able to stand, his foe sagged to the floor, drool oozing from his open mouth in an all-too-familiar curling line.

Grant turned, judging the weight of the sword in his hand. Though short, it was a heavy blade, ideal for what he had in mind. Swiftly, Grant switched the short sword so that he held it in a reverse grip, the blade pointing downward.

Then the three remaining guards were upon him, thrusting their own blades toward him as he darted and dodged their three-sided attack.

As he spun out of the way of the nearest attacker, Grant drove his elbow back, slamming it into the gut of the guardsman who stood behind him. The man let out a blurt of expelled breath, and Grant stabbed behind him with the reversed sword, plunging it between the man's ribs. Grant turned, pulling the blade free, and saw he had been just an inch too high to hit his opponent's heart. Still, the guardsman struggled woozily on his feet as blood oozed over his bare chest.

Then Grant heard a swish through the air as another of the guards swung his blade at the ex-Mag's face. Grant met the blade with his own, pushing it aside with a clang of sparking metal. His opponent stepped back, swishing the blade through the air left and right in a showy but useless display.

Grant went to meet with the attacker again only to find his progress blocked by the remaining swordsman, striking his blade across Grant's flank. The thick material of his coat and his shadow suit took the impact, and Grant just grunted in irritation as he continued on to meet with the other man, driving the point of his sword upward to penetrate between the man's ribs.

The sentry hollered in agony as the sword cut through his stomach, nicked the spongy tissue of his right lung. Grant reached for the crown of the man's head with his free hand, his fingers entangling in the man's thick hair. Then, with a brutal yank, Grant pulled the man's head forward and down in the direction of the floor, forcing his blade deeper into the man's torso in a gushing geyser of spilling blood.

To Grant's side, the remaining swordsman gasped as his friend was torn apart, and in the distance Grant heard Papa Hurbon's rolling laughter come to an abrupt halt. Grant turned his attention to the remaining guard, fixing him with a no-nonsense stare as he pulled the blood-smeared sword free from his colleague.

"You don't really want any of this, do you, son?" Grant challenged, blood dripping from the sharp edge of his blade.

The guardsman looked at Grant, then at the sword in his hand, then back at Grant. To Grant's surprise, the swordsman ran at him then with a defiant cry, looking more determined—and more fearful—than ever.

As the swordsman reached him, Grant dropped and, timing his blow with precision, drove a punch into the man's hip. Grant's blow hit with such power that the guardsman flipped over himself before hurtling four feet through the air and slamming down jaw-first against the hard floor.

Ignoring the man's cries of pain that came from behind him, Grant stood, flipping the short sword over in his grip once more so that he held it upright again. Across the room, Papa Hurbon's eyes had gone wide, and he had ceased pawing at the naked slave girl with his pudgy hands. Grant pulled back his arm and threw the sword he had been holding. It flew across the room, end over end, until it embedded itself point first in the cushioned seat between Hurbon's abbreviated legs. The serving girl who had been sitting with Hurbon leaped up and burst into tears, running for the nearest pillar, where she cowered, sobbing loudly. Hurbon visibly gulped as he eyed the sharp blade that had missed him by less than an inch.

"I'm guessing you're about ready to talk now," Grant stated as he strode across the room toward where Hurbon sat.

Slowly, Hurbon nodded. "Don't think I ever did catch your name, son…" he began.

AT THE TOP of the staircase, Kane struggled in the grip of Ellie as she used her hold on his Sin Eater to thrash him against the wall. The plasterboard wall disintegrated as Kane hit it, and he let go of his pistol as he rolled through the weakened wall and into the disheveled room beyond.

Two of the fetus-faced women creatures stood in the room, using whips against two men who had been chained to the wall. For a second, Kane lost concentration, and he saw the room as the men saw it, a stylized dungeon draped with rich velvet curtains, in which two women dressed in leathers teased and tortured them.

Kane brushed his finger to his nose as he looked at the bemused clients. "Pay no attention to the man behind the curtain," he said before turning back to the gap in the wall, focusing his attention on seeing the real once more.

Ellie came bustling into the room, using the door that stood to the left of the newly created hole in the rotten wall. She was caked in the white dust from the wall plaster, her hair streaked with ghostly white. Kane watched as she brushed the dust from her face and ran her hand through her clumpy hair. Then he saw the final piece of the puzzle, even as the broad woman brushed the dust away. There, along the center line of her crown, a ridge of sharp spines ran through her hair in line with her nose. She wasn't a woman at all—she was one of the Annunaki. And what's more, Kane thought he knew which one:

Lilitu.

Except, of course, that meant that there were two of them.

Chapter 15

Two Lilitus. It almost didn't bear thinking about.

Kane girded himself as the broad woman who had called herself Ellie came rushing toward him, one of her meaty fists swinging at his head like a construction ball. Kane had never defeated Lilitu in combat. The last time they had met it had required the intervention of a third party to finish this monstrous foe.

He sidestepped, managing to just barely avoid the woman's incredible blow. Ellie's fist smashed against the wall, loosening a cloud of plaster and splintered wood in its passage.

Well, Kane thought as if in consolation, she sure has the strength of an Annunaki goddess.

Somehow that didn't make him feel better.

From somewhere behind him, Kane heard the cries of the other people in the room, shocked at this intrusion into their depredations.

With exceptional speed that defied the bulk of her frame, the woman grabbed Kane by his left bicep and yanked him close to her. Kane kicked out as he slid across the floor, and the heel of his boot connected with Ellie's lower leg, forcing her to pivot away from him, releasing her grip on his arm.

Kane lurched back in an unbalanced jig, but the fast-moving woman was already charging at him, her head down. Kane felt the sudden fiery pain in his chest as the woman butted him with the spines atop her head, and he fell backward, crashing into one of the lash mistresses who had been teasing her client to a zenith of sexual frenzy.

Kane's hand snapped out and he grasped the fetuslike creature's whip, shoving her to one side.

As the broad figure of Ellie hurtled toward him once again, Kane snapped the whip, using it to cut across her face with the force of a blade. Ellie cried out something unintelligible as the whip struck her, staggering backward and pawing at her face with her little, pudgy hands.

Kane looked at the half-formed thing from whom he had grabbed the whip, her childlike eyes open in dismay. "Much obliged, ma'am," he said, tossing the whip back to her. She stood stunned as the whip landed at her feet and skittered across the bare board floor.

Kane was already moving again, running for the gap in the wall that led out onto the staircase balcony. In the false dungeon, Ellie was recovering, a dark stripe across her face bearing mute witness to Kane's attack.

The Cerberus warrior ducked as the woman launched another powerhouse blow at his head, striking with such force that, if it connected, Kane felt sure he'd be nursing a broken neck. He rolled aside as the woman came rushing at him, ducking past her and out through the ragged hole in the wall.

Outside, the corridor seemed to be richly appointed once more, and Kane realized that the struggle with the crazed housemistress was affecting his concentration. If he didn't end this fast, he'd be sucked back into the illusion of the House Lilandera and he may just never escape it again.

GRANT WAITED as Papa Hurbon sent his people out of the temple.

"Normally I'd suggest we take a walk," Hurbon explained, "but given the circumstances…"

Grant shrugged. He had met Hurbon just once before, out in the Louisiana bayou where the man presided over the congregation of his voodoo cult. Hurbon had suffered terribly at the hands of his idol, Ezili Coeur Noir, whose demands had peaked with a sickening display of bloodletting in the form of both of her patron's legs. Grant was unsure whether Hurbon had given his limbs willingly or not, but he had met the man shortly after the second savage amputation and he had not been happy, feeling abandoned and betrayed by his dark goddess.

"What are you doing here?" Grant asked once the dancers, the musicians, the slave girls and those guards that could still walk had left.

"Making the best of a bad situation," Hurbon said bitterly.

"Is there a way out?" Grant asked.

"What? From this?" Hurbon looked affronted. "Now, why would anyone want to get away from this?"

"You know what this is, right?" Grant said. "It's some kind of weird painting brought to life. That doesn't bother you at all?"

Hurbon's face scrunched up in bitterness as he considered Grant's point. "When Ezili Coeur Noir came back she took my other leg and she left me for dead," he explained. "She was a sadistic bitch at the best of times, but I loved her. You understand?"

"I'm trying to," Grant admitted.

"But after that, your woman came—what was her name?"

"Ohio Blue," Grant said, naming the local trader with whom Cerberus had worked a few times over recent months.

"Yeah, Blue," Hurbon said. "Pretty blonde thing, seemed a bit soft and fluffy to me, like she thinks she's some kind of princess, but I'd do her anyway."

"You're a good man," Grant muttered sarcastically.

"Her people patched me together, but what was I left with? This!" Hurbon gestured to his missing legs. "So when she came back again," Hurbon continued, his voice calm once more, "how could I resist her call?"

"Who came back?" Grant asked, confused. "Ezili Coeur Noir?"

"Ezili, yes," Hurbon said. "But it was Maitresse Ezili." Hurbon watched as Grant scowled in confusion, and realized that the powerfully built ex-Mag was having trouble comprehending. "You never followed the path, did you?"

"You mean, voodoo?" Grant asked. "No, that's admittedly a gap in my education."

"The spirits take many forms," Hurbon told him, "different aspects responding to the different needs of their devotees."

Grant nodded, beginning to see how this might function. Over the past few years he had been forced to build up a working knowledge of the false gods called the Annunaki, and so he was aware of how so-called gods and goddesses took different guises depending on time and place and on which facade they wished to present to their worshippers.

"There is more than one aspect to Ezili," Hurbon said, "and each has her own field of expertise. Ezili Coeur Noir is her dark and vengeful side, the part of the *loa* that demands revenge on one's enemies, that calls out for blood. That's the crazy bitch who took my legs."

"But she didn't put you here," Grant concluded.

"That mad whirlwind of hate? Hell, no! This whole place would be verr-rry different if she had had a hand in it," Hurbon continued, gesturing around the temple. "You wouldn't want to be here if she'd been a part of that."

"I don't want to be here anyway," Grant pointed out miserably.

"My point being," Papa Hurbon continued, "Maitresse Ezili, she knows only love. She cares for her children, worships life and its continuance."

As Hurbon twittered on about his idols, Grant recalled something that housemistress Ellie had said when the Cerberus field team had entered the House Lilandera.

"What kind of house is this?" Kane had asked, his voice low and wary.

"A celebration of life," the dark-skinned woman had replied, smiling her broad smile as she intertwined her fat fingers, their rings glittering in the light cast by the chandelier. "A place where everyone can find a friend, my darling. Just you see."

"Shit!" Grant spit.

"What is it?" Hurbon asked, astounded at Grant's outburst.

"I think we've been hoodwinked by your goddess," Grant stated. Ellie, he realized now, was Maitresse Ezili who, in turn, was another face of Lilitu, dark goddess of the Annunaki. "What would happen if someone doesn't want to worship life in the way this Maitresse Ezili prescribed?"

Hurbon shrugged. "That would never happen. I don't imagine she'd take it well."

"No," Grant said, speaking his thoughts out loud, "neither do I."

STANDING IN THE BASEMENT of Lilandera, amid the glowing parts of the astrogator's chair, Brigid Baptiste holstered her TP-9 blaster and reached for the northernmost point of the pentagram that had been laid out across the floor. The headrest to the chair sat there, its eerie glow diminishing even as Brigid laid her hands upon it.

"Kane? Grant?" Brigid said, engaging her Commtact link with them. "I'm about to try something. Stand by— things may be about to get a little weird."

"Make that 'weirder,'" Grant confirmed over the Commtact. "And a heads-up before you start—Ellie isn't what she appears to be. I think she's an Annunaki."

"I'm about three steps ahead of you on that revelation, partner," Kane explained over the shared link. He sounded distinctly out of breath.

"Everything okay with you, Kane?" Brigid asked, her hands still resting on the headrest.

"JUST FUCKING DANDY," Kane snarled in reply to Brigid's query.

At the top of the stairs, Kane tuck-rolled across the rich scarlet carpet and scooped up his Sin Eater handgun where it had been knocked from his grip by Ellie a minute or so earlier. The large-framed woman came crashing through the polished wooden door, bringing half the frame with her in her haste, the brass door handle zipping across the hallway as it broke apart.

Kane rolled up onto one knee and crouched at the head of the once-again decorous staircase, leveling the Sin

Eater at the huge woman who was charging toward him like an angry rhinoceros.

"Just do whatever it is you have to do, Baptiste," Kane instructed as he unleashed a stream of hot lead at the rolling form of Ellie. "And do it quick."

ONE HAND ON EITHER side of the headrest, Brigid pulled it up from the floor with just a momentary struggle. It had been embedded into the floor a little, and the sharp point where the headrest had been broken from the chair itself seemed to be caught in a groove in the floor. But after a moment's effort, Brigid yanked it free with such a pull that she toppled backward, landing on her butt.

Sitting on the concrete floor with the chair head in hand, Brigid looked around self-consciously. "I'm really glad no one was here to see that," she muttered.

As if to put paid to Brigid's lie, a voice piped up just across from where she now sat in a heap. "Are you okay, my dear?" the voice said. It was the elderly woman, the one in the chair who had appeared to be comatose just moments before. The woman was awake.

THE SIN EATER PISTOL kicked in Kane's hand as he reeled off another swift burst of fire at the approaching figure of Ellie. The bullets struck her shoulder, neck and forehead, and she didn't even seem to slow down, just kept charging at him across the eight-foot gap that remained between them, the bullets bouncing from her skin and hurtling away.

Kane rolled at the last possible instant, over and over as he went down the staircase, protecting his head with his arms. Ellie crashed against the walnut balcony, unleashing a fierce cry of anger and frustration.

Kane bumped down the stairs. When he had begun his

roll, the stairs had been richly carpeted with cheerily perverse figures carved into the walnut banister. By the time
he reached the bottom, the banister was a rotten structure
with visible evidence of woodworm, and the carpet was
gone, in its place just bare floorboards streaked with dirt.
There was evidence of a campfire pit at the foot of the
staircase, a round, charred patch marring the dirt-streaked
floorboards there.

Kane righted himself, standing at the bottom of the
battered staircase, pointing his Sin Eater up toward its
topmost level where Ellie recovered from striking the banister. Like the bedroom and the corridor he had seen when
he had meditated himself into a calming state, Kane saw
now that the whole staircase was a shambles. High above
Ellie was a gaping hole through which the sky peeked,
and Kane saw several holes in the wall where bricks had
gone missing.

Brigid's voice came to Kane over the Commtact.
"Did it work?" she asked enthusiastically. "Did anything
happen?"

"Oh, it happened," Kane assured her as he watched
Ellie recover. "Things are looking mighty different to
how you remember them, Baptiste."

BEWILDERED, Papa Hurbon stared at Grant as the Grecian
temple seemed to fade around them. Suddenly they were
in what appeared to be a pantry, cold wind blowing in
through a shattered window high up in the room. Still
legless, Hurbon was sitting propped in a wheelchair
beside a shelf of rotted foodstuffs, a small leather bag of
his belongings hanging over the side of the chair like a
saddlebag.

"What's going on?" Hurbon asked.

Grant ignored him, turning toward the closed door of

the cool larder. "Brigid, Kane—I think we're in the back of the house, some kind of storeroom running off the kitchen. Could use some backup. Do you copy?"

"Little busy right now," Brigid replied.

"Ditto that," Kane added.

Stealthily, Grant moved on silent tread to the pantry door, pushing it open just a crack and peering outside. There was a kitchen out there, dilapidated with evidence of mold and the green shoots of weeds peeking through the tiles that lined the walls. It appeared to be empty.

Grant turned back to Papa Hurbon where the corpulent man sat, trying to take in the unexpected new sights all around him. "Did you do this?" Hurbon demanded, clearly unhappy.

"Man up, Hurbon," Grant barked at him, reaching around and giving the man's wheelchair a shove toward the door. "It's for the best. You can't live your life in a picture."

Looking up at him, Hurbon glared. "You have no idea of the forces you're meddling with here, boy," he snarled.

"No, I don't," Grant agreed, "but you seem to be something of an expert. Funny how shit works out sometimes, ain't it?"

With that, Grant shoved Papa Hurbon ahead of him into the kitchen, the tires of the wheelchair bumping over the cracked floor tiles as he hurried them across the room toward the hall.

BRIGID STARED in amazement at the elderly woman in front of her. She was still sitting in the living Annunaki chair, but she was leaning forward and Brigid could see that the chair had ceased to be attached to her with its weird, winding tendrils.

When Brigid had sat in that same chair months before,

back when it had still been in Papa Hurbon's possession, the chair had endeavored to absorb her, covering her in living tentacles that had been almost impossible to break free from. Quite how this woman had done the trick was beyond Brigid, and her naturally inquisitive mind insisted she ask.

"Are you okay?" Brigid asked.

The elderly woman smiled gently, her blue eyes showing compassion. "I believe I just asked you the self-same question, my dear. You appear to have fallen."

Embarrassed, Brigid pushed aside the broken headrest of the chair. "That chair and I have some history," the red-haired former archivist explained. "It has a habit of trying to swallow people whole."

The other woman laughed falsely, a polite social affectation and nothing more. "It behaves itself if you know how to talk to it," she explained. "However, I must admit I quite forgot myself. I feel as if I've been dreaming for a month."

"We all were," Brigid said with a knowing smile. Then she brushed herself down and, still crouching on the concrete floor, offered her pale hand to the woman. "I'm Brigid, by the way."

"Winifred," the woman replied, brushing her palm against Brigid's for a moment. "My friends call me Winnie."

"I think something's going on in this house," Brigid explained, "that's happening partly because you've been locked in that chair."

Winnie's brow knitted with concern. "That would never do," she said, and Brigid watched as the elderly woman slowly raised herself from the seat. She did so with such poise, such elegance, that Brigid felt entranced.

"How long have you been here?" Brigid asked, picking

herself up from the floor and reaching for the next part of the pentagram, a side panel of the chair that had been wedged upright in a crack in the old stone floor.

Winnie looked around the basement as the light of the chair continued to softly glow. "That's a question to which I have no answer," she explained reasonably. "Unless you happen to know what day it is."

"It's the last day of April," Brigid replied, indelicately shoving the side panel of the chair aside with a grunt.

"Le mange-les-morts," Winnie said, speaking the words with gravity.

Brigid eyed the elderly woman with fresh anxiety. She recognized the words if not their significance—it was French and it meant "the feast of the dead."

CROUCHING AT THE FOOT of the ruined staircase, Kane reeled off another shot as Ellie came charging down the stairs like a runaway train. His bullet struck her shoulder but the woman barely flinched and certainly did not slow down.

In a moment she was upon him, cuffing him across the face with such power that Kane was flipped over. The ex-Mag sailed across the wide lobby of the house before slamming shoulder first against one of the walls. The wall had lost its luster now, was just bare wooden paneling, much of which had rotted right through. As Kane pulled himself up, another chunk of the wall fell to the floor.

Ellie glared at him, and Kane watched as her eyes took on a lizardlike aspect, the whites turning yellow, the chocolate-brown irises narrowing into dark vertical slits. "You fail to acknowledge your betters, apekin," she mocked, and she began to charge at him once more.

"Yeah, and you have a god complex," Kane retorted,

aiming his pistol at the floor between them and blasting out a fierce volley of bullets.

Kane's bullets drilled into the rotten floorboards between himself and the charging woman. As her feet hit the boards, the whole structure collapsed beneath her weight. Kane watched as the rotund woman fell through the floor, sinking about a foot down and tumbling over herself, her rich skirts flailing in the air.

Kane sprinted toward Ellie, then leaping at her as she struggled to free herself from the destroyed section of the floor. He had no idea where he was running to, just knew he needed to keep his distance from the brutal powerhouse of the Annunaki goddess-turned-woman.

Just then Kane spotted Grant entering from the shadowy far end of the corridor. He was pushing a cranky old wheelchair within which sat the familiar—though still surprising—form of voodoo *houngan* Papa Hurbon.

"What the hell's going on?" Grant asked as his partner approached at a dead run.

"Back up," Kane shouted. "We have one out-of-control goddess and she is mighty riled."

From his seat, Papa Hurbon began to laugh, a great rolling sound like the crashing waves of the sea. "Oh, you are so naive it makes my sides hurt, it surely does," he muttered. Even as he spoke, his hand reached into the tanned leather bag that hung on the side of the wheelchair and he pulled out—a little object made of cloth and a black ribbon on a spindle.

Grant tipped Hurbon's wheelchair back and pulled it, dragging the voodoo priest back toward the kitchen as Kane laid down covering fire from his Sin Eater. Behind them, Ellie was struggling out of the rotten section of the flooring, tossing aside broken floorboards as she heaved herself out from the wreckage. In a moment she was on her feet once more, and began stomping toward the trio at the far end of the corridor. And then, incredibly, she stopped in place, standing stock-still as if turned into a statue.

In his seat, Papa Hurbon began to chuckle to himself, his busy hands working at the objects he had produced from his leather satchel.

"What the hell's going on?" Grant asked.

"You told me you don't believe in the path," Hurbon replied, his eyes still fixed on the round woman as she struggled against some invisible force that seemed to hold her rigidly in place.

Kane looked at Hurbon, then at Grant. "Voodoo magic?"

"That's what I think he's prattling about," Grant snarled.

Hurbon's hands continued moving, winding the black ribbon around and around until it had almost smothered the larger object he held there. Kane saw now what that thing was: a small doll, crudely sewn from red rags, two crosses of yellow thread used to create its eyes. The doll was a simple representation of a woman, and it looked bloated in its middle, more like a beanbag with legs. Kane realized that the doll bore a passing resemblance to Ellie.

"You make that just now?" Kane asked.

"This?" Hurbon replied with a raised eyebrow. "No, this is something I keep around for special occasions, white boy. See, this here represents the *loa* of love, Maitresse Ezili. Usually I'd use it to call on her when I was performing some love magic, but it seems that today she's not in such a loving mood, *non?*"

Kane looked from the rotund doll in Hurbon's hands to the portly woman struggling in place against the invisible barrier. "You're an observant little cuss, aren't you?" he drawled. "I guess you're doing this, but how long can you hold her?"

With the gravity of ritual, Hurbon wound another loop of black ribbon around the little cloth doll in his hand. *"Poupée de cire, poupée de son,"* he muttered. "It'll hold her for a little while yet, till she calms down."

Standing behind the wheelchair-bound priest, Grant met Kane's eyes and shook his head. "So, how are things?"

"Better for the moment," Kane replied.

A moment later a small door in the side of the staircase opened and Brigid Baptiste stepped out. She was accompanied by the white-haired woman called Winnie.

"This is going to take some explaining," Brigid said as she took in the debris and abject weirdness of the altered vista in front of her.

Kane smiled. "Ladies first," he quipped.

Chapter 16

In the end, it was Papa Hurbon who helped piece together the situation as the mismatched party gathered in the run-down kitchen.

"There are many aspects to the *loa*," he elaborated as he explained the nature of the voodoo spirit world. "Each *loa* has different sides, and each plays its role in a particular situation."

Kane waited at the doorway to the kitchen, his Sin Eater still in hand, watching as Ellie struggled against her invisible chains. Brigid, Grant and Winnie had taken up positions around the battered old kitchen table, while Hurbon sat in his wheelchair, making occasional windings with his black ribbon around the *poupée*—or voodoo doll—he held in his pudgy hand.

"Broadly speaking," Hurbon continued, "there are two sides to the voodoo spirits, the Rada and the Petro. These sides represent peace and aggression respectfully."

"You worship the Petro, right?" Brigid asked, and Hurbon nodded. "When we met before," Brigid recalled, "I figured you were a Bizango, a follower of the darkest path of voodoo."

"A path is only dark until it's been lit, little peach," Hurbon admonished Brigid, a little of his old bravado returning as he made another slow loop around the doll with his black ribbon.

Brigid ignored his comment, feeling her skin crawl with her proximity to this repellent man.

Kane spoke up from the door, his eyes still fixed on the struggling figure of Ellie. "We met a friend of yours earlier today, Hurbon—delightful lady called Ezili Coeur Noir. Anything you want to tell us?"

"That mad bitch is nothing but trouble," Hurbon snarled. "You need to keep away from her. She revels in death."

"We noticed," Grant said, his expression deadpan. "And we think she's about to do something that'll bring about the end of all life. Including yours."

"Ezili Coeur Noir is the queen of all things dead. She has always been a dangerous *loa*," Hurbon acknowledged, "but recently she's been unhinged. It's as if once she came back from the stars she lost all her self-control."

"'Came back from the stars'?" Brigid repeated, urging the crippled voodoo priest to elaborate.

"I found her in the wreckage of her spaceship," Hurbon explained. "She seemed confused and weak as a newborn kitten. I did what I could for her."

Nine months earlier.

ALARMS WERE SOUNDING in the air like jangling wind chimes and the docking bay was shaking with increasing violence as *Tiamat* began to rip herself apart. The mothership had gone into a self-destructive spiral that could only end one way—with her obliteration. All around, the slow, heavy tolling of the crystalline notes continued to echo through the vast chamber as the bulkheads sealed themselves in final preparation for the end. Lilitu strode out of the shadows of the chamber, beautiful and horrible all at once, her scaled face blood-streaked and stained with smoke, her right hand now a welter of blood, flayed tissue and bone chips where she had taken a blast. Her crimson scales shimmered beneath sparking bursts of electricity as she strode across the chamber toward where Overlord Enlil's skimmer waited, the promise of freedom reflecting from its sleek lines.

Then, as the dark goddess was about to take the skimmer, the elevator door to its left slid open on its groove and five familiar figures came rushing out, moving with such speed one might believe that their heels were aflame. Lilitu stepped back, merging with the shadows, conscious that she was outnumbered by these heavily armed newcomers.

The Asian woman—Shizuka—was still coughing as she emerged from the elevator car, and the powerful form of her lover, Grant, gave her a friendly shunt as they hurried toward the disk ship that waited in its docking pod. Shizuka, the samurai princess, looked exhausted, her head held low, her clothing torn.

Behind that pair of humans, the flame-haired Brigid Baptiste was scanning the docking bay left and right, the brutal length of a Copperhead assault subgun held in both hands.

Beside Brigid came Rhea, the traitorous hybrid who had turned to assist the Cerberus rebels, somehow managing to channel the thoughts of mothership *Tiamat* in the process. Like all hybrids, Rhea was beautiful, her sylph-like physique closer to that of an adolescent girl than a woman. Hers was a delicate beauty that seemed fragile and ethereal, more so as she stood in front of Brigid's taller and more shapely form. The hybrid's pale hair was feathery like down and she was dressed in a one-piece tan coverall.

Kane brought up the rear, keeping his head down as

he sprinted across the hangar bay, feeling dangerously exposed. It was incredible, Lilitu thought. Even here, in what appeared to be relative safety, the man's finely honed instincts were trying to alert him to the fact that he was being watched; she could see it in his every movement as he hurried toward Enlil's docked skimmer with his allies.

The group halted at the disk ship itself, finding it locked. "Now what?" Brigid asked, her breasts heaving against the weave of the shadow suit as she took deep breaths. "How do we get in?"

Rhea laid her hands against the sensor plate of the hull of the skimmer. The sensor plate was artistically hidden from view yet obvious to any who knew the functionality of the Annunaki craft. On her command a section of the hull parted in a triangular shape, magically appearing like the sun's rays through a gap in the clouds.

"Oh," Brigid said, pushing a wayward lock of hair from her face as a ramp began to extend outward from the skimmer, its glistening surface forming in front of her eyes from smart metal. "It must be keyed to Annunaki genetic material. Right?"

The traitorous hybrid was hurrying the others up the boarding ramp now, feet clattering on the extended smart metal strip. "Something like that," Rhea told Brigid with an enigmatic twinkle in her curiously expressive eyes. "Now we must tarry no longer."

Idiot apekin, Lilitu thought as she watched from the shadows at the edge of the hangar. The ship had opened like a blossoming flower because Rhea had pressed its key switch, nothing more sophisticated than that. Organic technology remained, she realized, far beyond anything even the smartest human seemed able to comprehend. Lilitu took a pace forward, her one good hand flipping open a plate on the diagnostic unit that the skimmer was still connected to, jabbing in the override command. The ship would automatically seal if it believed there was no atmosphere for the pilot to exit into; thus it was but the work of a moment to fool the system.

Behind Rhea, Grant urged the beautiful Shizuka up the ramp, her exhausted form almost collapsing as he helped her through the triangular gap in the hull. Brigid Baptiste followed them inside, with Kane just a few feet behind her.

Lilitu smiled her cold, reptilian grin as her hand moved away from the emergency override. Alone on the boarding ramp, Kane suddenly found himself facing a smooth wall, the hull sealing before he could join his companions inside the escape ship.

"Hey!" Kane shouted as he pulled himself up short. "I'm still out here!"

With the speed of a striking cobra, Lilitu reached out from her hiding place, grasping the back of Kane's thick hair and yanking him backward with neck-wrenching force. The others could wait, but this one had been a thorn in her side for far too long, ever since her days wearing the body of Baroness Beausoleil.

To Lilitu's surprise, the ex-Mag relaxed his body in an exceptional combination of his instinct and training, and she found him racing toward her head-first, like a battering ram.

With a sneer, Lilitu stepped out of the way of her hurtling foe, detaching her hand from his hair even as he sailed across the hangar floor. Kane crashed into the deck, grunting as his left shoulder smashed into it with incredible force, and he was flung several yards forward before finally skidding to a halt on grazed skin.

Lilitu moved toward her fallen foe at a dead run, punting

the toe of her boot into his stomach even as he struggled to recover. Behind her, the Annunaki goddess knew Kane's colleagues were watching through the portholes of the sealed skimmer. There was nothing they could do; Kane was hers now. She kicked at him a second time, this boot so hard that the ex-Mag rolled over, slamming into the deck plating with bone-numbing force.

Yet with that ghastly streak of pluck that humans seemed to possess in the most unlikely of circumstances, Kane pushed himself up on his elbows and glared at her.

"How'd you get here?" the ex-Mag snarled through clenched teeth.

Lilitu laughed, admiring his spunk. "I never take the chance of being trapped," she assured him. "I always have an exit in mind, unlike you, apekin."

Beneath her, Kane pathetically attempted a leg sweep, forgetting how interminably fast she was. Lilitu shoved one of her feet down into the base of Kane's neck, grinding her heel against his throat. She felt the edges of her mouth curling up into a smile. "No," she told Kane, her voice a hoarse whisper. "You will not escape. I sealed your friends and my traitorous slut of a sister in the ship."

Trapped like a bug beneath her heel, Kane struggled uselessly to free himself.

"Only I can free them," Lilitu added, thinking of how the override had sealed the skimmer, "and I will not. All of them will die, trapped like vermin. And you, Kane, you will die as all humanity will eventually die—beneath the heel of the Annunaki!" With those words, Lilitu pressed all her weight down on Kane's throat, either to suffocate him or to snap his worthless neck, whichever came sooner.

But then, impossibly, Kane shifted his position subtly, and his knee slammed against Lilitu's thigh, sending

driving pain through her nerve ganglia and forcing her
to fall with a howl of rage. She landed atop Kane's struggling form, and immediately attacked his face where it
appeared directly in front of her. The stump of her left
hand swept at Kane, then her right batted him in the face
and cuffed him several times so that he reeled with the
disorientation.

Even then, Kane glared at her with those steely gray
eyes as if in accusation, and Lilitu cursed him. Lilitu
reached for those penetrating eyes then, her sharp nails
outthrust, wrenching the skin from Kane's face in four
deep red streaks even as he turned away to avoid being
savagely blinded.

The two of them thrashed against the decking in some
strange mockery of love-making, until Lilitu's hand found
Kane's throat and began to crush it with all of her incredible strength. Yet even this close to death the human still
struggled, driving his fist at Lilitu's nose. In an instant,
she ducked, and Kane's hand slammed against the cranial
spines that decorated her skull like a sadist's tiara.

Still, the impact forced Lilitu to regroup, and her grip
on her accursed foe's throat loosened for just a moment. In
that instant, she heard Kane gulp down a desperate breath
even amid the racket of the alarm's tolling that sang frantically through the air like wind chimes in a hurricane.

Something hit the right side of Lilitu's face then, and
she found herself toppling backward, Kane's left fist pulling away from the punch he had somehow managed to
plant on her.

Lilitu landed awkwardly, her ruined hand beneath
her, and she shrieked as the white fire of agony burned
along her whole arm. Across the decking, Lilitu could
hear footsteps as Kane righted himself and put a little
distance between them. It was a wise move, the rational

part of her brain realized, for she was far stronger than her opponent.

Tamping down the pain in her arm, Lilitu pushed herself up from the deck, searching for Kane's form through the smoke of the shuddering hangar bay. He was watching her, taunting her, it seemed.

With a howl of agonized triumph, Lilitu urged herself forward, charging toward the insignificant human and ducking beneath his right fist, sidestepping a failed body blow. Then she had him in her grasp, driving him back, until he was slammed bodily against the hull of Enlil's skimmer where his friends remained trapped. With the brute strength born of fury, Lilitu pounded Kane against the side of the skimmer, forcing the air from his lungs as she tried to crack his ribs. His eyes rolled, losing their focus, she saw, and in that moment Lilitu was sure that she had won.

But she had not.

Suddenly, Kane's arms swung around until his cupped hands slammed against Lilitu's ears like a thunderclap inside her brain. Lilitu ignored it, pushing Kane hard against the skimmer's shell once again and driving her crown spines into his chin.

Impossibly tenacious, the apekin brought his hands around again, meeting with Lilitu's ears with such an impact that she went momentarily deaf, the sound of the alarm turning into a distant thing as if heard through a body of water. She staggered backward, her grip on Kane loosening as she howled in agony like a wounded animal.

It was all just a blur then, Lilitu acting on something primal, some deep-rooted instinct to kill whatever stood in her way. They tumbled to the decking of the hangar bay, writhing in each other's embrace until Lilitu stood over Kane's form once more, her voice a strangled screech of frustration.

"You are a fool!" she told Kane. "This is the night you dance to oblivion, screaming for the mercy of *Tiamat!*"

In that instant the blur of combat finally righted itself, seeming to slow time down. Two figures were standing behind Lilitu, and she turned as she heard the familiar voice of the first.

"Scream for it yourself," Rhea stated emotionlessly, and Lilitu saw the ASP blaster attachment wrapped around her sister's right wrist. Beside the hybrid woman, Lilitu saw Brigid Baptiste poised with her Copperhead subgun, tracking the Annunaki goddess's every movement.

"How were you able to open the seal?" Lilitu demanded, her voice shrill. When Rhea didn't answer, she realized that the bond of blood between them was even now too deep, that Rhea had escaped the skimmer but she would never turn on her own blood kin. "Come to me, sister," she said, her arms spreading out to hold her, perhaps even to crush her.

Rhea did not move. She merely stood there, a look of disgust forming on her smooth features. "How can anything so beautiful be so evil?" she asked in a horrified whisper.

Lilitu scoffed at the question. Evil? What was evil? What did morality matter to a goddess? The Annunaki were above such infantile concepts as good and evil. She would explain it to Rhea, make her see the truth of good and evil, how the whole thing was a game, the distinction no more important than the opposing colors on a chess board, good and evil defined only by who made the first move. But as she began to speak, the ASP blaster flashed in Rhea's hand and an energy bolt zapped out, plowing a hole straight through Lilitu's chest.

For a moment Lilitu stood motionless. Blood bubbled over her lips and her beautiful lizard's eyes rolled up in her skull. And then, finally, Lilitu fell backward, slamming into the deck with a violent shudder, her limbs outspread.

And that was how Lilitu had died, her blood seeping into the decking of her mothership *Tiamat*.

Tiamat was dying, too, in that moment, but the spilled blood of one of her children acted as a strange wake-up call. Even as her bulwarks and decking shook with the aggravated pain of her destruction, *Tiamat* extended a mother's caring hand to her daughter, absorbing Lilitu's corpse into herself even as Kane joined his companions and the skimmer launched from her deck. Patiently *Tiamat* was engaging the rebirth sequence that had been used just a few years earlier to re-create her children across the planet Earth, the sequence that had allowed the Annunaki to live again.

Outside, beyond the limits of *Tiamat*'s dragonlike body, Enlil's skimmer was rocketing through space, the Cerberus rebels and their hybrid friend installed safely within. It would not be long now, the celestial mother knew, until she lived no more. But still, there was time to re-create beautiful Lilitu, to fix the damage the apekin had done to her precious princess daughter.

Her other children were finding their own escape routes, *Tiamat* felt. The Annunaki legacy would live on. Even now her most prized son, Enlil, was plucking at the seeds that would become a new *Tiamat,* that she too might be reborn.

Lilitu's blood seeped into the living deck of the spaceship womb, and *Tiamat* saw—or, more accurately, sensed—the terrible damage that had been done to her child. Lilitu's hand was missing, and a gaping rent had been opened between her breasts. Her shell, her body, was ruined. The Annunaki could grow new forms and alter them like a snake sloughing its skin or a caterpillar becoming a butterfly, moving from chrysalis state to a new and better shape. Each of the Annunaki had been hidden as a hybrid, a form that had simply burst open when *Tiamat* commanded it, revealing their beautiful actuality within, like an oyster revealing a pearl. But there were many forms for the immortals, and each one needed to be grown.

As her walls shook, dying in the heavens high above the Earth, *Tiamat* absorbed the essence of her daughter and engaged the birthing sequence, piping the command through her veins to an escape pod hidden in her belly.

The burning had started within *Tiamat* by then, the final purging of her own system by fire that would result in her death. She felt the burn surging through her, and if the mother of all the gods can truly be capable of cursing, she cursed then, cursed that even immortal things occasionally ran out of time. As fire ripped through her, blossoming across the heavens like a beautiful orange flower, *Tiamat* launched the escape pod with Lilitu's essence within it, activating the rebirth sequencers therein.

And then *Tiamat* exploded, pale ectoplasmic waves shimmering out along the curving lines of the vessel, a pallid borealis fanning slowly out until it formed a mile-wide shimmering across the firmament.

Within the escape pod, the rebirth sequencer struggled to make sense of the hurried data flow it had been given. Lilitu's corpse sprawled unmoving in the astrogator's chair, the chair's tendrils trying to make contact with the dead goddess in their presence. The rebirth sequencer scanned her and understood it was to create a dead thing, one that was new and yet that was like the old Lilitu.

The escape pod was no more *Tiamat* than a single leaf is the tree that it fell from. It merely understood that it had been a part of the spaceship womb, and that its job now was to do what *Tiamat* could not, to re-create this beautiful goddess that lay in its midst. The data of Lilitu's life flowed through the escape pod's circuits, and it seemed there was too much information. How could this be the life of just one person? This Lilith, Lilu, Lilitu. This first wife of Adam and this snake in the Garden of Eden. This Queen of Sheba who seduced King Solomon. This Baroness Beausoleil. How could all of this be just one person? How could all these aspects fit into just one creature?

The escape pod made a decision as the flames from *Tiamat*'s pyre scorched its rear, frying the circuitry that powered its own logic centers, fragmenting the data it had been given to safeguard. Rocketing through space, hidden in the shadow of the dark side of the Moon, the escape pod began to carve a new body for Lilitu, a body that would be split into many parts.

Chapter 17

There is no shame in crying. Even for a god or goddess, whose comprehension is so much more than that of a mere mortal, there is no shame in crying.

It had hurt, she admitted. It had been excruciating. And yes, she had cried, for even she was only but a god.

Once, she had been called Lilitu, and perhaps she remembered that at some deeply buried level the way one remembers the passion one must have once felt for a lover long departed, the way that emotion sometimes returns in dreams.

The escape pod had followed *Tiamat*'s commands, had given the goddess a new body via the chalice of rebirth. But the information had been jumbled, confused, and the whole package had become fragmented when *Tiamat*'s explosion had rocked the escape pod.

They used to say that the stars in the sky were the gods themselves, each one representing another member of the infinite pantheon that watched over the planet Earth. If that was the case, then a whole galaxy of new stars must have been born that day nine months ago when Lilitu had died and been re-formed.

First Body had been the most dominant. She had been everything that Lilitu was, only messy and jumbled, every aspect of her personality entangled with the death of *Tiamat*. In some primal way, First Body remembered dying, although the details—the battle with Kane, the blast from her sister as the mothership rocked around her—were all forgotten. The single most frightening thing for an immortal is to discover that death can happen, even to them. Mortals—humans—no matter how much they run from and hide from it, were able to accept death. Some even philosophized that death was the one thing that made life worth living, for without its promise one would just go on aimlessly forever.

All the aspects of death were wrought across the new form that had been conjured as First Body, the black-hearted id that knew no boundaries, had no concept of morality. And so the First Body had emerged from the smoking wreckage of the crash-landed escape pod, lusting only for death.

They had landed in the bayou, close to where Lilitu had once made her home when she had assumed the form of Baroness Beausoleil. The escape pod had intended to take Lilitu—whatever she now was—home, but the damage it had taken when *Tiamat* had blown up in its proximity had been too great. It had not had the energy or stability to reach its intended destination.

First Body stood amid the smoldering wreckage, shards of the hull and great chunks of the interior strewed across the swampland, smart metal forming and re-forming as it sank into the waters of the bayou. The navigator's chair, the responsive technology that painted pictures inside its sitter's mind, lay in a heap amid the burned leaves of a fern, its base missing. First Body reached for it, but found her legs could not carry her. Instead she stumbled and fell, sinking into the moist soil that the bulk of the escape pod rested upon.

After a while, a man approached through the mist, First Body saw. A portly man, with dark skin and a gap-toothed smile, wearing a loud Hawaiian shirt and knee-length cargo pants that left his glistening calves exposed. He was using a walking cane to help him through the boggy soil and as he came closer First Body saw that he was sweating profusely, thick beads of perspiration running down his lined face like miniature rivers.

When he reached the astrogator's chair, the fat man halted, studying it from a few paces before jabbing at it with his cane, muttering something at it. First Body looked at the man, watching from her hiding place amid the shadows of the escape pod's wreckage. As she watched, her malformed body like something pulled from a grave, she became conscious of movements coming from deep within the ruined starcraft, more bodies being formed by the struggling tech hidden in its depths.

Standing out in the open, the man turned, peering around the clearing and seeing more of the wreckage of the escape pod until he noticed the large hunk that lay camouflaged among the trees. He whistled as he took it all in. "Anyone in there?" he asked, his voice deep like the low rumble of distant thunder.

Warily, the corpulent man took another step toward the wrecked spaceship. Then First Body stepped out into the open the way a baby fawn lurches its first steps, her flesh dark as if it had been charred. She was tall, a towering frame of near-fleshless bones, her spindly limbs like those of a bird.

"I know you," the man said, much to First Body's astonishment. "Ezili Coeur Noir. My sweetheart. *Ma chérie.*"

First Body looked at the man, her yellow lizard's eyes narrowed as she assessed this fat fool. He bowed in front of her, not an easy thing for a man carrying so much weight and yet he did so gracefully, kneeling in the wet marsh as he exposed his neck to the visitor.

First Body knew who she was then, knew her role on

Earth. The man had called her Ezili Coeur Noir, not a goddess but a *loa,* a voodoo spirit. It was a form Lilitu had assumed before now and it was not a gigantic leap for her to assume this personality once again; the information was buried deep within her, among the jumble of traits she had been infused with during her botched rebirth. All the gods and spirits and idols of Earth are the same gods and spirits and idols, just hiding behind different names, wearing different forms.

"You will help us," she instructed the large man, her voice like dried leaves. She reconsidered the statement, trying to feel how many personalities she was now. "You will help me," she amended.

Still kneeling, the portly man looked up and offered a gap-toothed smile that seemed to engulf the whole width of his impressive, bucketlike jaw. "My name is Hurbon," he said, "and I am yours to command, my mistress."

With Hurbon's help, First Body took the astrogator's chair away from the wreckage, knowing its abilities were precious. The chair contained star maps, and promised the only true way for her to find her way home. Hurbon, it transpired, was a voodoo priest, governing a small following out here in the middle of the Louisiana swampland. He took the chair willingly, hiding it away from prying eyes and nourishing it with blood at regular intervals as his mistress instructed. It was a living thing and it required protein now that true interaction was denied it. Unused, the chair would die unless it was provided with food in the form of blood.

In her newborn weakness, First Body herself had been drawn deeper into the swampland, hiding like a wounded animal, covering herself in the shadows as she tried to amass her strength. The technology that had been used to create her, an Annunaki chalice of rebirth, had somehow become imbedded in her during the crash landing. It wasn't visible; the physical chalice pit was not actually a part of her. But at a deeper level, the submolecular level, something of its programming had been hard-wired into her DNA during the escape pod's desperate attempt to create new forms, new shapes. First Body, now branding herself as Ezili Coeur Noir, harbored within her a whole strain of rogue DNA operating as a chalice of rebirth. She could feel it calling to her, like some strange motherly instinct yearning for children.

So she sat there in the dense swamp and reached out with one of her spindly hands. Already the hand had blackened, the skin there drying and becoming hard like leather, an armored sheath within which her body hid. Even then, she looked like a dead thing, her physicality had adopted the dried-out look of a husk, a walking corpse. Without a mirror, the irony was lost on her as she reached out, the chalice-of-rebirth technology deep inside her yearning to bring things to life.

There were things under the soil. She felt them somewhere deep in the back of her brain, in the part of the brain that knows things by instinct alone, the part that remembers up isn't down and down isn't up. Seeds had scattered from the ferns and the trees, and had been buried in the earth by the animals, the insects and the elements that moved in cyclic patterns around the swamp. Placing one long-fingered hand against the moist earth, Ezili Coeur Noir clawed at the soil, delving deeper and deeper as she searched for the seeds. In her mind's eye, they glowed, like the bones of an X-ray. It was the way she saw, not an aside or an overlay to her vision, but simply the way her vision was now, altered by the unfinished business of her own birth. It saw things beyond the simple limitations of solids and liquids; it saw through and into the ground and the plants around her, the life bubbling all around.

When her hand made contact, Ezili Coeur Noir had let out a gasp. It had been an ugly thing, spouting from her dried-up throat through cracked, pencil-thin lips, the sound of a man choking on his own vomit. The seed beneath the soil seemed to throb with energy it could barely contain.

I want to live, the seed cried out. I want to live and to feel the touch of the golden sun.

Ezili Coeur Noir felt the thing inside her, the chalice of rebirth, reach into the seed. It sent the signal for the seed to begin growing, overwhelmed it with pleasure until the seed began to sprout, tiny green shoots bursting from its hard shell.

Even then, First Body had not truly embraced her nature, had not truly understood—or at least reasoned— what it was to be Ezili Coeur Noir. She remembered from the first time, and yet she had forgotten, had dismissed the broken, malformed memory of her other lives.

Thus, it had come as a surprise to her, the queen of all things dead, that the seed had grown from green to brown to dead in a matter of seconds. In less than a minute, a new fern stood where the seed had been pulled from the soil, its spines brown and drooping, a carpet of dead leaves around its base. Ezili Coeur Noir looked at this thing she had grown, this dead fern, with wonderment, her lizard-slit eyes wide with astonishment. And slowly the smile had formed on her terrible face. She had grown a dead thing and the knowledge pleased her.

Her eyes, which saw the things hidden in the soil, which saw the layers of history on which she rested, searched for more things to grow and to corrupt. And for a while she had amused herself, growing new things,

dead things, making things that should live into things
that would only ever be dead.

Could a thing that had never lived truly be dead? she
wondered. Must a thing first be alive to then embrace
death?

Whatever the rules of the universe were, Ezili Coeur
Noir knew she could change them. That mastery of death
began by having no life, by expunging the concept of life,
eradicating life from history. And so her dark plan began
to take shape.

For a while Ezili Coeur Noir had toyed with the things
of the ground, had tested the extent of her abilities, wit-
nessed them grow with each passing day. At that stage,
she had yet to experiment with animals, with sentient
things, amusing herself only with the plants of the Earth.
But as the months passed, she began to feel the call of
blood, the need to feel its warmth upon her desiccated
flesh, in the same way she had instructed Papa Hurbon to
bathe the living chair.

And so when Ezili Coeur Noir was feeling strong
enough, she had returned to Papa Hurbon's voodoo temple
and begun testing the limits of human beings, finding herself drawn more and more toward death and dying. She
showed Hurbon how to see visions from the chair, how to
make them dance in front of his eyes as if real. In return,
she had demanded blood, pouring it on her body and on
the chair.

She appeared at dawn one morning, as the sun was
just nudging over the immutable line of the horizon, mist
clinging low to the ground. Papa Hurbon lay asleep in his
magnificent four-poster bed, perhaps not snoring loudly
enough to wake the dead but certainly loudly enough to at
least attract them to his home. Silks decorated the ceiling

of Hurbon's room, their soft colors, purples and pinks, fluttering in the breeze like clouds that had been dyed and somehow penned indoors. Beside Hurbon two women lay asleep on the bed, sisters, the eldest just seventeen. The corpulent voodoo priest had exhausted them; Hurbon was, as he frequently admitted, a man of discerning taste and no little energy. He woke with a start, straight from asleep to wakefulness with such abruptness that there seemed no transition. Something had woken him, some primal instinct.

Hurbon rolled the teenager—pretty with youth if not in looks—from his chest and reached out to the side of the bed, where he kept his trinkets and fetishes. There were several fith-faths there, popularly known as voodoo dolls, poppets that were believed to trap the spirit, to guide the will. Hurbon grabbed one, pulling it close to his chest as he sat up in bed. The doll was plain, just a simple rag thing in the form of a human being, shaped by wax and sawdust.

There was a woman standing at the foot of Hurbon's bed, her face in shadow. She was tall, her skin shadow dark on her emaciated frame. He knew her straight away.

"Mademoiselle Ezili Coeur Noir," Hurbon said, his voice coming out as an astonished whisper. "You look more beautiful than ever."

In the darkness, Hurbon saw her yellow eyes flash, the brief appearance of her brown teeth as she granted him just the slightest smile. Blessed, Hurbon had done something foolish then, something he would regret months later, when his sadistic mistress had returned for her final visit. He had placed the poppet aside, that little doll of wax and dust, believing himself safe in the presence of this beautiful *loa* spirit of death.

Ezili Coeur Noir spoke then, her voice distant but forceful, like death itself. "Wake your people," she said. "I have need."

Hurbon leaped from the bed, tossing the covers aside and calling to the devotees who had slept with him. As the two girls groaned themselves awake, Hurbon wrapped himself in his silk dressing gown and waddled from his bedchamber, his voice loud as he roused everyone who had slept in the temple after the preceding night's ceremony. Hurbon's temple welcomed all comers—it was as much a flophouse as a temple, and his followers a mishmash of the lost and the lonely. So long as he had a steady supply of willing believers in the path, Hurbon didn't care.

Alone in the bedchamber, the two sisters brushed their hands through their messy hair, wondering what was going on. "What's crawled up his ass?" Nina asked, her voice still slurred with sleep.

Beside Nina on the bed, her sister, Nadia, started to answer but her words stopped as she became aware of the other presence in the room.

"What is it?" Nina asked, reaching for her lipstick amid the trinkets and junk that Hurbon kept beside his bed.

Nadia continued to look into the shadows, her eyes so wide she could have been high on an old stash of their father's jolt. Nina pouted, applying lipstick without needing a mirror, and peered to where her sister was looking. There, standing in the darkness of the bedchamber, she saw the naked figure of a woman, thin as a bird, watching them with eyes the yellow of sickness.

"Who the fuck are—?"

Ezili Coeur Noir did not let the girl finish her sentence. "You will be the first to honor me," she promised in a dry voice drained of all emotion.

Nina shied away from the end of the bed, at a loss for words and suddenly very terrified. Beside her, Nadia began to vomit.

GOOD AS HIS WORD, Papa Hurbon had roused his followers. They didn't follow him, he reminded himself; he was merely their guide on the path. They were tired and confused, but they gathered in the *djévo* room where newcomers were initiated into the faith. Ezili Coeur Noir rested on a wooden chair, watching from the shadows; she could be seen, but she seemed to fade into the background as Hurbon's initiates danced and sang and drank. The sounds of drums echoed through the whole of the temple, and could be heard for miles around, attracting new followers even as the celebrants danced themselves giddy and let the spirits ride them, almost sixty people, young and old, dancing maniacally to the beats of the drum, the crashing of the bell. There was food, too, cooked meats and bowls of stew and rice, arranged on a side table and constantly refilled, everyone taking turns to help with the cooking. A roasted sheep lay spread out on a silver platter, a cleaver beside it for anyone who wanted to carve themselves off a hunk of its richly spiced meat.

The celebration continued through the day, fifteen hours of nonstop dancing until exhaustion and hysteria began to show. The *djévo* room was hot by then, thanks to the flaming torches that lit it, the candles on every surface. The smell of sweating human bodies filled the air. People had thrown aside their shirts; some of them had even stripped naked. Papa Hurbon sat on a chair on a raised stage in the room, and he had become drunk on heady wine as his initiates continued to twirl and cheer. It was a party, a celebration of the *loa* spirits who had walked the path before them.

Ezili Coeur Noir stepped from the shadows then, the giddiness of life spread in front of her. She bent until her mouth was close to Hurbon's ear.

"It begins now," she told him in a whisper that seemed to have all the power of a crashing tidal wave.

Hurbon, her obedient lapdog, nodded and stood, swaying a little with drink. The *ku-bha-sah*, a ceremonial sword used to part the corporeal world from that of the voodoo spirits, sat in its decorous sheath beneath Hurbon's chair, where he had placed it hours earlier, when all of this had started. He pulled the sword from its sheath and the blade glinted in the flames as he carved an extravagant swirl through the air.

The music stopped, though Hurbon did not remember commanding it so, and a hush descended on the room. "The blade, *ku-bha-sah*, has cut through the gossamer-thin veil to the spirit world," Hurbon explained, "and revealed to us a mighty *loa*, our protector, Ezili Coeur Noir."

She had been there among them all along, and yet it seemed as if she was being seen for the first time. Blessed ceremony and its effect on the weak-minded was an Annunaki weapon from days immemorial. Ezili Coeur Noir appeared, in that moment, to become taller, as if her very bones had elongated inside her emaciated frame. A cheer went around the room as she parted the shadows.

"You will show your devotion to me," the queen of all things dead instructed, "by letting blood."

There was a gasp from the people in the *djévo*, sixty-something people taking in their breath as one, followed by nervous laughter from some of the younger members of Hurbon's congregation.

Hurbon himself did not feel nervous. This would be a beautiful act, he knew—why should a *loa* knowingly hurt him or his people? It was beyond credibility.

Ezili Coeur Noir's sick eyes scoured the crowd for a moment until she saw Nina, her shirt open to the navel, her smooth, coffee-colored skin glistening with sweat. "It's your time," Ezili Coeur Noir said, her eyes fixing on the girl's like a rattlesnake hypnotizing its prey.

Without a word, the girl stepped forward, stiffly marching to the raised area of the room, her arms frozen at her sides like an automaton.

Ezili Coeur Noir had watched Nina for many hours. She was graceful and she clearly loved to dance, used it to flirt with the men, to draw attention to herself. Dancing brought her joy.

"Give me your leg," Ezili Coeur Noir said, her yellow eyes still fixed on the girl's.

Without hesitation, Nina reached for the meat cleaver that rested in the remainder of the sheep's carcass, her fingers wrapping around its handle without looking, her eyes remaining fixed on Ezili Coeur Noir's. Then she swept the blade down, the reflected candle flames sparkling across its silver edge, and hacked into her own leg, just below the thigh.

She grunted just a little with the effort, but Nina didn't scream, even though her sister was shrieking with terror from her place in the crowd. Nina withdrew that square blade and a thick line of blood appeared along the top of her leg like some magician's trick as she swayed just a little in place. Then the blade of the meat cleaver swept down again, and she had embedded it in her own leg a second time with a savage blow. This time, the blade sunk so deep it hit bone, and Nina toppled over, sagging to the floor as her blood gushed over the raised wooden stage. And, as she hit the floor, Nina began to laugh and to weep with joy.

Ezili Coeur Noir watched as the girl withdrew the blade and swept it down again, plunging it into her own limb, hacking through the flesh and the bone there. Her own face was as death, an emotionless mask, but she felt the blood spilling across the stage, its warm, red fingers reaching out until it touched her bare toes.

Nina was the first. Another twenty-three people amputated their own legs for Ezili Coeur Noir that evening, including Papa Hurbon himself, screaming that he could see the spirit world even as he drove the ceremonial blade of the *ku-bha-sah* into his own flesh. Ezili Coeur Noir had been born of pain, and pain was all she truly understood. Pain and death.

By dawn, Ezili Coeur Noir was satiated. Blood painted the whole of the temple, that ragged, disheveled little wooden structure out in the middle of the swamp. Blood was the link that made life in people. Ezili Coeur Noir was, or would be, the queen of all things dead. And since all things must die, she was, by default, the queen of the Earth. Blood was hers.

Chapter 18

Papa Hurbon's busy hands looped another twist of black ribbon around the little doll as he sat in the kitchen of the House Lilandera with the Cerberus rebels and the elderly woman called Winnie watching him.

"When she came and took my other leg," Hurbon admitted, "I thought I would die from the pain alone. Didn't matter about the blood loss, just the pain was enough to finish me. You know?"

Grant nodded solemnly. "I have an idea."

"Your boss—Ohio—came along," Hurbon continued, "and she patched me up. I would have died otherwise, but she wouldn't have that on her conscience now, would she? Like I said, soft and fluffy little princess, that one is. I think she only came back to ransack my place, figured she could overpower me after the mess you'd all made of my people."

Hurbon was talking about Ohio Blue, the independent trader with whom Kane's team had worked in an undercover capacity, posing as her lackeys so as to access bottom-feeders like this voodoo priest who had stumbled upon alien technology. Now was not the time to correct his assumptions, the Cerberus team knew.

"After that, I got the fuck out of there," Hurbon finished. "I couldn't face her if she came back again—I'm running out of limbs." And he began to laugh at his own sick joke.

"So how did you end up here?" Kane asked from his guard position at the open doorway. "Or is it obvious?"

"Maitresse Ezili called to me," Papa Hurbon explained.

Kane nodded, encouraging the man to go on.

"That's the one standing outside," Hurbon said, holding aloft the rotund doll he had wrapped in a long strip of black ribbon, "the one I'm binding. She's another side of Ezili, dedicated to passion and to love."

Brigid brushed the hair out of her eyes as she spoke, "She's the same person, then? The same as Ezili Coeur Noir?"

"The same but different," Hurbon replied, "like branches from the same trunk. Each one goes its own way, finds its own path, but they are all still a part of the tree, are they not? Ezili takes on many faces depending on emotion. Ezili Dantor, Ezili ze Rouge, Ezili Freda Dahomey—these are all parts of the whole."

A silence fell upon the kitchen as Hurbon finished explaining the nature of the voodoo spirits and each member of the group there tried to take in everything he had told them. In that silence, Hurbon twisted another loop of the black ribbon over the voodoo doll in his hands. In the corridor beyond the room, Ellie—or more accurately, Maitresse Ezili—was still struggling to move, but she remained held in one spot, unable to go forward or backward.

Brigid began to see it all now. It was mixed and confused, like some fever dream brought to life, but it did finally seem to make some kind of sense. Lilitu had died in combat on *Tiamat*—Brigid had seen this with her own eyes—but the living spaceship had revived her, her motherly devotion absolute. However, *Tiamat* had been dying at the time, too, her body disintegrating as fire took hold in her depths.

"The rebirth process couldn't be completed," Brigid concluded. "Things were wild at that moment, explosions firing off everywhere, so it produced a fractured version of Lilitu."

"Fractured?" Kane queried uncertainly.

"Ezili Coeur Noir and Maitresse Ezili—or Ellie, as we know her—are parts of the same person, but they're physically separate," Brigid said. "It's like Lilitu's personality was split across two people.

"With no moral shackles constraining her darker personality, the aspect we've met as Ezili Coeur Noir has become nihilistic, devoted to death and destruction," Brigid continued. "An id freed from the restraints of the ego."

Brigid's cheeks flushed as she warmed to her subject matter. "This is basic Freudian psychology, manifesting itself in a literal, physical form," she continued. "Ezili Coeur Noir is the id, while the loving, life-affirming Maitresse Ezili out there is the ego."

Sitting across from Brigid at the table, Grant shook his head, confused. "Care to run that by us again?"

"The ego is the organized and realistic part of the psyche," Brigid explained as she drew on the wealth of information stored in her encyclopedic memory. "Effectively, Ellie out there has been trying to do good. Like she said, this whole house is dedicated to the affirmation of life. Even the name of the place—Lilandera—is just another corruption of her real name, Lilitu."

"It's a whorehouse," Kane pointed out. "And your organized and realistic personality out there trapped us in illusions and tried to kill me when I broke her hypnosis."

Brigid nodded thoughtfully, trying to see what it was she was missing. "Maitresse Ezili is operating like some kind of extremist," she mused. "Just like the Ezili Coeur Noir aspect, her personality isn't being constrained by anything."

Out in the corridor, the figure whom they had identified as Maitresse Ezili was still struggling as if against an invisible cage, but her efforts had diminished, and the fight seemed to be going out of her.

"There are other people here," Kane told Brigid. "Once I saw through the illusions I saw they were…well, weird-looking things, like fetuses, only grown to adult size in that form. They tried to seduce me."

There was a stifled gasp around the room, and the elderly woman called Winnie fanned her face as if embarrassed for Kane. "You poor, poor dear," Winnie said. "That's a terrible, wicked thing."

Kane thanked her with a stern nod. "They seemed to be guided by just one thing—desire. You think maybe they could be parts of Lilitu, too?" Kane suggested.

"More bodies," Brigid agreed, nodding, "malformed parts that didn't grow properly, operating with only the most primal personality traits. Lilitu's rebirth process must have been like something out of a nightmare."

"There are so many aspects to Ezili," Hurbon agreed, understanding the situation from his own frame of reference.

Brigid ran her hand through her brightly colored hair, trying to see what it was she was missing. "Id, ego and superego," she said, speaking to herself. "There's a third major aspect out there that's missing from this equation."

"Could it be these seductresses that Kane met with?" Hurbon asked.

"No, they're vessels," Brigid concluded, "mindless abortions that I believe only have the most basic components of Lilitu's personality within them." In her mind's eye, Brigid was tracing back through the literature she had read on the pioneering psychologist Sigmund Freud. "We still need to identify the superego, the moralizing, critical aspect of her personality. The judge keeping the id and ego in check."

It was suddenly so obvious that Brigid almost fell from her seat, her breath catching in her throat. "Mr. Hurbon," she asked, "is there an aspect of your goddess that you'd associate with judgment?"

Papa Hurbon scratched at his jowls for a moment, his fingernails grinding against the darkening line of stubble there. "Ezili Freda Dahomey, I guess," he proposed. "She's above the normal folk, like a landowner or—" He stopped then, too, following where Brigid was looking.

They were all now staring at the elderly woman with the exceptionally pale skin, the aristocratic lady who had called herself Winnie.

"You told me that your name was Winifred," Brigid said, and the woman nodded.

"Freda," Hurbon said, his voice soft. "Freda Dahomey. As I live and breathe."

Like a grandmother proud of her children, Winnie smiled and gave them a single nod. "A pleasure to meet you."

Nine months earlier.

FIRST BODY CLAMBERED out of the wreckage of the escape pod as the man called Papa Hurbon bowed. She lurched forward on malformed legs, her ungainly gait a series of stuttering, rocky steps. He had called her Ezili Coeur Noir, Ezili the black-hearted, and she had begun to recall a life that might yet be.

Behind her, still hidden among the wreckage of the spacecraft that was gradually sinking into the bog, another figure had emerged from the chalice of rebirth to observe this exchange. Unlike the first, Second Body was more finished, a properly crafted thing. Where First Body had dark, rough skin like a lizard's scales, Second Body glowed with luminescence, and the ooze of amniotic fluids still clung to her pallid form. Her hair was chalk-white and her flesh was pale, too, almost without pigment. Where First Body had been born almost as a dead thing, Second Body seemed vibrant with life in that moment, a beautiful, shapely young woman's body within which surged the memories of Lilitu, rushing in to fill an empty vessel.

When First Body stalked away from the crash site, Hurbon struggling beneath the weight of the astronavigator's chair beside her, Second Body took her first tentative step out into the open air. Lilitu's memories slotted gingerly into place. This was Earth, the primary outpost of the Annunaki, she recalled.

Second Body brushed at her cooling skin, wiping the amniotic goo from her bare arms, shaking it from her naked body. High above, out there at the edges of the atmosphere, *Tiamat* had self-destructed, and the burst of ectoplasmic force was only now dissipating from the ionosphere. Second Body looked up, as if sensing her dragon mother still up there in the stars. There was thick tree cover here in the bayou, and Second Body tilted her head as she sought a gap in the leaves through which to see.

Her form was graceful where First Body's had been ugly and strained, with shapely legs taking long strides across the boggy marsh with surety and poise. Her white hair seemed to shimmer in the light as she walked toward the spot in the clearing where the golden rays of the sun struck the ground. As Second Body reached that spot, the sun struck her body for the first time as it carved a path through the cover of the trees.

Second Body seemed to wither beneath the sun's rays, her skin blistering. She stepped back into the shadows, her skin smoldering as if she had been on fire. Something is wrong, the still-forming mind of Lilitu realized. The rebirth procedure had failed to complete; this body was defective, flawed. There was an absence of melatonin in this body, so it could not color, could not tan. Without such simple protection, the sun's rays were deadly to Second Body, and having been touched by this elemental enemy, her body seared with burning pain.

There had been a disease that struck the Annunaki, a rare genetic disorder called scarabae sickness. It scarred the body, causing it to fail and forcing its sufferers to hide themselves from the sun, lest their bodies burn away.

Cowering in the shadows of the escape pod, Second Body watched as her pale form became wizened, wrinkles of age puckering the flesh, making it old before it had ever managed a proper taste of youth. Second Body hid in the darkest shadows of the wreckage as her body spasmed and her pituitary gland fizzled, popping with the hormones that should have made her grow. For an hour or more she remained there, racked with searing pain so potent that it obliterated all other thoughts.

When she had finally emerged again from the ruined escape pod, Second Body was no longer a shapely maiden. Like the Moon, she had gone from maiden to crone, living in a pale, twilight body close to the end of its life. Lilitu's memory had almost entirely wiped, a kindly, bland sort of senility taking its place.

Strangely, from the point of view of the old Lilitu, Second Body would be broken, for she had nurturing qualities unutterably alien to Lilitu's true nature. In actuality it was a self-preservation instinct gone awry—her first steps on Earth had almost killed her, the sun's fearsome rays poisonous to her new form. In defence, she had sought to shelter herself and so, by extension, those she came into contact with.

This old woman, this Second Body, would be Ezili Freda Dahomey. The seeds of the identity dwelled somewhere deep within her, and Papa Hurbon had stirred them when he had named her sister, her deathly First Body.

"YOU WERE CASTING the illusions," Brigid said to the old woman sitting at the kitchen table. "You used the mechanics of the chair to somehow… I don't know, make people see perversions. Why would you do that?"

"Because the perversions were there anyway," the woman who had been revealed as Ezili Freda Dahomey, voodoo *loa,* explained. "I simply tried to make them palatable. Admittedly, I became a little caught up in the dream after a while—sitting in that chair can become very confusing."

"So," Kane said, making his way from the doorway to address the white-haired old woman, "you're basically Lilitu." As the final word left his mouth, Kane raised the Sin Eater in his hand and targeted the woman right between the eyes.

"Kane—wait!" Brigid cried.

"What? And let this worthless parasite on the human race escape us once again?" Kane snapped.

Across the table from Brigid, Grant pushed his chair back and commanded his own Sin Eater into his hand, adding its threat to Kane's. "Let's ace one of these lizard faces while we—"

"No!" Brigid insisted. "Listen to me. Hers is a personality so fractured that it has taken on three distinct physical forms. If we don't put her back together, Lilitu will became increasingly insane. The black-hearted aspect—Ezili Coeur Noir—is already gearing up to wipe out all organic life with the Red Weed. We'll need all three of them if we're to halt this madness. It'll take all three personalities to make Lilitu sane again."

Kane brayed a mocking laugh. "You must be thinking of a different Annunaki overlord, Baptiste." He spit. "Lilitu was never sane." He shoved at the elderly woman in front of him with the muzzle of his blaster, making her cower back into her chair.

"You're mistaking sanity with morality, Kane," Brigid insisted, "and the two are not the same. I don't think for a moment that what Lilitu did to us or to humanity was right, but she always applied logic in her schemes. She may be repellent but she was never insane. Right now she's two hours away from destroying everything. And that woman at whom you're pointing your gun may well be the key to stopping her."

Kane's blue-gray eyes flicked from Winnie to Brigid and back. The elderly woman sat there quite calmly, not making any sudden movements the way the other one— Ellie or Maitresse Ezili or whatever she was called—had when Kane had challenged her by the upstairs rooms. Reluctantly, Kane lowered his pistol. "You've never steered me wrong before, Baptiste," he said. "And you had better be damn right this time."

A moment later Grant followed his partner's lead, commanding his Sin Eater back to the wrist sheath beneath his coat with a flinch of his tendons. "So, how do we do this, then?" he asked.

"Three distinct beings, each carrying a fractured thread of Lilitu's personality," Brigid mused. "What we really need to do is to find a way to pull these three people together into one being again."

"Impossible!" Papa Hurbon retorted. "These are separate aspects of a most wonderful spirit. You cannot simply...fuse them together."

Kane fixed the voodoo priest with a stern look. "This ain't your goddess, buckaroo. This is just some crazy alien whose only real desire is to enslave the human race, crushing us under her heel." Glancing at Winnie, the ex-Mag added, "No offense, ma'am."

Winnie smiled, saying nothing. She seemed somewhat bemused by the whole conversation.

Then Brigid spoke up, her words coming slowly. "No, what he just said," she began, looking at Hurbon, "that's it. We'll fuse them together again."

"Care to repeat that for the slower members of the class?" Kane asked.

"Fusion," Brigid said. "The cold-fusion generator at Redoubt Mike, the one that had been moth-balled when the mat-trans prototype was switched for a different power source. If we could open that up somehow and—" she gave a sideways look at Winnie, but the old woman seemed to be oblivious that she was being spoken about "—join them back together."

"You mean place—" Kane began and stopped himself, too.

"You don't need her," Hurbon interrupted, realizing how both Baptiste and Kane were tiptoeing around mentioning the need to use the aristocratic old woman who was really Ezili Freda Dahomey. "Voodoo works with pieces that represent the whole, so you'd just need some part of her."

Kane glared at him. "What, so suddenly you're all for this?"

Hurbon met the ex-Mag's fierce gaze. "Ezili Coeur Noir is out of control," he said, "and if what you and your companions say is true then we—which is to say I—am very much in danger. Now I love her and will worship her until the day I die, make no mistake, white-bread, but I sure as hell want that day to be a long, long way off."

Kane looked over his shoulder then, down the corridor to where the plump form of Maitresse Ezili remained struggling within the invisible binding. "Are you able to keep that one busy?"

"Not forever," Hurbon admitted, nervously fiddling with the little doll in his hands.

"What about Ezili Coeur Noir?" Kane asked. "You have anything in your bag of tricks that can stun her temporarily so we can hold on to her for long enough to try this fusion thing?"

Papa Hurbon reached into his saddlebag once more and produced another doll, this time wrapped like an Egyptian mummy in ribbon of the purest white. What little could be seen of the doll showed it was thin, with yellow eyes and dark skin on its face like a lizard's. It looked like Ezili Coeur Noir, and it also bore a striking resemblance to Lilitu, albeit with her skin blackened. "I made this to hide myself from her," he said. "While the doll is wrapped in white she won't come near me."

Kane looked at the strange fetish, realization dawning. "That's why the undead can't see this place, isn't it? That's why they won't come near. Because your little dolly there repels them."

"It blinds Ezili Coeur Noir to my presence," Hurbon confirmed. "Little wonder that her servants are confused."

Grant checked the corridor, shaking his head. "Now, I understand guns a whole lot better than I understand dolls," he said, "but I'm starting to wonder if we don't have us an arsenal here that could take on the gods."

"Well, one goddess at least," Kane agreed.

Sitting at the table, Brigid seemed to be doing some

swift calculations in her head. "I don't have the expertise to pull this off," she finally admitted. "The fusion generator works by meshing atoms together using hydrolysis, but how we might apply the same principles of attraction to a personality…I don't know."

Across the room, Kane fixed Brigid with a serious look. "Baptiste," he said, "we have access to the smartest living scientific brains on the planet. Speak to Lakesh, speak to Philboyd, get Bry on it—whoever. If anyone can get this working, it's you."

"You're asking me to remotely coordinate a dozen scientists to engage an energy system deemed too unstable for use," Brigid said, "so that we can try to bind a false goddess back together into one functioning psyche."

"Who's not mad," Kane added. "Remember that part—that's crucial."

Brigid narrowed her eyes in disdain. "You really have no conception of the impossible, do you?"

Kane smiled his cheery, lopsided grin. "Not yet."

Chapter 19

Brigid explained her idea to Lakesh via Commtact.

"I'll be honest," she said, "it's not really a plan, just a concept for one."

In the Cerberus ops center located in the Bitterroot Mountains of Montana, Lakesh nodded his head sagely as Brigid's familiar voice piped out from the speaker at the communications desk. "It is, however, one with intriguing possibilities," he mused. "Cold fusion was discarded as a viable energy source in the 1990s because of the difficulties involved in stabilizing the procedure. Indeed, for many years scientists argued that it was pathological science, which is to say that it produced false-positive results."

"But we utilized the cold-fusion generator to engage the Louisiana redoubt's mat-trans," Brigid said, "so we know that the sequencer there works."

"Indeed," Lakesh agreed. He felt a little rejuvenated having taken a three-hour nap, but he had been woken as soon as Brigid's query came through to the ops center. Now, the head of the Cerberus operation sipped at a cooling mug of tea in an effort to revive himself as the other core members of the ops room bustled around, making notes off of Brigid's suggestions.

The ops center was manned by a number of top-notch scientists, so-called "freezies" who had been placed in suspended animation at the end of the twentieth century and hidden on the Manitius Moon Base, to be revived about two hundred years later in the world of the outlanders. Lakesh, too, had been a well-respected scientist in his day, specializing in physics and cybernetics. His early work with the mat-trans units had been considered ground-breaking for its time.

With a snap of his fingers, Lakesh caught the attention of Brewster Philboyd, who sat at the monitoring desk, nervously polishing the lenses of his black-framed spectacles with a cloth. "Brewster, what is the status of Mike's reactor right now?" Lakesh asked.

Brewster tapped a brief sequence into his terminal as he responded. "The cold-fusion reactor at Redoubt Mike is currently powered down," he confirmed. "We curtailed its output five minutes after CAT Alpha arrived on site."

"What if we leave the reactor powered down, Brigid?" Lakesh offered. "The security locks would disengage and you could access the core with the applicable maintenance codes. Once the access hatch was open, you could lead your prey there and thus trap your problem inside. At that point, we could reengage the system and—"

"Negative," Kane's voice came over the Commtact link. "This is Lilitu we're talking about. Right now she's a pumped-up, out-of-control psycho goddess. We might be able to trick her into the reactor but we wouldn't have a chance of containing her long enough for you to get the thing operational."

"Just how powerful would you estimate she is right now in her current form?" Lakesh asked.

"She's bringing the dead back to life with a touch," Kane argued. "I saw her holding a file of papers, and they were literally deteriorating at her touch. Paint blisters at her approach, flies die when they near her. We're talking some really serious mojo."

"So you think she could atrophy the casing around the cold-fusion reactor before we could power it up?" Lakesh asked, unable to keep the surprise from his voice.

"If you mean, could she rot it with her touch," Kane said to summarize, "I'd go with a distinct maybe."

"Kane's right," Brigid agreed. "We're going to need the reactor operative when we lead her inside. It's…" Brigid's voice trailed off.

"Brigid?" Lakesh prompted after a moment, wondering if the radio connection had been somehow severed.

"Still here," Brigid said in her chirpy voice. "I was going to say 'it's our only chance,' but I honestly don't know that this will actually work. We're proposing to unlock an admittedly dangerous system of energy creation to use to imprison a would-be goddess of death. I wonder if we're not creating more trouble here than we're solving. It seems a hell of a risk."

Lakesh took another sip of his steeping tea before he answered. "Risks are what make life interesting, my dear," he reminded Brigid.

Over the loudspeaker, Lakesh and Brewster heard Brigid take a deep, steadying breath. "Okay," she said, "so can we get the thing live and open in time for us to get Ezili Coeur Noir and her other physical manifestations inside?"

"We can override the security protocols from here," Lakesh suggested, "but getting the access paneling open will be an on-site job. Someone there will have to do it."

There was a momentary silence over the comm network then, as a decision was reached one thousand miles away in a dilapidated mansion house in the Louisiana bayou.

"Okay, we have us a volunteer," Kane said.

"Excellent," Lakesh replied. "We'll start working on

the security system at our end, and I'll amass a brain trust to look into the possibility of igniting the reactor once those protocols have been paralyzed. We'd need to employ a specific output to do what Brigid has asked, of course, which may require a little theoretical experimentation at our end. I have Donald already working up a computer simulation model that should be able to give us some insights in about—Donald?"

At one of the plain desks of the room, the dour-faced Donald Bry was working at a computer terminal, his fingers playing furiously across its keyboard as he brought up a schematic of an energy reactor. At the call of his name, he looked up from his frantic programming work. "I've found a reactor simulation in our database which we can adapt, but it will take a day to jiggle it to represent the cold fusion system."

"Eight hours minimum," Lakesh reported over the Commtact.

"Scratch that," Kane replied. "Remember that Red Weed virus we spoke about earlier? Remember I saw a batch of it being mixed while we were inside the redoubt's main hangar. I'd estimate we have maybe three hours to clear this thing before the Red Weed goes live."

"Heralding the cessation of all life on Earth," Lakesh concluded, speaking as if to himself.

Brewster Philboyd glanced up from the communications array with an expression of concern. "Dr. Singh?"

Without answering, Lakesh strode across the large room until he stood at the foremost point, where all of the terminal operators could see him. "Listen up, people," he announced, projecting his loud voice. "We have a critical situation here, and it's all hands to the pump. I require a full analysis of the prospective effects of cold fusion on a living body, both human and Annunaki. I also need a working theory of how we might combat an outbreak of a genetically modified and very virulent strain of anthrax. This needs to be done now—I require your answers in one hour." With that he clapped his hands, and the staff gathered themselves into teams to work out their theories.

Then Lakesh turned to Donald Bry. "Donald, you may as well abort the simulator program," he regretfully explained.

Bry brushed his hand through his tousled copper curls. "I'll start on breaking the security protocols instead," he said, his enthusiasm not dampened.

Then Lakesh was back at the communications station, advising Kane's field team that they were on the case. "We'll report back in one hour," he assured Kane. "Just figure out what you need to do on-site and if you require anything else from us."

"Well, if you've got any luck going spare..." Kane began flippantly.

"I'll send it along, old friend," Lakesh assured him before curtailing the Commtact link.

Around the hectic operations room, clusters of like-minded scientists were drawing up flow charts and diagrams as they began to brainstorm ideas. Lakesh looked around, proud of the way his people rallied when asked. Once this crisis was over—*if* it ever was over—he would have to thank them personally.

In one corner of the ops room however, close to the doors, an ex-Magistrate called Edwards rubbed his forehead with the palm of his hand. "All this science geek stuff is giving me a headache," he muttered to Domi.

Edwards was a tall man whose broad shoulders seemed to strain against the confines of his white jumpsuit. His right ear had a nick in it where it had been caught with a bullet almost a year before.

Along with Domi, Edwards had been tasked to guard the ops center, but he felt the driving need to get some fresh air, having been cooped up in the bunker for almost three days. His headaches had been getting worse over the past few weeks and he wondered if he may be coming down with some sickness.

Quietly, Edwards slipped out of the busy room and made his way along the vast arterial corridor toward the accordion-style doors that served as the redoubt's exit. While the science boffins were busy with their theories, Edwards figured he would take a few minutes to himself, out on the rock plateau overlooking the Bitterroot Mountains.

Outside, the afternoon sun beat down, barely a cloud in the sky. Edwards smiled as he took in the magnificent vista, and a strange tune came to mind. As he tried to recall the tune, he could already feel the weight of his headache beginning to abate.

Nearby over a hundred pairs of eyes watched as Edwards walked out onto the rocky plateau, humming a few bars of the tune that seemed to be caught in his head. Edwards took another step out onto the rocky plateau, taking in a deep lungful of the fresh mountain air, entirely unaware of the watchers observing him.

After a moment, still humming the strange tune that was stuck in his head, Edwards turned and strolled slowly back to the open entrance to the redoubt. As he did so, one of those sets of eyes flashed bright as molten lava for just an instant, so brief that an observer would have thought that they had imagined it had they not been looking specifically for it.

MEANWHILE, one thousand miles distant at the House Lilandera, Papa Hurbon was cooking something up in the kitchen.

Hurbon had produced a small stub of a chalklike substance and, with Grant's help, had eased himself to the floor where he sketched out an irregular circle on the ruined tiles. The chalk was in fact farine, the flour used in voodoo ritual, and the corpulent priest pressed it against the rotted tiles of the floor to create the specific markings he knew by heart within that circle.

"What are those marks supposed to be?" Grant asked as he pushed the table back a little to give Hurbon more room.

Brigid scooted her chair to follow, for she was busily sketching something of her own in a little notebook she had retrieved from her pants pocket. She wore a pair of glasses now, perched at the end of her nose. Brigid was slightly far-sighted.

"They are called *vévés*," Hurbon explained. "If we are to enter into battle with the *loa,* we must pool as much strength as we can."

"Seems reasonable," Grant acknowledged, feeling like a fraud. He had grown up in the strict regime of Cobaltville. To him, this hocus-pocus seemed anything but reasonable—it felt as if they had stepped back one hundred years, to the days when superstition had ruled the old Deathlands, before the Program of Unification had brought rationalism and enlightenment to the world.

Hurbon drew a large symbol that took up more than half the kitchen's floor space. The symbol looked a little like a surrealist sailboat to Grant's eyes, with a triangular shape at its bottom and a base line and mast above that.

"This is the *vévé* for Ogoun," Papa Hurbon told him. "He is warlike, but he truly represents authority, and I believe that is what we will need in this quest. Authority over the rogue *loa* who challenge the natural order of things. Authority over the queen of all things dead."

Moving like a crab across the cold floor, Hurbon continued sketching for a few more minutes while Grant watched. Hurbon's strokes with the marking flour were bold and sure, creating designs he had doubtless drawn a thousand times before. When he was finished, the floor looked like a spider had gotten loose with a stick of chalk. Scribbled symbols were all over, forming a loose circle that congregated in the center of the room.

Outside the house the shambling figures of the undead began to shuffle with more direction, as if becoming alerted to something new in their presence.

While Hurbon had been working and Brigid continued making her own notes, Kane went to check on Maitresse Ezili. She seemed almost as if she had been frozen, her mouth stuck in a silent scream that showed off her pearl-white teeth. As Kane neared her, the woman's yellow eyes flickered toward him, watching his movements.

"You want out, don't you?" Kane taunted. "Meanwhile, we're trying to figure a way we might be able to fix all this."

He took another step closer to the constrained woman standing in the center of the hallway. "See, you're not complete, you're half a person." Kane pointed back to the kitchen and told her, "Baptiste in there—she's book-smart like you wouldn't believe. She says you're an ego without an id or a superego, you've become detached from them somehow during a messed-up rebirth. That's what's made you so crazy, trapping people into this little love factory. Baptiste says that if the ego is the rider then the id is the horse, whatever that means. I guess she's really saying that you aren't going very far while you're in pieces like this, you're just trudging over the same little furrow."

Maitresse Ezili glared at him with her lizard's eyes, the fury burning deep within them like a curse.

Fearless, Kane brought his own face close to the woman's. "Oh, sure, you feel that way now but you'll thank me when it's all over," he told her. "If it makes you feel any better about this, the last time we met and you were whole, you almost killed me. Maybe you'll get better at it next go around."

With that, Kane strode back to the kitchen, leaving the magically incarcerated form of the Annunaki goddess-turned-voodoo-*loa* alone in the dilapidated hallway. "Don't expect me to cut you a break, though," he added before disappearing into the kitchen.

When he entered the kitchen, Kane saw that Papa Hurbon was back in his wheelchair, a half-dozen strange designs sketched out in white across the floor.

Hurbon's hands were toying with the little doll wrapped in white ribbon as he spoke. "This ribbon blinds Ezili Coeur Noir to my presence," he said. "As long as it is wrapped around the doll, she will be turned away the way you dissuade a cat, as if smelling something unpleasant."

Grant was about to say something as he stood downwind of the sweaty voodoo priest, but he thought better of it.

"What about us?" Kane asked as he paced into the room, glancing back at the statue-still figure of Ellie standing in the corridor.

"It works by proximity," Hurbon told him. "Which means that so long as you're near me and the doll's intact, Ezili Coeur Noir won't come near you. That's why she hasn't come here, and her zombie people avoid the place. The spell drives them away."

"Ingenious," Grant said.

"Yeah, but it's no good," Kane huffed. "We need to

be near this psycho bitch to trap her. If your spell keeps turning her away, she's going to start looking for another date."

"Some good-looking dead guy with a full set of teeth," Brigid mocked.

"So what do you require?" Hurbon asked, turning the doll over in his hands.

"Catnip?" Kane ventured.

Sitting at the scarred kitchen table using a short pencil to jot notes in her small pad Brigid Baptiste glanced up at Hurbon and the others arrayed around the table. "We need to depower her for long enough to hold her and move her without getting ourselves killed." She raised the pad and showed Hurbon the simple sketch of the layout of the redoubt that she had drawn.

"I could hold her in the same way I have Maitresse Ezili out there," Hurbon mused, "but that would require me to drop the spell of concealment. I don't know…"

Grant slapped the voodoo priest on the back. "Don't worry, we'll take care of you."

Papa Hurbon laughed then, a full basso roll like distant thunder. "That is not as reassuring as you think it is, Grant," he told the towering ex-Mag.

Grant shrugged. "It's the best we can do."

"To bind Ezili Coeur Noir as you've requested," Hurbon stated, "I'll need to remove the hex that blinds her to my presence."

"How soon would it be until she sees you?" Brigid asked.

"I could keep out of her way indefinitely," Hurbon said with a smile. "But that's not what you want me to do now, is it, my pretty little peach?"

Brigid shook her head. "If we can capture her at the redoubt we have a chance of using the fusion generator to entrap her," she said. "So we need her there."

"And we need her calm," Kane pointed out. "Lilitu fought like a hellcat when she was alive. I don't want to begin to imagine what she'll be like this time around, what with being half-past dead and all."

"I can hold her for a limited time," Hurbon said, "but I'd need to tread into the Kafou, the crossroads of our world and hers."

"Land of the chalk drawings here not enough?" Grant asked, gesturing to the newly decorated floor.

Hurbon smiled, a grossly wide display of teeth in his bucketlike jaw. "The *vévés* charge the batteries, but we still have to use the equipment," he explained. As he spoke, he struggled to reach behind him for something stored at the back of his wheelchair.

Grant stood and offered the crippled voodoo priest a hand. "What are you looking for here, man?" he asked.

"There's a hidden panel," Hurbon explained.

Grant ran his fingertips along the back of the wheelchair until he located a disguised popper beneath the material that covered the seat. He snapped the popper open and the dark cloth covering the back panel folded back on a triangular crease. Grant saw now that the seat contained a false panel within which items could be stored. Inside, held at a sharp diagonal, was a long length of decorated leather—it was a sheath within which sat a sword of two feet in length. With the impressive length of the blade, the scabbard had just barely fit beneath the hidden panel.

"You find it?" Hurbon asked.

Grant held out the sword, laying it across his palms

in the way of ceremonial presentation. "This what you're looking for?"

"The *ku-bha-sah*," Hurbon said with a nod.

Winnie gasped and shied away from the weapon as Hurbon accepted it.

Standing by the doorway, Kane peered across at the wheelchair-bound priest as he unsheathed the sword. "I seem to remember borrowing that little pig-sticker from you not so long ago."

Hurbon nodded. "Indeed, but you had no concept of its true power."

"Care to enlighten us?" Kane asked grimly.

"The *ku-bha-sah* is a ceremonial blade," Hurbon explained as he placed the empty sheath on the table. The blade glinted in the daylight that spilled into the kitchen through the dirt-smeared windows. "It is used to cut a rent from our world to theirs."

The three Cerberus warriors nodded warily. They had come across a knife that possessed similar properties to those Hurbon described, and it had created a dimensional rift—an infinity breach—that had very nearly ended in disaster.

"You said 'ceremonial,' didn't you?" Brigid clarified after that pregnant pause. "Not actual."

"The *ku-bha-sah* represents the cutting of the cross point," Hurbon agreed, "where worlds meet."

Then Hurbon gave out a list of instructions, things he required to perform the ceremony he had in mind. They didn't have much time to perform his ritual, but he insisted that he would need blood to complete the arcane procedure. "Sacrifice is key," he said to assure them.

Brigid considered querying this, wondering that it was just a populist myth concerning the voodoo religion, but she chose not to. Hurbon was a practicing Bizango, she reminded herself, the darkest and most secretive of all voodoo schools. His ways were bound to seem extreme to an outsider.

"It matter what you sacrifice?" Grant asked.

"I have preferences, but it's about the circle of life," Hurbon said.

"There were mice upstairs," Kane pointed out. "They do?"

Hurbon nodded.

"In which case they're probably all around, then," Grant muttered. "I'll go look."

Thus, with eminent practicality, Grant pushed out the back door of the mansion house to search in the undergrowth there.

Outside the door, just three feet from where Grant exited, an animated corpse was waiting, as if poised for him. It unleashed a banshee howl as it came rushing toward him.

Chapter 20

Before Grant could react, the walking undead man tossed something at him from one of his deteriorating fists. Automatically, Grant's hand went up, batting the thing away in a flinch reaction. It was a rock about the size of a baseball, and Grant yelped as it was struck from his arm.

Then the undead man was upon him, jaws extended as he reached for Grant's throat with black, leathery hands.

Grant gut-punched the undead man, his big fist driving into his body like a pile driver. Appropriately, it was like punching deadweight, the corpse-thing barely moving under the force of Grant's blow.

Kane was in the doorway by then, his eyes going wide as he took in the remarkable situation. "The hell…?"

Grant reached for the undead man's wrists as his hands clenched around Grant's throat. "They may not be able to see the house," Grant rasped as he fended off his gruesome attacker, "but they sure as fuck can see *us!*"

Kane scanned the immediate area as he rushed to help his friend, making sure there weren't any more of the living dead things waiting to ambush him. The backyard seemed otherwise clear, but the vegetation was so dense it was hard to be sure.

The corpse-thing secured a grip on Grant's throat, jagged nails ripping into the skin of the ex-Mag's neck as he pressed tighter. Then Kane was behind the moving undead man, getting a solid grip around his blackened body and yanking him away from Grant.

Grant choked out another breath as he found himself pulled along by the struggling corpse-thing. The thing had, quite literally, a death grip on his throat now, and the breath was being squeezed from him in a painful rasp.

Behind the animated corpse, Kane struggled to pull the attacker off his partner. "Let go, dammit," he snarled. "Let go!"

The corpse-thing swept its head back, smashing the back of his crown against Kane's face with such brutality that the ex-Mag's nose began streaming blood. Kane held on, shaking his head as dark spots whirled in front of his eyes.

Unable to breathe, Grant sank to his knees in the dirt. Desperately, he grabbed both hands around one of the undead abomination's wrists and applied all the pressure he could. His vision was swirling; he needed to take a breath. Grant pushed against the pressure points of the corpse-thing's wrist, trying to force him to release his uncanny grip, but the undead thing had no pressure points.

A trail of blood spattering his face, Kane kept pulling at the undead man, digging his heels into the moist earth of the yard as he tried to get him away from his friend. Some sixth sense—that legendary point man instinct of Kane's—kicked in and the ex-Mag glanced over his shoulder. Kane's steely gray eyes narrowed as he spied movement. At the edge of the overgrown garden, where a low fence of rotted wooden slats could just barely be seen amid the greenery, another walking corpse came trundling toward them. Perhaps she had been called here by her undead colleague or perhaps she had simply heard the sounds of the frantic brawl in the yard. Whatever, the thing lumbered toward the Cerberus warriors even as they struggled with the first corpse-thing.

The second corpse-thing appeared to be a tall woman, gangly in death even if perhaps she had not been in life. Her lifeless eye sockets were fixed on the struggling figures by the house, and she groaned in grim determination as she reached for Kane's head.

Brigid appeared in the doorway at that moment, alerted by the noise of the scuffle. She held the metal bar she had freed from the truck, and she rushed into the yard, swinging it at the corpse-thing like a baseball batter. At the same time, the undead woman grabbed Kane's face from behind, pulling him with such force that his back arched as he struggled against her. The metal pole slammed into the corpse woman's chest, breaking multiple ribs and knocking her back, forcing her to let go of Kane's face with a tangle of torn hair in her hands. The corpse woman hissed, struggling to retain her balance as she tottered back from the blow.

Brigid swung again, smacking the undead woman across the face with the end of the metal stick, keeping her distance as she slashed her again.

Kneeling by the back door, Grant gave one final, desperate shove against the wrist of the undead foe who was strangling him, and he heard a loud crack. The intense pressure of that grip suddenly eased, and Grant found himself still holding the corpse-thing's wrist as he took a desperate breath. The left wrist bone had snapped, breaking apart. With no flesh to hold it in place, the hand had just broken away.

Still behind the undead man, Kane yanked again and found himself toppling backward with the corpse as its grip on his partner finally failed. They rolled in the dirt, the weight of the undead man pressing down on Kane's chest.

Kane grunted as he slammed across the hard soil, his fists jabbing at the corpse-thing atop him, trying to shove him away.

Then Grant was standing, and he grasped the undead man by his remaining hand, pulling him up to his feet. Kane pushed himself off the ground and assisted Grant. The two of them grabbed an arm each and propelled the corpse-thing across the yard. The undead figure sailed eight feet in the air before hurtling into the deep grass, limbs in disarray. As he landed, chunks of diseased flesh broke away, and the two ex-Magistrates watched in disgust as his head snapped off and rolled across the ground, still hissing out a weird, angry screech long after it had been disconnected from the neck.

Behind the ex-Mags, Brigid was finishing off their other undead opponent, slamming the corpse woman repeatedly with the metal staff. Each vicious blow knocked a chunk from the undead thing's decrepit body, and after a while it had become more a battle of savage erosion than actual combat, until there was no longer enough of the undead woman to fight back. Brigid removed her glasses and wiped the crud from their lenses.

"Let's find this sacrifice and get out of sight," Kane advised as he scanned the area around the house, his eyes flicking past the two corpses that lay unmoving in the dirt. "Won't do to be caught out here again until we're prepped for the endgame."

Standing beside Kane, Grant was hacking, trying to clear his throat. It felt scarred, and he spit into the grass before turning back to the building. "Didn't realize how localized Hurbon's black magic shit was," he snarled.

"Guess once we're out of the house we become targets again, huh?"

Brigid leaned down at the rain gutter that ran beside the back door. Beside the drainage outlet, a small grate covered an airbrick, several of its clay grill struts missing. She cupped her hands and waited. It took two minutes, but finally a mouse poked its nose out and came to her as she held out a morsel of rotten zombie flesh. She waited until it stepped close enough that she could grab it.

They had their sacrifice.

"ONCE THE *ku-bha-sah* is charged," Hurbon explained after he had sacrificed the mouse and drained its blood in a pattern across the floor, "it will work in a manner that can help you."

"'You'?" Kane repeated, standing close to the back door entrance to the room. "You mean, me?"

"You've wielded the *ku-bha-sah* before, Kane," Hurbon said with a nod. "Besides, you don't expect a crippled old bastard like me to do battle with my mistress's army of the dead, do you?"

"And what are you going to be doing while I kick me some zombie butt?" Kane asked, glancing nervously over his shoulder to make sure nothing else was moving out there in the yard.

Hurbon reached into his leather satchel again and removed a spindle of black ribbon, placing it in his lap beside the doll that represented Ezili Coeur Noir. The doll was currently wrapped in white cord. "I'm going to hold her for you," he said as he began loosening the white ribbon.

Then Papa Hurbon unwound the ribbon that had been coiled around the cloth fetish of Ezili Coeur Noir. Though white, the outer layer looked suddenly dirty when the hidden turns of the ribbon began to show, for the doll had been handled many times since the voodoo priest had first cast his binding weeks before.

Kane watched, feeling uneasy as he saw the doll for the first time in two months. It was a remarkably ugly thing, made more so by its subtextual association with a child's toy in Kane's mind. Its body was a dark color like charred wood, and twin eyes had been sewn into its face in a cotton of bright, putrescent yellow sealed with wax to make them shine. Kane had seen the doll months before, when he had visited Hurbon's shack-cum-temple for the second time. Back then, Hurbon had been crafting the thing, shaping it for his purpose of repelling Ezili Coeur Noir. Even then, Kane had recognized the thing as Lilitu; the simplicity of its design somehow made the connection more obvious than the physical presence of her decaying body.

"Once this comes off," Hurbon told his little audience of four in the Louisiana kitchen, "we can't turn back. You folks are sure now?"

Kane nodded. "Quit showboating and let's get this thing done."

Hurbon nodded, pulling back the final fold of white ribbon. "May take a few minutes, depending on how close she is," he explained, "but she'll be able to see the house if she comes looking now."

Grant had made his way back to one of the dirt-streaked windows of the kitchen, and he watched the over-grown vegetation there suspiciously as the other spoke.

Brigid folded up her little pad and removed the square-framed spectacles she wore at the end of her nose. "What's next?" she asked.

"You want to combine her aspects," Hurbon stated, "you need to get them all together."

"Can't be done," Brigid said, tapping the front of her pad. "I thought we might be able to use an interphaser to do it, but I can't see any way to make it work."

"So long as we know where they are," Hurbon said, "I can do it." He peered back over to where the old woman who was Ezili Freda Dahomey was sitting. She appeared to be watching the whole ceremony with rapt attention. "Freda won't move now," he said.

"Say again?" Brigid requested.

Hurbon pointed to the symbols he had drawn on the floor with the mouse's blood. "She sat and watched as I trapped her," he explained with a chuckle. "Always was too trusting, that side of her."

Moving over to the doorway that led into the house, Kane checked on the figure of Maitresse Ezili. As before, she remained held in place in the corridor by the foot of the stairs, her struggles diminished to nothing. From a distance, Kane thought, she appeared dead, as if embalmed and placed in the hallway like some perverse decoration.

"So, what's next?" Kane asked.

Hurbon reached into his bag one last time, bringing out a small, sharp knife with a black handle. It looked like the kind of knife one might use to pare fruit. "Now," Hurbon explained, "different people do this in different ways but it works best if you can get a part of the person you intend to control."

Grant eyed the knife. "Like a finger?"

Hurbon smiled indulgently. "I prefer a lock of hair," he said. "Ever since Ezili Coeur Noir paid that final visit, my keenness for blood-letting ceremonies has soured. Mice notwithstanding."

"Understandable," Kane acknowledged.

"This here is what's called an *athame*," Hurbon said, turning the knife over in his grip. "I borrowed it a few years ago from a woman in Sao Paulo. A magic woman, fucking ancient she was. What they called her was the Bruja, said she'd lived forever.

"This knife is like any other knife," Hurbon continued, "only she'd charged it up with magic. She was crazy powerful in the ways of her craft, and she'd had this knife a long, long time."

Hurbon wheeled himself around so that he could cut a lock from Winnie's hair. The elderly woman sat still, staring straight ahead as if caught in a trance, as Hurbon cut a curl of her hair with a swish of the little blade. Once he was done, Hurbon took the tiny clipping and began to fiddle with it between his fingers, working at it until it became three distinct strands. Then he plaited the strands, his pudgy fingers surprisingly deft for such an operation. With that done, he handed the tiny plait—perhaps two inches in length—to Brigid Baptiste. "I guess you'll be the one who needs this," he said.

"We'll see," Brigid replied, taking the lock of hair and placing it safely in her glasses case along with her spectacles. A moment later she returned the case to its pocket in her jacket.

"Now, we also have the passionate one to deal with, huh?" Hurbon said, wheeling himself toward the door. "Passion sometimes comes out as anger, don't it?" He chuckled.

"You seem to be taking this in your stride," Kane observed as he stepped aside to let Hurbon wheel past and out into the corridor. "As it were," he added self-consciously, acknowledging the man's disability.

Papa Hurbon glanced over his shoulder to Kane. "This whole thing is a mess," he said. "Just happens to be the mess I've been practicing my whole life to deal with."

"That's how it happens sometimes," Kane agreed,

thinking of his own strange life's journey. He had been trained from birth to protect order; it was only later in life that he found out the order he had been duped into believing was the wrong one. So, in a sense, he really was still a Magistrate; it was only his jurisdiction that had changed

While Kane followed the voodoo *houngan* down the corridor, Brigid and Grant stopped to study the unmoving figure of Winnie, or Ezili Freda Dahomey. Grant waved his hand in front of the old woman's blank eyes, but she didn't move, didn't even flinch.

"Like she's not here no more," Grant said.

Brigid placed her hands to her face, rubbing at the tense feeling she felt around her nose from wearing her glasses. "That woman has slept through most of this little adventure," she said. "It seems somehow appropriate that she's out of it again, here at the end."

In the corridor, Hurbon stared at the impressive figure of Maitresse Ezili as she squirmed against the invisible bonds that held her.

Realizing the *houngan* was too short in his chair to reach for the woman's hair, Kane offered to cut a lock from her head. "You want me to do it?" he asked.

Hurbon handed Kane the *athame* blade and Kane took a lock of black hair from the back of the woman's head, two inches in all.

Then Kane gave the blade back to Hurbon along with the pinch of hair. "We about done?" he asked.

"Not yet," Hurbon said, still studying the woman. "Take her ring, there, from her finger. That one—" He pointed to the ring finger of her left hand. It was a gold ring holding a shining ruby, the gem a fierce red even in the ill-lit corridor.

Kane reached for the woman's hand and stopped, peering back at Hurbon. The man had produced the other doll, the one that represented Maitresse Ezili and had been entwined in black ribbon.

"Is this safe?" Kane asked.

"Why do you think I asked you to do it?" Hurbon replied with a knowing smile, clutching the doll tightly in his hands.

Nine months earlier.

SECOND BODY LAY shivering beside the wreckage of the escape pod as night mercifully fell in the Louisiana bayou. Naked, her skin still felt as if it was on fire from the punishing effects of the sun, red welters bubbling across her arm and forehead where they had been touched just briefly by the sun's fearsome rays.

The spacecraft itself had sunk lower into the mire, and Second Body could see now that it would be gone by the morning. She should be gone then, too, for being in the sun like this was dangerous for her. It had aged her terribly already, and her arms were covered in the beetlelike blotches of the sickness. She would hide those scars over time, clothe herself so that they could not be seen. The thought of clothes made her realize that she required a hiding place.

Behind Second Body, something within the sinking wreck moved, and a stream of garbled noises came from a still-forming throat. Afraid, Second Body shuffled away, putting more distance between herself and the figure who emerged from the wreckage, enough that it could not touch her. In appearance this one was larger, wider, and it looked to Ezili Freda Dahomey—to Second Body—more like a waddling sphere than an actual person. This was Third Body.

Third Body's skin was dark, far darker than Second

Body's but lighter than the desiccated flesh of her first-born sister. A balance had been struck by the malfunctioning sequencers of the chalice of rebirth, it seemed. Third Body was, in a sense, a halfway house between her two sisters, an amalgamation of them and a buffer between their traits. An ego, then, to sit between base instinct and overarching morality.

As Second Body watched, Third Body called her over. "Come now, sister," Third Body said. "I won't hurt you."

"The sun hurt me," Second Body stated, as if this explained her fear.

"I need your help," Third Body said, "before the ship sinks and we lose the others. I love them but I cannot free them on my own."

Love would be the guiding principle for Third Body, and all because the first thing she had been tasked to do after her birth was to decide whether to help the other newborns or to ignore them. The original Lilitu template would have left them to die, concerned only with her own survival. Once again, the personality growth had fractured, corrupted, made of Third Body something she should not have been.

Second Body, the one who would be Ezili Freda Dahomey, helped her larger sister, dragging other bodies from the escape pod. Each body had been generated there, made in the production line of the malfunctioning chalice of rebirth. They were half-formed things with fetus faces and pulpy limbs like dough. These were the failed attempts that the broken logic of the escape pod had tried to create as a body for Lilitu. Had they grown they might have looked like the old hybrid barons, but they had been aborted as soon as they had been birthed, the mush of the swamp finally leaking into the circuitry and ruining the birthing procedure. Instead, these half-born things had just the barest of personality traits: to want. Third Body would care for them, though, and for her older sister, too.

"We shall find a place where we can all be safe," Third Body announced. Beside her, the rag-tag group watched the escape pod sink without a trace beneath the marsh, in much the same way as the sun had set a few hours before, when Second Body had finally been able to stop cowering from it.

"We shall find a dark place for you," Third Body said to assure her Second Body sibling. "A place beneath the earth."

Second Body smiled, the old woman's wrinkles creasing her pale face. Third Body was love, and Second Body approved. Already, Second Body had an inkling of who her sister would be, of which face of the voodoo Ezili she would adopt. It would be the most loving aspect, the one known as Maitresse Ezili. She would take care of Second Body and she would take care of her sister-abortions. And she would care, too, for strangers and wayfarers; Maitresse Ezili would care for any outlanders who came into her reach. It would be nothing like her time as Lilitu or Lilu or any of the others. And it would be a beautiful life.

IN THE HALLWAY of the House Lilandera, Kane warily reached for the woman's hand. As he touched it, he felt a jolt go through him like electricity, powering through his hand and up his arm, sending shooting pain across his chest. As the jolt hit, the servo motors of his wrist holster began to whir automatically, and the Sin Eater tried to launch itself into his hand, finding its path blocked by Kane's bent wrist. "What the hell, Hurbon?" Kane shouted.

"You'll be fine, man," Papa Hurbon said. "Just remove the ring."

Kane shook as the strange power racked his body, feeling it running all over him, head to toe, as he clung to the hand of the housemistress.

"It's the binding," Hurbon said simply. "Didn't think she'd fight this much."

As he said that, Maitresse Ezili began to inch forward, her feet still in place but her body keeling slightly toward Kane. Still clinging to her hand, tremors running through his own body, Kane snagged the ring Hurbon had indicated and yanked it free, stumbling back three steps with the effort before striking the nearest wall with his back.

As Kane looked up, the woman he still thought of as Madam Ellie reached forward, her left hand clawing for his face. Automatically, Kane drove his own hands forward like a wedge, pushing Ellie's grasping hand away from him. She was terrifically quick, however, far more so than he had expected, and already her hand was reaching out, grabbing him by the throat. Before she could secure her grip, Kane grabbed Ellie's wrist, forcing her hand away from his neck.

Kane was backed up against the wall, nowhere to move to get clear of the woman's grasping hand. She was still stuck in place, too, he realized, unable to get her legs to move. But that didn't seem to diminish her determination to hurt him. Whatever his touch had done, it seemed to have fractured the invisible binding that held Maitresse Ezili in place, allowing her the freedom of movement in her hand and arm. With a sinking feeling, Kane recalled how strong the Annunaki overlords were in their original forms. If Ellie has half that strength…

Kane grunted with the effort of driving that reaching hand away. It seemed that somehow this Annunaki abortion had become stronger as she was held in place, and now all of that fearsome power had been centered into her single mobile hand. Fingers outstretched, the house-mistress Ezili drove her hand at Kane's eyes, endeavoring to blind him in her desperation.

Three feet from Kane, sitting in his wheelchair, Papa Hurbon wheeled himself backward even as Grant and Brigid appeared in the kitchen doorway after being alerted by the sounds of the skirmish.

"What's going on?" Grant snapped, the Sin Eater materializing in his hand.

Hurbon ignored him. Concentrating, the voodoo priest turned the *athame* blade over in his hand as he watched the now-moving form of Maitresse Ezili grab Kane's throat with her lone, mobile hand, driving the ex-Magistrate back against the wall with such force that the plaster crumbled, dust spewing across Kane's bloodied face.

"She's loose," Brigid screamed, her hand moving automatically to her hip holster.

"I can't make the shot," Grant snarled, trying to get closer. Papa Hurbon's wheelchair blocked his path and Kane's struggling form made it too dangerous from even this brief a distance.

As Grant tried to slink past the voodoo priest, Hurbon slapped the voodoo doll of Maitresse Ezili against the wall and drove the *athame* knife into its heart with a clunk, pinning it there. As the blade struck, Maitresse Ezili herself ceased moving, her eyes rolling up in her head, and her grip slackened on Kane's throat.

Kane stood against the wall for a moment, struggling to catch his breath and holding back the urge to cough. In front of him, Maitresse Ezili stood stock still once more, her body locked in place, the once-grasping hand fixed in a clawlike shape.

"That supposed to happen?" Kane asked, his voice sounding raw as he cleared his throat.

Papa Hurbon held his hands up in innocence. "She's got a mad one for you, *non?*"

Irritated, Kane strode down the corridor and handed Hurbon the ring he had removed from the woman's hand. Hurbon took the ring and weaved the lock of hair around it, threading the black hair carefully through the claws that held the gemstone in place. Once he had done so, he handed the strange totem to Brigid.

"You take care of this one, too," Hurbon instructed, fixing her with a no-nonsense stare. "And if anything goes wrong, you get rid of it and you get far, far away. You won't want to be anywhere near if Maitresse Ezili comes back for it, you understand me?"

Brigid took the ring and pocketed it. "I understand."

Grant, meanwhile, had made his way up to the far end of the corridor, past where the trapped form of Maitresse Ezili stood. He stared at her warily as he passed, wondering that she might make a grab for him as she had Kane.

Then Grant was at the front door to the House Lilandera, the Sin Eater still clutched in his grip. He pulled open the door.

"What is he doing?" Hurbon asked as Kane and the others shuffled along the corridor.

"Checking for hostiles," Kane explained simply.

"Who are we expecting?" Hurbon asked cheerily.

Kane gave the man a stern look, and Hurbon fell to silence.

"There's three of them out there," Grant confirmed, leaning against the rotten wood of the old door.

Like so much of the house, once the illusion cast by the

vision chair had been dropped, the front door had been left revealed as a tatty, ancient thing, hanging wonkily on rusted hinges, evidence of woodworm all over its blistered paintwork. Seeing this, Kane recalled how Brewster Philboyd had described the house when he had first located it on his satellite surveillance feed. He had said the place was in a state of disrepair, and Kane had been surprised to find it appeared to be in such spectacular condition when they had seen it with their own eyes. With hindsight, Kane realized that should have tipped them off from the get-go. With a sigh, Kane reminded himself of Womack's Law: hindsight is 20/20.

At the doorway, Grant watched as several half-alive figures strutted along the shingle drive. They had been aimless before, unable to see the house that stood right in front of their dead eyes. Now, they walked with purpose, not really striding but at least walking in a definite direction. There were three of them; the others had presumably returned to the redoubt or found other things to occupy their time, whatever the undead did with their time.

Three, we can handle, Grant assured himself. Then he turned to his companions, holding his Sin Eater aloft and using it to gesture outside. "Okay, ramblers, it's on."

Chapter 21

Grant led the way onto the grounds of the House Lilandera, now just a dilapidated old building hidden by the overgrown vegetation that surrounded it.

Behind Grant, Brigid Baptiste and Kane fanned out, readying themselves for another batch of the undead. The red-haired former archivist used a two-handed grip to hold the metal pole she had acquired, her semiautomatic securely back in its hip holster. Kane meanwhile appeared to be unarmed, and he watched the undergrowth warily.

Behind the Cerberus trio, Papa Hurbon wheeled himself from the house in his wheelchair, bumping down the rotted wooden stairs there and freewheeling across the shingle pathway where plants and weeds had untidily sprouted.

Up ahead, Grant strode boldly toward the road, his eyes never leaving the three shambling figures who lurched along the path toward him and his companions. As he reached the first, a man with his rib cage on show through his unbuttoned shirt, the zombie moaned and made a grab for him. Grant wanted to be sure before he engaged more of these abominations in combat, and that grab was all he needed to confirm that he and his companions could be seen, that Hurbon's spell had worn off.

The zombie's jagged brown nails slashed through the air, and Grant sidestepped in a swift, two-step dance. Then Grant's right fist lashed out, using the barrel of his

Sin Eater to smack the undead man in the face. As his blow hit, Grant squeezed down on the firing stud, and the Sin Eater came to life, unleashing a volley of bullets into the undead man's head at point-blank range. Head smoldering, the zombie staggered backward, while his undead companions turned on Grant.

Grant focused his attention on the one he had shot first. He had had time while in the House Lilandera to consider the most efficient way to deal with this seemingly infinite army of undead. He and Kane had concluded that his best option was to put each one down in succession, rather than allow their energies to be split between two or more. So Grant punched the first zombie with his left fist, smashing it across its still-smoldering face with a blow like a hammer. The undead man staggered backward under the force of the punch, and Grant raised the Sin Eater again, snapping off another burst of fire at the thing's torso. Grant turned then, as the first animated corpse fell over, his feet snagged by the roots of a weed that had spread over the pathway.

As his first foe fell, Grant turned on the next undead man, saw that this one was carrying a thick branch it had snagged from one of the nearby trees. Grant leaped over the path of the swinging branch, landing agilely on both feet and delivering a rocket-fast jab to the zombie's jaw. Even as his fist struck, Grant popped off another burst of fire from the Sin Eater, peppering the undead thing's face with bullets.

Though bullets had little effect on these revived corpses—other than perhaps whittling down their bodies by miniscule degrees—Grant had concluded that the shock to their bodies, plus the burst of light involved, served as enough of a distraction to give him some small advantage. As such, he used his Sin Eater like an extension of his fist, landing blows and lacing them with quick bursts of gunfire as he struck.

As the undead man with the branch sagged backward, Grant rammed down with his left fist, bringing it hard against the back of his adversary's head. The moving corpse-thing toppled forward, getting a face full of shingle as he struck the path.

Grant used his strike to springboard from the moving zombie, leaping through the air and catching the third one with a scissor kick that threw them both to the ground. As the third corpse-thing struggled to fight back, Grant drove a knee into his windpipe, slamming his head against the solid ground. Then his right fist struck out again and again, smashing the zombie's moldering face, with a burst of gunfire punctuating every blow.

"Stay…the hell…down!" Grant ordered his gruesome opponent as each punch struck.

In a few seconds the undead thing's rotten face looked barely like a face at all, and thick black liquid leaked from its empty eye sockets like an oil spill.

Kane and Brigid had joined Grant by then, mopping up the struggling corpses that Grant had put out of action. Together, the three of them worked as one unit to finish off the undead figures.

"This is going to take forever," Kane complained as he put the last of their relentless foes down for good, decapitating him with a solid kick. "We need to be back in the redoubt inside an hour to make this plan work. After that, the Red Weed catalyst will make whatever we do irrelevant—everyone will be dead anyway."

Grant gave his partner a stern look. "We can only keep going," he said. "If it happens, I'll deal with these dead things while you and Brigid make a run for it to the redoubt."

As Grant made his statement, Brigid's Commtact came to life and she listened as Lakesh outlined his discoveries.

"Regarding the reactor, I think we've found a way to make it work," Lakesh explained. "It's a back door to the security system, but by using a false power surge to the electrics we can fool the system into believing it's been shut down. Once we do that, it will automatically engage a systems check and reboot sequence, giving you about two minutes during which the access hatch can—theoretically—be opened."

"You say about two minutes…?" Brigid said.

Donald Bry's strained voice came over the Commtact link. "The reboot takes two minutes and eight seconds," he explained. "The system will believe it's been powered down during that period and will allow the access hatch to be opened. That's your window."

The trio of Cerberus warriors and Papa Hurbon had reached the scarred blacktop now, and warily began to trudge along it, back to where the overgrown dirt track led deeper into the swamps.

"That's not long," Brigid mused over the Commtact, "but I think it's doable. How much notice do you need at your end to start this security glitch?"

"We've set the sequence in place," Lakesh told her. "We're monitoring your progress via our satellite surveillance and we can go live as soon as you're ready."

"But you can't see once we enter the redoubt and our Commtacts are unreliable inside," Brigid observed, speaking her thoughts out loud. "Kane?" she asked, knowing her partner was listening in on the conversation.

"We'll be there in an hour," Kane decided. "Have to guess it after that."

"But what if you're not there?" Lakesh asked.

"Then you'll finally get to throw that end-of-the-world party you've been planning for," Kane stated.

Over the com link, the Cerberus warriors heard Lakesh discuss the plan with his personnel. Then he came back to Brigid and Kane. "We'll monitor your progress via the satellite and start our sequence ten minutes after you reach the door."

"What about the catalyst?" Brigid asked.

"By Kane's timing that would be ready in ninety minutes," Lakesh said. "Donald and I have a team working on possible counteragents, but no answers yet, I'm afraid."

"Great," Kane said sourly. "Anything else?"

"Good luck," Lakesh offered.

Kane, Brigid and Grant checked their wrist chrons as they continued down the scarred tarmac roadway.

"Roughly ninety minutes before the world ends, huh?" Kane pointed out with grim humor.

Wheeling himself along the blacktop behind the Cerberus teammates, Papa Hurbon spoke up. "We have, on occasion, been on opposing sides of the fence during our brief meetings," he told Kane and the others. "But I believe today that fortune is waiting to be kind."

Brigid looked at the strange voodoo priest and smiled, clearly touched. "I hope you're right, Mr. Hurbon."

Hurbon shrugged. "In a situation of this magnitude, my natural instinct is to call upon the *loa*—to pray to my gods," he clarified. "Somehow, that seems inappropriate. We are going to kill one, are we not?"

"We're going to stop a god gone mad," Brigid lamented. "Things like that—they just have to be done."

"You make it sound like you do this regularly," Hurbon observed with a chuckle.

"Yeah, sure," Kane huffed. "Every three months. Set your watch by it."

Thus, the foursome made its way onto the dirt road that led to the underground entrance of the redoubt. Kane took up a position behind Hurbon's wheelchair, grasping the handles and pushing the corpulent man along since he found the uneven track heavy going under his own power.

"How far away is this place?" Hurbon asked, reaching into the bag at his side.

"Fifty minutes on foot," Kane said. "Maybe a little less if we don't meet anything too hostile. Or if you lost weight."

Hurbon produced the spindle of black ribbon from his saddlebag and began unraveling a length of it, speaking under his breath. He was blessing it, Kane guessed, preparing the ribbon—and himself—for this final showdown.

Within forty minutes the group had reached the entrance to the redoubt. Other than the clutch of undead wandering around near Lilandera, there had been few signs of life—or unlife—during their trip. There had been just two encounters with wandering corpse-things, both of them mercifully brief. It seemed that Ezili Coeur Noir had called most of her troops to her side, and Brigid proposed that the undead things may have trouble living—as it were—beyond a certain proximity to her.

As if to confirm Brigid's theory, Grant spotted several shambling figures waiting by the large rollback door to the redoubt. "Company," he stated, his voice low.

"I see them," Kane acknowledged. "We're ahead of schedule. Let's keep it that way."

With a single curt nod, Grant hurried forward, his body crouched low, the Sin Eater present once more in his hand. His companions followed but held back a little, both Brigid and Kane remaining alert if Grant needed their help.

In his wheelchair on the dirt track, Papa Hurbon brought out the doll that represented Ezili Coeur Noir, its black rag body sagging with the loose sawdust stuffing inside. "Get me to some cover, eh?" he instructed Kane. "Give me a chance to finish this."

With a silent nod, Kane pushed Hurbon's chair to the edge of the dirt road while Brigid kept watch, hiding the voodoo priest among the greenery there. The greenery was actually turning brown, much like the dead plants in the immediate vicinity of the redoubt itself. It seemed that the longer Ezili Coeur Noir remained here, the more death spread out around her. Her powers were growing, Kane realized.

"You think I'll be safe here?" Hurbon asked as Kane parked the wheelchair.

"I'm fresh out of guarantees," Kane replied grimly as he turned back to the dirt road leading to the redoubt entrance.

Open, the door to the redoubt was wide enough to fit a vehicle through. There were three zombies trudging around, not really guarding the entrance so much as wandering aimlessly. They turned as Grant approached in his half crouch.

The lead undead thing was a woman, with tangled locks that fell down her back like lines of blood. This was the same one whom Kane had battled with earlier, the one he had dubbed Dreadlocks who had thrown him through the glass wall of the laboratory. She hissed like a rattlesnake when she saw Grant, and he could not help but smile, repulsed but faintly amused by the terrible thing.

Behind her, two other undead figures waited, and then Grant spotted a third hanging back in the shadows of the tunnel. The closest of the undead figures was skeletal with a walking stick. Next was a small figure whose skin had shredded, leaving only his white skull for a face. The third figure remained in the shadows of the entryway, looming there with unspoken menace, at home with this swath of death that now surrounded the redoubt.

As Grant took another step, Dreadlocks stopped hissing and lunged at him. Grant was ready, mentally prepared for this move. He had stepped forward only on the toe of his foot, and he kicked backward so that he reared away as the undead woman swept a clawlike hand at his face. Her hand cut through the air, and then Grant was upon her, his right fist driving a blow low to her torso, the Sin Eater's trigger depressed as he struck.

The female zombie's body shook and chunks of her desiccated guts spewed from out of her back as Grant's bullets cleaved a path through her rotten flesh.

This close up, Grant could smell her, and his nose wrinkled in disgust. Her breath reeked of disease, while her body carried the musty smell of old books, mildew and dust. As the undead woman doubled over with Grant's punch and tumbled to the ground, the undead figure with the walking stick turned on Grant.

Grant's eyes opened wider as the animated cadaver took his stick in both hands and wielded it like a bat. Behind the scarecrowlike skeleton, the white-faced one bared his teeth and hissed, his hands poised like knives.

"Crap," Grant muttered. They were fighters, dead or alive.

Grant ducked low as the stick came slashing through the air, swishing just inches over his head. He jabbed out with his right fist, blasting off a volley of bullets at his skeletal adversary.

Behind Grant, Kane and Brigid had just joined the

fight, even as the undead thing with dreadlocks struggled up off the ground, her rotten guts hanging from her torso.

"I'll take her," Brigid instructed. In a second she had flipped around the metal pole she held, striking the female zombie across the side of her face and knocking her back to the ground.

Kane didn't stop to argue. He was already rushing at the shorter figure, leaping into the air as he reeled off a stream of bullets from his own Sin Eater pistol. The short, skull-faced zombie stood there as the bullets rattled against his bony hide. Then Kane was on him, his foot kicking out into the undead thing's jaw. The zombie fell back, but had recovered in a fraction of a second. Despite being dead, these things still seemed able to move pretty damn fast when they needed to, Kane lamented, and it seemed they had more life in them when they were close to their terrible mistress, Ezili Coeur Noir. She had to be inside the redoubt, then.

Then the white-faced zombie lashed out with his right hand, driving it like a blade at Kane's exposed throat. Kane managed to turn just a fraction, and the undead thing's hand caught the edge of his neck, the talonlike nails ripping away curling shreds of skin.

Kane struck back, driving his left knee into the zombie's gut with such force that the animated corpse-thing was shoved backward, arms flailing to keep his balance.

Kane's right fist whipped out and he drilled another burst of fire at his opponent, then he followed through with a roundhouse kick, spinning in place until his heel met with the tumbling form of the white-faced zombie. The zombie crashed to the ground, skidding in the dirt until his chalky head slammed against the side of the redoubt door. Kane stood over the struggling, undead body for a moment, blasting shot after shot into his back. He spasmed, like an insect with its carapace cracked, still trying to right itself despite the fact that its body was ruined.

Kane drove the heel of his boot into the back of the undead man's neck, slamming it down into the ground as he tried unsuccessfully to get up. Kane became aware of the looming figure just a few feet back from the redoubt entrance. It was the big man with the eye patch hiding his empty left socket. Kane peered into the shadows, watching as that broad-shouldered undead man strode into the light like some prizefighter from another era, an era when legends still walked the Earth.

"Guess it's you and me," Kane said, and he raised his Sin Eater, snapping off a quick shot. The bullet zipped through the air and struck the zombie's face, leaving a hole dead center of the eye patch. The animated undead man seemed utterly unfazed as a wisp of smoke smoldered from the hole in the ruined eye patch. "Yeah," Kane muttered to himself, "just you and me."

A few feet away Grant vaulted and ducked as his own undead opponent slashed at him with his walking stick. Then the zombie came at him again, swinging with his walking stick, and Grant met the stick with the muzzle of his gun. The two weapons clashed together, and a sliver of the aged stick snapped away.

Going low, Grant dipped and blasted off another burst of bullets from his weapon, peppering the emaciated body of the zombie with titanium-coated 9 mm steel. The scarecrow-thin figure shook as the bullets drilled into his soulless body, dancing in place as if caught in a quake.

Grant leaped then, his Sin Eater still spitting death at the revived old corpse as he barreled through the air. The corpse-thing raised the walking stick once again but

Grant's right foot kicked out, anticipating the move and kicking the stick aside. The aged stick snapped in half as Grant's blow struck.

As the walking bag of bones turned, pulled by the momentum of the blow to his walking stick, Grant landed feet-first on his chest, driving the old figure into the ground. The zombie let out a hissing curse as Grant's weight broke his rib cage, and the ex-Mag rolled from his body, turned and drilled another blast of gunfire into the zombie's face.

A moment later Grant was standing over the animated corpse, one foot to either side of the undead thing's long head as he stabbed at Grant with the abbreviated length of the broken stick. Clamping his feet there, Grant shifted position and snapped the awful thing's neck, wrenching it hard to the left. When the ex-Mag stepped away, the old corpse lay still on the ground, head turned at an impossible angle, the creamy bones at the top of the spinal column peeking through his ragged frock coat. After a moment, the hand holding the stick drooped, sagging to the ground and loosening its grip on the walking stick for a final time.

While Grant was dispatching his foe, Brigid was using her metal pole like a staff to bat her own blood-haired foe backward into the siding of the buried redoubt entrance. Incredibly, Dreadlocks reached out and snagged the end of the staff as it came at her face for the fifth time. Brigid suddenly found herself losing her footing as the pole came to an abrupt halt in midair.

Then Brigid was lying on her back, the metal bar wrenched from her hands by the blood-haired woman. Dreadlocks held the metal bar, staring at it with her soulless eyes, and Brigid would swear that a grin crossed her wasted, time-eaten face.

The undead woman swung the metal pole at Brigid, turning her opponent's weapon against her in a flash. Brigid rolled out of the way as the bar slammed down against the ground, burying itself several inches into the moist soil beside her head. The female zombie recovered in a second, and drew the metal pole back for another swing at her opponent, even as the red-haired former archivist struggled to her feet at the edge of the path, where the dried-up tree cover began.

The metal shaft whizzed through the air again, cutting a savage strike against Brigid's ribs as she righted herself. Once again, Brigid fell, tumbling over and over with the force of the blow. Dreadlocks kept coming, pulling back the pole to try for another swing at her living opposite, the blood-smeared metal bar swinging through the air like a gross baseball bat.

Still lying on her back, Brigid's right hand fumbled for her holster, and she produced the TP-9 semiautomatic even as the pole came crashed down toward her face. Brigid turned her head at the vital instant, and the heavy metal bar slapped against the loam, kicking up another gob of wet soil.

Brigid swept the TP-9 around, blasting bullets at her attacker even as she came at her again with the metal bar. "I don't plan on following you into oblivion," Brigid promised as her bullets struck the zombie figure and pinged off the hard surface of the swinging metal bar.

The metal pole swept down again, striking Brigid across her left shin, forcing her to scream out in agony.

Her mind racing, Brigid saw her chance and she altered her target in an instant, turning her TP-9 on the dead branches of the overhanging tree. As the zombie with dreadlocks charged at her, Brigid's bullets clipped the branches above them, cutting them from the trunk of the cypress tree. The zombie figure disappeared amid a tumble of crashing foliage, and Brigid rolled aside once more as the metal bar slammed the ground beside her.

"Too close," Brigid muttered as she breathed a sigh of relief.

WITHIN THE SHELTER of the military redoubt doorway, Kane tussled with the animated corpse he had tagged as Eye Patch. The moving corpse-thing lunged forward, knocking Kane's Sin Eater aside even as Kane snapped off another shot. The undead man was fast, whatever else, and Kane assessed his fighting style even as the brutish zombie drove his knee at Kane's groin. Kane turned, blocking the move with the side of his leg, and jabbed out with a swift ram's-head punch at the undead man's jaw. The zombie's head snapped backward with the force of Kane's punch, but it didn't seem to slow him in the slightest. Already, Eye Patch was powering forward and he head-butted Kane in the face. The ex-Mag's nose showered red across his face as something inside burst.

Kane snapped off another punch at the zombie with his right fist, rattling off a burst of bullets as the blow struck him across the rotted remains of his face. As the corpse-thing staggered back, Kane took a breath, wiping at the blood that had splashed from his nose.

His opponent was a fighter, Kane realized. Not necessarily schooled, but without doubt able to hold his own, even against a trained Magistrate. If he had still been alive, Kane knew he would have been an almost impossible challenge to stop, more like an elemental force than a man at all. As it was, even dead the man seemed absolutely determined and incredibly powerful.

Head down, the undead man charged at Kane, his booted feet kicking up dirt as he raced across the gap between them in the shadows of the redoubt doorway. Kane timed his next move carefully, sinking to the ground at the exact moment that the one-eyed zombie would have struck him, and kicking out with both legs, propped by his arms. Kane's feet struck the undead man as he raced on past where the ex-Mag had been a fraction of a second earlier, and suddenly the corpse-thing was rolling over himself, arms flailing.

Still crouching, Kane turned, snapping off two quick shots before the undead man had ceased rolling, clipping his foe in the hip joint and gut. The zombie struggled for a moment before righting himself and standing on unsteady legs. Then he lowered his head, and Kane knew he meant to charge again.

From his crouch, Kane stilled his mind and targeted the zombie's right knee as he ran forward, pumping off a burst of fire from his Sin Eater. The bullets met their mark, and the onrushing zombie's knee popped in a explosion of cartilage and desiccated gristle. Kane rolled away as the zombie toppled over himself, crashing to the unforgiving tarmac of the redoubt's sheltered road.

OUTSIDE THE ENTRANCE, Brigid scrambled through the fallen branches, outrunning her foe as the zombie recovered. Brigid called to Grant as she rushed toward him, her arms pumping at her sides.

"Grant, I need an assist!"

Grant was still standing over the fallen body of his own adversary and he turned at the sound of his name to see Brigid sprinting toward him in a limping manner, the pant leg torn below her left knee. A moment later a tall, shambling, undead thing crashed out of the undergrowth behind his partner, Brigid's metal bar clutched in its hands. Momentarily, the undead woman used the bar as a walking stick, pushing herself upright. Then she began to march after Brigid, her long-legged strides eating up the distance between them.

Without a moment's hesitation, Grant leveled his Sin Eater at the undead woman and began blasting off a steady stream of fire, spraying her rotting body with bullets as he ran at her. The undead woman ran on against the barrage, even as Brigid turned and added her own fire.

Then Grant's gun clicked on empty, and the ex-Mag just smiled. The undead woman was running at him, pulling back the metal bar to take a swing at him now. The bar cut the air as it raced toward Grant's head, and his hand snapped out and grabbed it, stopping it in the same way the woman had when she had taken it from Brigid. For a moment the two fighters faced one another, alive and dead, both clutching the metal bar.

Then, with a twist of his wrist, Grant snagged the bar, wrong-footing the zombie woman in the process, making her sink to one knee. Taking a swift pace forward, Grant kicked out, booting the woman full in her ruined face. Her neck snapped back and she sagged to the ground, letting go of her grip on the bar.

Brigid rushed over, helping Grant dispatch the loathsome animated corpse as she struggled her last, finally giving up the fight once her head had been wrenched from her spinal column.

"I hate this," Brigid admitted.

"It's dirty work," Grant lamented. "Just have to get on with it. How's our timing?"

"Fifty minutes," Brigid said as she checked her chron. "There's still time."

Once they were done, Grant and Brigid turned to see Kane standing over his own foe, who sagged as he knelt on the road leading into the redoubt. Kane had his gun at the undead man's head.

"Whatever you were," the ex-Mag snarled, "you ain't nothing but history now."

A moment later the undead man's head exploded like a ripe melon as Kane blasted a stream of bullets through his skull until his weapon clicked on empty.

Wiping at his bloodied nose, Kane looked up at his partners. "Tough bastard, but I don't think he'll bother us again."

Both Grant and Brigid nodded in agreement as they stepped over the fallen corpse of the undead man, his skull shattered and spewing thick brown drool across the entrance to the redoubt. A moment later Papa Hurbon reappeared from his hiding place at the edge of the swamp road and wheeled himself along to join them, the black rag body of the Ezili Coeur Noir doll lying in his lap.

It was time to put an end to this madness.

Chapter 22

One thousand miles away in distant Montana, Mohandas Lakesh Singh and his team cheered as they watched their teammates enter the redoubt via the live satellite feed projected on the main screen.

"Excellent news," Lakesh said, smiling broadly. Even though it wasn't over yet, Lakesh found he had the strangest urge to hug someone or to pat them on the back. Thus, he turned to look around for someone with whom to celebrate and the first person he saw was Reba DeFore—and while the stocky physician wouldn't object to a hug, Lakesh could see she had a far weightier issue on her mind. "Reba?" he encouraged.

"We've been unable to find a way to counteract the virus, I'm afraid," she said, but Lakesh saw the trace of a smile appearing on her lips.

"Do go on," the Cerberus director said encouragingly.

"Well, I think I've figured out what to do with the Red Weed," DeFore explained, unable to hide her smile now.

At one of the nearby desks, copper-haired Donald Bry was giving instructions to begin the security shutdown on the reactor, and Brewster Philboyd related the timing to Brigid over the Commtact link.

Lakesh touched DeFore's arm gently, guiding her to a quieter section of the operations room. "That sounds like remarkable news, Reba," he said. "What do you have?"

"We've concluded that the thing Kane saw being mixed

wasn't the Red Weed itself," she said. "It was the catalyst. It needs to be mixed with the virus to make it go live— without it the Red Weed remains inactive."

"That's correct," Lakesh confirmed. "But the only way to halt that process is to keep the catalyst away from the batch of Red Weed stored in the redoubt."

"No, it isn't," DeFore explained. "We can do an old homeopathy trick. The Red Weed is stored in the lowest level of Redoubt Mike, waiting for the catalyst compound to charge it. But if we effectively flood the room that it's in, the catalyst will become so watered down by the time it makes contact that it will be useless."

Lakesh raised his eyebrows as he looked at the physician. "That could work," he agreed. "Rather than block the catalyst, we'd effectively ruin the batch of the Red Weed itself. That's certainly thinking outside the box. We've all been tackling this as something to halt, not to dilute!

"However," Lakesh continued thoughtfully, "while the facility is underground and located in swampland, there's no way Kane's team could get sufficient water to the site, not in the time they have left now. I fear that the ingenious solution you've proposed is impossible."

"No, it's not," DeFore said. "We've already tapped into the security system for the reactor. If we send a false report that there's a fire in the lower levels, wouldn't it set off the sprinklers?"

Lakesh nodded thoughtfully. "They've been unused for two centuries," he said, "so there's a risk that the system has been drained or simply run dry, you realize?"

DeFore looked chastened.

"All we can do is try," Lakesh told her, placing a reassuring hand on her shoulder. "And hope."

"Why?" she asked. "What will happen?"

"The Red Weed is stored on the lowest basement level," Lakesh said, "which is the same place as the mat-trans and the reactor core. They're going to be trudging through water before this is over."

A moment later Lakesh was talking with the field team over the Commtact once again.

AS THE COMPANIONS trekked along the silent underground passage leading to the vehicle elevator, their Commtacts came to life once more. It was Lakesh, and he sounded jubilant.

"Well done getting to the doors," Lakesh began. "We may have come up with a solution to the Red Weed problem."

"We're all ears," Brigid assured him over the Commtact.

"We're going to use the sprinkler system to flood the redoubt, including the lowest level where the inactive Red Weed is stored," Lakesh explained. "This should have the effect of diluting the catalyst if it's added—a roundabout but perfectly serviceable solution to our problem."

"I sense a 'but' coming on," Brigid said as another of the shambling undead men came toward the group from out of the shadows of the tunnel. Grant and Kane peeled off ahead, their reloaded Sin Eaters blazing as they dealt with the new threat.

Over the Commtact, Brigid heard Lakesh sigh. "Assuming the sprinkler system still has water in it," he said, "then we'll be flooding the facility, specifically the level with the mat-trans and the reactor."

"How deep?" Brigid asked, the practicality of the scenario dawning on her.

"Maybe a foot," Lakesh mused. "Not terrible but—"

"Getting Ezili Coeur Noir to the reactor in that environment is going to be like wrestling a bear in quicksand,"

Brigid concluded. "Plus, we have a wheelchair user with us. Hurbon here won't be able to manage that terrain."

Up ahead in the tunnel, Brigid saw Grant punch the skull of the rotted undead figure, blasting with his Sin Eater again and again as each blow made contact. Realizing that his partner had this one in hand, Kane had trudged on ahead, checking the dark tunnel for more of the soulless stragglers.

Brigid turned her attention back to her discussion with Cerberus. "Flip on the sprinklers," she commanded Lakesh. "I guess we'll figure something out when we get there."

Beside Brigid, Papa Hurbon continued fiddling with the dark rag doll that represented Ezili Coeur Noir, providing their only defence against her terrible atrophying powers. He was wrapping the doll tautly in black ribbon.

Shortly thereafter, the group stepped into the elevator at the end of the access tunnel and waited as it began its shuddering descent into the redoubt.

"Time to face the music," Kane said.

"Let's just hope it's not a funeral march," Brigid added.

IN THE CERBERUS operations center, Donald Bry prepared to give the order to engage the sprinkler system for the distant redoubt. He had rapidly programmed in a computer sequence that would alert the automated fire safety system to a false fire within the redoubt's walls.

He turned to Lakesh, who stood a pace behind him, anxiously watching the code flash across the computer screen. "If we lock this to one location it will shut down in three minutes," Bry realized. "The system will detect no heat or smoke and so presume the fire's out. What can we do?"

Lakesh pondered for just a second. "Tell the security

system that the whole redoubt is on fire," he decided. "Flood the whole facility."

Bry nodded as he ran the coded sequence and sent the order.

Behind them, at the entry to the ops room, Edwards had returned to his post. But he was not alone.

FAR BENEATH THE SURFACE, Ezili Coeur Noir stood behind the glass-walled laboratory of Redoubt Mike, watching the timer on the centrifuge that was mixing the catalyst for the Red Weed. As her undead servants shambled around, adding the final items to the mixture, the glowing green figures there showed she had eighteen minutes before it was completed.

She smiled then, a death's-head grin in her deteriorating face. By the humans' projections, the Red Weed would spread in the space of a single night. By dawn's first light, humanity would be doomed. It pleased the part of Ezili Coeur Noir that was still Annunaki—that was still Lilitu—to think that the humans would be responsible for their own destruction. It seemed just after the problems the apekin had caused her.

As the timer ticked down to seventeen minutes, water began spraying from above the queen of all things dead, drenching her and the equipment all around. Ezili Coeur Noir peered up above her, grimaced as she saw the sprinklers coming to life across not just the laboratory but the whole hangar area that contained it. Indeed, the sprinklers had been set off across every level of the redoubt, a pouring stream of water jetting from the pipes that webbed the complex.

Ezili Coeur Noir tracked the path of the sprinkler pipe far above, seeing how it came down the wall there. She reached across to the wall and placed her hand against the pipe. She would stop this artificial rain, she reasoned, through the simple expedient of breaking that pipe. Her hand clutched the old metal that ran down the wall and her grip closed even as the eerie taint of death took hold and caused the gray paint coating to peel from its surface. In a moment, the pipe had burst beneath her powerful grip.

But instead of halting the flow, the pipe's destruction did the opposite; it opened it up so that water could shoot across the room, spraying the lab like a hose.

Angrily, Ezili Coeur Noir stepped away, even as the floor of the lab began to glisten with an expanding puddle of spilled water. As she strode from the lab, her undead servants continued to work at their task, oblivious to the watery assault that drenched them. But something struck her then, not physically but as if from within. It felt like a bubble expanding in her black heart, like a prison cage expanding from inside her.

Ezili Coeur Noir called to her people to help her, her voice something from the far side of the grave.

It was at that moment that the main elevator doors opened and Kane and his companions stood revealed.

WHEN THE ELEVATOR doors opened, Kane's team found themselves looking out across the hangarlike floor of the redoubt, seeing the army of the damned who waited for them. There must have been forty of them now, Kane guessed, and each undead figure was standing ready in front of Ezili Coeur Noir. From above, a light rain seemed to be falling, spraying out from the fire safety system and slowly drenching the room.

From the corner of his eye, Kane watched Papa Hurbon for a moment as the corpulent man sat in his wheelchair, binding the home-made doll with a strip of black ribbon.

It was his spellwork that had caused Ezili Coeur Noir to falter, the proximity of the hex affecting her now.

"Think you can control her?" Kane asked.

Hurbon nodded once, very slowly. "I'll try my best, Kane. I owe this mad bitch, remember?"

"Baptiste," Kane said, his eyes still fixed on the army of zombies that stood at the midway point of the hangar, like a wall of death. "Get to the reactor and get ready for Bry's signal. I want you opening that baby up the second the access plate becomes demagnetized."

Brigid looked at the undead army blocking the way that they had used before. "How do I get there?" she asked.

"I saw another elevator just off the lab," Kane recalled.

Brigid looked across to the entrance to the laboratory area, its glass walls shattered where Grant had rammed it with the artillery truck just a few hours—and a butterfly's lifetime—ago. There were shambling, undead figures moving around within the large room, working at their designated tasks.

"I'll get there," she assured Kane.

"Grant," Kane said. "Protect Hurbon and let Brigid do what she needs to do."

Grant looked at the vast army of rotting flesh that blocked the way out of the room. "Will do, but we're going to need to get Ezili Coeur Noir downstairs sooner or later."

Kane reached behind him for the ceremonial sword that Hurbon had handed him in the elevator, drawing it from its ornate sheath. "I'll handle it," he told his companion grimly.

With that, Kane strode across the empty section of the huge room, his boots splashing in the pool forming there, marching toward the army of the undead. From overhead, the fierce lighting glinted off the puddles and glimmered along the sleek blade of the *ku-bha-sah* sword.

"I'll give your boy this much," Papa Hurbon told Grant as the ex-Mag rested his grip on the handles of his wheelchair. "He may be a naive fool, but he's sure as hell a brave naive fool."

"Only kind there is," Grant told the fat man as he eyed the approaching army of cadavers.

Behind the line of undead, Ezili Coeur Noir gestured, her spindly finger pointing out toward the interlopers in her presence. "Kill them," she told her followers, "that they may better learn a life of servitude."

Thus, the first salvo of shambling figures made their toward Kane, staggering figures trudging across the wet floor in their strange, unsteady gait, determined to destroy the abomination of life. As the first of the undead got within six feet of Kane, he swung the *ku-bha-sah,* its sharp edge glinting like a ray of sunlight in the enclosed space. The animated corpse stepped straight into its path and the blade cut a line across his torso before sweeping clean at the far end of the arc. Kane stood his ground, the sword held in both hands. The corpse-thing stopped in place, too, standing still as his swollen, maggot-eaten guts spilled onto the floor. His hideous, rotten figure had lost integrity, and in a moment he fell to the floor, his foul-smelling innards staining the metal plating like some terrible accident.

"That's the line," Kane shouted, his eyes fixing on Ezili Coeur Noir's yellow orbs. "Any of your people cross it and we will have ourselves a problem."

Ezili Coeur Noir held Kane's gaze, the lids of her lizard eyes taking a slow blink as she considered his statement. "I like you," she said in her rasping voice that sounded like crushed leaves. "You shall take pride of place as my castrato once the new dead world is born. And I shall make you sing."

But as Kane watched, the corpselike woman seemed to shudder, as if struck by a seizure. That was Hurbon's doing, Kane knew—the binding was taking effect, casting some supernatural hold on the half-life figure of the Annunaki goddess that Hurbon had created when he had accidentally given her her new name.

And then the awful, lifeless army charged at Kane through the pouring water and he found himself batting them away with swift strokes of the two-foot-long sword. As Hurbon had promised, the sword had some exceptional power over these creatures. It seemed to be devastating, far more effective than their bullets or other weaponry had been. Kane swung the sword in a long arc from high to low, cleaving the head from a stumbling undead man and snagging a chunk of his shoulder away before the *ku-bha-sah* sword cut the shambling undead woman beside him through the neck, continued slicing and powered through two more corpse-things, high in the rib and across the belly respectively. All four figures staggered backward, and the suddenly headless one grasped for where his skull had been before toppling backward into the next wave of zombies.

"Come on," Kane snarled. "Who's next?"

There were plenty of undead atrocities just waiting to take him up on that taunt.

IN HIS WHEELCHAIR, Papa Hurbon continued wrapping the thin black ribbon around and around the fetish representing Ezili Coeur Noir, winding it tighter and tighter to bind his wicked goddess.

"Poupée de cire," Hurbon chanted under his breath as the sprinklers soaked the ribbon, *"poupée de son. Poupée*

de cire, poupée de son." It was French Creole, and the words meant "doll of wax, doll of dust." So long as he repeated the binding spell, the *houngan* would hold Ezili Coeur Noir's powers in check, prevent her from assaulting Kane and the others. However, he had no way to stop her undead army attacking.

"Keep it up, man," Grant said, glancing across the room to where Ezili Coeur Noir stood. "Whatever it is you're doing seems to be working."

Hurbon made another twist of the binding ribbon. "The way of the path provides power you can't possibly understand," he told Grant.

"I don't need to understand it," Grant replied, "just so long as it works. That's my best friend fighting out there, while I'm stuck here protecting your sorry ass."

Ahead of them both, Brigid Baptiste sprinted across the decking toward the lab, the metal bar clutched in one hand, its surface stained with dark streaks of blood. One of the undead figures in the laboratory turned as she entered, and Brigid swung the pole around in an upward movement, knocking the undead man in the jaw with such force that he was driven almost a foot up in the air before falling onto his back with a loud crash. Even as he dropped, two more of the undead figures turned and rushed at the infiltrator, their busy work with the lab equipment forgotten.

Brigid grasped her staff with both hands, readying herself for the next onslaught, but her emerald eyes were on the timer at the centrifuge spinner unit. The digital readout showed they had fifteen minutes left before the catalyst was mixed and ready for use, fifteen minutes before the end of the world began.

The zombie to Brigid's left—a female figure with a

large chunk of her forehead caved in as if it had been struck with an artillery shell—made to grasp for Brigid with one of her deteriorating hands. The flesh there was a dark, pitted streak that barely clung to her clacking, bony fingers. Brigid stepped back and brought the metal staff up, striking the undead woman on the breastbone. The animated corpse took a step back at the impact, then tucked her head low between her shoulders, fixing Brigid with a glare from her soulless black eyes.

To Brigid's right, the second zombie lab technician swung one arm at her, and Brigid saw almost too late that he had tossed a beaker full of boiling liquid right at her face. Brigid ducked, just barely dodging the impact, as the water and the glass beaker flew through the air.

The beaker smashed against a filing cabinet behind Brigid, shattering into pieces as steam puffed from its contents. The red-haired former archivist was already in motion then, swinging her metal pole low so that it tripped the male zombie off his feet. However, the first one was coming at her again, reaching out with hideous, clawlike fingers.

Brigid rolled backward, watched in horror as the undead woman leaped after her, not so much diving as simply falling, her rotting black mouth wide open. Brigid could smell the corpse's terrible breath as she landed just inches from her face, and she slapped her left hand against the woman's concave skull, holding her back as the savage undead thing tried to bite off her nose.

"Get…off me," Brigid said, the words coming staggered as she struggled to keep the snapping jaws of the undead woman from snagging her.

The undead woman's hands came around, clawing for

Brigid's face even as her jaws clacked shut once again on empty air, closing just an inch from the tip of Brigid's nose.

KANE STABBED the three-foot-long blade of the *ku-bha-sah* through the rotting torso of his next opponent, using both hands on the grip to drive it through the zombie's black heart. Pus and congealed blood spurted from the back of the undead warrior as he fell from the blade and toppled to the floor.

But there was no time to congratulate himself. Kane saw another dozen shambling, undead figures making their way toward him on all sides, surrounding him and tightening the circle that would entrap him.

Kane dived at the floor as the closest of the zombies swung a heavy metal wrench at his head, a makeshift weapon found among the artifacts in this motor pool of the old redoubt. Kane's hand slapped against the metal plate floor and then he sprang up, twisting with the sword as he drove it up between the ribs of his latest opponent. The walking corpse let out an awful, choked gasp and thick, brown-colored blood oozed out over his front teeth. Standing once more, Kane pressed his foot against the zombie and gave him a hard shove, pushing him from the end of his blade.

The zombie staggered backward, dropping the wrench to the floor with a splash of the pooling water. The undead man hissed, the spittle of his black-brown blood spraying out at Kane's eyes as he did so, and he reached for Kane's throat. Kane delivered a swift left punch at the zombie's face, snapping his brittle neck with the force of the blow.

Then the ex-Mag was moving once again, turning to face his next attackers. There were two—a man and a woman dressed in the tattered remains of their wedding clothes, their faces a patchwork of diseased skin. With a one-handed grip on the ceremonial sword, Kane swung it toward the undead woman's head, slicing her rotten ear off and bringing with it a clump of matted hair that flew past him in the air. The undead husband made to grab Kane, his gristle-and-bone arms reaching around Kane's torso and pulling the ex-Mag off his feet. Then the wife was upon Kane, battering her small, bony fists at his chest before clutching him by the throat.

The undead woman's grip was not tight enough to strangle him, but Kane felt her sharpened nails ripping into the flesh of his neck, drawing blood. He kicked out, driving a bent knee into the woman's abdomen so that she doubled over, ceasing her horrifying attack.

Then Kane was bending forward, shrugging out of the grip of the undead man and throwing him to the floor. The moving corpse hit the metal decking with brutal force, and he writhed there, struggling to right himself.

Kane placed a firm foot against the struggling undead figure's back, stomping hard to drive him back to the floor. Then the *ku-bha-sah* blade swung once more, and Kane decapitated his struggling foe with a vicious sweep of supernatural metal through desiccated bone. As the undead man's head rolled away across the water-slick floor, Kane looked up to see further animated corpses making their unhurried way toward him. While the ceremonial blade he wielded was exceptional, he was beginning to feel exhaustion deep in the core of his being. He had been on the run all day, and the perverse incident in the House Lilandera had drained him in other ways. But there was no time to stop.

With grim determination, Kane gritted his teeth and urged himself on, his sword glinting and flashing as it swung through the air.

WHILE KANE WAS DOING an admirable job, it was perhaps inevitable that a few of the deathless zombies would break through his assault. Thus, as Papa Hurbon continued chanting his confirmation under his breath while he bound Ezili Coeur Noir, Grant found himself fending off four of the grave-busters who had been brought to life by their terrible mistress.

"Keep going," Grant instructed the priest. "I've got this."

Grant threw himself at the first of the undead men, a tall, gangly sort with a face so rotten it was hard to distinguish his features at all. Grant used his bulk to block the zombie's path to Hurbon, and his fist lashed out in a hammer blow, knocking the zombie where his left eye had once been. The undead man stumbled backward, and Grant spun on his heel, whipping out with his other leg to trip the zombie, forcing him to the wet floor in a splash.

The undead man hissed, and Grant recalled the Sin Eater to his grip before blasting a face full of lead at the uncanny creature. Even as he did so, a second soulless wretch reached for Hurbon, his hands grasping for the voodoo doll the man was working. Hurbon was no wallflower; his meaty left fist snapped out and he struck the zombie square in the face, driving him an ungainly step backward.

As the undead man recovered, Grant lunged, bringing him to the ground in a football-style tackle. The animated corpse toppled backward, crashing to his knees as his back was arched by Grant's thunderclap blow. The ex-Mag leaped to his feet in an instant, unleashing another unforgiving round of gunfire at the undead man's skull, the bullets ripping thick gobs of flesh away in their urgent passage.

"Get back!" Grant instructed, turning for just a moment to look at Hurbon.

The voodoo priest did not bother to argue. Immediately he began wheeling his chair back toward the wide-open doors of the vehicle elevator. The wheels kicked up water from the surface of the hangar in twin sprays as Hurbon retreated.

In front of Hurbon's startled eyes, Grant fearlessly tackled the undead people who had come after him. The powerfully built ex-Magistrate kicked the closest high in the chest, sending the undead woman hurtling backward as she struggled for and lost her balance. Grant ignored her, turning his attention to another of the fiends, this one armed with a metal bar. The bar whooshed through the air as the zombie tried to brain his living opponent, but Grant leaped out of the path of the lethal hunk of metal. Then the ex-Mag had his gun up and was directing a long burst of fire at the zombie, riddling his face and chest with bullets.

The undead man with the bar took the impacts of the bullets without complaint, lurching just a little to retain his balance beneath the shock. The shots were all the distraction Grant needed, and he came at the corpse in a blur, his left hand reaching out in a vicious grab for his foe. Grant's fingers grabbed the zombie by his rotten face, his digits sinking into the ruined flesh. Then the ex-Mag was pulling the undead man forward by his face, sickening hunks of graying flesh tearing away. With a final yank, Grant let go of the zombie and stepped aside as his forward momentum drove him straight into the decking.

But there was no time to stop. Grant found himself facing two more of the zombies, one of them the woman he had first brought to the floor just thirty seconds earlier.

In his wheelchair, Papa Hurbon continued winding the

black ribbon around the doll, determined to keep their mistress's deathly powers in check.

IN THE CLOSED-OFF laboratory area, Brigid dived away from the undead woman who was trying to eat her nose, sweeping her legs out from under her with a turn of her metal staff. As she crashed into the watery decking, the undead woman grunted through a broken voice box, the sound like nails down a chalkboard.

For a moment a strange sense of tranquility seemed to settle on the glass-walled room, and Brigid looked around her, searching for her next foe. There were several other walking undead men or women, making their unsteady way through the aisles of equipment toward her as water gushed from the broken pipe. And there, not six feet from where she stood, Brigid saw the timer counting down atop the centrifuge, timing the release of the Red Weed catalyst. Twelve minutes left.

She could stay here, she realized, deal with the catalyst, add something to the mixture or simply break the device. But there was no time left. She needed to deal with the reactor first and foremost or Kane's battle would be for nothing. She had to trust that Lakesh's plan would work.

The set of her jaw showing brave determination, the red-haired former archivist hurried through the lab and out to the tiny corridor beyond it that held a two-man elevator. Brigid stabbed at the call button, watching the open doorway as two more zombies hurried toward her from the lab.

The elevator door slid back on its silent tread and Brigid stepped inside. She jabbed at her floor button with an outstretched finger and waited as the elevator doors began to languorously close while her two would-be attackers stumbled into the abbreviated corridor. As the elevator doors were about to meet, one of Brigid's undead foes reached out and jammed his hand between the doors, halting them and preventing the elevator from descending.

Without a moment's hesitation Brigid swept down with the two-foot-long metal bar she had appropriated as a makeshift weapon, rapping the solid metal across the zombie's wrist. With a wrenching snap, the man's wrist broke and the hand was ripped from the undead man's arm.

"Sorry, but I'm in a rush," Brigid said as the doors whispered shut. "Can't hold the elevator for anyone today."

The doors sealed and Brigid felt the elevator shake as it began to descend through the redoubt complex. As it sank through the shaft, Brigid let out a breath in relief. At her feet, the hand twitched as a spasm went through the dead fingers one last time.

THE FLOOR of the hangar was over a foot deep with water, and the sprinklers continued to spray the room with freezing cold water like icy rain.

Kane had worked through over thirty of the undead men by then. Both he and the *ku-bha-sah* blade were smeared with the detritus of human corpses, the water from the overhead sprinklers making it cling to them like some kind of muddy paste. Now, however, there were just two more of the undead men to dispatch before he reached Ezili Coeur Noir where she stood proudly like some strange statue of Cleopatra from ancient times. The revived corpses fought Kane with the grim determination of things that never want to die again, ripping and clawing at his flesh as he ducked and leaped away from their punishing assaults.

Elsewhere in the large hangarlike room, Grant was

dealing with the last of his own foes, protecting his team's ace-in-the-hole—Papa Hurbon—until he could finish his binding spell.

With two swift swipes of his sword, Kane dispatched the final two undead men and they fell to the floor as one, their guts curling out across the decking, their heads rolling away from their twitching bodies.

"Your party's over, Lilitu," Kane said as he wiped the grime from his face. "Time to pay the band and go home."

Twelve feet away, standing at the doorway that led from the hangar at the back of the room, Ezili Coeur Noir narrowed her sick yellow eyes and let out a hiss, sounding more like a snake than a person. "Tomorrow's parties are canceled, flesh puppet," she told Kane. "All tomorrow's parties end today."

And then Kane was running at the emaciated form of the queen of all things dead, and that terrible flower of carnage was shrieking as she called on her supernatural powers to destroy this apelike foe who challenged her projected reign of death.

Chapter 23

Brigid Baptiste hurried from the elevator and out into the sub-basement corridor, her boots splashing in the eighteen inches of water that now covered the floor.

She was in a service corridor with white-painted walls, the emergency lighting above fizzing and buzzing as it flickered on and off. In a moment she had reached the end of the corridor, and she burst through the fire door and into the main artery of the redoubt. She was back in the corridor with the red stripe running across its bottom third. Two of the walking corpses stood there, turning at the sound of the heavy door as it crashed against the wall on its hinges.

"Dammit," Brigid swore, "I just don't have the time for this."

The zombies—a woman and a man—groaned angrily as they spied Brigid hurrying toward them.

Brigid swung the metal bar in a high arc, and it struck across the undead woman's face, knocking her back into the white-and-red wall with bone-jarring certainty.

As the female corpse-thing fell backward, the man lunged for Brigid, and she drove him away with the heel of her hand, smacking it against his breastbone as if pushing a button on an old-fashioned game show.

"Come on," Brigid muttered as she brought the metal bar back into play. "Give a girl a break already."

The undead man either didn't hear or, more likely, didn't care.

TWO FLOORS ABOVE, Grant turned to Papa Hurbon at the vehicle elevator that only came as low as the hangar.

"You should probably get out of here," Grant said.

Hurbon looked at him sadly, the strange rag poppet still clutched in his hands. "You don't need my help?" he asked.

"Your help's great," Grant said, "but if we can't contain this psycho bitch then you're going to be the first to die. You've done a lot for us—I can't have that on my conscience." Grant's hand reached around as he said this last and he pressed the ascend stud on the elevator control board.

"You took away that beautiful dream world," Hurbon lamented as Grant stepped from the large elevator and its jawlike doors began to close. "I could have lived there and been happy, you know?"

Grant nodded once, respectfully. "Sorry, but it had to be done. You know that."

Hurbon nodded as the doors closed between them and the elevator began its shuddering ascent to the surface. "I know," he replied, even though Grant could no longer hear him, "it's all about sacrifice. Just have to know when to hold 'em and when to fold 'em." And then Hurbon began to laugh.

THE *KU-BHA-SAH* SWORD slashed through the air, cutting through the falling droplets of water as Kane forced his deathlike foe to retreat from the redoubt's hangar area and into the corridor beyond. Ezili Coeur Noir held her forearms up to deflect the sword, and sparks kicked out with each strike. To her surprise, her colossal powers seemed diminished, and the striking sword almost seemed to hurt.

"What can you possibly hope to achieve, thing of flesh?"

Ezili Coeur Noir snarled contemptuously. "Do you think you have a chance to stop me now?"

"See this water all around us?" Kane asked as he raised the sword to a ready position once more. The sprinklers were still raining down on them both. "This is your plan being washed away. The Red Weed you intended to unleash—the catalyst agent doesn't work in water. We've diluted your whole evil plan out of existence."

Ezili Coeur Noir smiled tentatively, as if it was a joke. "Impossible," she retorted.

"Hey, you read the file," Kane said. "You tell me."

The ex-Mag had backed the coal-skinned, skeletal figure to the end of the corridor by then, and she stood with her back to the elevator. Ezili Coeur Noir balled her hands into fists, a howl of utter frustration coming from her throat as she lunged for Kane. The ex-Mag leaped into the air, his clothes heavy with water, and plunged the tip of the *ku-bha-sah* into the grim figure of Ezili Coeur Noir even as she tried to bat him aside.

Kane landed in a splash of water, watching as the fractured Annunaki goddess-turned-voodoo-*loa* collapsed against the sealed elevator doors, the sword poking from her chest. She wasn't dead—Kane could tell that immediately—but she seemed almost asleep, as if struck by some incredible weariness. She was no longer struggling. Whatever Papa Hurbon had done to charge the sword had worked; its supernatural nature had stopped the queen of all things dead.

Warily, Kane stepped up to the elevator and pressed the call button. From behind him there came footsteps splashing through the water that formed a layer across the floor.

"Hurbon's safe and all the dead are *really* dead," Grant

explained as he joined his old Magistrate partner. "You need a hand?"

Kane glanced over his shoulder, acknowledging his partner with a lopsided grin. "I think I've got this one," he said as the elevator doors opened and, leaning against them, the static form of Ezili Coeur Noir tumbled backward into the cage, the sword poking up from between her breasts.

Grant looked mystified for a moment, stunned that his partner had succeeded in stopping the self-styled queen of all things dead.

Seeing the bemused look in his partner's eyes, Kane shrugged. "Hell of a sword," he explained.

Together Kane, Grant and the sagging body of Ezili Coeur Noir took the elevator to the lower level where the mat-trans and the cold-fusion reactor were located.

BRIGID BAPTISTE DROVE the metal bar—end first—into the final remaining zombie, parting his ribs and leaving him struggling there on the floor like a crushed bug. She had smashed the other one to pulp, and while her remains still twitched, she no longer posed any threat to Brigid.

Ignoring the struggling corpse, Brigid hurried on down the red-striped corridor and back into the room where they had initially arrived. In the corner of the low-lit room, beside the armaglass walls of the mat-trans chamber, Brigid saw the reactor waiting for her like a promise. Even as she approached it she saw the operation light blink from green to amber—Donald Bry's security glitch had come into effect right on time. She had two minutes and eight seconds to remove the access panel and get the corpselike form of Ezili Coeur Noir inside.

When Grant and Kane entered the room just forty seconds later, struggling with the lifeless body of Ezili Coeur

Noir, they found Brigid kneeling on the floor by the reactor. A clutch of screws was arrayed around her where she had removed the physical lock from the security panel door, the magnetized lock having switched off with the false data spike.

"Quickly," Brigid said, her hands reaching for her pockets.

Kane and Grant dragged the deadweight that was Ezili Coeur Noir to the reactor's access hatch where a small, reinforced window could be used to peer within. At the same time, Brigid Baptiste produced the two plaits of hair that Papa Hurbon had ritualistically weaved.

"How much time do we have?" Kane asked.

"We just passed the fifty-second mark," Brigid said, consulting her wrist chron. "So about seventy-five seconds."

"Open it," Kane instructed, and Brigid pulled open the access panel. As she did so, the sound of the cold-fusion reactor filled the room. No longer muffled by the layers of metal that surrounded it, the reactor sounded like an aircraft taking off, and Kane and the others could feel static electricity playing in their hair. As if they hadn't realized before now, the feeling confirmed just how dangerous this was—opening an operational reactor core as it continued to generate energy. Brigid leaned close, tossing the two plaits of hair inside where they skidded across the metal plating of the interior.

But the burst of static in the air had another effect. Suddenly Ezili Coeur Noir was moving again, wrenching the sword from its resting place in her chest.

"And now you will all take your places in my private choir." She shrieked as she tossed Kane and Grant from her.

Kane smashed against the side of the reactor, while

Grant was slammed over one of the desks that had been used two centuries earlier to monitor the prototype mat-trans. Semiconscious, Kane's head sunk down and suddenly his head was underwater.

Brigid leaped back as Ezili Coeur Noir took a stride toward her, the movement of her insectile leg something hideous.

"Once inaugurated you shall sing the songs of the dead," Ezili Coeur Noir assured Brigid as she took another ominous step toward the red-haired former archivist, "until your vocal cords burn out like stars in the sky."

The queen of all things dead was so close that Brigid could smell the fetid stench of her foul breath. Kane was still lying facedown in the water beside the reactor, delirious, a trail of bubbles coming from his mouth.

Brigid pulled her TP-9 from the holster and, as Ezili Coeur Noir took another menacing step toward her, snapped off a quick burst, ordering the sickening creature to keep back.

Grant meanwhile found himself lying on the far side of the aisle of observation desks, his head fuzzy from the reeling blow he had just taken. He looked up, blinking to clear his vision, and saw the emaciated goddess standing in front of the reactor, looming over Brigid, who drilled another burst of fire into the monster's dead chest. He didn't need to think, just needed to act.

Grant's boots splashed in the shallow water as he launched himself, leaping over the desk in front of him and careening toward the black-skinned figure of Ezili Coeur Noir. He tucked in his head and shoulder-slammed the abominable creature, driving her like a battering ram through the open access panel of the reactor.

Then Grant was inside the reactor, too, where the noise was so loud that he couldn't even process it, just heard it like white noise. Ezili Coeur Noir crashed against the metal-plate floor of the reactor, her skeletal body sprawled in front of Grant as he struggled to his feet.

"Grant!" Brigid called from outside. "Get out! Get out now!"

Grant didn't need telling twice. He was already running, leaping over the fallen body of Ezili Coeur Noir even as she made a grab for him.

Grant barreled through the open access hatch, rolling over himself in his haste. Behind him, Brigid Baptiste slammed the door closed, sealing the reactor even as the amber warning light switched back to green. In that second, the automated electromagnetic lock came back to life, and the reactor was sealed for good.

Grant turned back, clutching at his shoulder where he had struck the deathlike woman, feeling the ache of the blow. "Singing lessons will have to wait, bitch," he snarled as the reactor hummed behind the metal walls.

Atoms collided as the fusion reactor powered up, its core creating energy from hydrolysis. Lying beside the reactor, Ezili Coeur Noir, the unliving remnant of Lilitu, struggled to her feet. The reactor sounded unspeakably loud this close to her insect-bitten ear, and she hissed at it, swearing the way a cat swears.

The reactor was charging up, its core spinning faster as the fusion process went into overdrive, the external security system intact once more.

To Ezili Coeur Noir, however, it wasn't a reactor but a cell. Just another place from which she must escape.

Outside the reactor, Brigid hurried over to where Kane lay, pulling him from the water by his hair. Kane took a gasping breath, his eyes unfocused for a moment as he tried to work out what had happened.

"You're okay," Brigid said to assure him.

Kane made to reply, but instead blurted a mouthful of water over Brigid Baptiste.

Through the window into the reactor Kane saw Ezili Coeur Noir push herself unsteadily to her feet, her putrid yellow eyes fixed on the door that Grant had leaped through just ten seconds earlier.

In silence, Ezili Coeur Noir reached out for the door and shoved against it, trying to make it open. It was locked, she realized, but that did not matter to her. Outside, when she had found the redoubt, she had used a whole zombie army to dig out the door and break inside. Here, with just a single metal door barring her way, its surface painted a clean white, she would be out in a moment.

Ezili Coeur Noir—the First Body of the crashed escape pod—placed her hand solidly on the door, laying her palm flat. Then she called upon the corrupted chalice of rebirth, felt its leakage as it sang its song of death in the air. The paint on the door blistered then flaked away, leaving the shining metal of the door itself revealed.

Just outside the reactor, Kane watched as Ezili Coeur Noir pressed against the door, the paint on the outside peeling away under the power of her deathlike touch. "She's coming through. We have to do something."

"Wait," Brigid said. "That's all we have left to do now."

Inside the reactor, Ezili Coeur Noir pressed her hand against the metal, and the outer surface began to oxidize, rusted chunks flaking away in a shower of copper-colored petals. Behind her, the reactor kicked into full fusion mode, and the queen of all things dead merely smiled, feeling its power shrugging against her back with all the irrelevance of a wave striking the shore. In a moment she would be free. In a moment she would recruit these terrible apes into her new choir of death.

Another chunk of the door fell away in a shower of

rust, revealing the thick, inner core of the double-layer door. Ezili Coeur Noir's hand brushed it and a streak of rust showed there, twinkling like a seam of gold. She pushed her finger into the soft line of rust, her ragged nail poking through it and into the center of the reinforced door, the halfway point.

And suddenly—nothing. Ezili Coeur Noir pressed against the door, but it stood there, immobile, sturdy as it had always been. She looked at her hands, looked back at the door, and she saw the call of the dead things fading from her vision. On the floor of the reactor, two tiny trinkets were being smashed together by the nuclear reaction: a plait of hair as white as snow and a ring through which was threaded a weave of hair as black as night. As the atom collider crashed the things around it together, fusing them to create new energy, Ezili Coeur Noir found herself buffeted by the trinkets and, at some spiritual level, the things that they represented.

While she still looked like a dead thing, in that moment Ezili Coeur Noir changed, and Lilitu stood in the reactor, her psyche fused together once more. Through the window in the little safety hatch, Lilitu saw the face of Kane as he stood spluttering for breath and spitting out the water he had swallowed.

"Nooooo!" Lilitu screamed as her body was pummeled by atomic forces, ripping itself apart in a tremendous implosion.

Out in the swampland, in a dilapidated house that had acquired the name of Lilandera, two figures shook in place as they were called back to the core personality.

Standing in place in the hallway, the voodoo doll just out of reach where Papa Hurbon had jammed it into the wall, Third Body Maitresse Ezili shuddered as her portly figure was reduced to a heap of dust. Her last thought had been of love.

Just a few paces away, sitting at the kitchen table, Second Body Ezili Freda Dahomey rocked as if drifting off to sleep. Then she, too, was gone, the only evidence of her passing a single fleck of skin, a dark scar on it in the shape of a beetle.

Deep beneath the ground, in the reactor room of Redoubt Mike, First Body became whole even as she ceased to be. The process took less than two seconds and it sounded like nothing, left nothing in its wake. It was as if Lilitu, or Ezili Coeur Noir, or whatever other aspect she had taken, had never even existed.

In the mat-trans room outside the reactor, Brigid watched as the readout needles shuddered then stabilized, the water still raining down on them from the overhead sprinklers. As the needles finally returned to their base level, the beautiful redhead breathed a sigh of relief. "It's over," she announced.

Kane looked around, as if seeing the room in a new light. "I expected it to be louder somehow," he said, "when she finally went."

Brigid peered through the tiny security window of the reactor. "This is what it sounds like when gods die," she said as the reactor powered down.

Together, the three warriors made their way to the mat-trans unit that waited at the front of the room. The reactor charge would remain for ten minutes yet—more than enough time to send them on their way back home.

OUTSIDE THE BURIED entrance to the redoubt, the light was turning to dusk, April turning to May and taking with it the *Mange-les-Morts*. Papa Hurbon wheeled himself along the dirt road that trailed through the bayou. He peered over his shoulder now and then, but there came no evidence that anything had changed, just the dead leaves and the sounds of distant insects and birds, as it had been when he had arrived.

Still, he liked to think he knew that it was over. Because, if it wasn't over, he was pretty sure he *would* know; something would be crawling or seeping or shambling from the entryway.

Hurbon smiled then, as he took the little doll from his lap, the black material that made up her body still wringing wet from the traumas inside the redoubt. With pudgy fingers, he loosened the black ribbon that he had used to bind the doll, loosened it just a sliver, just enough to let the doll breathe, as it were.

"Doll of wax, doll of dust," Hurbon muttered as he brushed dirt from it. "You're all fixed now. Soon you'll come back, my precious little girl, and this time it is I—not you—who will be making the demands."

Papa Hurbon smiled as he wheeled himself down the dirt track toward the tarmac road beyond.

Epilogue

Once again there came the strange sensation of nonmovement, the stomach rolling of sea-sickness.

Then the mist began to clear and Kane, Grant and Brigid found themselves standing within the mat-trans unit in the Cerberus ops center, the familiar brown-tinted armaglass materializing behind the swirling mist.

"Good to be home," Kane said, brushing at his wet hair.

Brigid nodded as she tapped in the door code that would release the lock and allow them to exit the mat-trans chamber. Her own damp hair clung to her face. "I need a shower," she said. "A warm one this time, with soap."

"Sounds good," Grant agreed as he rubbed at his aching shoulder, following Kane and Brigid from the mat-trans chamber and out into the familiar ops room.

What confronted the three Cerberus warriors was a scene of carnage.

Something had paid Cerberus a visit.

Something bad.

The Executioner
Don Pendleton's®
ENEMY AGENTS

American extremists plan a terror strike....

When California's Mojave Desert becomes the training ground for a homegrown militia group with a deadly scheme to "take back" America, Mack Bolan is sent in to unleash his own form of destruction. But first he'll have to infiltrate the unit and unravel their plot before it's too late.

Available in June wherever books are sold.

Don Pendleton's Mack Bolan®

Kill Shot

**Homegrown radicals
seek global domination!**

The terror begins with ruthless precision
when the clock strikes noon, gunfire
ringing out in major cities along the East
Coast. At the heart of the conspiracy,
sworn enemies have joined for the nuclear
devastation of the Middle East. As blood
spills across the country, Bolan sights his
crosshairs on their nightmare agenda.

*Available June
wherever books are sold.*

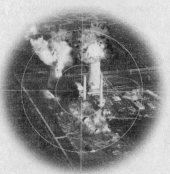